BETH W. PATTERSON

THE WILD HARMONIC

Hidden World Books
Cleveland Writers Press Inc.
31501 Roberta Dr., Bay Village, OH 44140
ClevelandWritersPress.com

Printed in the United States of America

Paperback ISBN-13: 978-1-943052-38-7
eBook ISBN-13: 978-1-943052-39-4

First Edition: March 2017

10 9 8 7 6 5 4 3 2 1

Smoke & Shadow Books is an imprint and trademark of Cleveland Writers Press, Inc.
The publisher is not responsible for websites (or their content) that are not owned by the publisher.

Library of Congress Cataloging-in-Publication Data on file with the publisher.

Cover and Interior Design by Monkey C Media

Author photograph: Marc Pagani, copyright 2015 Marc Pagani Photography. Glyph "Birch Block" by Aidan Wachter.

Dedicated to the memory of
The Lord of Garbage,
the greatest shape-shifter of them all.
Rest in peace, you sick bastard.

CONTENTS

ACKNOWLEDGEMENTS

Warmest thanks to my mentors, advisors, and beta readers: Bill Fawcett, Jody Lynn Nye, Kevin Dockery, Gena Valentine, James P. McCormick, Wayne R. Oliver, Ben Waggoner, Sarah Neilson, Elyn Selu, Soner Çiçek, Gerald Trimble, Maria Ferguson at Wolf Howl Animal Preserve, Dan Lively, Shandy Phillips, Mark Soderquist, Lisa "Ronicus" Davis, Lisa O'Hara, Bob Craven, my real-life pack (Stephen "Salty" Randall and Rob "Buckshot" Schafer), and Woha the wolf.

Major kudos to my awesome editor Patrick LoBrutto for steering this endeavor in the right direction and to Paul Huckelberry for making this all happen. Also to the real Darren Cook, aka Captain Thylacine of the Never Never.

And extra special thanks to every musician with whom I have played. For better or for worse, you all made me what I am. And thanks to my family and friends for loving me in spite of this.

ACT I

TRACKING

"And those who were seen dancing were thought to be insane by those who could not hear the music."

—FRIEDRICH NIETZCHE

CHAPTER

1

PRELUDE TO A HOWL

"It's time to flip the switch from 'standby' to 'on' and unleash the beast!" Raúl the drummer shouts, and I bare my teeth in assent. He starts us off with a mighty cadence across the tom toms and we all jump in on a tight downbeat. We hit the crowd hard with a clenched fist of bass, drums, keyboard, horns, electric guitars, and the commanding presence of our menacing-looking Rasta frontman. The mural of Bob Marley behind us stares out at some unseen vision. Gods, I've missed playing reggae.

Frenchmen Street, just over the border of the French Quarter and into the Marigny district, is a hot bed of music, less touristy than Bourbon and full of authentic bands, unique restaurants, and art markets. And while the Jamaican-themed Café Negril hosts bands of every sort, on the weekends reggae is king. It's been years since

Hurricane Katrina, but the aftereffects have still filled the denizens of New Orleans with an even fiercer need for ceremony, and the long, narrow club is crammed with people hungry for life.

And I am hungry, too.

As Nigel, our lead singer, calls out a tribute to Haile Selassie, Raúl and I drop out for eight bars and I grab the moment to dislodge a strand of my long, Creole mustard-colored hair from the strap of my tank top. Onstage in a packed club, it doesn't matter that I am not a pretty woman. For even in a musical city like here in New Orleans, no one plays bass quite like I do. Oh, sure there are better players, with better tone and timing, who can hold down grooves that would keep a train from derailing. They can play soaring solos, or raise a band to new heights from the ground up. But I'm the one who stayed in the spotlight all these years. I have instinct and a ferocity that allows me to dive so deeply into the sound, I don't see anyone's judgment. When I become one with the music, I am a pair of eyes, a pair of ears, a pair of hands, and frequencies. At the same time I'm holding in the core of my being a darkness that I can't let the rest of the world see.

My bass is a comfort in my hands, the thick strings gliding under my fingers, the familiar weight balanced across my shoulder, and the smoothness of the body leaning into my right side like a favorite dance partner. I forget to be uneasy, and let myself ease into the pocket. Raúl and I sit out when only the guitar and keys play together in what they call *riddim,* then dive back in when it's just bass and drums together in *dub.* We all close in together and raise our voices. The vocal harmonies are especially tight tonight. We are all just a bunch of misfits come together, and tonight we are creating a sound. It's who we are.

Many people, including voodoo drummers, Jesuits, and music therapists, have told me that repetition of rhythm can induce a trancelike state. You can also see this in mantras for meditation. These structural *riddims* certainly have gotten me into another universe altogether. In reggae, there is no showmanship allowed for a bass player. Just create solid bass lines without variation, and pay attention to the spaces between the notes as well.

A current of sound energy connects Rowan and me. Just thinking of him makes my breath quicken. Even if he weren't working as the soundman tonight, I would still be able to pinpoint his location. His dark, laughing eyes are shining in the back, even though the spotlights prevent me from seeing past the edge of the stage. Much as I'd like to, I'm not going to try to seduce him tonight. Maybe I'll just lunge for his throat. That would be safer. Something is going on; it scares me. We have more in common than he knows.

The PA system here at Café Negril isn't great, but at least I don't have to worry about how I sound when Rowan is behind the board. He can do a world-class job of slaying feedback and balancing a mix. Most folks who have worked with him have remarked that they don't know how he does it. Live or in the studio, it's as though he can hear notes before they even start. I would bet my bass that his keen auditory senses are because of what he really is.

Trust in Rowan has been creeping up on me. That never happens, not in years. Not for those like me. It's like something magical, or something much darker. I wish I knew why, or even how he is doing this. Sometimes I feel as though he would understand me better than anyone on this planet . . . and I am terrified of how crushed I'd be if I were wrong.

A hoarse, high-pitched screeching from around the corner of

the bar tears the fabric of the night air, jangling my nerves. A cat seems to have just met an untimely end in the street. Helpless to the animalistic desperation that stabs at my senses, the scent of death assaults my nose: bodily functions shutting down, blood flowing, energy shifting. I don't lose the groove, but I give the room a desultory glance. The crowd continues its oblivious dance, but Raúl and I exchange a fleeting glance of concern. One side of my upper lip peels back from my teeth.

Nigel calls for riddim, which I accidentally interpret as dub. Among the crisp guitars skanking on the upbeats and the keys filling in the smaller gaps, I suddenly stick out like a low thumb. I try to make my blunder sound as deliberate as possible, sliding my note slowly down the neck and into oblivion. Why couldn't my friend at the voodoo shop find a potion that wards against stupidity?

I have to free myself, if this is not real. This unhexing charm had better work. I'd have been better off tucking the gris-gris bag in my bra, held against my skin, but that would have been too distracting. The comforting lump of it in my pocket will have to do. The scent of pungent smoke and the sweet herbs tucked into it promise a miracle. My lungs creak as I try to inhale some sort of immunity to this obsession with Rowan, because if I continue to feel like a bloodhound on a scent trail, I'll never get through the gig.

What is really frightening is that I don't want to fight it. It's like a delicious drug, which scares the hell out of me. If Rowan is doing this, he does not know the danger he is putting us both in. But I can't seem to resist it. Is it wrong to crave dangerous toys? There is a big, swollen full moon in the sky, and I think it's making us all a little mad. The glowering disk always has affected me more than others.

No! I have to focus on the gig, and I watch Raúl's bass drum pedal to ground myself. Raúl and I have been working together for a number of years now on various blues, funk, and reggae gigs. I can always count on him to keep everyone in line, signaling the changes with his clockwork playing. Nyahbinghi chants are next. Even though I myself am not a Rastafarian, this piece needs to be given the respect it deserves: Babylon and Zion and freedom and fire.

The intensity of the show increases. Assorted scents fall into complex olfactory harmonies of their own: sweat from the dancing audience, the acrid tang of cheap, spilled booze, and cilantro from the tiny grill past the bar where many a starving musician can get an insanely good taco on a thrifty nickel. A fainter odor: I can tell that someone *almost* made it to the grimy restroom way in the back. The girl dancing by herself up front is putting on an impressive veneer of joy, but the scent of her loneliness is so far in the olfactory foreground, I have to shield myself from her secret melancholy. Time to dig into my strings, ground, and bring myself back to task.

We launch into a ragga dancehall song next, the sharp accents of the intro shooting across the stage and up my leg bones. Raúl shoots me a comical grin, and I chuckle. It's going to be okay. We always have fun when we work together. Raúl never tells me what made him decide to settle in New Orleans, but he seems to love it here. Even though he expresses no desire to leave this crazy town, he always teases me that he's going to steal me away and take me to his native Mozambique with him . . . exaggerating his accent, occasionally switching to Tsonga or Portuguese, describing his native African culture in outlandish caricature. Perhaps I would like to meet his brother? He would just eat me up. Once you go Mozambique, no other will you seek. (Or it will hurt to take a leak, or it will make your whole week—there's a different rhyme every time he goes into this act.) Most of us musicians are a crude bunch, and Raúl's antics never fail to get a laugh out of me. There's a genuine harmlessness to it all, and I'm quite certain that he can sense that my affections secretly lie elsewhere.

I squint through the lights at Rowan. Either this little gris-gris bag doesn't work, or I really am in love with him. No way to know for sure until the bag does its magic, literally. So there's nothing to do except lose myself in the music for now, swaying to my own spell.

But with the trance-induced groove, an awful realization creeps over me.

Rowan hasn't bespelled me at all. Why would he? He could have any woman he wants, and I am not exactly a prize. My heart does a nosedive into my gut. I am so screwed. It's far easier to lift a curse than it is not to feel an emotion.

Finally we are on the last song in the set. Most people have begun to trickle out as Nigel brings us down with a song about feeling *irie,* mellow and agreeable. But the ones who are sticking around are still craving more. As much as I am feeding on this power surge, I can't wait to get home. This is Frenchmen Street, not touristy Bourbon, but it's still getting too crowded. It will be too risky to even tell Rowan goodnight. I simply don't trust myself.

But he is gone before I've even packed up my bass. I am torn between the relief of keeping my secret and the empty longing for something I have never known.

◆ ◆ ◆

Back uptown in my tiny one-bedroom apartment, I heave a groan of relief and frustration. Surrounded by my comforts—my books, my Rush posters, hazardous toys, and knickknacks, I am in my territory now. I can keep my secret, even during the full moon, but it's physically draining. It's time to fully be myself.

My blinds permanently drawn, it is now safe to throw self-consciousness to the wind. Stripping off my stage clothes and throwing my little gris-gris bag onto the floor, my body finds much needed relief as I drop to all fours and allow the change. It feels good: stretching my spine, extending my tail, and feeling my fangs protrude, as if the beast of me has been cramped in a kennel all month. As long as my playing doesn't sound pure white, I don't mind if my fur is. Another growl that can't be helped resounds, this time from my stomach. Between the long gig and now my body's change into a large wolf, it voices its displeasure at me for not having grabbed a burrito at the venue.

Only one more day of the full moon, and tomorrow's gig is a showcase. It means that I'll have only forty-five minutes onstage, and I'll get to see some friends. It should be far easier than what I had to deal with tonight. A lot of my musical peers will be there. Comradeship in the music scene is invaluable.

There's my fellow bass player Teddy Lee. Teddy is going to go places, but right now he doesn't seem to be in a rush. Like Raúl, he's one of the few people on the scene that I feel I can trust. He's also one of the best musicians I know, but most people can't seem to get past his high falsetto singing voice and abnormally large chin. When Teddy's not onstage, he's outright hilarious . . . cheerful and cuddly-looking, like his name.

My childhood best friend Sylvia has promised that she'll there too. I am so relieved to have her back in my life, a pillar of comfort in these dangerous and uncertain times. She and her family had disappeared suddenly when we were in our teens, and one blessed night when we were reunited a few years ago on a gig, she explained that it was a witness protection program. And just like that, we picked up where we left off. I still find her new job hard to wrap my head around, but I know it's the same old Sylvia I knew from our days of sleeping over at each other's houses and playing games to scare ourselves silly. Fed up with the madness of the music scene, she quit gigging as a progressive rock keyboard player to become a nun and a church organist in St. John Parish. She was always wise beyond her years, and a beacon of reason. But she'll still be eager to hear my gossip and recent discoveries of gloriously bad movies.

And Rowan will be running sound again, dammit. This stupid gris-gris bag was a rip-off. Some miracles can't be bought or sold. There are charms to heal broken hearts, charms to attract love, but nothing is going to kill my feelings for him.

A high-pitched whine escapes my sinuses like a whistling teakettle, and then I remember that the neighbors can hear me. Growling to let off steam is not an option, so I pin the offending cloth pouch beneath my paws as I would a mouse and snatch it in my teeth. With a violent shake of my head, I imagine its neck snapping. Shredding the gaudy fabric, I roll in the pieces, twisting and turning like a decapitated snake.

The oils and crushed herbs permeate my coat to my skin, and the scent soothes me. A moment to let my heightened sense of smell pick up on every subtlety, and the bag's contents begin to work their magic. They make me drowsy and relaxed, and my physical shell flows back to human form. The magic can't break my love, but it can keep me from fretting about it for a while. Naked, I drag myself to the fridge for a post-change snack of high proteins, sliced turkey breast and yogurt. Then I crawl into bed and ready myself for mystical dreams.

Only one more night of the full moon to go while I have to see Rowan. Then for a few weeks I can go back to being a normal musician—whatever that is.

◆ ◆ ◆

I could bite my own leg for choosing this line of work sometimes.

As it is, I'm already irritable—I've had a hell of a day. Now my bass is strapped to my back in a padded gig bag tough enough to withstand a grizzly attack. Ahead of me on a hand truck, I'm pushing my rig, which when cranked at full volume, could blow the toupee off of a crooked attorney. Remaining positive was possible until just a second ago, when I reached for the door of the club and some patron of the arts decided to call out, "You *play* that thing?" Would he ever dare ask a female police officer, "You *shoot* that thing"? Grrrrrr . . .

I've often wondered if my male bandmates get asked any of these dumb questions, but now I need to focus on more important things. Namely how I'm going to pull off this show for the second night in a row without throwing myself at Rowan.

Before my eyes have a chance to adjust to the dim light of the club, I can sense him. Without looking I can locate him behind the mixing console. But of course, he would be. His punctuality defies the musicians' lackadaisical stereotype. But then again, Rowan is not your average anything.

Rowan steps out from behind the board to help me carry my

gear. I try not to think about his Hispanic-Cajun good looks, and as he greets me with a kiss on the cheek, I pray that my rising temperature doesn't accidentally singe him. "How was your day?" he gently murmurs as we hoist my gear onto the stage.

Oh, dear *gods*! I was planning on being Miss Cool, but I can't help myself. I have all of the social graces and aplomb of a warthog in a tutu, and before I even realize it, I find myself spewing about my adventure.

"You're not gonna *believe* this. This afternoon, I was trying to drive across Camp Street, and this dude yapping on his cellphone and driving at this idiotic speed, ran a stop sign. Somehow I knew he was coming, and I swerved as hard as I could, but he totally plowed into me. Luckily there was no one riding shotgun. If there was, it would have been *ugly* . . . we're talking major injury or death, and three generations to pay off medical expenses." He nods sympathetically.

"And when we got out of our cars to exchange info, he recognized me! Remember when I told you about that gig I played in the Quarter where this drunk dude cursed me out for *three solid hours* from the bar, and the rest of the patrons were getting pissed, but the bartender refused to throw him out because he was tipping her so extravagantly?" I don't wait for a response. "It was *him*, and I wanted to kill him right then and there, but I had to act rational because by that time a cop had arrived on the scene. As they were towing away my poor crumpled car, he nonchalantly apologized for ruining my vehicle and my gig, as if he'd done little more than knock over my drink. I was so mad I was practically foaming at the mouth! So I asked him if that was all he could say, and he said that in fact, he had more he wanted to tell me. He asked me if I was aware of massive changes about to take place and the coming of a new heaven on earth. And he pulled a *pamphlet* out of his pocket . . . like I really want to be preached at by a *religious freak!* What kind of man tells you 'join the angels' right after he's demolished your vehicle?"

His expression never changes. "Other than that, Mrs. Lincoln, how was the play?"

And in a split second, I am laughing. And then I realize that while I've been running my mouth and emotionally barfing, he's set up my mic, run my amp through a DI box, and materialized a guitar stand for me seemingly out of thin air. He knows just by the sound of the room's acoustics what settings I should use, and he's surreptitiously adjusted my tone on my rig—I 've been known to forget to do this myself when I'm really flustered before a gig. There's even a bottle of water for me. If I didn't know any better, I'd swear he was a freaking ninja.

But I do know better. I wonder if he knows that I know? I'm terrified to ask him about it.

It's an extremely risky boundary to cross. It seems that many people choose to turn tail and shun the things that make them who they are: their quirks, their flaws and foibles, their hopes and fears, their heritage, and their private demons. It didn't take me long to figure Rowan out, and the fact that I seem to be the only one who has caught on is extremely unnerving to me.

A beverage-enhanced voice bellows from the crowd, "Hey, miss! You gonna play us a song tonight?"

No, actually, I'm going to land a helicopter. Deep sigh. I have to be grateful that we live on a planet with only one moon. Especially on nights like tonight, when it looks so ripe, and when it plays with the tides of our bloodstreams.

I glance at our band's backdrop. Even the scowling Lion of Judah looks exceptionally ferocious in this light.

◆ ◆ ◆

I hate checking sound while audience members are trickling in. We try to get the right levels—play a little, adjust a little, play some more, the sound person tries to dial up the right tone and volume, tries to get us decent monitor mixes so that everyone in the band can hear each other—and in the midst of this, someone always screams, *"Play a song!!!"* We go to check our microphones ("One, two . . . one, two . . .") and some genius shows off his intellect with *"Three, four!!!"* (This is why I always check my mic in Scots Gaelic.) The band that goes on last usually checks sound first, so at least I can get this over with, swap a few jokes with Raúl, and sneak away before I'm tempted to stare at Rowan.

Now that there's nothing left for me to do—except catch the other acts and wait my turn to go play—I have to step outside for a spell. Hanging out in the employees' parking lot helps me clear my head, even in the humid evening air. Flanked by the back ends of adjacent businesses, it's a good, private little spot to prepare mentally before a show, and with three other bands sharing the billing with us tonight, the green room is a little too crowded for my taste right now. The sun begins to set over the defiant buildings: intricate wrought iron balconies interspersed with the occasional potted fern contrasted against rugged walls. We haven't had much rain yet this season, so the mosquito population isn't too awful tonight. I lean against the sun-warmed bricks and begin to relax.

Someone in the distance is having a crawfish boil . . . I can smell the highly concentrated spices and the salt used for purging the live crustaceans, and I can imagine how some nice, fat mudbugs would taste . . . small cobs of corn, potatoes, heads of garlic, and mushrooms boiled with them, absorbing all of those complex flavors and washed down with a cold Abita Amber beer. Farther off in the distance, a lone trumpet player is warming up outside another club. Long tones in some easy intervals, then an ambush of chromatic runs. Some jazz licks are flushed out of hiding . . . they run amok in whatever chord changes are playing within the unseen musician's head.

There's a reason that New Orleans seems to attract the absurd. All sorts of misfits are more likely to be accepted here. Some people come here to be noticed, and some to hide. And it is indeed a supernatural town. The bright is just a little bit brighter, and the dark a whole lot darker. All of the frenetic tales, all of people's secrets, hopes, and broken dreams get carried down the Mississippi river—all the way from the source. They end up here at the mouth in highly concentrated energy that pools near the Gulf of Mexico and runs this area like an unpredictable power grid. People flock from near and far because of the hype about voodoo, the cemeteries, the ghost stories, and endless books about vampires that take place here in the Crescent City.

I suddenly snap out of my musings. Something doesn't smell right. It's not even the ubiquitous skunk-and-gasoline smell of pot that seems to loom over the music scene. That I don't mind; it's as ever-present as a backdrop these days—especially on reggae gigs like this one tonight—and although I don't partake of it much myself, I'd rather deal with stoners than drunks. But it's the three kids in the farthest corner who are trying to get their jollies who have caught my attention. And now it seems as though I have caught theirs.

On my own turf, I am suddenly regarded as an intruder to their little party. I suddenly remember why drab colors are important for survival in the females of many species.

They begin to approach me. I don't even know what they want, but I do know that they're not employees, nor are they here to contribute to the conservation of any endangered species.

"There she is, the one that got away! You better be careful, or someone gonna bite you back!"

I have had a crappy day, I'm trying to focus on the gig tonight, and I absolutely do not need these punks messing with me now. I stand as still as a stone until they step a little too close for comfort. They make the mistake of making eye contact with me. It's an act of aggression that tips me right over the edge.

A subtle feedback loop gnaws at my eardrums, and I'm dimly aware that an angry little song is rumbling in my throat. I think it's an old Scottish call to battle that I learned as a kid, but I'm not really paying attention to anything other than how to make these kids to back off—*now*. One foot takes an involuntary step forward.

And as if summoned somehow, Raúl is suddenly at my side, snarling what appears to be some choice words in Tsonga. He could be reciting the nutritional content off of a bag of Chee-Wees for all I know, but it sounds menacing enough to make these punks step back very quickly, palms up in the universal "We don't want no trouble" gesture. They wisely decide to move along.

Trying to maintain some semblance of bravado, one spits on the pavement as a final gesture of defiance in the middle of his hasty retreat, marking his territory. They duck into an alleyway.

Raúl resumes his relaxed smile, as though he's just enjoyed this showdown like a funny film. "They don't know much about who the real 'brothers' and 'sisters' are, do they?" he says. "Mess with one musician, you mess with the whole lot. Now let's go back inside, before you attract any more attention. Who would it possibly be coming after you next time, hmm?" he teases. "Some mobster? Maybe some James Bond villain . . . no, I've got it! Disgruntled rodeo clowns. Come on, *baixinho* . . . if you weren't like a little sister to me, I would marry you this instant. Since I have these scruples, I guess I can't be a true Louisianian then, can I?"

I look back to track our adversaries' retreat, but there's no sign of the kids. Only a cluster of rats skitters down the streets and into the gutters. One creature turns back to fix me with a menacing glare in its beady eyes before joining its scaly-tailed brethren. This clearly isn't over.

◆ ◆ ◆

Teddy checking sound when we walk back into the club is such a welcome sight, I forget about the near attack. Raúl gives him a wave, and the comfort of friendship grounds me. I've borne witness to so much backstabbing and outright swindling over the years amongst club owners, equipment dealers, producers, and fellow musicians, so it seldom goes unnoticed by me how refreshingly real Teddy is. When you're a bass player, you don't often hang with your fellow low-end jockeys (the annual Mardi Gras "Bass Parade" notwithstanding), and I'm grateful that Teddy and I have each other's backs.

Tonight he's playing with self-proclaimed guitar god Maestro Dude Holstein, a man known for his grandiose ego, pretty golden hair, and faster-than-the-speed-of-musically-pleasing guitar licks. I don't know why Teddy is wasting his talent in a backing band for Maestro Dude Holstein. He seems content to just make his musical statement and then disappear into the shadows again. Not all of us are career-driven, I suppose.

The Maestro, however, is a notorious asshole, and right now he happens to be mouthing off to my beloved Rowan. I try to mind my own business and appear casual, but the hair on the back of my neck and arms is beginning to rise. Maestro swears at Rowan over the mic, insulting his aptitude, his musicianship, and his manhood. Rowan calmly diffuses the situation by suggesting a different setting on Maestro's rig. Maestro tweaks a few knobs, fails to see any more problems, then storms off the stage into the green room.

Teddy makes a beeline for me as the next band sets up. "Can you *believe* that dipshit? I can't take dealing with these asshats any more." He grins as Raúl, who has also worked with Teddy, comes trotting over to commiserate. "I've been dying to take that guy down a notch or two, and tonight's the night." I must appear concerned, because he chuckles reassuringly, "Don't worry. It's not going to make the night go askew. But this douchebag might think twice before fucking with his fellow musicians. You guys in?"

No need to ask us twice. With soundcheck officially over, and the canned music flooding the PA once more, we have a few minutes to spare before the showcase begins. Maestro has stormed off somewhere—he doesn't seem to be close, as the smell of his rancid cologne (which I think is probably Chanel Number Two) is very faint. In a millisecond, Teddy has swiped the set list and procured a Sharpie.

"Um, isn't he going to notice . . .?" I venture cautiously.

Teddy grins like a mischievous wild animal. "Who do you think had to write up his set list at the last minute while he was fixing his hair?" He flips the paper over, and we set ourselves to the task.

Now there are three of us, huddled into a tight knot, howling with laughter. We substitute quite a few nouns in the song titles with "penis." We compete for the most heinous plays on words, trying to keep our voices down.

"Okay . . . now we have 'Rising Farts' and 'Gland in Hand,' and I think we're good to go! Holstein is gonna have a *cow!*" Teddy triumphantly snatches the newly altered set list and is back at the edge of the stage so fast, he defies physics, while Raúl and I try to alleviate the pain in our faces from laughing by mashing our cheeks in our hands.

I'm still wiping the tears from my eyes when I spot Rowan across the room, casually leaning against the railing intended to protect the sound board and crew from drunken idiots. He seems unfazed by the exchange with Maestro, but his mouth holds the barest hint of a smile, as if he's actually heard our wicked plans. It's hard to imagine him as potentially dangerous, as all I can see in him are sweetness and beauty. I am a little ashamed at how quickly my pulse begins to race again.

◆ ◆ ◆

I actually enjoyed Bad Pillow, which was a trio of cello, African percussion, and theremin, an early electronic instrument that sounded eerily reminiscent of early horror films. I endured Sofa King Bad, who probably did not intend to be New Orleans' answer to The Shaggs. But with Maestro Dude Holstein up now, Raúl has managed to tear himself away from two lovely German ladies to sit with me. Women are crazy about him, with his high African cheekbones, exotic accent, and charming manners; pure animal magnetism.

But apparently to Raúl, not even female attention can measure up to the impending hilarity. It is quite entertaining to see the megalomaniac Maestro Dude Holstein verbally shoot himself in the foot a few times, then scowl at his band and carry on the rest of the set with the proper titles, face darkening with each song. I'd swear that Teddy can see us, even through the blindingly bright stage lights that always make a dark club seem pitch black from the stage. He grins, and he throws some utterly sublime bass riffs my way. Between his amazing playing and what it meant to him that I was there, it was worth it.

"I *told* you I'd make it!" hisses a familiar voice next to me. As I whirl around to face my best friend, Sylvia flashes me a toothy grin and raises one copper-colored eyebrow at me. "I'll have to say at least a dozen Hail Marys for lying to Father O'Flaherty to get out of my chores. But he believed me when I told him that polishing the silver would soften my callouses, affecting my ability to play."

I nearly snort my water out of my nose as I hug the nun. *"Callouses?* You don't need callouses to play keyboard instruments, you crazy Penguin!"

She snorts. "I know that, but the priest doesn't. I hate polishing silver. That stuff they give me to work with stinks. Why hello there, Casanova," she says by way of greeting to Raúl.

The Maestro hops off the stage to stand by his little table full of merch, and Teddy comes over to join us. It's too late to holler out a request for a reprise of "Rising Farts." My turn to do my thing.

◆ ◆ ◆

I'm been psychologically revving myself up for this moment. Now it's as if my frustrating day never even happened, and a warm glow begins to kindle in my belly. Rowan's obsidian eyes are shining behind the board. Sylvia is sitting at the bar, wearing her full habit of a black tunic, veil, and wimple and beaming at me. A million punchlines to this scenario of the nun at the bar come to mind, and it's obvious by the glint in her eye that she's found the humor in it too. A few curious young men begin to cluster around her, but she shoos them away with a comically stern glower. Friendly Teddy has already struck up a conversation with her, and the two are chatting like old friends. He is trying to keep a straight face at her theatrics before turning to me and giving me a thumbs-up, that huge chin of his turning on the full force of his generous grin.

We're the headlining act for this showcase and the final band, and we have to give the crowd its money's worth. And we're up, and it's time to go. Now is not the time to think about future gigs, paying bills, or even Rowan.

I may be a woman in love, I may be not entirely human, but all that matters right now is that I am a musician. And we're off.

The pull of the moon higher in the sky draws the crowd in a tide of swaying, weaving bodies. The songs seem to fly, one right after another . . . I can't believe how quickly the set is going. We switch to a reggae adaptation of an old Hebrew chant, Nigel the singer lunging with conviction. The mix is intoxicating. A frequency thrums down my spine from the base of my skull to my tailbone, playing my body like a vibrating string. It feels so sweet and delicious. I shiver with pleasure and surrender completely to the groove. It carries me like a steady river, and I navigate through it easily in the boat of my musical mind.

The lapse between my heartbeat and the pulse roaring in my ears creates a complex polyrhythm. Not only that, but the faint sound of the other players' hearts adds to this vibe . . . just bass and drums now, and it's a huge heartbeat.

Lub, dub . . . lub, dub . . .

Too soon we're coming to our final crescendo, and now it's my turn to shine. Solos for bass aren't often called for in this kind of music, but I've just been given a cue. I've never taken a bass solo quite like this. The notes just choose themselves. My beats ever so slightly behind the solid bass drum, it seems that some sort of door has been opened. It's as if I just haven't been paying attention all my life . . . until now. I'm beginning to hear partials, overtones, harmonics, and all sorts of dimensions that I somehow should have known were there all along. I don't know how Rowan is coaxing a sound like this out of me.

Rowan. He's not behind the board.

It's hard to make out the audience with the spotlights in my face, but the movements of my friends swim into view. Teddy is looking worriedly at me. Sylvia is pacing like a caged animal. In spite of their sudden concern, they look so hilarious somehow that I let out an involuntary bark of laughter. I must have forgotten to shave my legs this morning . . . *why is this occurring to me now?* My knees begin to bend into a slight crouch, and my stomach does a sudden lurch. I've lost the groove. Or has the groove lost me? Something's wrong. The hairs on the back of my neck stand up. Someone in here is afraid, and it stinks . . . pungent and sickly. But why? And of what? The audience seems oblivious, but the keyboard player and guitarist start inching away from me. Even tough-talking Nigel looks uncomfortable.

The kick drum pounds through the floor and resonates up my spine in an unmistakable cue. It appears that Raúl is just going to close us out with a drum solo. Not at all the way we rehearsed the set, but it seems like a great spontaneous idea, and the crowd is digging it. So I let my solo fade, and Rowan is suddenly appearing from the backstage shadows—unseen by the throng that is now transfixed by Raúl—and silently leading me by the arm back into the wings. The mere notion that his hands are on me at last makes me giddy beyond description. He wordlessly slips a pair of shades on me. *Oh, my, I'm a celebrity now* . . . I lean my bass against one of the equipment cases and follow like an obedient little lamb.

The urge to reach out and stroke his short-cropped black hair suddenly overtakes me, to trace my fingertip along that fetching widow's peak of his. I can barely bring myself to look him in the eye for fear that I would drown in the dark intensity of his gaze. What would it be like to bury my nose in the hollow of his throat and breathe in his scent? Would he taste spicy, like his blended heritage—of cayenne and gumbo and chilies and cinnamon? Would he mind how lunar-white my skin might appear against the café au lait hue of his own?

He leads me down the corridor toward the back exit. The music is still singing in my blood, and I'm savoring the feel of Rowan's fingers on my arm. The sensation of the tiniest bit of his skin against my own is electrifying, and his body feels turbocharged with energy, which seems to flow into me through his firm grip. My tongue lolls out of the side of my mouth in pleasure. In spite of my dizziness, I haven't had a drop of alcohol tonight (although I had been planning on a few glasses of celebratory post-gig wine). Another power surge from Rowan's touch, and I start laughing deliriously again.

We're in the employee parking lot. The whole area seems oddly deserted, as if invisible to everyone but us.

"What the hell was *that* just now?"

I've never heard him raise his voice before. "Rowan . . ." I mumble weakly.

"I don't have much time. Tell me what's going on with you. You need to be honest with me if we're going to keep working together like this!"

"Rowan . . . I need . . . to shpeak wif you . . . ." I can't even get the words out. The moon is so bright that even through the shades, the parking lot nearly looks like the weirdly shadowed afternoon of a solar eclipse.

"I'm not asking you again. Come clean this instant, or I'm leaving right now."

Now that the moment I've been equally fearing and wanting is staring me in the face, a surreal wave of calm washes over me. Instinct steers me into something that is neither surrender nor risky move. This is the proverbial straw, the tipping point, and it's now or never.

"Rowan!" I can feel his body heat, breathe in his richly alluring scent, and all resistance flees into the night. Mustering up all of my courage, I take a huge, deep breath until my lungs creak. The feeling of my chest expanding and my spine stretching means that there is no turning back now. In one frantic moment, I've stripped off my clothes and dropped to all fours. My hands are padded before they even hit the ground, with a click of claws on the pavement. My pale coat shines white in the moonlight.

And there he is beside me . . . our noses touching, tails wagging. I rear up onto my hind legs in utter joy. He licks my muzzle.

And then the others appear. Big, gray Teddy with his powerful furry jaw. Raúl with his mottled coat and huge rounded ears, closer in appearance to an African wild dog, his shining white teeth parted in a lupine grin. Soft, slender Sylvia, still wearing that damned wimple held in place by her pointed ears, most likely intended to ease any shock I might feel over this huge revelation. "We thought you'd *never* come out of the den!" she snorts thickly through her long canine mouth. The words are garbled, but the message is clear. I must be giving her a *look,* because she continues, "I'm sorry! I was sworn to secrecy, and you know how I can keep a secret! You had to figure it out for yourself."

My mind reels with incredulity. How long have they known that I was lycan? Why did it never occur to me that there might be a reason for my connection to Sylvia, Teddy, and Raúl beyond music and friendship? Have I really been *that* self-absorbed all this time? Or so myopic in my feelings for Rowan that I had a nose for only him? Did I really believe that by burying myself in my music career I could stall my fear and denial about my true nature forever? How did the others find the courage to reveal themselves to each other? Which of them were born into it, and which ones were bitten? I want to *understand,* almost as badly as I want to *be* understood at long last. I have so much to learn from this newfound pack of mine.

The outside humidity makes my nose sweat, and the stench of human agenda surrounding the club is no picnic, but in my joy and relief I couldn't care less at the moment. Common sense keeps me from howling to the world, *I belong somewhere at last!* I fix my gaze on Rowan, his dark widow's peak markings framing his intelligent eyes—now golden, but every bit as smoldering. He smells spicy and clean-of musk, passion, and superhuman self-control. Someday, hopefully, when we're laughing over a glass of wine in his den, or even—fingers crossed!—lying in bed together, I'll tell him, "You have no idea how long I've wanted you to sniff my butt!" But now is not the time for joking. And I'm not going to try to seduce him tonight. It's that time of a big, swollen full moon in the sky, and it's time to gather together in a different kind of intimacy. I look around, but there's still no one else in sight.

We all close in together and raise our voices. Packed tightly and banded together, a single unit

celebrating its uniqueness. Humans would call it noise, or cacophony, or "the crap young people are listening to these days." But they can't hear what we can: the subtle beating between notes, the intricate countermelodies, the descant, the way that multiple melodies weave around each other so expressively. It's a frequency that no one else can hear, save others of our kind.

There's no way we could be tracking this in a studio. It would never sound this good on a recording, not even done with state of the art equipment. We are among a very small few who can hear it anyway. All we can do is live in the moment and be grateful that there will be more nights like this. This is our secret, and we will leave no tracks. We are all just a bunch of half-human misfits come together, creating a sound. It's who we are . . .

CHAPTER
2

CADENZA

Journal entry, March 15th: What does it mean to be a werewolf musician? Most days I really strive to be ahead of my game, playing to the best of my ability, always learning, always growing, and feeling the music. Other days I have to suppress the urge to tear people's throats out. In short, this makes me no different from any other kind of musician.

I'm not all here. My body is on autopilot, instinctually perusing the upscale boutiques on Magazine Street, but my mind has been elsewhere since that life-changing gig. And Sylvia's briefing over the phone this morning has given me even more to wrap my head around.

There is a definite ebb to the erstwhile frenetic energy all over the city now that Lent is finally in full swing. I don't follow the custom like my clerical pack-sister Sylvia does, but the relief of Mardi Gras stressors being over is enough to make me want to embrace it. Multicolored strands of rogue plastic beads are still caught in the trees lining the streets, generous offerings that never quite made it from the floats to the hands of parade goers. I feel a smile creep over my face as the warming weather caresses my bare arms. As always on days I don't have to be on stage, a t-shirt, jeans, and sneakers are my seasonal coat. My tarnished yellow hair is pulled back in an unceremonious ponytail, although my personal code forbids me to go out in public without my ritual mask of heavy black lines around my eyes. I like to think of it as a tiny trademark disguise that gives me power, like a Superman cape or a Lone Ranger mask.

"Birch!" a boisterous male voice calls out. "Heyyyyyy, Birch! Where y'at, dawlin'? You were great the other night! How ya been?" In my line of work it's not at all sordid to hear a total stranger, like this man in a Hubig's Pies t-shirt, tell me how great I was last night. Judging by the matching shirt the woman with him is wearing—*his mate*, I can smell—I can only guess that they are tourists. They are obviously trying to get the hang of some of our local vernacular, and I wonder if they know how to pronounce the name of the city. Nobody around here really says "Noo Or-LEENZ," but there are endless songs about our town, and nothing good rhymes with the way it's really pronounced, "Noo OR-lins."

The man's façade of over-familiarity makes me stiffen. I am always introduced onstage by my real name, "Birch MacKinlay," but my close friends call me by my childhood nickname "Buzz". An instinctual reflex turns on my automatic smile. These well-meaning people obviously don't know me, of course, but I always want to be gracious, albeit guarded. I nod and exchange pleasantries with the couple, get a whiff of their enthusiasm, and move on. Finding my cognitive bookmark, my train of thoughts resumes rocking on its tracks in time to my footsteps. As the memories of last night flood back, butterflies dance in my stomach and a ridiculous grin smears itself across my face. *I'm not a freak! There are others like me! Not only that, but they are people I care for . . .*

Too often I have taken this city for granted, but now my reawakened senses allow me to see it through a different lens. In this town, strangers chat like old friends. Brass bands, jazz funerals, and second line parades are part of everyday life. I spend much of my time playing for carnival balls and eccentric pub crawls.

Icons range from Satchmo and Fats Domino to salt of the earth heroes like Mister Okra—the last of a dying breed of people who drives through the Marigny neighborhoods selling produce from his truck, announcing his wares with a bullhorn in the old tradition of street criers. And of course there's the late Ruthie the Duck Lady, a famous schizophrenic woman who traversed the French Quarter on roller skates and always had live ducks trailing after her.

And the Mardi Gras Indians are another element that is difficult to describe to the outside world. They have their longstanding traditions that span many generations of Big Chiefs and Big Queens, elaborate handmade costumes, jagged edge tambourine rhythms, Wild Men, spy-boys, flag boys, signals, and Creole patois. African tribes meet First Nation tribes, blended beings all.

So why wouldn't this be a place for lycanthropy as well? Like the Mardi Gras Indians, lycanthropy isn't a mantle that any person can just take up. It just happens to you, and you can either walk away from it or celebrate it.

So many labels have been slapped on me over the years: diva, monster, angel, prize, and white trash whore. I have drifted between shores of identity, an uprooted tree trying to blindly navigate its way through the floodwaters. And now I have been swept onto the shore of the Promised Land in a way that no street preacher could have ever foreseen.

This transformation. I am still incredulous that it happened in front of others, let alone four people I love. I had never let a soul know until now, and shame had burned up most of my energy trying to stifle my dual nature. Even before I had any clue that I would someday become a werewolf, I was simply *different*. And anyone who has ever been different knows that that is a near death sentence in school.

I don't know what I would have done without Sylvia back then. She was a misfit redhead with her nose constantly in a book, and I was a restless tomboy with complete disdain for authority and the inability to blend in. Luckily Sylvia lived two blocks away from me and was quick to soothe me, helping me to transform my frustration into humor as we explored the most ridiculous 'what if' scenarios in our heads—usually pitting our nemeses against each other in imaginary cage wars. She was always immersed in her piano lessons, yet always had time for me whenever I showed up at her house, bass in hand—the oboe that my folks thought I should learn just wasn't satisfying to me. She was ready for us to jam out on "Light My Fire" or any number of songs over which we could bond.

I wish I'd known that we were both born lycans. We were, after all, the ones who spent our teenage years secretly swapping horror novels, playing "Light as a Feather," and sitting up all night with Mountain Dew and the Ouija board in her family's game room. My parents were always so preachy about hellfire and damnation, and

I didn't trust many of the other girls enough to let my animalistic curiosity slip to them.

I had been devastated when Sylvia had suddenly disappeared with her family, not knowing that her entire household was lycan and about to get its cover blown. And then, with no other friends, the bullying started. It was that time when cruelty at school was an epidemic for which there was no cure. There wasn't even an official name to call attention to the issue of this merciless persecution, and the teachers neither cared nor intervened. The other kids could not smell it on me, but they knew that I was somehow different, which is a pre-teen death sentence. The bullies and their disciples might have spared a girl with a physical disability, but an able-bodied kid was fair game for getting punched, tripped, taunted, and—worst of all—labeled. I always felt a fire of rage in my belly, but I would always freeze for fear of what I might actually do if I unleashed it.

I had no outlet. So nearly every day I would run through the woods in which we used to play, screaming out my despair. If I could not preserve my innocence, I was going to slaughter it as brutally as possible—before someone or something else could beat me to it. I wanted to watch it die, wanted it to beg for mercy so that I could show it none, the way none was shown to me. But of course this was impossible, because my innocence was already gone. So I took out my beastly anger on my surroundings. The trees and ferns, the paths and creatures, the things I had loved so were now my targets. Anything in my way was slashed, torn, and mangled on my rampages. And then one day, there no turning back, and I realized exactly *how* different I was.

As my body made its transition to adolescence, I seemed to have inherited a curse—or was it a blessing? In recurring dreams I received visitations from shadowy entities, enticing and frightening. Their silky voices were more tangible than audible: *"Your time has come. Arise and hunt your destiny."* Wolf-shaped with diamond bright eyes, these were the most perfect creatures I had ever seen, and I wanted more than anything to be accepted by them. After fighting this growing instinct for years, it was a relief to finally accept this lycan life, the only thing that made me feel protected and powerful.

The option to fight it never entered my mind.

I received some sort of warning before my first complete metamorphosis, although I hadn't figured it out until many years later. The last time I had seen my grandmother was during a trip back to Scotland. Before she died, she was trying to tell me something: *"You're alikened to . . . alikened to . . ."* *Alikened to what?* I'd wondered for years. It wasn't until my first transformation that I realized she'd been saying, *"You're a lycan, too."*

The only thing that prevented my savagery from ruling me was my first bass guitar. My rants in the woods subsided as I immersed myself in its healing low tones. And so began my dedication to this safe haven of music, and my instrument became my first real shield. Learning some bass lines and their foundational structure became the path to tame the destructive flame within, to soothe the beast of me, and to hide it during full moon phases. No matter what anyone said or did at school, it no longer mattered. The monster that was trying to surface within me went back to its lair, and I found some kids my age to play with in a little garage band. At last I was able to connect with other people, and the nightmare was over for a spell.

My trials had taught me to blend in with my surroundings. They showed me that it was possible for a she-wolf to get through college, play gigs, cultivate friendships, and keep her wildness stifled during the full moon. I had managed to land a lucrative gig, playing bass with the world-famous bluesman Slackjaw Harrison, which suddenly put me in the best of clubs and festivals all over the world. I had even dated.

I shouldn't have worried about my wolfishness being exposed to my suitors, for in dating who wants to see the true person anyway? They only saw a gal with a good gig. Some of the young bucks just wanted to be bought lavish gifts, some betrayed me, and some wanted to be seen with me but lacked interest in getting to know me. So when Calvin O'Quinn came along, with his keen attention to my playing and his acceptance of my wild nature, I ignored the warnings my instinct was screaming.

I wonder if my lycan life was the only thing that allowed me to survive my former relationship with Cal, or if my preternatural senses caused me to be more deeply entangled with him. He tasted of money and power, both of which had intrigued me, for I had never known these things. He had a penetrating stare that could draw me in and hypnotize prey. At close range he could choke me singlehandedly, and from afar he could suffocate my spirit.

I paid dearly for the boost he gave my career. His input included coercion into tanning beds and controlled food portions. I began to get weaker, and his power grew. I recall my promo photo from several years ago. I looked as close to beautiful as I would ever be, but in truth I was starving.

Perhaps werewolves aren't inherently vicious. Perhaps most of us simply go mad from being given this gift that is taboo to use, like a beautiful and deadly weapon that is illegal to own.

I finally reached the point where my raw instinct took over, and one day I fought back. He was grabbing me by the face so hard that my back teeth were cutting into the insides of my cheeks. I lashed out and bit him on the hand. A scrap of his skin, dry and oddly patterned, came off in my mouth. We both stared at the scrap before he turned on his heel and disappeared from my apartment so instantaneously, I could have sworn he had vanished into thin air. And just like that, I saw him no more. Should I have fought harder? Should I have tried to run away sooner?

Shame boils in my belly.

I finally recognized that I was better off alone. But then I began recording with Rowan and found that we laughed easily together, sharing a love of "outsider music" and egregious B-movies. I had stopped daring to dream of true love by then, and tried to bury the notion of more than friendship with this compelling music man. But at my first whiff of his lycanthropic scent, I could no longer repress my hope for a deeper connection.

Now, everything is different. I have my pack: Sylvia duBois, Raúl Makamu, Teddy Lee, and Rowan López. My whole world has just expanded. I will give the gigs my all and try to be an asset to the pack.

What do I really want in life, true love or a successful career? I am supposed to be hard-wired to strive for a successful music career. It's the eternal hunt, always pushing for more. According to the masses, performers aren't supposed to feel pain. They aren't supposed to have hobbies, confidantes, or even boundaries. This is the age of instant gratification, and we are expected to be available to the public at any given moment. But the tiny bits of glory, the places I've gone, the things I've seen . . . I've tasted enough to want to stay in the game.

But at some point, happiness and true love would be a nice option.

Perhaps the simple, basic necessity of belonging is enough. It's going to be a fine line to tread: a balance between pack, career, and hope for love. I hope to every higher power that I don't screw this up.

I shake myself out of my musings like a dog come in from the rain. I've just walked almost three miles, and haven't even thought about it. I'm almost to the New Orleans Music Exchange. I need new bass strings, and it will be good for me to drop in and say hi to everyone. A dose of the normal would be good medicine, if hanging with musical equipment dealers could be considered normal.

Just before I reach the cross street of Louisiana Avenue, a shriek nearly makes my heart stop. It isn't a human cry of terror, but it sets my every nerve on edge. Ignoring the traffic and indignant horns, I go pelting across the road, off to the side of my destination, and find the source of the sound. It's a dead mockingbird draped over the roots of the old oak tree down the block. I shrug off any advice I've ever heard about handling dead wildlife and lightly put a finger to its breast. The bird is still limp and warm, eyes and mouth wide open as if to scream, and I stare until my neck prickles.

Mingling with the outside world no longer appeals to me, and the safety of my own house screams my name. I buy my strings as quickly as possible, catch the bus home, and lock myself inside. Lighting some candles and incense, I choose my favorite bass, my Rickenbacker, plug into my small practice amp, and dial up some comfort and grounding. I play into the late hours in a vain attempt to drown out the shriek that still resonates in my mind.

CHAPTER

3

THEORY AND PRACTICE

My phone rings just as I am waking up, and I silently commend this caller for waiting until a decent hour to summon a nocturnal musician. Then I see that it's Teddy, which makes sense. "Hey, pack-mate," he croons. "We need to have a rehearsal."

"Huh?" Having two basses on a gig isn't unheard of around here. I've seen groups with two electrics, electric and upright, or even electric and sousaphone. Teddy and I have often considered covering the two-bass masterpiece "The Maker" by Daniel Lanois, but I don't recall having been booked for a two-bass gig with him.

His familiar chuckle wrests a grin from my lips. "Code talk. It's our first pack meeting together. You know, like if we're going to be a pack, we have to actually be in one place now and then. Rowan has a room at the Fountainbleau."

"The *Fountainbleau?*" Tipitina's Fountainbleau, just off of Tulane Avenue, is a former Mid-City hotel turned complex of rehearsal spaces and studios for musicians to rent long term. It seems like an unlikely meeting place for a bunch of potentially dangerous shape-shifting carnivores, since there are people all over the facility at every hour.

He laughs again at my pre-coffee stupor. "Okay, so we're freaks of nature, but we're musicians nonetheless. What better place to hide than among a bunch of fellow nutjobs? Especially since so many of them are insomniacs anyway. I know your car is still in the shop, so I'll pick you up in an hour. Bring your bass, but don't worry about backline—Rowan says that we have amps."

Hiding in plain sight. He's right, of course. Congregating in nature within a day's drive might only tempt some yahoo with a shotgun. I can't wait to see what this rehearsal is all about.

◆ ◆ ◆

The old eight-story building is a familiar sight to me. From many varied rehearsals and recording sessions out here, I am already well acquainted with the pleasant, slightly musty smell of hundreds of individual A/C units tempering each room—or not. On the ground floor just before the elevators is a large vending machine replete with nearly everything a musician might need in a pinch: individual guitar and bass strings, picks, drumsticks, earplugs, blank CDs, and nine-volt batteries. Going deeper into the giant hive I can hear the bleed-through of sounds from assorted bands. Unbeknownst to the players, they create a private cacophonous symphony for the outsider's listening pleasure, comprised of funk, blues, and heavy metal. At the top floor, we pad silently down the long halls that could pass for hotel corridors save for the cement floors and uncarpeted walls. It looks more like a disciplinary school for wayward players, a strict institution that no longer carries any threat or shame.

Raúl and Sylvia appear to have arrived a split second before us, standing in front of a small door on the left. Raúl grins and queries, "We should have some sort of secret knock or something, shouldn't we?" He raps out a flurried rhythm with his knuckles. Teddy snorts, "Morse code for the Toronto airport isn't exactly a secret knock, you caveman drummer!" Before Raúl can retort, the door jerks open.

And then we enter the tiny room, and I step into what feels like another universe.

Aside from the expected small size of a practice room—probably sixteen by twelve feet—this space is like no other cell here in which I've done rehearsal time. The soft illumination seems to come from everywhere, easy on light-sensitive eyes. A whiff of something rich and familiar, maybe cedar, blurs the olfactory traces of the outside world. Instead of the usual band stickers and grimy concert flyers hanging on the pressboard walls, there are vibrant tapestries of mandalas and colorful cushions offsetting our pack equipment. There is a pristine seven-piece drum kit with state of the art cymbals for Raúl to use, a few brand-new amps for everyone else, some mic stands, three vocal mics, a small monitor, and a modest mixing console. There's something else different about this room, a soft veil that can only be detected with a gut feeling. It's the same sort of hocus-pocus protection about that enabled us to go unnoticed in the parking lot the other night. This explains why, unlike the other rooms, there is no sonic bleed-through in here, which probably means that no one can hear us either.

Rowan is waiting inside, and he is a completely different man.

Gone is the passive, patient veneer, replaced by his stronger nature: flame and steel and ferocity. His cheekbones are more pronounced, and although his form looks the same, something beneath his skin seems harder, leaner, and more intense. But he smells the same, and his eyes are still kind.

I smile at him with a mixture of joy and shyness, like greeting a lover in the morning after a first tryst. His black eyes sparkle. "Buzz! Welcome to your new life of fully accepting who you are," he greets me in a voice that seems to have gained overtones. "We are, after all, a hybrid of the two most misunderstood creatures in the world: the wolf and the musician. And welcome everyone else! The pack is complete at last." This is met with a few cheers and yips.

I am at a loss for words. "This is . . . quite the private facility!" I blurt out.

"It needs to be for what we're going to be pulling off," Teddy supplies. "Let's face it: musicians can be narcissists, substance abusers, swindlers, eccentric assholes, and just plain crazy. And werewolves . . . well, we can be almost as bloodthirsty as any other musician. This is why in this combination of lives, we have to work twice as hard to not make waves. Can you imagine what would happen if we were the worst of both worlds?"

I shudder. "I would hate to imagine. At least it feels secure in this room, almost like no one knows that we're here." And it really is a safe haven, part den, part temple, and part playground.

Rowan turns his smile on me, and my heart flips. "Secrecy is one of the most important things of all," he explains. "We are far more endangered than we have ever been dangerous. Now that you have come into your own, you need to be aware of how surreptitiously you need to live your dual nature. You also need to know about warding and shielding. This is crucial to remaining undetected. Using the power of your consciousness, you can disguise your scent, even to other lycans. You can also obfuscate your energy signals, keeping yourself safe from humans."

"But wouldn't a whiff of a rumor that I am potentially a little dangerous make people back off?" I blurt out. The infinite patience in Rowan's eyes smarts worse than a jab. I get the hint: apparently I have "stupid question Tourette's syndrome" today.

Raúl suddenly appears grim and pensive. "Trust me, little one: if we were so invincible, we wouldn't have to go into hiding. Humans are capable of genocide toward other humans . . . how do you think they would react toward a people like us? Fear brings out true monstrosities. Remaining warded will spare you a lot of danger, not to mention heartbreak."

Rowan cuts off the solemnity at its knees, interjecting, "Ok, enough already. Let us howl!" He ends his command with a dramatic flair, releasing the tension.

I notice that there are cushions on the floor for five people, but it isn't laid out in a perfect circle, or even a symmetrical pentagram if the lines had been connected. Rowan's seat is the largest, and the rest of us take up smaller stations in a semicircle facing him. One large and four small, and then I realize that the layout from above resembles a wolf's pawprint.

"Buzz, you were an oboist once. How about giving us a note?"

"Come again?" is my dumbfounded response. I haven't played oboe since college, and even then, it was only so I could get that sweet scholarship that enabled me to attend without the threat of paying off student loans until the end of time.

Teddy chuckles. "Many musical packs tend to think in terms

of a starting note. You know how the principal oboist gives the orchestra an A, and everyone tunes up to that note? You have the best sense of pitch . . . I think you ought to be the one. What do the rest of you guys think?"

I am dubious. "Should the alpha be the one . . .?" I don't know much about wolves, but I do happen to know that in true wolf packs, there tends to be an Alpha male and Alpha female, lower ranking Betas, and an Omega, who is not a low man on the totem pole, but rather a peacekeeper or court jester.

Rowan appears thoughtful. "Many conventional rules go out the window when it comes to lycan bands. One of the biggest mistakes that people make is to apply human traits to wolves, and the reverse is also true. We are not entirely wolves, and we are not entirely human, either. Because we belong to neither one nor the other, some lycans remain loners, but most naturally gravitate toward each other and form packs. Different packs find each other based on common strengths of our lupine senses—for us it is our sharp hearing, while others bond based on their sensitivity to lunar phases, group dynamics, or smell and instinctively form small groups of preternatural communities. For example, many lycans make superb wine experts, social workers, oceanographers, or in our case musicians. We all channel it different ways."

I recall that my cousin Bonnie MacKinlay back in Scotland is a whisky expert. I wonder if she's one of us, and if she could be harnessing her lycan skills with enhanced sense of smell.

Rowan cuts through my tangent. "Earth to Buzz! Do you want to give this a shot?"

I am oddly pleased to be asked, almost pathetically so. I never had any aspirations of being a great oboe player in college—I was having too much fun playing bass on Frenchmen Street every night, much to the dismay of my advisors. I had a good tone, which made me come across as a better player than I actually was, but my heart was never in it. My days as principal oboist came to an end when I could no longer contain my subversive humor, and decided that it would be funny to give the orchestra a B-flat instead.

Now I sit back and clear my throat. No, throat clearing is bad for voices. The rest of the pack is looking at me with kind patience, waiting for me to figure something out. At first I feel stupid. I have howled in complete wolf form, but something about doing this in human form feels something cross between childish and disingenuous. I decide that I'm overthinking this, and unfocus my mind a little. I take a deep breath and a yawn bursts forth: a yawn with a high-whistling overtone, sounding much like a big, lazy dog. I can feel it in my sinuses and soft palette. I think I'm onto something. I raise my head and instead of trying to land directly on the note, I croon a gentle rising howl that eases its way into the standard A concert pitch. Nothing resonates.

Finally I try shutting off my mind and reaching for a *feeling* in the note vicinity, a bit lower in pitch but with feeling, something that no orchestra has ever required of me. This time something opens in my mind and a tingle runs down my spine.

The others gradually join in. Not in the perfect fifths and fourths that string players play, striving to all become a perfect colony. Not the flurry of wind players, running across their favorite licks to get into their comfort zones. This is something simpler . . . and at the same time way more intricate. Tones glide around each other, not limited to any paltry western scale of twelve distinct notes. I had no idea how limiting absolute pitches and perfect intervals could be. In the howl, the musical potential is infinite. It's the difference between a paint-by-number kit and a finely blended oil painting. In a slight trance, I feel the tones swirling around with all five of my senses.

It reminds me of a music therapy workshop I once attended years ago. We learned a technique called "vocal toning". Someone started with a vocal note, and everyone joined in, relative notes somehow finding each other, tonal centers changing and everyone gradually going with the flow, like a school of fish all changing direction at once, or thousands of starlings in flight—natural and primitive. It had nothing to do with performance and everything to do with raw emotion. I had been nearly lightheaded at the end, feeling as though I had been slightly tranced out . . . it had been a powerful experience.

This goes beyond even that. I am more than a voice box musical instrument, a speaker cone, or a radio receiver. I surrender to just loving the sound of my note as it merges with other tones, drifts away from them into complex intervals, and then reunites with the drone. All the pleasure centers in my brain have been short-wired to my auditory perception. I feel the pull of the tides in my veins and I feel the wind over the earth. Human minds judge a performance, but lycan minds are all about a connection.

The music naturally begins to decay and fade out, and with a satisfied sigh we all turn towards Rowan. It's obvious to me that Rowan is the Alpha, and everyone else just sort of falls into a natural order like notes in a chord, with Rowan as the tonic.

Democracy in a band is a nice concept, but everyone knows that it's seldom the reality. It's also far less stressful in the long run to have someone have the final say-so, so long as there is mutual respect.

I can no longer contain myself. I glance at Rowan. "So, are you the Alpha of this organization, or what?"

Rowan's smile is maddeningly ambiguous. "We may be part human and part beast, but we are all musician. A traditional ranking does not apply as it does in other packs of lycans or true wolves. There are different rules for different packs, not unlike different systems of government for different nations. Basically what works for most musical packs is just *'stay in the groove.'* Don't give it too much thought. Musical lycan packs are unlike most bands—we are *loyalty*-based, with the intent to have no backstabbing or power struggles. We have to set our egos aside in order to survive."

"But yes, Little One, Rowan is our Alpha," adds Raúl. "When we discussed forming a pack a few years ago, I more or less insisted. He has the most musical experience and sharpest instincts. His wisdom has been legendary for decades, and forming this pack was his brainchild." It occurs to me that I have no idea how old Rowan really is, or even Raúl. Wolves don't tend to live much longer than a decade in captivity—even less in the wild—and humans decline altogether too soon. I wonder if the two factors cancel each other out?

"I am happy to be his right hand man," Raúl continues, now speaking to us all. "As far as finding the rest of you, we didn't have to try very hard to decide who we wanted. All we had to do was sit back and observe the scene over the past year. The cream always rises to the top, and the answers became obvious. Teddy, with his fluid social skills and teamwork ethos, was eager to join the party. Sylvia was already clinging to her newfound reclusive life, and took a little more convincing. But when she realized how much good she could do as a spiritual advisor to other lycans, she welcomed the prospect."

"Hey, I didn't want to miss *all* of the fun!" the nun gently protests.

"But you, Little One," he says turning to me, "you were the most stubborn!" He lightly raps my skull with his knuckles. "Hardheaded! You hang onto your secrets so hard, you should be part bulldog! And that is actually a very important trait, to be able to guard secrets."

"Let's take a break," Rowan's voice is a benevolent command. "We need to address a major issue, here. We old farts—Raúl and yours truly—know most of the shifters in the local music scene. Buzz, I have a feeling that no one has told you yet that shapeshifters are far from limited to lycanthropes. You'll catch up on all the lore during your training. In any case, we lost one of our own yesterday. Have you guys heard of Alma's passing?"

Alma! I didn't know her well, but am saddened to hear this news. They called her "the little bird that could," and she was the darling of Frenchmen Street. She could sing anything, from gritty torch ballads to vulnerable tunes, breathy and childlike. I recall her sunny disposition and fearless array of tattoos.

"I heard something about that," Teddy pipes up. "They found her on Louisiana Avenue by the roots of that big ol' oak tree, just down from New Orleans Music Exchange. Autopsy reveals some sort of poisoning."

"She was a *shifter?* Oh gods, no . . ." I hear myself moan. "I saw a dead mockingbird yesterday in that same spot. That was *her?*" I try to fend off the wave of guilt, even though I don't know what I could have done to prevent it.

"I have been receiving information over the last few months through a network of other Alphas," Rowan continues. "Something is harassing shifter existence. We don't yet know how widely spread the threats are outside of New Orleans, but some clandestine movement is at large."

"Sounds like some sort of government conspiracy to me," Teddy murmurs pensively.

Rowan shakes his head. "For the government to want to use us, they'd have to admit that we exist. The repercussions would be too severe if there were ever a leak; not just about the secrecy, but also the indentured servitude. We're not talking about Roswell rumors, we're talking American citizens . . . mostly." He finishes this sentence with a respectful nod at Raúl.

"Does anyone have a clear reason why?" I ask. I am only just now embracing this new life and this new sense of belonging. I can't bear to have another precious thing violated.

Sylvia is the voice of reason. "Does it have to be complicated? Do you remember the principle of 'Occam's Razor'? Basically the simplest explanation is probably it. It's most likely either greed or fear. The same reason that countries are at war, that greed battles empathy, that prejudice sends the masses on proverbial witch hunts."

Raúl lets fly an abrupt chortle. "What, they're out to get women in long black cloaks?" he teases her. With lightning speed, my best friend whips out a ruler from seemingly thin air, grabs Raúl by the wrist, and smacks him smartly across the palm of his hand. "A hundred Our Fathers, you scandalous child!" she castigates him. The big man pretends to cry like a little boy as the rest of us double over in hysterics, shattering our tension and fear of the unknown threat. I wonder if Sylvia always keeps that ruler handy, like pepper spray.

The ensuing hard laughter that springs from us all breaks the tension, and I am grateful for this tiny morsel of relief. Then Rowan wipes his eyes and continues the discussion. "There are more packs out there that any of you can possibly imagine, and all packs are united by some common factor; for us it is music. And even more groups of other kinds of shifters exist, even for the non-gregarious ones; more like a kind of union without all the fees and restrictions.

"Some of the more high-falootin' shifters and I are in the process of organizing a combination awareness rally and musical showcase this coming harvest moon to send out a warning through cryptic lyrical messages and more complex wordless signals through harmonies, polyrhythms, and energy signals. Our task is to alert our people, as well as dispense healing and courage. It's most likely going to take place at The Howlin' Wolf, publicly billed as the standard ambiguous 'private party, but Teddy suggested that we call it . . ."

"Howlapalooza!" Teddy chimes in on cue.

"The powers-that-be will listen if they get word that Rowan has written lyrics and will be performing, which he seldom does anymore . . . this is why he does not write or play live, save special occasions," Sylvia explains. "Our Alpha is a much bigger deal than he's been letting on."

"One good piece of news is that we have an organization of our own trying to pinpoint and eradicate whoever is behind all this," says Rowan. "Shifter Infiltration Network, or SIN, is a covert intelligence operation dedicated to keeping our kind safe and out of the public eye. Which leads me to the next topic: modern communication."

We are each given a special cell phone with the rest of the pack on speed dial, as well as the numbers of a few other top-ranking lycans in the area. The contacts are highly encrypted, and the ringtones are designed to be only heard by other lycans—like a dog whistle of the highest technical innovations.

The different members of the pack are assigned different tasks for my training in different aspects of lycan life. I am thrilled to have this new world opened to me by the people I love and trust. But a tiny shard of self-doubt nags me. I am the neophyte, and worry that I will be the weak link in the chain. *A band is only as strong as its weakest member,* I have so often heard, and hope that this also does not apply to a pack. I push the worry with a mighty sweep to the back of my mind and try to refocus on everything that lies ahead for my new life.

I am the only member of the pack who has never had any training, but the others are eager to show me the ropes. "I wonder what would have happened if you guys hadn't finally called me out," I muse. The image on the "Join or Die" flag —a snake hacked to bits—comes to mind, and I barely repress a shudder.

"This is why it's a hard road for a lone wolf coming into its own," Sylvia assents. "Imagine having to grow into adolescence without anyone warning you that you were going to get boobies or periods! Sorry . . ." She aims the apology at the remaining males. "The rest of us had training by various elders. Rowan and Raúl had their families, I had family friends who were lycans, and later special factions of the Church . . ."

"And I had the Boy Scouts!" finishes Teddy with a grin. "Believe me, kiddo, the others had it way easier. There is much more to being a werewolf that just trying to suppress your state every full moon. You have to learn the physical, spiritual, social, and mystical aspects of it all."

For physical training, Rowan urges me to spend more time at

the gym. I freeze. The last person to suggest that I do that was Cal, and it was because he was forever telling me that I was fat. I try not to hear the echo of his cold, silky voice in my mind . . .

Rowan picks up on my distress. *Damn!* So much for controlling my emotions.

Mercifully, he pretends not to notice. He explains, "Two different sets of metabolism for two different corporeal forms can really throw your body out of whack. You burn more calories and body fat when you're in wolf form, but when you change back to human, your metabolism won't know what to do, and it will try to overcompensate. If your human form stays in good physical shape, you'll have an easier time switching. Have you ever seen a fat wild animal?"

As a matter of fact, I have. "The captive tiger at that truck stop in Grosse Tete." I remember seeing this poor creature come waddling out of its hiding place in its cement cell, looking more like a neurotic Garfield than an exotic beast.

He nods. "Exactly. A body designed to hunt for its prey can gain more weight if it's not challenged. Werewolves can get out of shape just like any living creature, no matter what our advantages may be in strength and speed. If you spend a good amount of time at the gym, you will not only have a prolonged life, but also everything— your mind, your reflexes, your endurance, and yes, even your bass chops—will benefit."

"Oh, by the way," he adds, "you'll want to stretch and rehydrate your body as much as possible after switching back to human form. You know how your muscles can get sore after a strenuous workout? Imagine how sore you'll be after a complete metamorphosis of your muscular-skeletal system and them back again. But don't worry . . . just like exercise, it gets easier and easier to adjust the more you do it. Don't overtax your body, and remember to meditate afterward."

Raúl is placed in charge of overseeing this training. His expertise lies in the body, the physical vehicle through which we live as musicians and as wolves. I have a feeling that he's going to tease me through my struggles, and that I'm going to be flipping him the bird a lot.

Social training is the mission given to Teddy, and I grin. We get to be *drinking buddies?* Of course, there's more involved than that. A lover of world music and a walking encyclopedia of cultures, Teddy is the teacher of communication, social mores, protocol, and codes.

Sylvia is, of course, assigned to guide me through the spiritual process. I am relieved not only to be able to continue to confide in her, but to hopefully learn what I so desperately want to hear: that I am not a monster, but something inherently good, instead.

Rowan will talk me through the more eldritch musical theories and emotional shielding. I will learn to let the waters of my feelings flow, freeze, or evaporate. He tells me that energy shielding is sometimes crucial to survival. He will teach me more about warding. We are to meet on a weekly basis. My heart does a cartwheel. Life just gets better and better.

Before we adjourn we test out the backline equipment provided for us. I am like a babe in toyland: the brand new Markbass combo has a wide range of tones that I can coax out of it. Teddy tries out the SWR bass combo, and we swap back and forth, comparing sounds. Rowan answers my silent question about where all this stuff came from: the combination of his Alpha heritage and years of careful financial planning and people-watching have allowed him to form a nest egg and put together what he considers the perfect musical pack.

We are all supposed to meet to play music together on a regular basis. Playing, I am told, helps ease any tensions in pack hierarchy. It also strengthens the bonds.

I have Teddy drop me off on St. Charles Avenue at the edge of Audubon Park, and I walk home along Exposition Street the rest of the way. It's a nice day, and I need to savor the howl still ringing in my ears for a spell.

◆ ◆ ◆

On my way back from our "rehearsal", I am more than a little bit overwhelmed. My life has changed so drastically, and I've kept my secret guarded for so long.

Until I met my pack, I had never told a soul. Yet somehow only one person seemed to figure it out. No words were ever said, but his implications were enough to make me sick with fear.

The echo of his words rings in my ears. *You're just a stupid little bitch . . . you'll never be anything but a stupid little bitch . . . I know just what to do with girls like you . . .* I shudder at the memory of his fingers gripping my hair, my eyes filled with tears from pain and bewilderment as he nearly ripped my locks from my scalp.

Calvin Quinn had been tall and charismatic. He would never be what anyone would consider handsome, but his presence was compelling from the first moment I saw him in the audience at one of my gigs with old Slackjaw Harrison. He was well liked by many bigwigs in the music industry. His veneer was generous and chivalrous. Fond of fine dining, fine wine, art, and music, he was a collector and a connoisseur. My bass playing and stage presence were definitely things he wanted slices of.

I had been playing with Slackjaw for a few years, and Cal had bought every CD of his that I appeared on. Next thing I knew, he had booked the band to play for a private show at the house of a famous NBA athlete. Next gig was for a major corporation, which paid us more money in one night than any of us had seen in six months. And then it became a blur of parties, dinners, galleries, and studios. Sometimes we would meet for dates, and sometimes he would disappear for a few weeks at time. It was all a bit surreal, but I never questioned it. I had never been prized by a male like this before, especially by such a jet setter.

My parents had found Cal utterly charming when they came into town for a visit, and he took us all to lunch at the establishment of one of the most prestigious chefs in the city. The vintage wine was flowing freely, and he had an expert tongue for the perfect region and year to compliment our entrees. There was nothing not to like; he was wealthy and polite, and they thought he would be good for their self-employed daughter who lived from gig to gig. He discussed art history with my mother, fishing and science with my father. He was a canny businessman who would buy property or land, increase its value through shrewd marketing, then resell it for twice the amount, and start all over again. He never stayed with any one endeavor for more than a few years, but was always on the move. And his ventures took him everywhere. New York. London. Dubai. Bangkok.

And he had a major dark side, as I had discovered too late. I couldn't help but wonder if Cal was affiliated with some sort of organized crime.

When I began to sense that something was not quite right about him and began to withdraw, he began to insinuate that he knew that something was not quite right about me in turn. And then the questions in that light and dangerous tone began: "Does your family even know what you *are?*" By then I had had a feeling that they already knew on some level, but would be devastated that I had not only chosen the curse willingly but also had actually relished it, dreaming of the day that I could one day terrorize and kill and maim. My parents would never be the same if they knew, so I was willing to take this shameful secret to the grave. And Cal somehow had sensed this, becoming a sword of Damocles hanging over me, ready to strike at any moment.

I shudder hard, forcing myself to focus on the present, the sunlight, the beauty of the huge oak trees, and the passing horses from Cascade Sables. Cal was somewhere far away now—in Vancouver, last I'd heard. And now I am a stronger, wiser wolf with a whole new life ahead of me.

◆ ◆ ◆

Back in the little hidey-hole of my apartment, it's a relief to focus on the mundane for a spell. I let my gaze fall upon my collection of potentially harmful toys and my stash of exquisitely bad movies—*I am still the same old me.* Reassured, I settle down to my writing desk, which is partly my "altar," adorned with nothing more than a candle, a trio of Rush bobblehead dolls, and a pair of tiny resin foo dogs that somehow got named "Rocco" and "Prestia." I flip open my computer and check for messages from my website. I haven't had a steady lucrative gig since Slackjaw's passing, but refuse to let this be the only high point of my career. This site not only lets folks know where I'm playing, but also shows some samples of my playing as a way to get new work. I'm hoping to get back onto a big bandwagon soon.

The very first message makes me audibly suck in my breath. It's from the late night talk show I had auditioned for, *Past Your Bedtime with Titus and Ronicus*. I had submitted a video of a one-woman one-bass show, singing Joni Mitchell's adaptation of Charles Mingus' "Goodbye Pork Pie Hat." I was especially proud of that little gem, since I'd arranged it for six-string fretless bass, able to alternate between walking basslines and some jazzy little chords, singing the whole time. It had taken me months to prepare, and I click on the message with such alacrity, I almost accidentally delete it in the process. This could be my big break at last.

> *Dear Ms. MacKinlay;*
>
> *We regret to inform you that your video was not chosen for our show. However, we encourage you to continue to pursue your creative endeavors.*
>
> *Yours truly,*
>
> *Management*

Continue to pursue my creative endeavors? How condescending is that? What else am I supposed to do, throw my bass in the Mississippi River? A snarl rises in my chest as I delete the message with a hard click, as if punching the key with any more force could somehow make this unidentified management feel it. The hard lump in my throat and tears stinging my eyes only aggravate my humiliation. It would be simple to text one of the pack and vent, but I would rather try to take it like a grownup. A few deep breaths ground me. Curiosity is the final nail in the coffin, provoking me into checking out show's website to see who did make the cut, and it isn't a name I recognize. It's some female world music performer from Syria or Turkey or something like that.

"You guys have been through this too, haven't you?" I ask my bobbleheads. "But you eventually made it. You're even in the Rock and Roll Hall of Fame now. I just want to get one stinking crack at national exposure. Is that too much to ask?" They don't have any answers for me, but they nod in sympathy.

I take a moment to get a grip before perusing the rest of the messages in my inbox. A couple of them are nice notes from people who had seen me on other gigs. No inquiries about new work, though. Six different people have asked me when I'll be playing next, or will I be playing on this date or that date—even though my entire gig schedule is posted on this very same website. By the time I have answered everyone's emails, an entire hour has gone by. One complete stranger has even invited me for a romantic dinner, which creeps me out, and I politely decline. *What am I, an escort?* By now I just want to punch something, which wouldn't be good for my hands.

Social media offers me even less comfort. Local news reveals the murder of an NOPD cop, a mounted officer named Debra Colt. Policewomen are sometimes killed in the line of duty, which always saddens me, but what raises the hair on the back of my neck is a paragraph about the abnormal levels of distress the horses have been experiencing in the wake of Colt's death.

I close my laptop with a sigh.

It dawns on me that I can sanctify my frustration without shame. A slightly obsessive-compulsive check to reassure myself that all of my blinds are drawn and all three locks—chain, sliding, and deadbolt—on my front door are bolted, and I strip. Unfolding into my full lupine form does bring me a sense of relief, as part of my animal brain is able to overlook ego and hurt feelings. The rest of me vents with a growl. It feels pretty wonderful actually, the vibrations resonating from my skull to my chest. Tension rolls off of me in waves, and the growl becomes a lullaby to myself. I leap onto my bed, lightly chiding myself for being allowed on the furniture, curl into a ball, and let this savage rumble lull me to sleep.

◆ ◆ ◆

It's so awesome to have my little Honda back in one piece that the voyage out to the river parishes seems to take no time at all. Tires crunching on gravel, I pull up into the church parking lot in shockingly bright daylight. The old tree behind the building sways its branches in a new familiar light, as if throwing me a secret wink. The others have told me that the aspect of spirit is what needs to be most urgently attended. I am grateful to have Sylvia as my first instructor, comforted to be in the company of another woman in my early stages of initiation. Not that I can't trust the others, but Sylvia is the person I know the most intimately.

I have to address her as "Sister" on church grounds, of course, but I don't really mind this. She is the closest thing to a real sister that I have ever had, and if I keep a familial mindset, I actually feel that it only strengthens our bond. I just have to remember to stop calling her The Penguin or tease her about her habit in front of other clergy. I am relieved that she wants to meet me in her little office on the church grounds, as I'm not certain that I want to set foot into the nearby convent.

She is exactly where I expect her to be: in the sanctuary, practicing that fearsome pipe organ. The music could pass for Bach, and I can't suppress a grin in spite of myself—I certainly won't tell Father O'Flaherty that it's really the progressive rock creation of Emerson, Lake, and Palmer.

I'll be there! I'll be there! I will be there . . .

She turns around so suddenly that I jump. Even though I now know she's a werewolf, this is going to take some getting used to.

Her grin smears her freckles across her face in a cosmic pigment whirl. "I figured you'd be coming around about now."

I trot across the marble floor, aware of how loud my feet sounded in the bright room, even in my soft Chuck Taylors, and we embrace fiercely.

"Sylvia . . ." I begin.

She shushes me. "It's Sister Jean-Baptiste as long as we're in here, okay?" I give her a tight nod.

"Come on." She indicates the side door, leading to the yard and the huge old live oak tree, so very much like the ones on whose roots we used to play as kids. "We'll have some privacy in my office . . ."

Her private study is sparsely decorated: just a plain wooden cross and painted portraits of Saint Cecilia, Saint Clare, Saint Francis, Bob Moog, and an old photograph of Rick Wakeman live onstage with Yes in the late seventies. A laminated Steely Dan backstage pass hangs casually from a nail on the wall, and an ornate rosary hangs from another. She's ardently studying a book entitled *The Letters of Lupus of Ferrières,* but puts the book down to give me her familiar tackle-hug.

"Letters of Lupus . . .?" I inquire.

"Saint Lupus of Ferrières, one of many saints named Lupus. Pull up a chair. I'll filch some wine for us when Father O'Flaherty isn't looking." I can't tell whether or not she's teasing me, but she knows how to loosen me up.

I shamelessly peruse her bookshelf. Assorted memoirs of missionaries reside next to the biographies of Thelonius Monk and

Kate Bush. I poke and sniff around a little more, but everything still smells like the same old Sylvia. Awkwardness melts away at last. Content to commence my training, I pull up a chair next to my childhood friend, who grins sympathetically.

"Relax, Buzz! Don't you remember how we used to suspend our disbelief all the time back when we were kids? Playing with Ouija boards and watching horror movies!"

A bark of laughter tears its way out of me. "Oh boy, if we only *knew!* So *pray* tell me, Sister … what does it mean to be a werewolf in a world of right and wrong?"

Her expression sobers. "Much of what I'm about to tell you cannot be traced back to written records. It has to be documented in lycan-song, not unlike the oral tradition of the Celtic bards and the West African Griots. It is a sacred task." She reaches across the desk and pats my hand soothingly.

"First and most importantly," she says gently, "let's see what we can do about this shame you've been dragging around with you for all of these years. There is a term called 'Taming the Beast Within.' Have you heard the story of Saint Francis and the wolf?"

I nod. "The critter was killing the animals and people of the town known as Gubbio. Seems like it had issues." I can sense my growing discomfort, and chide myself for going into levity mode as usual when unease strikes.

Sylvia is steadfastly patient as always. "And of course, there was another kind of shape-shifting. Remember how his prayers mentioned, 'Where there is hatred, let me sow love. Where there is darkness, let there be light.' And so forth. Do you see where this transformation allegory is going?"

My brain hurts. "No idea," I reply.

Sylvia takes a deep breath. "There are *some* who believe—by way of this aforementioned word-of-mouth tradition—that this allegory is even more cryptic and that Saint Francis *was* the wolf."

I feel myself jump, and look furtively around the tiny austere room, as if something could get us.

"Not only that," she continues, pretending not to notice my , "but it has been said that Saint Francis was one of many holy lycans who overcame the beast within by becoming one with it, thus gaining enlightenment through sacrifice. They came in droves to the monasteries to escape persecution and to learn how to use their condition for the highest good. It wasn't until later that other werewolves over time gave lycans a bad name. Just as there have been corrupt police, clergy, lawyers, and politicians who have done the same for their kind, they besmirched a role that should be used to establish justice and safety."

"Sylvia . . . that's *heretical!!!*"

She cocks an eyebrow. "Any idea can be heretical if it isn't popular enough. Many works of early art depicted manger scenes in which wolves were standing guard over the holy family. Sometimes they were portrayed howling in grief at the foot of the cross. The Church destroyed most of these works, save the few in which people were convinced that the wolves were actually dogs."

"As if dogs aren't capable of atrocities, too," I grumble.

"Yes, but the symbolism of domesticity they exemplify gives humans the illusion of control. Now let's discuss the 'nature of the beast'. Wolves have been vilified in folklore for millennia. Even the word 'beast' has gotten a bad rap in one of our international bestsellers." She nods her head in the direction of the Bible on her desk. "A wolf is not inherently bad, of course. It simply IS. It is the human influence on the wolf, not the other way around, that can lend itself to making our kind a monstrosity.

"Wolves have no agendas," she continues. I know this in my heart of hearts, but I relish hearing it from someone else. "They do not seek revenge, they kill only for food or other means of survival, and not out of anger, jealousy, or greed. They do not care for the affairs of packs in other nations, or what the world makes of their own community." She pauses to offer me some coffee and give me a moment to let all this new knowledge soak in. I'd have taken notes, but the idea of any written records of this taboo topic makes me uneasy.

"This is to help you get out of your old way of regarding yourself, and of what 'Taming the Beast Within' really is," she tells me. "So really, it should be called 'Taming the Human Within,' but should this term leak out, it could potentially cause problems. But it is the human race that falls prey to greed and genocide. Fearful humans ban minority ideologies, and the dominant thought across many societies is 'If you are not like the rest of us, you must die.' People often fear anything that they cannot control, and so must tame it or destroy it."

And my lesson continues until my mind threatens to explode. I learn about lost ancient letters, destroyed sacred texts. I am given the scoop on Church reformations that reduced our lycan histories and origins to speculations and rumors, scarcely fit for late night radio and implausible television specials. It was said that lycans –in addition to many other half-human species—originated before the flood of Genesis as the result of man's crimes against nature. Those that survived the deluge were faced with a choice: they were to either be the combination of the best of their dual natures or the worst. Those who did not choose wisely quickly died out, and the rest disguised their kind for millennia. Not until the seventeenth century or so did records resume of these man-beasts as monstrosities.

This is about all I can take in for one day, and Sylvia pours me another cup of coffee before I head back to New Orleans. She leaves me with one final piece of advice as I walk to my car. "Just remember to use compassion as you look through this new lens of your learning. After all, humans are people too."

◆ ◆ ◆

Teddy's house is tucked away in the French Quarter. It's a very convenient place to live if you walk to most of your gigs, and complete hell if you need a parking place or a good night's sleep. I leave my car parked uptown and catch the Tchoupitoulas bus to Canal Street, then hoof it down Dauphine.

Even blindfolded I would have known the unmistakable sounds of the Quarter. The jingling overtones of rattling harnesses a split second before the clop of metal-shod mules' hooves accompany the buggy tours. Sharp smacks of bottlecaps nailed to the shoes of young tapdancers in tandem with the bright claps. The distant calliope sounding from the Creole Queen steamboat on the river that is blessedly more in tune with itself than it used to be. And there are the ubiquitous tunes from myriad street performers, ranging from beloved longtime local staples to the carpetbaggers who only pass through like locusts.

I compose a little bass riff in my head to the sound of my footsteps as I clear each cross street. *St. Ann . . . Dumaine . . . St. Philip . . .* I finally reach the front door to his typical shotgun house, and reach up to ring the bell, but he's heard me coming and opens the door on silent hinges. The grin on his face is one of lupine hilarity as he puts a finger to his lips.

I giggle before I even know what's funny. "Teddy, what is it?"

He whispers in my ear, "The Maestro got kicked out of his house a couple of nights ago by his girlfriend, and seeing how he's been such a douchebag, none of the other musicians will take him in. Except me, since I'm such a nice guy, right? But now he won't leave. He's been here for two solid weeks, and I figured it would be worth it to have an audience to my Dude-riddance ploy." He stifles his laughter with a Muttley-esque wheeze. "I've been patient long enough, but when I glanced at his duffel bag and saw that the dude was planning to swipe my copy of *The Adventures of Lord Iffy Boatrace*, I made up my mind that this means war."

Ah yes, *The Adventures of Lord Iffy Boatrace*. An out-of-print gem penned in the eighties by Iron Maiden frontman Bruce Dickinson, it is nothing short of hilarious, perverted genius . . . and it's one of Teddy's most prized possessions.

We slink into the living room where sprawled comatose on Teddy's couch is the one and only Maestro Dude Holstein, golden hair sticking every which way like a dried-up fern, mouth open like a brain-dead frog. Opposite the luxurious furniture is Teddy's stereo with floor-to-ceiling speakers. I watch him pop in a CD, crank the volume to eleven, and duck snickering behind the sofa like a kid who's just lit a firecracker. The room suddenly detonates with the low growling sounds of the Tuvan group Huun-Huur-Tu throat singing at a frightening decibel level rattling the walls, and the Maestro shoots off the couch as though fired from a cannon. He charges down the stairs and out the door, his open duffel bag leaving a trail of possessions in his wake, including a dilapidated stuffed rabbit and a soiled-looking sex toy.

"Teddy . . .!" I gasp, nearly asphyxiating from laughter. As I let the hilarity run its course, I pause to take in his half of the duplex. As often as I'd been to Teddy's apartment, I'd never stayed long enough to hang out much. Now it seems like a crime that I never did. After Teddy gathers the rest of the Maestro's things—careful to use a paper towel to pick up the adult novelty—we spend some time just catching up, reconnecting on a mundane level.

We spend a great deal of time swapping bass lore, of course. Teddy not only plays electric, but also upright bass. He is always full of compliments about my quick ear, but he can read music notation, tablature, and even the Nashville number system. We discuss the importance of ear training versus the ability to sight-read: instinct versus reason.

We also listen to world music—tons of it. I had heard of things like Tuvan throat singing and Sufi singing, but Teddy's CD collection enlightens me further. I hear recordings of Swedish *nyckelharpa,* Balinese *gamelan* ensembles, West African *Ewe* dance-drum interlocking rhythms, and the *pamiri rubab* of Tajikistan. He tells me a chilling story about the Greek godfather of *rebetiko.*

"What's this all about, Teddy?" I ask, holding up a CD. The lettering on the cover is in Roman characters, with strange punctuation that reminds me of French, but I know it definitely isn't that. The instrument in the cover photo is long-necked and graceful, with strange-looking tied-on gut frets placed at odd-looking intervals. The intricate inlay makes it look too pretty to play.

He smiles. "It's a Turkish *bağlama.* You really need to hear some of this stuff. It's perfect for an ear as fine as yours."

I frown a little. "It looks like a bouzouki." There's a chick in town who plays the Irish bouzouki—an adaptation of the Greek instrument—but I'm not all that crazy about her.

"It's a relative of the same family. Check this out . . ." He shows me some pictures of Turkish instruments in the CD booklet of the entire *saz* family, from the tiny cura to the mighty divan. "They tend to have seven strings clustered into three groups. Notice the soundhole isn't in the top . . . it's down by the bridge. And the irregular looking frets are laid out for a much more complicated scale than our twelve-note system. With your pitch-sensitive ear, you will appreciate all of the little microtones that make up the music." He pops the disc into his player.

The sound sends tingles up my spine. It's rasping and droning, with notes bending between notes, giving the expressive sound of a human voice. I hum the drone, thinking of the infinite possibilities of creating music with more than twelve notes. The track eventually fades and I can feel myself beaming gratefully at Teddy. He reluctantly switches his stereo off, swinging his body around to face me. I recall that we have work to do, but I'm eager to train.

"Now, for your first lesson," he says, all business now. "You need to know about some other kinds of shape-shifters, and there are a lot of them! Technically, the term 'shape-shifter' refers to a wide range of people, real and mythological alike, including fae, plant people, and folks that can take on the forms of other humans. The true name for our animal-shifting kind is *therianthrope,* or 'beast person.' 'Shifter' is the most widely accepted word for us therianthropes, though sometimes we are referred to as 'blended beings.' Want to know something even cooler? We hail from nearly every land on the planet. But we lycans are the only shape-shifters who can pass along our gift through a bite. Isn't that a relief? Otherwise, can you imagine how many weremosquitos there would be?

"We *parahumans*—or people with genetic elements of both humans and animals—are as diverse as any culture, and I have a sneaking suspicion that public knowledge only scratches the surface of what's really out there. It would take me forever to tell you about all the ones I know, and I'm still no expert. I can only give you a crash course today. Let's begin close to home. You may have heard of our First Nation shifters, such as the Native American skin-walkers, the Central American naguals, or Inuit Iljiraat. Just a few of the blended beings across Ireland, the UK, and Faroe Islands are selkies, pookas, and kelpies. Nordic berzerkers, or literally 'bear shirts' also come to mind. Let's see . . . the shifters from Oceania have gotten a pretty bad rap, but I've heard that the taniwhas of New Zealand, the atai of Melanesia, and the bunyips of Australia are making an effort to appear more benevolent these days. The Antarctic ningen are known to communicate with these neighboring shifters, but are otherwise pretty aloof. We have fellow canine shifters from other parts of the world such as jackal folk and kitsune, or Japanese foxes, which can have up to nine tails. Feline shifters hail from all over, and they're usually tied to the cats of their native lands: jaguar people in Central and South America, werecats in Europe, and weretigers in Asia. Leopard and lion people are common in Africa as well as shifters there who become hyenas or owls. Who have I left out? Oh yes, in India we have nagas . . ."

"Nagas?"

"Snake people. They originated in India but now have infiltrated every ethnic bloodline. In some cultures they are considered to be sacred, many humans fear them, and a lot of these slippery folks have let both of these factors go to their heads. Some say that the snakes gave dawning consciousness to humankind, and even introduced the written word. There aren't too many nagas who choose to reveal themselves, but you've probably played gigs with a few. You'll know them by their charm and their fearlessness, sometimes to the extreme. Because of their bite, they are said to be immune to things like hepatitis-C and other blood-borne illnesses, though they may still be able to carry the disease like everyone else, including shifters that take the forms of bloodsucking animals." I pause to let this sink in. Teddy fetches a couple of cans of NOLA beer from the fridge, discreetly giving me time to digest all this. He returns with a wolfish grin, hands me one, and I imbibe gratefully.

"Take some time to wrap your brain around all that info. We shifters are still learning more about each other every day! Okay, there is also social stuff you need to learn. You might not believe how much protocol there is to being a werewolf, but it *is* a culture as well as a race, after all. First up, let's talk about manners." He takes another swing of his beer and releases a giant belch, causing me to laugh and ground myself.

As then he begins to tutor me. I can't believe all of the things I've been missing. I might as well be preparing for a Japanese tea ceremony with all of the decorum and subtleties.

First and most importantly, there is the issue with eye contact. Teddy explains how breaking eye contact can mean anything from deference to signaling respect. And like true wolves, sustained eye contact is almost always a challenge for dominance. He compares this to eye contact in other cultures, which can mean anything from flirting to empathy. He talks about how exaggerated eye contact can sometimes indicate a history of occult abuse.

"Respect and boundaries are the keys to survival of so many different packs. We all *have* to get along, as we know from other bands. There's no room in 'the world's biggest small town' like New Orleans for acrimony, and when it exists, it's rough.

"On to the howl: it's one of the things that defines us. The way we howl together in our pack is our art, and a way to let off steam while strengthening our bond. But sending out a message is a completely different animal, pardon the expression. When wolves howl, it triggers a chain reaction, and so for us the need to automatically join in is visceral. It's as infectious as a yawn. But because we have a scheming human nature, we must rein this in and really listen to the message that's being conveyed.

"We can't allow it to get out of hand. It's fine for humans to mindlessly raise their voices at football games, but if we start howling frivolously, the meaning becomes taken less and less seriously, like . . ."

"The Boy who Cried Wolf!" we say in unison.

"It's bad enough with humans," he continues. "With the human race, collective focus can take the form of everything from prayer and chants to mass hysteria and riots.

"You know who knows the most about this stuff?" he suddenly brightens. "Abuelo." I smile at the realization that the wise old Honduran busker and everyone's "grandfather" figure is actually a shifter. "Come on," says Teddy, rising from his chair and pulling me to my feet. "Let's go pay him a visit."

But when we arrive at his home on Saint Claude, we discover his doorstep buried under a pile of newspapers, some of which are crumbling from the elements. I don't know him well enough to have noticed his absence, but my flesh begins to prickle. We wander the perimeter of his house, but see no signs of struggle and smell no traces of fear. It's as if he's simply vanished into thin air.

The neighbors all report that they too have seen no sign of this kindly old *catratcho*. Teddy says that it's not like him to simply up and migrate like his monarch butterfly form.

Sometime during the night I awaken to find myself inside my apartment, standing at my front door, and locking all three locks compulsively, over and over again. The button on the doorknob, chain latch, and deadbolt go through a ritual before I realize that my anxiety is causing me to sleepwalk. Ripping off my clothes, I flow into the beast of me and sleep with one eye open, ears always attuned like satellite dishes.

◆ ◆ ◆

Tonight my role is the Enhancer. I'm playing with the Round Pegs at Big Mama's Lounge, the box office lounge of the House of Blues. We're celebrating an EP release. It's a satisfying job for me: I'm on the record, I had made some good money for the session work, and got a little credit for my bio without the responsibility of being a bandleader. So it's a nice little ego trip when they gobble up CDs and ask me to sign them.

I am, of course, dolled up for the show in an informal but graceful tunic over black leggings and short boots with soles soft enough for me to feel the vibrations through the floor. Not exactly rock star, just enough effort to look like I give a shit about my image. I am painted and scented as befitting a gal who is going to be watched under bright lights by many. I've even remembered to run a brush through my long hair. I step back, tap into my pack mentality, and feel the connected energies of everyone.

The horn players are a tribe unto themselves. Some have played together on assorted gigs for years, and at least one is a newcomer. But history doesn't seem to matter. One minute they are clustered in a black-jacketed cackling bunch, good-naturedly ragging on each other and blowing scattershot notes. Then Salty the drummer gives a countoff and they jump in together as a single entity: dynamics, chords, tasteful rhythms that lend themselves to each song, as if they had practiced this music for years. I grin. It's very similar to how the drummer and I lock into each other, enhancing each other's ideas, even occasionally trying to crack each other up.

The breaks are short but jovial. Tonight we are a ten-piece lineup, and many of us haven't seen each other in a while. Some folks do shots, some sip on beers, the cloud of smoke thickens, and I get drawn into the assorted clusters to catch up on gossip and exchange the sickest jokes possible. John the guitarist and I try to out-shock each other before it's time to hit the stage for a second set.

As I settle back into position and we wait for everyone else to reassemble onstage, Salty beckons to me from behind his kit. I lean in and he hisses, "Guess what I bought the other day? An authentic 1978 Battlestar Galactica Colonial Viper!"

My hand instinctively grabs his shoulder hard. He knows my obsession with these collectibles. "No way!" I bark. "I remember those! They took them off the market after a kid shot a pellet down his own throat! A deadly toy that I don't have! Where the hell did you *find* it? I've wanted one forever!"

His feral grin drives me nuts. "A garage sale," he brags. "The little spacecraft was still in its original box." If I didn't love Salty so much, I could choke him. But now the break is over and it's time to get back to work.

Tony Fox, one of our trumpet players, is still out wandering around somewhere. Some musicians are notoriously flaky, but it's not like the clever red-haired man to be this unprofessional, and we're irritated. Finally P.H. Fred the bandleader calls a song, Salty counts us off, and it's back to the show.

We engage the crowd, we try to unseat each other, we laugh at ourselves, and we alternate between intense virtuosity and goofy histrionics. I suspect that some of these players might also be shifters of some sort, but we are all one hundred percent musician.

By now anything goes. We seldom stick to the set list, and just go with the flow. P.H. Fred is on a roll. We ease into a vamp and he dives headlong into a shocking monologue that has the audience alternately laughing and gasping. The crowd is digging the spontaneous absurdity. Somehow a cheesy mashup of Bon Jovi and Styx is born under the spontaneous title "You Give Blue Collar Man a Bad Name." A few times the bari sax player and I find creative and amusing ways to flip each other off. By the time the gig is over everyone is hugging. A few musicians swap numbers with the hopes of more gigs together in other settings. These "warm fuzzy" nights are rare, so I stand back and just savor the energy.

As we pack up our gear after the gig, Salty ceremoniously presents me with a box wrapped in a plastic Rouse's shopping bag. I don't even have to ask what it contains, and I throw my arms around his neck, positively giddy.

"How much do you want for it?" is my next question.

He bats his hand at the air. "The lady selling her stuff didn't even know what a collector's item she had, and charged me all of five bucks for it. Come sing one of your Cajun French songs on my Big Easy Playboys record and we'll call it even." I love Salty's Cajun hybrid project, so it's a win-win deal for me. Clutching my new treasure to my chest, I make my way to the bar for one last celebratory beer, insisting on buying one for Salty too.

My elation is short-lived, though. Tony is still missing, his prized trumpet still on its stand onstage. I don't know him as well as I know the others, but I'm concerned all the same. Half the band members are on their cellphones trying to get word from the police or hospitals. Ian, another horn player, gathers Tony's things and says that he'll keep them safe. Someone else volunteers to swing by his house and check up on him.

I don't want anyone to see me constantly looking over my shoulder as I load up my car, so I let my nose and ears rule my senses. There are no unusual sounds or scents, but a drunk man weaving past me pauses and calls out, "Out here by yourself? You need to find yourself a guardian angel, baby!" Every nerve suddenly screams a warning bell, and a low growl resonates in my collarbones. I manage to control myself until I am safely in my apartment, and the beast comes out. Anger is safer to process in animal form, for human rage is far more deadly.

No! I say in my mind to this invisible threat. *This is* my *territory. Leave our musicians alone.*

◆ ◆ ◆

Raúl and I go to the New Orleans Athletic Club, which blows my mind once we enter. The colossal old building—old for an American establishment, anyway—established in 1872, is a tribute to a nearly obsolete sort of reverence for the betterment of human physique, before the age of refined sugar, processed foods, and the equally deadly unrealistic body image.

This place is like an ancient temple with modern trappings. Huge columns with ornate molding support the rooms that are softly lit by delicate lamps hanging on chains. No amount of space is wasted, yet there is enough room here to prevent claustrophobia. Rows of myriad workout machines sit opposite a small pub serving everything from wine, martinis, and beer to smoothies and protein shakes, all on the first floor. The second has a huge ballroom that looks better suited for a lovely old dancehall, but is dedicated to classes: yoga, boot camp, body shaping, cardio kickboxing, and others. Still, the floor-to-ceiling Palladian windows and gilt-framed mirrors make me wonder what I'm doing here. Across the hall there are more machines for spinning classes, some basketball hoops, and a pool on the other side of the building. The third floor has a track that runs around the perimeter of the court. Even the rooftops are used for running.

He talks me through some of the weights, and then sends me to the class called Boot Camp held upstairs in the ballroom.

Boot Camp is a rude awakening. I consider myself to be in fairly good shape, but realize that too many of my muscles have been long-neglected from too much playing and little else in lieu of physical activity. We go through a rapidly paced alternation between running laps, planking, weights, push-ups, squats, and stairs. Still I am able to keep up with the rest of the class. The only person who betters me is an exotic-looking woman; tall and raven haired, sporting a single blue glass eye around her neck that is striking against her golden skin. I hazard a guess that she is a model and has to maintain her figure through training every day. She barely appears winded. Her only sign of effort is a heart-shaped patch of sweat on the small of her back.

By the time I meet Raúl on the landing halfway down the stairs, I am trembling from exertion. "How did it go?" he asks, knowing full well what I am going to say.

"I hate you," I snarl. He laughs, throwing a towel over my face.

We sit for a spell in the bar. "Raúl, this gym must be a playground for you. Lots of fit women for you to ogle, all the heavy machinery you could ever want. I'm sure they have stuff like this back in Mozambique, but is it the combination of absurdities that keeps you here in New Orleans?"

Raúl's normally cheery face becomes grim. "I can never go back to Mozambique. I have no passport."

"Then how did you get . . .?" I venture, then snap my jaw shut. He's never opened up to me about his past before, and I know better than to push the issue.

He quickly changes the subject by humming a mantra. "Did you know that mantras are much more powerful for lycans? Try this, Little One. *Wahe Guru* or *Waheguru* is a Sikh mantra that means 'Wonderful Teacher' but it can also mean 'the Divine.' Not only is it a direct pathway to bliss but it is also a word you can still utter when you are in full wolf form." He brings to mind those viral videos of talking husky dogs, and I am grateful for this tiny bit of knowledge.

I sing *Waheguru* in my car all the way home, until I stumble up the front steps of my apartment. My newly-sore muscles protest, and my mantra changes to some inarticulate swearing.

◆ ◆ ◆

Alma's second line parade starts at The Spotted Cat. Raúl is on snare drum, and I've got a metal *guiro* that someone brought me from Brazil that makes a satisfying raspy sound with its steel-toothed scraper. I see members of Alma's band congregating, as well as a few of the guys from Egg Yolk Jubilee. Trumpets, trombones, drums, a sousaphone, and assorted people who just want to march along all cluster as we start down Frenchmen Street with "Down By the Riverside."

As we cross St. Claude Avenue and go deeper into the residential area, people hear us coming and run to the curb to clap along. One man I've never seen before stands on his porch and plays along with us on his trumpet. "This Little Light of Mine" has never given me such goosebumps before.

A lost-looking young man with boundless energy comes trotting into the fray. He seems sweet—fresh-faced and eager, a blank canvas carrying an insanely heavy-looking backpack. "What is the occasion?" he asks me.

I pick up on his accent. "Where are you from?" I ask him first.

"I'm from France," is his breathy reply. "I am just arriving today, and I want to know what this ceremony is?"

So I switch to French; I haven't spoken much since I moved to New Orleans from the Cajun area of St. Landry Parish at age eighteen. But it seems that this parade can be better explained in my second language, which forces me to simplify. It comes back to me in a mélange of the standard European French I learned in school and the Cajun French I grew up hearing from my friends' parents.

I tell him, "Our friend is dead. Her funeral was yesterday, she was buried yesterday. Today we celebrate her life. She was a formidable singer, and all the world loved her. This parade commenced at the bar where she sang, and will end at her mother's house."

He is incredulous. "A funeral *parade?*" he asks in French.

"Yes. Come with us," I command. Alma would have loved to have introduced a young foreigner to our unique customs.

And with the same zeal as those of us who knew and loved her, he dances alongside us for the remaining mile and a half. He does not lay down his heavy load until we stop, where Alma's mother emerges from her house, crying and smiling and offering us drinks.

◆ ◆ ◆

Stepping into Rowan's studio, I try to keep my pulse down. My eyes adjust quickly from the blazing daylight to the soft energy-saving lighting of a building humming with electricity on a palpable grid, and his intoxicating scent seems to come in from everywhere. This is, after all, his territory. I grit my teeth and will myself into self-control.

He's in the control room finishing up a session, tweaking a few rough bounce mixes before storing them to the hard drive and giving copies to the band. I park my butt on the couch behind him in the "sweet spot": the point between the two speakers that gives the truest sound of the mix. My ears are captivated by his magic, yet my eyes wander and I find myself staring at the nape of his neck, which I have a wild urge to nibble. I try to rein in my desires and my gaze wanders with a will of its own to the backs of his calves revealed by his shorts. His legs appear to be surprisingly muscular and defined, especially for a guy who sits at a studio console all day. I snap my head in a sobering shake and drop my gaze to ground level, where the whiteness of his sock stands out in stark contrast to his caramel-colored ankle.

I bite back a groan. *Sweet spot, indeed.* I can't look at him anymore, decide to rifle through the stack of books on the table next to me, and busy myself with flipping through a copy of *Zen and the Art of Producing*. The words of the pseudonymous author Mixerman are both bitingly true and amusing, and I attempt to get swept away somewhat in his sage advice.

My eyes dance across the page, but sound hits me from all directions. I hear him pad softly into the main room and gently instruct an intern: "Now, the way you need to wrap a mic cable is by alternating your loops . . . over and under . . . clockwise and counterclockwise . . . so that it won't develop any kinks and it will unroll smoothly just like a lasso. See . . .?" I hear the thump of cable hitting the floor. He is a born instructor. I hear equipment being gathered, instrument cases closing, and the volume swell of goodbyes as musicians begin to trickle out of the studio. I know a few of these guys on the session, and we pause to make small talk as they depart.

The intern finally leaves, and it's just Rowan and me in the control room. We've worked alone together in the studio before, but this is something new. Intimate. He rolls up his chair to face me on the couch, picks up his guitar, and casually noodles around with a few blazing licks. I find it an absolute crime that he does not perform live anymore. We take a moment to indulge in our unique shared humor, pulling up some videos on You Tube of some exquisitely bad music. We have a good belly laugh at some songs by Shooby Taylor—arguably the world's worst scat singer. By the time we get down to business, I am finally relaxed enough to begin my tuition.

We get comfortable in the drum room, which is a five-sided chamber. Rowan has hinted before that there are more advantages to its shape than just acoustics, but for now we have to touch on the most urgent skills.

He cuts to the chase. "Warding takes practice, but it's the most basic and necessary measure of protection. When you're with the whole pack, or even with one of us, we can cover you while you learn. There is a subtle energy that connects us all. While warding doesn't make us truly invisible to the senses, we can disengage from this flow so thoroughly that we don't even enter the thoughts of someone whose attentions we don't want. There is a safety in removing your imprint from the energy patterns that can be seen by others. You are still one with the oscillations, for if you were to stop vibrating, you would begin to die.

"Now, about shielding. It's different from warding in that it's strictly on an individual level. This is what some would call 'emotional control.' Do not deny your feelings, only tuck them away until you are safe. I think of it as 'freezing,' allowing the emotions to thaw later in a secure environment. Until then, the show must go on, so to speak. Trust no one."

He talks me through a simulated pattern, asking me to imagine situations in which I am afraid, angry, and even relaxed and off guard. Each time I am instructed to visualize a hard, clear ball protecting me, or a gossamer veil that extends to cloak my immediate surroundings. The trick is to draw on the energy that feeds both the woman and the wolf of me. I'm failing miserably at this, and decide that if I express resistance, he won't see that it's largely because I desperately want to prove myself worthy of him.

"Why is this so necessary?" I grumble.

The mirth in his eyes fades. "Other shifters, as well as many people, are likely to alter their treatment of you—intentionally or not—based on your emotions that they perceive. If they cannot detect an energy pattern, then they cannot detect a weak spot. But don't disconnect with yourself. Your emotions—and instincts—will save you. This is more like scrambling an outgoing radio signal, or making it undetectable, so that others can't know what's up your sleeve. An energetic poker face, if you will. It's kind of like shielded cable.

"Survival is a process through a combination of actions, body language, eye contact, emotions, reason, kinesics, instinct, scent, and pheromones. Humans have a hard time with many of these because human reasoning has evolved faster that instinct can keep up. This is why they often make so many drastically poor choices."

I want so much for this man to be proud of me it hurts. Then I realize what I'm doing and slam the imaginary globe around myself. A bizarre sense of an imploding force field crackles around the outline of my body. Rowan tilts his head, and his black eyes shine.

"Very good," he says. I keep the shield wrapped tightly around myself, hoping that he won't notice the elation over his approval that now sings in my blood.

"This brings us to the subject of intuition," he continues. "It's basically evolved instinct. The trouble is that most of us have been taught by adults to ignore it while we are still pups. All we have to do is let go of the counterintuitive lessons we were taught as children and learn to trust our gut feelings again. We have to pay attention when the hair on the back of our necks rises, when we 'smell a rat,' when someone rubs us the wrong way for no logical reason. When the rest of the world is talking, we should be listening and paying attention to signals. There is a reason that dogs can predict seizures and low levels of insulin or sniff out cancer. There is no reason why our kind could not do the same if we would only balance our egos with the world around us. We lycans potentially have the best of both worlds.

"Now about vibrations. A wise man once said, 'If you want to find the secrets of the universe, think in terms of energy, frequency, and vibration.'"

I can't tell if he's pulling my leg or not. "Is this some sort of mumbo-jumbo new age glurge?"

He grins triumphantly. "Close enough. It was Nikola Tesla. 'Vibration' simply means 'oscillating motion,' whether it's in the form of an atom, a sound wave, or a solar system. They hold the very atoms of the physical world together. So everything is in motion, even when it appears to be still. We create vibrations with our thoughts, our voices, our emotions, and our minds. You can see the effects in water and sand sound experiments and moving particles around into patterns. There is an inexplicable bliss that comes from being completely one with them. And when the time is right, it is worth every risk."

Before I leave, he suggests that I experiment with tuning my bass to a slightly lower pitch. He tells me that it's a more relaxing frequency. "Besides, you'll find that it's accordant with much that is found in nature." It occurs to me that a slightly lower pitch was what opened up the magic in our very first collective howl.

"Next session we will discuss The Wild Harmonic, for it is the most powerful thing that you can sing," he tells me. My brain hurts, and I can't even ask him to kiss it better.

By the time I reach my car, I lose my grip on the shielding. The harder I try to regain control, the worse it gets. Several dogs in nearby yards begin howling at my uncontrollable release of pheromones. Just pushing the speed limit, I head down the street in the direction of my home, in hopes that this novice attempt hasn't alerted any of the unknown bad guys.

◆ ◆ ◆

The rhythm of my footfalls creates a cadence in my mind, then a groove, and last a melody. Walking to the grocery store rather than driving is much more conducive to songwriting. Heading with such purpose, I still remain on the alert, and the slowing of an old Volkswagen combi bus behind me kicks my instincts into overdrive. With the crunch of tires and the squeal of brakes, I turn to face whatever it is that wants my attention.

I barely recognize the elderly lady emerging from the vehicle like a malnourished cicada molting from a steel exuvia. "Mrs. Peacock!" I chide my former next-door neighbor with careful affection. That was the only moniker by which I knew her, and whether or not that was her real name I haven't got a clue. "Someone said you were moved to assisted living, and you never even told me goodbye!"

Little remains of the spry old woman I once knew. Her usual impeccable sense of fashion is gone, her habitual elegant garb replaced by a grubby white jogging suit. Whenever I'd dropped by her house for visits, she never answered the door without lipstick on. Now her unmade eyes are hollow and her white hair is wild— what hair remains, anyway. A massive chunk of it is missing across one side of her head, exposing speckled pink scalp.

"You there," she croaks. "Come with me." She fumbles in her handbag and begins pulling out some sort of net. Her arthritic talons become entangled in the fibers, and my gut instinct is to assist her even as I know that the net is meant for me.

I take several steps backward. "Mrs. Peacock, what are you *doing?*" I intone, calling up a slight whistle-whine.

She pauses, blinks, and straightens her jeweled cat-eye glasses. "Buzz? What are you doing here?"

Is it Alzheimer's? Dementia? I wonder. I take a deep whiff and smell drugs on her.

Her red-rimmed eyes fill with tears. Her hands begin to shake, which I'd perceive as frailty if I couldn't smell her unshielded terror. "Get out of here, Buzz. Stay safe. God loves you the way you are. Don't ever *change!*"

The double meaning of the warning could not be clearer. *How did she know about my protean nature?* But before I can grill her with questions, she totters back into the driver's seat of the combi. With a roar of vintage engines, she drives away, leaving me in a cloud of exhaust and panic.

The grocery store no longer seems important.

◆ ◆ ◆

Back in Sylvia's office the next day, I rehash the encounter with Mrs. Peacock. I'd spoken to Rowan about it the instant I'd gotten home, and his protectiveness of me in his tone had nearly made me weep. My best friend confirms our suspicion that my former neighbor was under the influence of this mysterious boogeyman.

"I used to deliver the old lady's groceries, and the next thing I know she almost attacks me," I moan.

The nun's face is completely neutral. "According to a two-thousand year old study, nine out of ten lepers are ungrateful bastards."

"You are ever the holy archivist," I reply dryly. "So what have you got to show me today? Be easy on me, wise one, for I'm totally freaked out."

"Then let's chill with some music first. Have you ever heard of shape note singing? Check this out." She hands me a book full of old choral music arranged in three- and four-part harmonies. The note heads all have different shapes: round, square, triangular, and diamond. The tradition is an American one dating back to the mid-1800s. Sylvia tells me that the notation was used to facilitate sight-reading for singers, the shapes indicating the degree of the scale.

"There is still the normal number of notes, but only four syllables in this scale: fa, sol, la, and mi. The act of replacing lyrics with the syllables is called 'fasola.' Julie Andrews would have had to truncate her little song had she lived in early America! See, in this form it's no less of a note, in fact it's far more. The shape represents a note as well as a solfège syllable."

"Isn't that sort of metaphorical for us musical lycans?" I muse aloud. "Shifting shapes in order to be more widely understood, and always about the music." My best friend silently commends my quick learning with the sparkle in her eyes. She pops a CD into her player and I am washed in the glory of the severe harmonies, pure and primitive. The hair stands up on my arms. I begin to believe that religion would be much more effective if it involved a lot less talking and a lot more singing. We sit in silence for a minute, savoring the aftereffects of the sonorous spell.

"So ... I have been thinking a lot," I say at last. "There are so many myths about werewolves, and sometimes they contradict each other. We're good, neutral, or evil. We can't fight the change, we're at the mercy of the lunar phases, or we can change at will. Transformation can be brought on by anything from rage to sexual desire. Change is sometimes an excruciating process, or some say that it's ecstasy. What is the real deal here?"

She appears pleased with my question. "It doesn't matter any more than what we are really called: werewolves, lycanthropes, *Úlfhéðnar*, Loup-Garou, or Rougarou. There are many different stories and theories throughout history, literature, and folklore, branching even further variety in pop culture and entertainment. Here's the lowdown on the myriad beliefs: all are false and all are true."

I can't hold back the huge sigh of exasperation. "Please don't tell me that this is one of these holy mysteries that we're not designed to fathom . . ."

She chuckles. "Getting predictable, am I? Well, not to worry, because the reason is quite simple. First of all, look at the different kinds of wolves there are all over the world. At least thirty subspecies exist. Then you have to look at the varieties of people in general, from a cultural standpoint, an ethnic standpoint, and an ideological standpoint, to name a few aspects of humankind. Now if some sentient being from another world asked you to objectively describe 'people' in a few sentences, a few paragraphs, or an entire book, could you do it?"

I know where she's going with this. "I know I'm supposed to say 'no,' but I think I could still give an overall snapshot of the basic natures of the human race."

Her eyes meet mine in a compassionate challenge. "People are bigoted, true or false?"

"Well, some people certainly are, but not . . ."

"People are generous and empathetic, true or false?"

"Sylvia, I see what you mean, but you're giving absolutes here, and it's more complicated than that."

"So is the nature of your original question. You asked, 'what is the real deal here?' And I said that they are all false and all true. Wolves are diverse, people are even more diverse, and lycanthropes are the most diverse of all. The answer to your question is: what kind of lycanthrope do you *want* to be?"

Growing frustration burns in my veins. *Just give me a fucking answer!* is what I want to scream at my best friend, and yet I know that this is for my own good—which further annoys me. I rein in my temper and force levity, trying to practice some shielding while I'm at it.

"Damn you, Penguin!" I growl, tugging her black sleeve in mock aggression. "Why do you have to answer a question with a question? Aren't you tired of being right all the time? Shouldn't you go back to fighting Batman or something?" She expertly parries my sleeve tug and imitates the comic book villain with a nefarious waddle.

Of course, that has to be the moment that Father O'Flaherty decides to walk past the office. Upon sight of our impromptu superhero battle, he rolls his eyes to the heavens, throws up his hands in a helpless gesture, and mutters something that sounds like *"Jesusmaryandjoseph . . ."* before continuing on.

It melts away my agitation. We clap our hands over our mouths and pinch our noses shut to stave off the snickering until we finally hear his footsteps fade down the hall.

"We will continue," Sylvia finally wheezes, wiping a tear from her eye, "with the teaching of the holy lycans of India—the dhole people—and how mantras can assist you. I am more versed in the history of lore-songs, but Raúl knows more of the actual mantras themselves. Now go on, Batman, before I get into any more trouble!"

I laugh all the way back to Orleans Parish.

◆ ◆ ◆

My second day of personal training with Raúl is two days later. He gives me a lift, since he says he has to run some errands Uptown anyway. I am trying to key myself up into the mood, and Raúl plays a CD in his van of the Mozambican group Ghorwane. I ask him if he ever heard them live back in his native country, and he shakes his head. "They are after my time, Little One. I came to the States so long ago, I even missed out on the Mozambique's independence from Portugal." And we leave it at that.

After a women's self defense class with the renowned trainer Dalia, Raúl meets me by the weights. We go upstairs this time to shoot some hoops. It's for increased coordination, he tells me, but I know he's just itching for a little one-on-one playing, which is fine with me.

As he readies to aim yet another slam-dunk over my head, he suddenly stops dead in his tracks and cocks his head. I sense something as well. Someone in here—a female—is warded, but the physical exertion is causing her to let her guard down a little. We both detect the unmistakable energy of a strange lycan and begin surveying the room. I feel a stab of something territorial as my eyes fall on the strikingly beautiful woman from Boot Camp. She's running laps above us on the track that wraps around the court. Her jaw is set determinedly, but her eyes tell me that her mind is elsewhere. *Is she or isn't she?*

Raúl makes a chuffing sound in his throat, a canine equivalent of a throat clearing politely for attention, a note intended to be heard only by others like us.

She comes to a dead stop and her head snaps in our direction, eyes wide in disbelief. Raúl waves. There is no need for any of us to verbally disclose what we are. In a heartbeat, she's down the spiral stairs and standing before us, her energy a mixture of curiosity and apprehension. Her large, dark eyes are liquid, her lips full and pouty, and her long black hair lustrous. Her olive skin is fresh and young. She has a body like a racecar.

She nods at me. "I've seen you in Boot Camp class. My name is Aydan." I can't place her accent.

Raúl's smile is annoyingly generous. "Where are you from?"

"I am from Izmir, in Turkey. I am a musician and I want to stay here awhile and learn everything I can about jazz and funk."

"Well, it seems as though my friend Birch and I could show you a few things, couldn't we? My name is Raúl, and I'm a drummer. Birch here is a bass player." I suppress the urge to kick Raúl in the ankle. I don't want to share my family just yet. It's a childish notion, but it appears that my territorial lupine side has just snuck to the surface of my consciousness to say hello.

I freeze my emotions and quickly file them away. "What instrument do you play?" I inquire politely.

"Bağlama. It's like. . . a guitar, but it has seven strings . . ."

"I know of the instrument," I chime in, grateful not to be completely out of my league already. "And the frets are laid out in microtones . . . very expressive. I've been listening to some recordings of Neşet Ertaş."

Her whole face lights up, further enhancing her loveliness. "Yes, I love his work! You know him? 'The Plectrum of the Steppe,' they called him. I got to meet him once in Izmir. I am so glad to have someone to talk to about this!"

And so the three of us chat, about odd meter music, funk, and local cuisine, with Raúl turning on the charm until I am nearly jealous. *Shield, Buzz, shield!* I tell myself. Not that I desire Raúl, who is like a brother to me. I don't like this unexpected side of myself. When we all leave, Raúl offers me a lift home.

I am quiet in the car, which I'm certain is uncharacteristic of me. Raúl says casually, "There is a whole world of music and a whole world of wolf people out there, Little One. We are only getting started."

His message is loud and clear. I may be a preternatural being but certainly no rare unicorn, and had better get used to meeting other formidable wolves. *As long as I have my chops and my pack, I have nothing to fear,* I assure myself.

◆ ◆ ◆

Being back in Teddy's apartment cheers me. I have secretly needed some comfort and good cheer in the wake of the nagging insecurity gnawing away at my belly, as well as the deep shame I carry for letting it bother me. Teddy has just finished a matinée gig on the upright bass near the French Market, and we are both happy to let the strains of Weather Report cleanse our musical and psychological palates. He sinks into his favorite chair with a can of NOLA Blonde and sighs, grateful for a moment's peace, but then frowns. "Aw, fuck, not *again!*"

The sound hits me too: an approaching rumble of about twenty pairs of tourists' feet, let by the righteous tromping of some tour guide's boots. Vociferous, whooping and hollering, they gather under Teddy's window. Teddy rises with a sigh and goes to his refrigerator. "Check this out," he bids me.

He's got a stash of about six cantaloupes in there. He chooses one, holds it up to his head for size reference, and grins. Trotting to his open window overlooking the street, he holds the melon, listening and waiting.

The tour guide rattles off a carefully rehearsed script. "This is a typical New Orleans home, called a 'shotgun house' because if you were to fire a shotgun through the front door, the bullet would continue straight out through the back."

"Unless you're a piss-poor shot," growls Teddy under his breath.

"This establishment," continues the guide, "is considered to be one of the most haunted buildings in the French Quarter. Legend has it that the owner, a wealthy entrepreneur, came home to find his wife engaged in a love affair with her slave. In a fit of anger, he grabbed his broadsword, sliced off his wife's head, where it *defenestrated*—that's 'flew out the window,' to you boys and girls —and landed on this very spot!"

This is Teddy's cue. With a blood-curdling wail that he usually saves for singing early Rush songs, he heaves the unfortunate melon out of the window. It smashes on the pavement with a satisfying thud, spraying the closest tourists with a light smoothie, as the startled screams immediately ricochet down the street.

The tour guide drops his character like a cheap souvenir mask. "Hey, watch it, asshole! I'm trying to conduct a tour here!"

Teddy bares his teeth. "And I'm trying to *live* here, motherfucker! Why don't you take your flock to a bar and make up some bullshit story about *that*? Every building in this city is haunted, so leave mine alone!" I join him at the window and we each give the tour guide a proud display of a one-fingered peace sign: the "Leland Sklar salute," in the tradition of one of our bass heroes. Teddy claps the window shut with a satisfying bang, denying his observer the last word. I grin, feeling a little adrenaline buzz. People can say what they want to about the benefits of yoga, but still sometimes there is nothing more therapeutic than the simple extension of the middle finger.

"Of course there's a ghost here!" he crows. "This whole house is full of energy, and it loves music!" He makes a beeline for his refrigerator again. "Care for some cantaloupe?"

I am in no mood for melon after that display, but I am too caught up in the hilarity to refuse. He carves up another ripe fruit and pushes a generous wedge toward me before feeding voraciously. We snarl together in parody of gathering around the kill.

"I meant to tell you," he mumbles through a juicy mouthful, "that you can learn a lot about basic lycanthropy decorum if you understand Japanese social protocol a little. In most situations for both races, someone is either your superior or your inferior. I would ask you if you've ever heard of *Honorable Bones*, but I know that the answer is going to be 'no.' Most people have never heard of this manifesto.

"It was written back during the Edo period by a monk who called himself Matsuo Ōkami. Because the original manuscript has been lost, and all we have is a translation, we don't know how 'Ōkami' was spelled, since Japanese has three alphabets. The word means either 'great spirit' or 'wolf,' depending on which alphabet was used. I wouldn't be surprised if the monk had intended for his pseudonym to be ambiguous.

"This set of guidelines is a good way of learning to err on the side of caution when dealing with other packs or foreign werewolves. Someone is either your superior or inferior, so it's always good to be overly polite and respectful. There is a protocol that you already know within the music community, which most musicians follow in order to get calls for more gigs and not be branded as douchebags.

"But when you step into other circles, be they social or work-related, you have to be aware of the subtleties of the vibes, lycan or human. This treatise is just a good thing to bear in mind when dealing with packs of military, nautical, or business lycans, for example. Kind of a universal code that everyone more or less follows. It's the effort that counts: it indicates that you wish to show respect.

"If there are any remaining lycans in Japan, we don't know. Both the Honshu wolf and the Hokkaido wolf are now extinct, so any wolves spotted in Japan would be a dead giveaway to something unusual. Individuality is not a Japanese lycan value. The shifters there today still cling to the old ways, and the more valued animal attributes are those of colony creatures, such as ants and bees."

I am overstimulated now. "I can't possibly learn all this!" I snap. "I had a hard enough time learning session etiquette while playing music in Scotland and Ireland! This shit's going to get me killed if I fuck it up!"

Teddy pulls me into an embrace. I don't want to be hugged, and growl. He hugs me tightly anyway, and the tension rolls off of me like waves. I am disgusted, for I want to stay mad.

"You won't get killed," he reassures me. "You have a pack to protect you. Every single one of us had to learn, so no one is going to judge you. And now . . . we are off for a drink at Flanagan's."

Flanagan's is only a few blocks away from Teddy's pad, and has a comfortable vibe. The only thing Irish about it is its name. In all other respects, it's a down-home local watering hole. To the right, the bar is low enough for people to sit at it like a table, and perfect height at which a large quadruped can stand around it. Subtle warding is coming from all directions, although there's no way to tell which patrons are doing it. The sign in the back reads EMPLOYEES AND WEREWOLVES ONLY.

"Teddy, are they serious . . .?"

He grins. "Know how there are vampire bars all over the Quarter? This is a werewolf bar. Of course, it's officially only in theme . . . we can't be too careful, but if we snort or howl, no one will take it amiss."

It smells friendly in here. There are, of course, a fair number of tourists, but assorted places at the bar distinctly smell like the favorite seats of various regulars. Everyone knows Teddy, and his relaxed attitude puts me at ease.

A half-human yelp of pain outside knocks us all to our feet. Closest to the door, I manage a glimpse of the sidewalk by the entrance before Teddy yanks me back in. Bob Felinus, a man who tended bar during my days playing at The Spotted Cat, is crumpled on the sidewalk, face contorted in pain. His arm appears to be caught in some sort of trap, and the scent of fresh blood permeates the atmosphere, sending us all into high alert. Another peek shows that it was some sort of bear trap concealed inside a cardboard box baited with books. Someone mutters that they're Terry Pratchett novels intended to look like a casual throwaway, and I happen to know that they're an addiction for the gentle soul who used to have a glass of wine for me at the end of every set.

Someone was out to get this specific man.

Teddy warns me to stay inside and joins the impromptu squad of rescuers, dragging the wounded man inside, trap and all. Once over the threshold of the bar, Bob collapses, not bothering to disguise his agony. His long sideburns are flecked with blood and foam, and he hisses as two men pry the trap open. They make him stretch out and elevate his feet, and a third man brings him a shot of his favorite Japanese whisky. I feel more than hear his breathing slow down to normal.

"He's all right," Huggy the bartender announces. "He's got a broken arm, and we're gonna get him to a hospital as soon as we can." And with that, a wall of patrons forms protectively around him. *It's safe in here,* I tell myself.

Amid the warding and the adrenaline, there is a strong sense of unity here. No one questions my presence. A few customers even give me conspiratorial winks and nods of subtle recognition. I have shielded myself so thoroughly (with a little help from Teddy) I can only assume that they recognize me from my gigs. I don't know how they could possibly know that I am a lycan, and in here I don't know if I fear this or hope so.

Perhaps I will fit in somewhere at long last, even if my life is continuously in jeopardy.

◆ ◆ ◆

Navigating around the ever-present potholes that give New Orleans another bit of its character, my little Honda responds to my touch like a polo pony. Fixing the streets is truly a Sisyphean endeavor, but we take good paving for however long it lasts. The time for repaving the Musician's Village, however, is long over due. Raúl's house is in this neighborhood, a post-Katrina rebuilding triumph by Habitat for Humanity. Spanning part of the Upper Ninth Ward, it allows many of the local musicians to live on musicians' wages and gather together with our kind. The brightly-painted houses are not ornate in structure, but sturdy and new. I pull up behind Raúl's van, unmistakable by the bumper sticker that reads SAVE A DRUM, BANG A DRUMMER.

Stewart Copeland's *The Rhythmatist* is playing at a humane level from his stereo. I forget about my longing for Rowan, my bass chops, and even what I might feel like eating for dinner later and allow myself to be swooped up in Raúl's strong, gentle hug, laughing unexpectedly when he gives me a noogie. He smells earthy, of comfort and strength.

"Are you ready to make some funny noises, Little One?" he asks with a grin. His teeth shining white against the undiluted darkness of his skin, beautiful striking cheekbones, and slight off-white tint of the whites of his eyes would make any person inquire, "You ain't from around here, are ya?" Which is why I have an even deeper appreciation for the Duck Dynasty shirt he's wearing, clearly as a joke. Laughter that ambushes you, that forces you to fall apart and regroup in spite of yourself, is often more purifying than any smells or bells of a ritual.

As per his earlier instructions, I am in sweatpants and a t-shirt today. Raúl goes to change, and instructs me to go through some stretches and hydration. I glance around his living room as I do, taking in the Tibetan prayer flags hung tastefully across the corners at reducing the harshness of the square room. The large flag of Mozambique hangs over his stereo and a handful of handmade drums. A promotional poster of Dave Weckl endorsing some drum equipment is placed reverently next to some framed prints by body painting guru Craig Tracy, whom the city is proud to claim as a local.

I sense some amount of warding taking place, albeit very subtly. No one questions noises coming from the neighbors here in the Musicians' Village, not when your neighbor across the street is a bari sax player, and two houses down someone might be trying out a new amp and some effects loops. Whether this is for our privacy or the sacrament of what we are about to try, I am grateful.

He returns in his yoga gear, looking for all the world like a movie star. "Part of your physical training must now extend to yoga. All of this is to not only increase your chances of survival, but to help you master your dual nature, as well as extend compassion toward those who do not understand you or even may fear you. The stronger we are, the more incumbent it is to champion the weak. Our kind would not survive without this understanding, for without balance, we would soon be killed off, and rightfully so.

"Ready to learn some mantras, *baixo?* Here is a little secret: it is no coincidence that many mantras can be uttered while a lycan is in full bass form, such as 'waheguru' and 'aum.' Your parasympathetic nervous system will kick in when we do this. It's literally 'getting a vibe.' Does that sound musical? It should. It's truly *vibration*— the essence of music, or the very thing that holds the atoms of our bodies together, and the dual vibrations that allow us lycans to change."

"Rowan was mentioning something about that," I agree, willing my heart to remain neutral.

"Mantras give the howl more energy and focus. And now here are some things you must know about these energies."

He talks me through a meditation that I can do whether in complete human form, complete wolf form, or some in-between phase, the last of which is something we will soon learn. I can feel a glorious vibrancy blossom along my spine as I stretch and flow into my change to wolf and back again. But something feels wrong over my heart. I don't know if it's my long history of repeated heartbreak, or the love I feel for Rowan that I am desperately trying to suppress. Something feels unmistakably blocked.

Old self-deprecating feelings creep over me, familiar and icy. I feel stupid, clumsy, and incompetent. *Where is this coming from?*

So I try the meditation again with the intention of not thinking at all. I quiet my mind and feel my immediate surroundings fade. In the absence of all present day life tasks—gigs, charts, oil changes, bills—other long-repressed feelings begin to surface. Now that it is safe to make full use of my gifts, my thoughts suddenly flash back to Cal. *"You need a halo. You're just a bitch, but I have the power to give you wings."*

Cal was determined to break down my resolve by keeping me awake all night, denying me food, and isolating me from my family and what few friends I had. In addition to all of Cal's abuses—for now I am finally able to admit that that is what they were—I now wonder if he was also trying to gauge the threshold of my senses to detect my lycan traits. Attempting to sneak up and startle me awake for seemingly his own amusement, forcing me to eat food that was too hot (his official story was that he had wanted me to associate food with pain so that I wouldn't overeat), and randomly flashing direct sunlight into my eyes with a mirror may have all been techniques to confirm his suspicions about my heightened senses. *Crap. There is no way I can make this meditation happen today. I should be born to do this. I can't even get being a werewolf right!*

I trust Raúl, so I don't attempt to shield my despair. He would never judge me, and I owe him this much honesty. He mercifully does not question me too much or try to push me too hard. Without prying he steers the lesson into related topics intended to keep me balanced as a "blended being." I learn through Hatha yoga how blended beings like shifters need equal amounts of solar and lunar energy to stay balanced. This time I shove Cal to the back of my mind and keep him there.

We end my training with a *namaste*. I cleave my train of negativity with a feeble quip, "Am I going to have to start ordering soy lattés and only eat organic quinoa?"

He rewards me with his usual deep smile. "No, Little One. My birthday is coming up soon, and I expect you to join me for some rare steaks and a few cigars. Maybe if the night goes really well, we can start a few fist fights and pick up a couple of hookers as well?" I laugh, and he gives me a huge hug, holding me in a bulwark of comfort before I leave. His scent is comforting, his energy strong.

As I head for my car, he calls out to me, "Don't forget to rest. It will keep your mind clear and your choices wise."

I am too relieved to feel discouraged on my way home. I have managed to control these feelings of love for Rowan for one more day. Right now that's all that matters.

◆ ◆ ◆

Next rehearsal is not only to recharge through the collective howl and practice for Howlapalooza, but also to learn everyone's stories. This is what the message on the pack phone reads, but as I step over the threshold into our Fountainebleau room, the tension in the room nearly knocks me to my knees.

No one can ignore Rowan's pacing. Any human musician might perceive it as some sort of foible, or a bandleader's concern for a forthcoming show. But in a rare display of exposed energies, Rowan has urgent news.

"Lorna Leatherwing was found dead in her New Hampshire home," he says, alarming in the flatness of his tone. A collective gasp flies around the room. I loved Leatherwing's music, in spite of her over-the-top stage show, which I found to be distracting from her songwriting. "Police discovered her hanging upside down in her closet, as she was prone to doing in her bat form. Only this time she was human, bound with ropes and her throat slit. Someone knows what she was. The media has been saying that is was some sort of lone crazed self-righteous vigilante that found her goth image unsettling. New Orleans isn't the only place where shape-shifting musicians are under attack."

He turns his gaze to me. "And not all of the shape-shifters under attack are musicians. A SIN agent bore witness to your former neighbor Hortense Peacock being shot. She said, 'You can kill me if you wish, but I will no longer comply with your ways.' The agent tried to intervene, but the gun went off and the assailant disappeared. We need to get our shit together if we are going to warn shifters everywhere. This is going to have to go nationwide, if not worldwide. And I need everyone's backgrounds today, even though this may make some of you uncomfortable."

The energy of the music today is more serious but focused. After an intense practice, we are all open and vulnerable, but connected and trusting of each other.

It seems that the pack has been somewhat aware of my background, but it's interesting to me how diverse we are in our histories. Sylvia, like me, was born into it with generational skips. Rowan and Raúl were born into it from long lines of shape-shifters, and Teddy was bitten.

Rowan reveals modestly that he is descended from a long line of Alpha males, mostly Mexican wolf with a little southern Red. I wonder how a Hispanic-Cajun man ended up with a name like "Rowan," but he doesn't reveal this. His father is from Mexico, and was a holy lycan before choosing a mate in Louisiana. It turns out that his father was the one who helped Sylvia find sanctuary when she decided to become a nun.

He describes his early musical career as "odd jobs," mostly playing piano for silent films. "Yeah, yeah . . . I'm an old man!" he jokes. "Sylvia, Teddy, and Buzz: you guys are going to have to come up with some interesting alibis over the years. True wolves are not particularly long-lived: only about eight years in the wild, and a little longer in captivity. But for some reason, being a 'blended being' causes the two factors to cancel out. It's about this time, in your late twenties and early thirties that you will find your friends asking what your secret is. In about twenty years, you'll all have to start saying, 'Yeah, yeah, I had some work done!' Eventually, though . . . well, you will have to decide on a new location and musical career. With a little luck, you won't have to fake your deaths like Elvis!" This is met with a hearty laugh, but a lump of ice grows in my gut. *Am I going to lose them all again one day?*

Teddy dispels my unease as he describes his unfortunate Boy Scout incident as if it's his favorite campfire story. It turns out that he is actually fifteen years older than me, still closer to my age than the two senior members of the pack, Raúl and Rowan. I can't help wonder if his having been bitten was just another way of having been chosen. Now that I know him even better since coming out of the den, I can't imagine him *not* being a lycan. With his nature of being a perpetual jokester and never quite playing by the rules, I am beginning to feel as if he is truly our Omega.

"My buddies and I were at a scouting event in Lake Charles. When we were told that it was going to be Boy Scouts and Girls Scouts working together for the weekend, we thought we'd died and gone to heaven. On the first day, we met some girls who seemed eager to sneak out of their tents and meet us by the lake after "lights out." And while we waited, we could hear something lurking in the bushes. The other two guys were acting like they were about to shit their britches, but I was convinced it was one of the staff just fucking with us . . ." He beings to chortle. "So I said, 'Look guys, there's nothing to be scared of,' and I dropped my fly and took a piss on this thing . . ."

"You *peed* on a *werewolf?*" Sylvia blurts out. This is the first time I have ever seen my nun friend visibly shocked, and a shout of laughter tears out of my throat, partly at Sylvia's incredulity and partly because of Teddy's infectious amusement. Raúl's deep brassy laugh echoes my own as he claps his massive hands appreciatively. Rowan simply buries his face in his hands, shaking his head slowly, but when he recovers, he is laughing along with the rest of us.

"Well, there you go. You marked it as your own territory," he snorts at last. "Did it have anything to say as it bit you?"

Teddy grins. "It said, *'Be prepared, bitch!'* "

All eyes look to me, and I know my own story is going to be a wet blanket after Teddy's epic. I am reluctant to tell my pack about the shame I felt from my rite of passage, but as soon as I open my mouth, I can't stem the flow of my story. I regale them with the bullying, the salvation through music that distracted me from my primal urge to tear apart everyone who had hurt me. The burning rage I had felt once I knew that everything I had thought I had known about life had turned out to be a lie. I even go into every gory detail about how struggled with my killer instinct, running through the woods and trying to create a path of destruction in a natural asylum where there would be no voices to report my monstrosity.

I tell them somewhat of Cal's gaslighting and threats to blow my cover. I voice my suspicions that he might have been something other than just an ordinary human being, with his uncanny ability to sense my weaknesses and fears, harnessing them to make me bend to his will. How I wish I could have just killed him, knowing that if I had failed in my attempt, I'd have been better off dead. I hadn't even cared whether or not I would have gotten away with it. Teddy and Raúl are barely able to suppress a few growls, so I decide that it is finally time to pass the talking stick to someone else.

Sylvia's story sounds almost like the Annunciation. It hits me that that since our adult reunion, I'd never gotten the full scoop on her mysterious disappearance past her "witness protection program" story. Now it goes beyond that: her parents had predicted what fate might befall her and somehow managed to find a way for her father to get transferred every few years in his job—before anyone could become suspicious of their daughter. Unlike my own parents, who had wanted me to choose the straight and narrow, Sylvia's folks had wanted her to trust her heart. All that had mattered to them was her happiness. And her coming of age was like a Rapture.

I know her well enough to know that she's certainly no Virgin Mary archetype, which makes her seem even more saintly to have walked away from so many earthly delights. It is a story very similar to my own in that we were both visited by some entity in the night on the cusps of our adulthoods. But whereas I regarded it as a deal offering knowledge and power like the snake in Eden, she chose to see it as a sacrifice in exchange for enlightenment. She harnessed her wolf to bring out the best in her music. And then one day she decided that she'd had enough of the outside world and gigs in dingy bars, for all of the occasional perks. It is one thing to try to preserve one's purity, and quite another to give up what you've already known. She traded earthly delights for solace—a gigging musician no longer, but still unable to quell the wolf within. When

Rowan approached her with the prospect of joining the pack, she finally found a balance.

Raúl is as still as a statue. No one dares to breathe as all eyes fall upon him. We reach out in wordless support, but it is Sylvia who finally breaks the silence. "Who are we to judge? We will never pry, but it concerns us how much of a burden you are carrying with you."

I am surprised to be just as in the dark as the rest of the pack. I knew that Raúl was reticent about his background, but I didn't know that he had been holding it inside for so long from everyone.

His eyes unfocus, and he allows himself to receive emotion like a huge satellite dish. We all tune in. His face remains stolid, but his eyes become stricken.

"My family and I lived near Gurúè in the Zambezia Province. It is diverse enough that we could disappear into the forests when we needed to change into our lupine selves, but we could still pick up work in the nearby tea estates. It was hard labor, but the tea estates of Mozambique are so beautiful, it would make the heart cry. I occasionally picked up gigs in Quelimane, or even as far down as the capital city of Maputo, but I preferred staying in the little homesteads when all was said and done.

"The painted wolf people of Mozambique tend to have large families, and laughter is an important value, both for the beasts and lycans. Our Teddy would have fit in well," he pauses with a grin, still keeping his eyes on the floor. Dropping his smile again, his eyes harden.

"There was a wealthy man from the United States who had heard of wild dogs and of a rumor that some new species had developed. My extended family is rather unique-looking in our lycan shape, since we carry mixed wolf blood. My grandmother was an Ethiopian wolf shifter, which is a rare and beautiful species: red and white like the foxes of Europe. Mixed with our African wild dog heritage, we were a distinctly unusual looking pack, and so tried to remain as hidden as possible. But someone had spotted one of us, and this American entrepreneur had ambitions for money and fame in his discovery of what he thought was a new subspecies. We had always been cautious enough to never change whenever we could smell any outsiders nearby, but someone eventually caught up with us.

"One day my little brother and I were hunting in our lycan forms near a wildlife preserve, and my brother wandered too close to an illegal trap. I saw it before he could get ensnared and ran at him, knocking him out of the way, but getting caught myself. If I had changed to human form to free myself, I was afraid that I would be seen in mid-change and our secret lives as lycans would be discovered. So I remained a wolf and let the man take me away, trying to close my ears to the cries of my family, even though they knew I had to do this for their protection.

"I was thrown into a crate with some raw meat and very little fresh water. What this man was doing was illegal, and he had to jeopardize my health in order to keep me hidden. I was given a sedative gas, so I do not recall if I was being transported by air or by sea. Hours, days, or weeks may have gone by, and I will never know. By the time I reached the States, I was little more than skin and bones.

"I did not want to encourage my kidnapper's belief in a new subspecies, so I focused on visualizing myself as a pure painted wolf and cast the illusion that I was no more than this. When we got to America, the poacher was disappointed that he had not discovered a rare and unique animal after all, so he drove me to some rural area and sold me to a collector of exotic animals. But this new captor did little more than keep me alive in an outdoor pen, throw me the occasional scraps of meat, and charge admission for tourists to gawk. I was the only shifter in his menagerie. All of the other inhabitants were pure animals: a caracal, a couple of douc langur monkeys, a hornbill, and an elderly mandrill baboon. There was nothing for any of us to do but turn around and around in the tiny little pens that he had constructed for us, standing up to our ankles in shit. The other animals screeched and cried all day. I knew that I must do something or else I would go mad, and then what? I begged my ancestors to either send me some hope of salvation or to call me home to be with them.

"The collector's daughter began to do more of the chores after that, including feeding us. She was a gentle soul of about eighteen. She was afraid of her father, and I often smelled him on her when she came to the pens to feed us. One day I reached out for the sake of us both. I spoke very softly to her in wolf form, and she did not find this to be unusual. 'You are beautiful,' I managed to say. It was not as clear as human speech, but she listened. Night after night I told her my story little by little. One full moon, I fully transformed in front of her, and she was not afraid—in fact she was enchanted.

"I continued to reveal myself as a man while trying to cover my nakedness so that she might not be offended. She appreciated my discretion and one night slipped something into my crate that she had told my father were rags for bedding. It was really a large hoodie and some sweat pants that she had gotten from the Salvation Army . . . enough covering that I could take human form in broad daylight if I ever escaped.

"One day she lifted the door to my cage and let me out. She said that her father was passed out drunk and would not notice. I had been cramped for so many months and my muscles so atrophied, I could not even stand up. But day by day she helped me to regain my strength.

"By the time I was able to run away, I was in love with her. She agreed to come with me. She had packed a bag for us with money, clothing, food, plus a forged ID for me. It was waiting for us under a tree at the edge of her father's property. On the morning we were supposed to leave I changed back into a man. I slipped out of my pen with the key she had slid into the crate, dressed, and waited for her. And then I heard the gunshot."

No one makes a sound. Raúl buries his face in his hands, curling up in his grief. He sobs, "Her own father had figured out what I was and shot her. I changed back into a wolf in a heartbeat and forced my way into the house, but I was too late; the bullet had gone right through her skull. He turned, aimed, and meant to kill me next, but I was quicker. I tore out her father's throat and left his body a shredded mess. The right thing to do would have been to run away, but the months of imprisonment combined with losing my redemption and the only woman I had ever truly loved was too much for me to bear.

"I left the animal cages closed as I transformed again, dressed, picked up the pack, and slipped away. It seems that it would have been kind to free them, but I knew that they would not know how to survive in this harsh and unfamiliar environment. Their cries would alert the authorities and that the animals would be transported to sanctuaries or zoos, where they would be given proper care. I wandered the land in search of respite. Even though

I found occasional jobs and places to live, I could never outrun the guilt. Because of me, this young girl I loved had been killed by her father."

"Why, Raúl?" asks Sylvia in a barely audible tone. "Because he found out that she was helping a werewolf?"

He is stone-faced again. "No. He shot his daughter because he found out that she loved a black man."

◆ ◆ ◆

Back in my apartment late that night, I decide that I can no longer keep my other side bottled up. I turn on my A/C window unit, which chugs and whirs a loud drone. While no substitute for central air conditioning, it's noisy enough to cover up any odd sounds that may escape. After double-checking to make certain that the blinds are drawn and the few lights are dim. I put on Sheila Chandra's *Roots and Wings*, and allow the music to help me wind down the day.

I disrobe without thinking and begin a mild meditation with a mantra befitting a wolf: *Om Chandraya Namah* ("Om Light of the Moon, the glittering or shining"). I begin in a child's pose, going within. In only a matter of seconds I feel the transformation as I rise to all fours. Spine stretching, chest expanding, my tailbone reaches for the ceiling in my down-dog yoga pose. The metamorphosis does not hurt; it only makes me feel extremely disoriented. I let forth an involuntary whistle-whine, feeling it vibrate down my elongated sinus passages. The connection from spine to the base of my skull shifts to allow me full range of head motion from a bipedal to quadrapedal stance. Humerus and radius adjust, femurs and tibias shorten, metatarsals grow, and heels become hocks. What were once fingertips and toes are now firm paws, distributing my weight, giving me stronger sense of balance and structure. Instead of being at the mercy of two barely mobile primate ears on the sides of my head, I can now cup and swivel them from the top of my cranium, picking up frequencies like two separately working satellite dishes.

I have lost my human concept of beauty in my shift, but I glance at myself in the mirror anyway. My fur is a whiter shade of pale, a fluke among the Southern Reds of Louisiana. Sometimes I wish I could remain in this form all the time. Other times like tonight I ask myself, why do I have to be so damned canine? It's so unglamorous. Out of all the shifters, why is my form the most common?

Human ego versus animal acceptance battle for a moment, then I simply surrender to what *is*. Curling up on my futon, I tuck my nose into the brush of my tail and sleep.

◆ ◆ ◆

Journal entry, April 15th: Dear beloved,

If only you would come a little closer and stay a little longer, I could knock you down from that pedestal on which I placed you. Then we would both be free.

The April morning is warm, with a hint of even fiercer heat yet to come, but I couldn't care less about that. I can't believe my good fortune in my assignment today. I am to spend the day hanging out with Rowan at the French Quarter Festival. The five-day free event gets too crowded for my taste, but it is one of the few remaining events that hires only local bands. I have a set to play with the Latin band Descendientes on the very last day, but today is one of those rare occasions in which I am completely free. I decide to leave my car by my uptown apartment on Tchoupitoulas, take a brisk stroll through Audubon Park to get to Saint Charles Avenue while the morning is still cool, and catch the streetcar across from Loyola University. I roll farther uptown where Saint Charles becomes Carrollton, and meet Rowan for coffee at Z'otz near his studio before we head to the Quarter.

"Normally French Quarter Festival needs every pair of hands that can set up a mic or work a fader, but let's just say that we got a hall pass today." He flashes a grin over the rim of his iced coffee glass, and I will myself to remain in control of my perpetual heat in his presence. "This will be the perfect way to practice everything you've learned so far."

It appears that this mission will inadvertently serve another purpose, which is getting to hear my cronies. I'm always so busy on my own gigs, I normally never have a chance to appreciate the jazz, funk, and blues that this city is famous for, not to mention a good many other groups that don't fit under those categories. And I get to do it all in the company of the man I crave. Climbing buoyantly into the passenger side of his Tahoe, I take note of the CDs in his console. Lots of guitar virtuosos, of course: Alan Holdsworth, Eric Johnson, Jeff Beck, Adrian Belew, and Steve Morse. And bands that feature collective killer musicianship: Mothers of Invention, Dixie Dregs, and local prog lords Twangorama.

And so begins my tuition put into action. Rowan shows me the ways of my lupine life, and like the Van Halen song, I am hot for teacher. I keep it to myself as best as I can, as he has taught me. We wander from stage to stage to identify power struggles between band members based on vibrations and scents. I detect an irregular spiky energy emitting from a fiddle player on one of the stages. Rowan is pleased with my observation, informing me that the

guy has a reputation for trying to take over other people's bands
and deliberately causing as much damage as possible if he doesn't
succeed. It seems that God created egos to prevent musicians from
taking over the world.

He then tests my ability to sense other shifters or to sense
warding. Sure enough, there are a few horn players out there
who are definitely something, based on my inability to tap into
any sort of energy pattern around them, like a glove obscuring
a fingerprint. *Ha, I knew it!* I gloat to myself, recognizing some
of them from The Round Pegs. Some of these fellows who play
regularly together have a slight energy pattern between them. And
there are some people who have no energy patterns because they
are simply burned-out. They are easy to tell apart from the warded
ones, for they just go through the motions. I try not to wonder if I
could ever reach that state.

Traipsing down Decatur, so proud of being seen side by side with
Rowan, I almost miss the slight hissing noise. Three gutter punks
are ogling me, unwashed and arrogant. In spite of their cardboard
panhandling box, it's obvious to anyone who knows anything about
tattoos that the ink covering their bodies couldn't have been cheap.
A dog on a rope leash raises despondent eyes at me—*not a shifter,*
but something is definitely mutable with these three young men.
The tallest one waggles his tongue between two fingers at me. Their
mocking laughter squeaks like a rusty hinge, and a flash of long
front teeth reveals their glirine natures.

"How about giving us something to eat? You don't wanna refuse
. . . we know where you live!"

The rumble I feel at the base of my skull sounds like a cargo
ship unloading a massive crate, but my brain decodes it a second

later as Rowan growling. I have never witnessed him hostile before. Then again, I have never before seen someone pose a threat to him or a pack member. Out of the corner of my eye, his face seems more angular, and his energy becomes harsh like a heavily distorted guitar.

The rat men slam to a halt in their tauntings. One mutters, "Dude, it's *him!*" They fidget and shuffle down the street at an uneasy pace, dragging the languid animal behind them. Rowan picks up the panhandling box and gets a scent. I try to make a mental note of the same, but the stench of unwashed bodies obscures their olfactory identities—perhaps deliberately. The box is just a discarded carton with ANGEL MINISTRIES printed on the side, but reveals no scent clues.

My Alpha slips his harmless veneer back on like a cloak, and we continue our route. His many facets have me enthralled, and I want to bottle them all: gentle Rowan, ferocious Rowan, and wise Rowan.

"I will now tell you about the Wild Harmonic," he says. "This is just one word for a special frequency to reach others, namely shifters, although humans and animals can sense it as well. It is based on the same law of physics that makes sympathetic strings ring out, with a touch of the esoteric. No one is really certain how it works, but it does two things: it gives strength to the singer, and it connects the singer with the audience. Sadly, this technique is almost always wasted on stage presence and marketing charisma. But it could actually save your life someday." He croons a note that I can barely hear, but I feel it resonate at the base of my skull.

We briefly encounter Teddy, who has a few hours to kill before playing his own set with Trombone Rusty and the Sackbuts, so we all wander down to The Mint to catch Raúl's set with Government Funk Soul. We stand together at the back of the crowd by the gate enclosing the grounds and watch Raúl set up his kit. He's too engrossed in his activity to glance at the gathering crowd. We ward ourselves from outside attention and Rowan instructs me to howl a greeting. "Go on, try it," he warmly encourages me. "Once warded, no one can hear The Wild Harmonic except other lupines, and there aren't any others in the crowd except our pack."

I have my doubts. But Rowan had never steered me wrong, ever. I clear my throat and timidly try. "Ra-Ra-Ra . . ." No one is paying attention. I fill my lungs, certain that I am going to be rewarded with strange looks. New Orleans is a tolerant city, but everyone has limits. "Ra-*aaooooooooooooollll!!!!*" I bellow.

No one even glances at me. Raúl, on the other hand, waves at me from fifty feet away.

We try other exercises, like how to locate others in the pack. Even though I am back to being limited to my primate ears and must swivel my whole head to pick up sounds, I find that I can still retain a few of my lycan auditory skills. After Teddy wanders away to get a beer, I find that I can still pick out his voice in the crowd. It has its own unique frequency, like radio station or a fingerprint. In time, without even consulting a festival program, I can even find my way to Sylvia's set with Cloisterfunk.

My tutelage goes on into the night, and by now I am overwhelmed from so much knowledge to digest. Paired with standing in the hot sun consuming crawfish pies and Covington Strawberry Ale all day, I am tired, but I don't want this day to end, ever. Intoxication with Rowan's company goads me onward, so I can't refuse his suggestion that we pop into Flanagan's bar for a nightcap.

I haven't been in here since Bob was caught in the trap, but not much has changed. Many of the regulars are in their favorite spots, and nearly all of them throw Rowan nods of respect. One of the locals has his toy poodle Samson on the bar. The tiny creature looks like a little fuzzy black lamb, but I've heard rumors that Samson is a shifter, forced to remain in dog form to avoid conviction as a registered sex offender.

I am about to question Rowan about this, when he turns and locks eyes with me. And I am slammed by realization that I want the love of Rowan Lopéz more than anything in the world.

My reaction is instantaneous. I can't tell if I feel it in my loins or my pounding heart most strongly, but my knees weaken. His dark eyes are serious now, and I flail desperately to try to understand what he is trying to tell me. I pick up a scent, but don't know what I am supposed to identify. Wait—that isn't his scent entirely . . . it's mingled with another signal coming from another direction.

I look around the room to discover several men staring intensely at me. Even Samson makes no effort to hide his stimulation, the red tip of his erection protruding from his woolly underside. With a rush of shock, I suddenly realize I've let my guard down. *Shit! Pheromones . . .*

I can't even look at Rowan now. I've just humiliated myself. This is a werewolf hangout, and I've not only let on my feelings for my Alpha, I've just inadvertently alerted every male in the bar that I am aroused.

I mumble something about having to go. I slam down the rest of my beer, give Rowan a quick hug, and am down the street before anyone can stop me. Perhaps it's my lupine Spidey Senses that help me to snag a cab so instantaneously, who knows?

Love is a kind of glamour that you cast upon yourself to keep another person beautiful. I would try to break this spell if I could be certain that I wouldn't feel completely lost without the enchantment.

◆ ◆ ◆

I am relieved that on tonight's gig I can be The Chameleon with Descendientes. Camouflage and contrast is the name of the game. I obviously don't resemble my Honduran bandmates—*dark and Hispanic like Rowan,* I reflect with a pang of longing, as I do every time I play with them. But when the music starts, I could have been raised in Tegucigalpa alongside these guys. Physically I stick out like a white thumb, but sonically I am blended. I sometimes tell the curious listeners who comment on my difference that it doesn't matter what your lineage is, or your skin color, or your family history. Only what's in your heart will make you truly transform. Even these fellows from Central America are called by the music and messages of South America.

These guys defy the cliché that has been stamped on what most of the gringo world has superficially dubbed "pan flute bands." While it's true that a person can hear Andean folk music played by buskers in many US cities, these guys use the traditional *quenas, zampoñas,* and *charangos* to play music from the *Nueva Canción Chilena* movement. Hermes the bandleader explained it all to me. General Augusto Pinochet had forced many of the founding groups into exile after the 1973 military coup d'état of Chile. Quilapayún went to France, Inti-Illimani went to Italy, and Illapu eventually ended up in Mexico. Other musical prime movers like Victor Jara remained in Chile and were killed for continuing to play their music—ironically for songs about love, peace, and social justice.

Like my bandmates, I wonder what I would have done had I been born under a similar regime.

Coming from a Cajun area of the world, I learned French as a child instead of Spanish. But I am fairly good with languages and accents, and soon raise my voice in harmony with my brethren, all of whom stand no higher than my shoulder. My body seems to fade as our voices blend in my favorite Illapu song, *Se Alumbra la Vida*—Life Lights Up. My hands chase the salsa-like bassline over the hunting ground of my fretboard.

We have our own "in" jokes between songs. As usual, they are alternately delighted and bemused by me because I not only find their coarse humor inoffensive, but I often try to top theirs with my own. Our final number is a south-of-the-border rendition of "Nights in White Satin" that makes the hair on my arms rise.

We are musicians. We are shape-shifters all.

Tearing down after the gig, I feel the hairs on the back of my neck rise. A split second later, a grown man I've never seen before in my life bears down me and tries to swoop me up in his arms. I can't suppress a growl as I squirm out of his embrace and push him away with more force than I knew I had. In a split second, the rest of the band is shoulder to shoulder with me.

I can't contain myself. "Dude, what is your *problem?*"

He looks crushed, eyes going maudlin behind his glasses. "I messaged you through your website. I told you that I was coming to see your show! Don't you remember me? I'm Gabriel. You know, like the angel." He nervously smoothes his mustache—I must have pushed his face away.

I have over two thousand people who follow me online, and this one person expects me to not only remember him, but also be overjoyed that we have finally met face to face. I recall the lyrics of Limelight, one of my favorite Rush songs about not being able to pretend that a stranger is a long-awaited friend. Oh yes, and about putting up barriers as well. Neil Peart certainly hammered that poetic nail on the head. I wish he'd written something about what to do when a creep is invading a person's personal space and staring as if at an art museum. *Now I understand why Neil doesn't do meet-and-greets anymore . . .*

I'm fairly certain that Gabriel doesn't speak Spanish, because if I properly understand the quip that one of my bandmates just muttered, he'd at the very least have the decency to be humiliated. Everyone keeps a close eye on him as he buys our CD, asking us all to sign it, which we do begrudgingly. Much to our relief, he finally takes leave of the venue, but not without a parting shot to me: "You're beautiful when you're angry!"

Shit. I still have much to learn.

CHAPTER

4

ARIA AND FUGUE

Today's rehearsal is going to be different, as I've gathered by Rowan's cryptic instructions to be well rested. Luckily we've had several days to recover after the exhausting weekend. Between the potential for heat exhaustion and the strain of multiple gigs over French Quarter Festival (both during the day and club gigs at night), the entire pack was beat. I am also glad to have had a few days to save face after letting my feelings show to our Alpha.

I have been told to bring my bass as usual, but also to wear loose-fitting clothing. Everyone is dressed comfortably. There is a case of bottled water in the corner. Even Sylvia has taken off her wimple to shake out her naturally red hair.

Rowan has news from SIN. "We have more information regarding more disappearance and deaths of shifters," he announces. "Not just domestic incidents in Baltimore and Asheville. Reports have come in from Istanbul, Krakow, and Paris. There seem to be several networks that want to harness the power of all parahumans, and then quickly eradicate us. Whether they are working together or competing with each other remains to be seen. SIN still hasn't been able to trace these incidents back to an organization, only confirm that they are correlated. It is more important than ever that you all remain in contact with each other. And you must remain in complete control of your protean natures at all times.

"Which brings us to the subtleties of shape-shifting!" he barks. "There are four levels, the process is called a fugue. Buzz, you need to be talked through this, and the rest of us need to *practice.*" I'm not sure if this last statement is as intended to reassure me that I'm not holding anyone back as much as it is to goad the others.

"Um, what is it we're going to do?" I am terrified that we will be completely shape-shifting in front of each other, and although I don't want to tear through my own clothes, I am suddenly filled with the same phobia I used to feel in high school when changing in the locker room for P.E. As much as I've dreamed of seeing Rowan naked, seeing him naked in front of the whole pack isn't what I had in mind.

Sylvia knows my fears forward and backward, and gently places a hand on my shoulder. "Keep your pants on, Buzz," she teases. "We will be in an in-between state. Lycans wouldn't have been able to survive for centuries without being able to do this. You will maintain your human form, but your senses will be heightened, and your looks will be . . . enhanced.

"There are several definitions of fugue. We have adopted this term because it's similar to multiple personalities, which lately they call 'dissociative identity disorder.' The musical definition of course, is 'contrapuntal composition with melodic themes announced or imitated by each voice entering in succession.' For us, each level of 'fugue' is a progressively deeper level of animal state. Like Dissociative Identity Disorder, same body, different personalities— or levels of fugue—to tackle different needs. But unlike this disorder, we retain our conscious identities, as the holy lycans learned to do so long ago, that they might be one with their animal natures and overcome the wild destructive urges that have unfortunately turned up in so many horror novels and films.

"This is what we call the 'alto stage' of the fugue. Let's start by toning . . . Buzz, give us a note."

I reach out with my mind and allow inhibitions to relax just a little. The temptation to surrender to the full wolf state is difficult to overcome, but the group energy gives me enough support and willpower to rein in my desire for excess.

I glance at myself in the mirror. My somewhat homely face is now symmetrical and coaxing. My murky eyes are now a deep gray, irises ringed in a subtle violet, just enough to be uncommonly striking without unsettling. My features take on a more chiseled appearance, my eyes larger. My normally thin, uneven lips are now full and red. Even my stringy blonde hair looks thicker, framing my face in gentle waves.

For the first time in my life, I am a beautiful woman. I can't stop staring at my reflection.

Teddy breaks my reverie. "That's enough, Supermodel!" he says jovially with a gentle shove. "In time you'll get used to it. Tell me what you notice about the world around you now."

I notice everything. Smells and sounds are enhanced. Even the various energies of people are nearly visible.

Sylvia's eyes are a more vibrant shade of green than normal, her red hair taking on a natural fire of its own. Raúl looks like an ebony-skinned incubus, radiating sex appeal. Even Teddy appears handsome, his chin giving him the appearance of a strong-jawed superhero, a quintessential "good guy," his bright blue eyes shining with mischief.

And Rowan . . . looks exactly the same. Am I the only one who can see how stunning he is all the time?

I wonder how he perceives me in return. My secret thoughts chime in: *Why can't I be this beautiful all the time? To be perpetually tuned into this magic would be an ideal existence beyond belief.* "This is . . . um . . ." I'm at a loss for words. "Kind of awesome . . .? I don't get it. Why can't we stay in this super-state all the time?"

Teddy sighs. "Trust me, kid, you don't want to. Maintaining it is physically taxing, it eventually begins to mess with your mind after long periods of time, and becoming more beautiful is a mixed blessing, too." I take his words to heart. His natural state is no more pulchritudinous that my own.

Sylvia smiles with her usual innate empathy. "It can almost be like a drug, Buzz," she explains. " Remember that 'alto' means 'height.' If you become too caught up in your heightened sense of awareness, you run the risk of missing vital clues right under your nose. This is meant to be more than cosmetic; in fact, the improved appearance can be a hindrance when trying to remain undetected. But it can enhance your ability to detect any danger going on that is out of range to your human senses. And yes, also to sniff out a potential mate, which is why we evolved to become more attractive during this phase. But you have to also be careful that your anger doesn't overtake you, because adrenaline will also heighten your instincts and bring this on."

This must be why that creep Gabriel was so turned on by my annoyance. I begin to suddenly slump, feeling like the slow kid who's holding back the whole class.

"You feel the ebb, don't you? You conserve more energy in the 'resting' phases of soprano—all human, and bass—all wolf. With practice, you can maintain this state for longer amounts of time."

Rowan's voice is gentle but firm. "Come back to soprano now. There are some things we all need to address. Someone fetch this poor woman some water?"

Being a novice is certainly taxing, and I am grateful that no one gives me any extra attention. Raúl hands me a bottle of water, whispering "I didn't have this down pat until I was well out of puppyhood."

Rowan grins appreciatively, then steers the conversation away from himself in a conversational sleight-of-hand. "Okay, everyone refreshed? On to tenor phase, which is the most intense of all. It's basically the stuff that horror films are made of. 'Tenor' means 'to hold,' named thusly back when polyphonic vocal music added the tenor to hold the pedal tone. Ironically, this is the hardest phase to maintain. It's not the most graceful, either. You will tend to look like some sort of wolfman from an old horror flick, neither person nor beast. But it is an important liaison between the two worlds. It is better to hold this in private, much like a yoga pose that you don't intend to put to use in public. It is merely to keep you strong and flexible."

My peers attain this state first, suddenly sprouting in height like a time-lapsed film of plants growing. Their fangs seem far too large for their mouths, menacing and protruding slightly at a vicious angle. Only Sylvia manages to maintain a dainty image.

I observe, imagining myself modulating into this form. My body heat flares up, and tenor phase comes naturally. My baggy jogging suit, suddenly tight around my waist, allows for my sudden increase of height and altered distribution of muscle mass. I feel a surge of adrenaline just before teetering like a wino. Standing bipedally is now a very difficult thing to do, as my foot bones are elongated, heels off the ground, and my upper body is overbalanced. My nose is something not quite human and not quite snout, and to my secret relief everyone else—save Rowan—has a little trouble remaining in this phase for long. I am the first to fall onto my butt with a snort. One by one my pack-mates follow suit, until we are all prostrate and glaring up at Rowan for further instructions. His yellow eyes crinkle at the corners.

"Bass phase you all know," Rowan manages to say articulately through a maw full of impressive dentition. "It's the completely corporeal wolf form. There's a reason that the word is also synonymous with foundation, as bass is both the foundation of music and the base form the very essence of who we are." Teddy and I glance at each other before flashing an exaggerated beam to the rest of the pack. "You all know how to fugue into that phase, so there's no reason to party naked here. Everyone come back to soprano now, stretch, and hydrate." We all exhale and shrink, collapsing onto the floor, and my insecurity fades when I hear the others groaning. My limbs are quivering as badly as they do after strenuous weight lifting. Dignity be damned, I just lie on the floor for several minutes before even looking at my bass in the corner. Someone hands out protein snacks. Some string cheese and three turkey slices land on my chest, and I wolf them down before playing.

Back in human form, we go over our piece for Howlapalooza and then wind down with a jam. Sylvia kicks it off with a Procol Harum riff, easing into a subtle variation, then modulates into another key and morphs the riff some more. Before long, she's created a completely original structure, and one by one we join in. The collective energy of musical and lycan bonding washes over me like a euphoric shock wave, ensnaring me into a slight trance. Time and space might still exist, but not in my mind. My world shrinks to this microcosm of five.

It's hard not to focus on Rowan's stellar playing, but the group vibe eventually sweeps me away. Teddy and I alternate between holding down the groove and playing a higher countermelody. At some point he sets down his bass and picks up the mandolin, which is a nice touch. This is the most killer lineup I've ever played in, and I can't help but wonder how a human crowd would react. The sweet irony is that we all came together so that we might truly be ourselves in secrecy and safety.

"I have to get to bed," I finally yawn. "I've got a gig tomorrow playing for the first time with Naj Copperhead at La Balcone, and I have to go over my charts. Copperhead's got a reputation for being a backstabber, but she pays her band well. If she keeps me on board, maybe I can finally give up the last of my Bourbon Street gigs."

Rowan's dark eyes are unreadable as usual. "Be careful," he murmurs.

I wonder if he's talking about this bandleader or this impending threat to the shifters. I have a couple of melatonin supplements at bedtime, but sleep does not come easily to me. What in the world could be after us shifters? An extremist movement? A cult? Or some crazy person with minions? I can't draw any conclusions because my mind does not understand why anyone would condone slavery and genocide. As a would-be monster, I can vouch for the fact that there are mysteries far more frightening than things that go bump in the night.

◆ ◆ ◆

I'm grateful to have found a decent parking spot not too far away from La Balcone at the end of Decatur Street, almost to Esplanade. Even with the advantage of my hand truck, rolling my rig through the French Quarter is still no picnic. The clusters of tourists often block the sidewalk, oblivious to the fact that some of us need to get from *here* to *there,* and neither streets nor sidewalks make for particularly smooth sailing. La Balcone has been many things over the years, but its recent incarnation has always been agreeable to me: nice, spacious stage to accommodate a large band, decent lighting and PA, and a courtyard in which to escape on breaks.

Naj mostly plays original blues songs, but she had emailed me a rough set list to let me know about the covers that we might occasionally play, so I had been studying that. Most of it is stuff any New Orleans bass player should know. *New Orleans Ladies. Pride and Joy. Use Me. Oh Baby Love. Stir it Up. Redemption Song. Bad Mama Jama. Drown in My Own Tears. Proud Mary. Tipitina. Fly Away. Something You Got. Signed, Sealed, Delivered. Piece of my Heart. Ruler of my Heart. Tell Me Something Good.* A few of them are not your typical club songs, such as the Sherman and Sherman song *Trust in Me* from Disney's *The Jungle Book* (I have been instructed to play it in a sultry rhumba style). Any of these gems I didn't already know I looked up on YouTube or occasionally downloaded for a thrifty ninety-nine cents, but I am as prepared as can be.

The woman lounging at the bar is surprisingly sweet-faced and cheerful. Not at all what I expected. Flame-red hair—a little too bright to be natural, but perfect for stage—frames her heart-shaped face and accentuates her dimples. Her snakeskin-print dress hugs her body as she uncoils from her seat to greet me. "Hey, Birch! Or it's 'Buzz', as your friends call you, isn't it? Where y'at, mama? Nice to finally meet you . . . I think this will be a killer lineup tonight."

I roll my rig into the corner and shake her hand with a neutral grip. "Nice to meet you . . . Naj."

She beams. "It's actually short for 'Naja,' which means cobra. My mom was in India when she discovered that she was pregnant with me, and had been in the midst of a spiritual experience. Anyway, I've heard so much about you, but had never had a chance to hear you play." She licks her lips, and I turn my back to set up my rig, though I can feel her eyes tracking me. "Actually, I saw you wandering around at French Quarter Festival," she continues. "Who's the pool stud? He's hot!" My shoulders tighten, but I practice my breathing. *Send no signals . . .*

She gives my shoulder a playful shove. "I'm just kidding. I've worked with Rowan in the studio before. He's a hell of a musician. He's a hell of a guy, period. But you already knew that, didn't you?" She nudges me in the ribs.

I can't figure her out. But I don't have to figure her out. All I have to do is play the gig, get my money, and get the hell out of here. Still, I feel oddly energized by this challenging exchange.

I give the room a cursory glance. There's a man watching me from the bar. He takes his drink and claims a table near the stage in front of my rig. This patron of the arts appears clean-cut but smarmy. He's so polished that from a distance he looks slimy, but I've been told that guys like that are actually cool and leathery. His tongue flicks out flirtatiously, and I try not to let him see me shudder. His unblinking stare is especially unnerving. Perhaps he has no eyelids.

I remember the rumors, Teddy's advice, and Rowan's warning, and with ample time to warm up and set my tone I head to the ladies' room to collect my thoughts and steady my energy. Past the stage and down the narrow hall I stalk, towards the doors in the back marked MEN and OMEN. A faint trace of the missing "W" lingers on the latter, but the hairs on my neck rise all the same. I shield myself to the fullest, reminding myself to trust no one. Talk is cheap, but falling for it is expensive as hell.

I am introduced to the drummer who only goes by the name "Sand," an unsmiling, unadorned woman with a long hair pulled back into a severe bun. She approaches me sideways, nods in formal greeting, but shows no warmth. There's an older black gentleman on keys who introduces himself as Tim, and we hit it off instantly. A tenor sax player and trumpet player are whispering and grinning by the courtyard entrance; again there is that universal tribal vibe within horn sections. I causally know these guys from other gigs, and greet them with my usual irreverent humor. I see out of the corner of my eye a rubber toilet plunger end go rolling out of someone's gig bag and I smile to myself. The unglamorous accessory means that we'll have a trombone player, as the household object makes for an excellent mute. The bone player turns out to be a tall, graceful woman named Lydia King. She has a powerful build and long braids swaying in intricate cornrows. She could pass for some sort of a Creole Amazon goddess. Every time I try to catch a name or get a better look at her, she vanishes.

We start out in a decent comfort zone. Naj calls it: "Blues shuffle in B flat, no quick four, chorus has stops, watch me or the drummer for cues." And away we go. I lean back slightly as a posture befitting a good, solid shuffle . . . my bass lines walk steadily, appearing to wander occasionally but always hanging on the right chord centers. I fall into a comfortable, loping gait. Given too much thought, it's like lumberjacks trying to balance on floating logs. Becoming one with the pocket, it's hypnotic. I often tell people that playing in the pocket is like focusing on your breathing. Think of it one way and you meditate, think of it another, and you hyperventilate.

The tourists dig it. The springtime shower has forced people into buildings, and the scent of rain and sweet enthusiasm fills the room. Even after the weather abates the crowd stays, attentive and generous.

Naj has them all hypnotized. Her precious bunny face belies her sultry movements when she wraps herself around the mic stand. Occasionally she pounces on the keyboard: her secret weapon, her hidden trump card. During these times Tim shifts with the ease of a shaman and becomes a killer clarinet player, melting into the shadows and giving her the glory. She's actually quite proficient on the piano, and it only increases the intrigue. *Naja . . . naga . . .* There is no doubt that this woman is one of the snake people Teddy had described.

For a pre Jazz Fest show, the bar ring isn't bad at all. Naj is generous in dividing the tip money, and even gives me a small cut of her CD sales. I shake hands with a few tourists who are full of glowing praise, and accept a beer from a handsome blond man with an untraceable accent and goes by the name of Yohan.

That wasn't too bad, I reflect, stowing my gear in the back of my car. That's when I notice that one of my tires is flat. I heave a huge sigh. I'm going to have to take all my equipment out again to get to my spare. As I unload piece by piece and place it far enough away from the recently dried mud, I can't help but notice the odd marks in the dirt surrounding my car, tracks shaped like a capital letter "I." Leaning in to examine the flat tire more closely reveals the cause: twin punctures, fang marks.

◆ ◆ ◆

I refuse to let the mysterious assault on my vehicle intimidate me, especially today. I have a lucrative recording session that could possibly turn into more prestigious sessions if I play my cards right, and I can't let myself get paranoid. The project is for a well-known female artist, Sarya Sheepsour, whom I won't actually get to meet, but that's fine with me. Others have complained about her caustic attitude toward even the most seasoned professionals. Last week, she was in the studio while one of my contemporaries laid down a blistering guitar solo, to which she responded, "I like what you're *trying* to do!" So nope, not getting an autograph won't exactly break my heart. With a little luck, I'll have a gold star on my discography and none of the headaches.

I've done so much session work by now, I seldom get "red light fever" (attacks of nerves as soon as the record button goes on) but I want to be on top of my game. I haven't listened to any music with earbuds over the past twenty-four hours. No dairy products for the past day either in order to reduce any gunk on my vocal cords to an absolute minimum. Although I haven't received all of the files of the works in progress to listen to, I've learned the form of the songs that the engineer sent me, and I can get a general gist of the songwriter's style. Not rocket science in general, but overestimating one's ability to play off the cuff is one of the worst studio crimes a musician can commit.

How can I put all of my recently acquired lupine lore to further my skills today? I shift to alto form, which is getting easier to maintain. My intuition and hearing will be enhanced, and while appearing more attractive might not make things any less complicated for me, it will most likely make them pay attention.

Raúl would probably tell me to be physically warmed up: not just my hands and upper body stretched, but all my whole body on alert. I listen once again to the files of the rough bounce mixes of a few of the songs, and try to feel the essence of the music up my spine. *Don't play your instrument; play the song instead,* he once told me.

I would imagine that Teddy's advice would be some sort of wisecrack. *Sniffing butts is part of protocol, whether you are a canine or a musician.* I make a mental note to watch for the subtle signals that most people miss when they are recording, especially eye contact and cues between the engineer and the producer.

Sylvia, of course, would warn me to tame the human within, the ego that is fair game for anyone to take a shot at. I have never worked with this producer before, but his reputation precedes him for shock value and crassness. I remember her lessons about power: *Blended beings can fuse two sets of consciousness and thus have a stronger impact on deliberate intention, whether you refer to it as magic, quantum physics, or prayer.*

And Rowan would have me pick up on the energetic fields. All of that electrical equipment is going to make it harder to pinpoint, but if someone stands near a monitor speaker, it might actually amplify someone's pattern. I will also be able to gauge their reactions to whatever I play. What would he tell me? *Be careful,* I would guess.

I bring two basses—my trusty Fender Precision and a fretless—a preamp, and a small rig, not wanting to count on whatever the studio may or may not have. I already know Mike, the engineer, and we hug warmly. And there is no mistaking Kim, the producer, who's looking down at me like a bird of prey. A man in his seventies, he is well over six feet tall, spine ramrod-straight. His gauntness only increases the unmistakably hungry look in his heavy-lidded, deep-set eyes. His wide, razor-thin mouth curves in a hint of a formal smile, as he says, "Welcome, Birch. Mike here tells me that you would like to do some basslines, even though I argued that this project needs a more masculine sound to it."

I breathe deeply, taming the human within. I smile politely, hoping I'm not accruing bad karma by rolling the third eye. "You know, Kim," I reply, "this *is* New Orleans. Don't be so quick to assume that I'm female."

This is a momentary standoff. I know for a fact that he enjoys trying to unsettle people, but I simply refuse to let it happen today. If I didn't have my guards up, he'd be interfering with my energy field and playing me like a Theremin. He smiles; he likes this game, and I realize that so do I. This is a fun sport.

Posturing and playtime over for the moment, it's time to get to work. Kim wants to hear backing vocals first. I let Mike set up a vocal microphone and gets some levels for me, making certain that what I'm hearing in my headphones is at a comfortable volume. I reciprocate the courtesy by testing at the loudest volume at which I realistically think I will be singing, preventing him from having to adjust my sound in mid-take or start over.

"I need for you to be the voice of the forgotten ones," Kim dictates, channeling his muse. "Your backing vocals should sound like lonely schoolgirls, the ones rejected by their parents, friendless and at the bottom of the heap. Sing their broken dreams splitting at the seams, these would-be sluts with no esteem. Dirty lives that cut like knives, only the damaged one survives, no future as contented housewives. Think frustrated lesbians, masturbating virgins . . ."

I am unable to keep my mouth shut. "Kim, it's going to take a major stretch of the imagination to pretend to be a virgin!"

He sticks his finger in my face to chastise me and I pull it, blowing a raspberry. He laughs in approval of my insolence and lets me just use my better judgment from this point on.

They can't put their fingers on it, but a combination of my new look—I've worn a purple blazer to enhance my eyes in alto phase—and something about my kinesics and subtle scent makes them trust me. Heightened senses and animal magnetism are still no substitute for hard-earned chops, though, and I give it all I've got. It's not just about projecting an image. It's about living up to it.

With a bottle of room temperature water and a handful of lyrics sheets I knock out vocal harmonies to four, five, then six songs. Usually they happen in one take and Kim says, "Good. Next!" Sometimes he has me do second and third harmonies on the fly. On one particular song I point out that adding a third harmony would actually detract from the push-and-pull of a two-part spontaneous arrangement I have just laid down, reminiscent of the Everly Brothers.

"Fine. You have a great musical mind. You work at L.A. session speed. Okay, let's see what you've got for those bass lines."

We try running my bass directly into the console through my preamp, but decide that miking an amp is the best way to go. I listen to the tracks and play with the dials on my instrument until satisfied with my tone in relation to the mix, which is of the essence. Actually there are five essential *t*'s: taste, technique, timing, tone, and touch. The tracks roll and I flesh out each song, sitting into the groove, my place in a makeshift pack of sounds that consists of me with the previously laid tracks. Then Kim asks me to throw in a few more basslines to songs I haven't yet heard. So I pay close attention, map out the songs in my head, and manage to get some decent tracks within three or four takes. I can hear their approval or indecision in their breathing, and I can hear the partials in the notes that they can only feel subliminally. I am hyper-focused, just like Rowan. I navigate my parts according to what I sense from them before anyone has to say a word.

By the end of the session Kim and I are friends, at least as close to being friends as one can be with this predatory bird. "I'll be calling you for some more work. New Orleans is a great place for me to live, since I like good food and I like to date strippers, but the people here have their heads up their asses when it comes to making money. You need to stop playing these shitty gigs and get your name on some gold records. Would you be willing to move to L.A.? Or do you have some boyfriend or husband who's just tying you to the kitchen, living off of your money, sitting around jacking off to your songs, and wishing that you were a lesbian?" I assure him that I have no such person in my life, but an unexpected dilemma hits my gut. *Would I be abandoning the pack if I came into some real success?* I remind myself that that is not an issue for the present.

I can't help feeling relieved that Cal is no longer around. He would have loved to have rubbed shoulders with Kim, and I feel a fierce satisfaction that he had no part in this magical—if not twisted—recording session. Whether he wanted to invest in my music and turn a profit on it, wanted his name in print on a record, or simply wanted to cage an unusual creature for his collection, it will never happen again. I am not some legendary leprechaun or golden goose. I am a wild animal and a survivor.

Perhaps the best thing about today is that I have been paid by the track. Now I can alleviate my credit card bill of the expenses I just forked over for my new tire, and still have a little to spare. No matter what adversaries try to unseat me, I'm going to survive. All I have to do is stay alert every moment.

INTERMISSION

"As the dawn was breaking the Wolf-Pack yelled
Once, twice, and again!
Feet in the jungle that leave no mark!
Eyes that can see in the dark—the dark!
Tongue, give tongue to it—Hark! O Hark!
Once, twice, and again!"

—Rudyard Kipling, "Hunting-Song of the Seeonee Pack"

I am getting antsy. I've been pretty good about getting home after gigs on full moon nights without any unnecessary fur flying, but I need to let my wild nature out. I have yet to run with my new clan, and I am trying not to climb walls. The others can feel it too. Although I am the last to join, I have discovered that the entire pack is still very new, forming piecemeal since Rowan officially met Raúl on lycan business a year and a half ago. We have yet to run as a group, and I still have not yet run in true bass form with anyone else.

Rowan has proposed a Moon Run, and even though I have never heard the term, I can easily guess what it is. Running together under the magnetic pull of the moon is something that all lycan packs need on a regular basis, and even playing music together is not going to feed that primal longing. Sylvia says that during the full moon the bond between heaven and earth is the strongest. I don't know if this is literal or allegorical but it doesn't matter to me. I still like the image, but the shock of so many recent deaths and disappearances knot in my stomach like curdled milk, and I voice my concern.

Rowan's eyes are steady and strong. "We can't let these mysterious terrorists stifle our wild needs. This is essential to the pack. The Spillway is a perfect location for a run," he suggests. "We have all been around too much electricity, and haven't had enough grounding. Literally. Touching bare earth would work wonders for us as individuals, and even more so as a team. We need to get back into our flow. Running with the pack is being in the flow . . . even flow spelled backward is *wolf*."

I wonder why I'd never thought to explore the Bonnet Carré Spillway before this. Built for flood control in 1931, the land stretches from the levees of the Mississippi to lake Pontchartrain, diverting the waters of the former into the latter. The forty-two acre wilderness is used for assorted recreation during the day: biking, four-wheeling, hiking, and fishing. At night, however, it seems the sort of place where a wolf can be a wolf.

I remember that it's also used for hunting, and although I know that we will be cloaked, I am discomfited by another nagging detail. "We will be warded, but not invisible. What about eyeshine should we encounter any oncoming vehicles or flashlights?" I'd seen enough glowing eyes of critters in my own headlights at night.

"I guess you have no way of figuring this out by yourself, since you're not exactly going to look at yourself in a mirror while there's an oncoming car," chuckles Raúl thoughtfully. "Don't worry, Little One. Somehow our kind has evolved to have no eyeshine. It's a way to stay hidden in the modern world. That's one of the only ways a human can differentiate a lycan from a true wolf at night. But no one will be looking for lycans on the Spillway, or even know what we are. People will not see what they are not expecting to see."

◆ ◆ ◆

Piled into Raúl's van and heading in the direction of Baton Rouge, we grow quiet. The Bonnet Carré Spillway between Norco and Laplace seems like an ominous location as we approach. The eternal flame of the oil refinery lights up the night sky, and I remember why they call this stretch of road "Cancer Alley."

We have agreed to meet Sylvia at the Spillway Bar in Norco. At first I don't see her at all until she steps in front of me and waves a hand in front of my face. I realize that she is fully warded, so the locals take no notice of the ill-fitting nun in their midst.

First we ward together before trotting down to the makeshift wilderness. This is my first time being a part of it with the whole pack. In a protective cluster, we growl a note to match the earth. I feel a wave of strength descend in a benevolent fog around us. It is a soft cloak of obscurity, a one-way tinted window allowing us to see all without being seen ourselves.

Gathered under the swollen moon, Rowan shines so brightly with power, it almost hurts to look at him. Desire mixed with awe force me to avoid eye contact with him. He's taller, leaner, and more savage than I've ever seen him in the mundane world. For all of his musical wisdom and gentle heart, he is still potentially dangerous.

Sylvia sings a hymn that I have never heard before.

Give thanks for moonlight, ever what we need
A shade of gray between instinct and lore
A hunger that propels us to the core
And music we create, on which we feed

A total satiation would mean death
But craving ever drives us to expand
Through fervent congregation, pack, or band
A pathway to wild places with each breath

A razor wire of truth on which we run
More delicate than glass the balance hangs
Between the hunt, the coarse display of fangs
And existential thought, the two made one

That moment when all four paws leave the ground
The savage breast supplanting human tears
The pounding of our thoughts ring in our ears
But pumping hearts that scarcely make a sound

Live for the sake of living, flesh and bone
Between two worlds the night bids, "Welcome home"

I am slightly incredulous that this holy woman is the same person with whom I once created such childhood mischief. Perhaps I, too, have lived many lifetimes without knowing it. I stand in awe and love as she now invokes a lycan blessing:

May you see in the darkness
even while your enemies would hide your light
May your ears always be attuned
to the music of the spheres and of the howl
May you always be downwind from the scent of friendship
May your hearts remain hungry, your bellies full but never satiated
And may the warmth of man-made flame
or the collective heat of the pack
still pale compared to your fire within.

Off come the clothes, but for some reason I don't feel self-conscious. In this palpable five-way energy connection, all human stigmas that I have been taught crumble and fall away like so much dust. These strange ornamental wrappings only hinder me and give me little protection from the elements compared to what my full animal potential has to offer me, and I shed them in my eagerness to feel the night air on my skin.

We flow into our animal shapes like a grove of nocturnal blossoms, a graceful unfolding of fur and fangs, reaching for the moonlight that nourishes us. This is a step back into Eden, before the first divine sacrifice took place. It is reminiscent of an ancient ancestral memory, before the dawning of consciousness, when all was pure. When we spoke as freely with animals as we did with angels, demons, and gods. Before we were cast out of our innocence with our newfound enlightenment, and set on our journey to discover Who We Are.

Rowan moves from wolf to wolf with his nose scrunched back, fangs prominently displayed in an act of something between asserting his dominance and smiling. Our warm-up consists of tumbling, rolling, playing, nipping, and generally being silly as we acquaint ourselves with this newfound collective freedom. Clustered together, our tails wag as we reassure ourselves and each other that it's still the same old us. We trot away from the highway and farther towards the river, comforted by the cover of night and increasing seclusion. Five is a small number for a true wolf pack, but for a band of shape-shifting musicians, it is just right.

Now that I have been in training, I am even more attuned to the howl, and it is like nothing I have ever experienced. One by one as everyone joins in, the crescendo swells to an otherworldly mantra, like a chorus of Tibetan singing bowls. The auditory spectrum shines like a prism and fragments like a kaleidoscope. An unmistakable line of energy connects us to one another in every possible combination like a star, a snowflake, and an intricate geometric pattern. There is a palpable pull like the ebb and flow of a tide, and I wonder if it is the moon or this wild new sense of unity that causes it. I am intoxicated by the music and at the same time more aware and alive than I have ever felt before. Is it because of my sharper lupine hearing, or is this something that only lycans can perceive: heightened senses with a human appreciation for beauty?

We are all tiny filaments of one sentient being, like five petals of a flower. Ten eyes look to the moon, a heavenly body that pulls at the tides of an endless sea of blood cells pumped by five hearts. Rowan points his nose at a star and we feel a surge of life force pulling us in a definite direction. He arcs into the air like a dolphin and aims himself like an arrow at the horizon. We surge together around him like a school of fish, like one complete organism as we take off at a hard run across the land. My center of gravity has shifted. No longer limited by the precarious balance of a bipedal run, my body now rocks into a different cadence as my weight is propelled across forelegs and hind. Tail extended, I am streamlined like a comet. The interlocking rhythm of twenty paws across the earth is the wildest music yet, a beauty that humans addicted to symmetry and patterns cannot understand. The moon holds the steadiest rhythm ever, a pulse that only the most eternal of beings can fully comprehend: a beat once every twenty-one days, with the occasional flam of a lunar eclipse.

I delight in the intense speed I can maintain; faster than anything I could ever experience in human form, and so effortless. It is like low-level flying: fast as a vehicle but devoid of any wheels or windshields to detract from my trajectory—the vehicle is me. My body elongates and contracts, a self-winding spring.

We carry the blood of the moon and the sun, our mothers and our fathers, our beasts and our people. Each breath is a gateway to a sacred duality. We are the stuff of fairytales and fables, a mystery that no one has ever solved. The hunt is eternal, for it is not in the felling but in the chase that brings us to our most aliveness.

We each alternately push ahead and fall behind like migrating birds. It becomes hypnotic, and for a split second I wonder if the others are in this trance as well. I look with my eyes, but I cannot even pick them out individually, nor separate my consciousness from the rest of the pack. We all melt together into a vortex of trust and strength. We are a single electrical current, a flow of blood through veins of instinct.

And then in a miniature bang, we splinter and expand. Our diaspora extends our consciousness. Gone astray, every one to his own way. I pick up a hundred different trails and take notes by rolling in whatever smells interesting: scent rolling is lycan social networking. I am an oxygen-seeking blood cell, gathering life force for all. I am a single tendril, a lone neuron eager to collect information and send it back to the brain center, the central hub that is the pack.

All doubt and confusion is somewhere far behind.

Run it off. Run it all off.

My inhibitions drop further as something breaks the concentration of my data gathering. Its long hind legs and white pom-pom tail make it an irresistible chase, and the closer I get to my quarry, the more myopic I become in my hunger. So single-minded am I, I don't even hear, smell, or feel the presences of two beings bearing down on me. Rowan and Teddy nearly collide with each other as they both strive to stop me in tandem. Only for the heightened awareness of each other is there no colossal lupine sumo splat. Rowan catches the scruff of my neck in his teeth, an act that reduces me to something between an abject puppy and a suddenly very horny woman. My body instinctively goes limp and he releases me. The rabbit is well out of sight for now, and I would do anything for Rowan to grab my neck again. I pant in exhilaration of the run, the profound high, the mystical experience, and *Rowan, Rowan, Rowan.*

Sylvia and Teddy catch up with us both, alternately trying to jump over each other and nip each other on the butt. Raúl grins at me and I manage to say, "Waheguru." He sneezes in amusement. We all just congregate for a long while, sharing the various scents we've picked up, sniffing, posturing, and wagging.

Back in the van, we feed our faces on protein bars and sliced beef. Rowan gently explains to me that if I'd caught and eaten the rabbit, I'd have had to either digest it fully before returning to human form or be horribly sick from lacking the capacity and enzymes to process it. And he knew for a fact that we wouldn't have enough time for the former, and Raúl would not be happy to have anyone barfing raw meat and fur in his van for the latter, pack mate or not. His eyes are shining, mouth curved in a reluctant grin. I have a gut feeling that he may have learned this the hard way in his youth, finally able to laugh about it now.

I wonder if this ritual will ever become less delicious over time. I am so ridiculously happy that I almost stay awake in the van on the ride home. Before fading out of consciousness, my last thought is how much I still want that rabbit.

ACT II

PHASE SHIFTERS

"The meeting of two personalities is like
the contact of two chemical substances:
if there is any reaction, both are transformed."

—CARL JUNG

CHAPTER

5

PHANTOM POWER

The New Orleans Jazz and Heritage Festival is upon us, and we are all suddenly insanely busy for two weeks. Even Sylvia, who is no longer publicly gigging, is off on a mission to Guatemala. Even if I'd had no Jazz Fest gigs, I wouldn't have been able to ignore the vibe. Not just in the Quarter, either. Across the increasingly gentrified Bywater, the Marigny, Mid City, Garden District, West Bank, and practically at my Uptown doorstep, festive visitors are everywhere. Most of us show our local pride subtly, such as fleur de lis jewelry around our necks and ceramic impressions of Water Meter lids hanging on our walls. But now I start to see the annual influx of tourists with straw hats and Hawaiian style shirts printed with chili peppers, washboards, and alligators. They support our music, bless their hearts. Even if they haven't yet learned the unique ways we pronounce certain street names like *Calliope* and *Burgundy*, let alone pronounce *Tchoupitoulas*.

Raúl and Teddy are the rhythm section of The Zydeco Sex Puppets at the Fais-Do-Do stage on the first Friday. I've got the early morning spot on the main stage with Descendientes the same day, then an afternoon set at the Lagniappe Stage with the Round Pegs. We each get passes for two in our performer packets, but parking passes are scarce, so we carpool in Raúl's van. I nag Teddy to put sufficient amounts of sunscreen on his arms, and then I have him slather my back. It's going to be a scorcher today, and my skimpy halter top is allowing skin that never sees sunshine to get burned to a crisp if I'm not careful.

The shuttle vans are efficient as ever, and both of my sets go without a hitch. I'm so busy catching up with the other musicians that I almost forget we have a job to do. I don't notice any glaring errors on anyone's parts, and my own are subtle enough that I don't think anyone notices.

Rowan is mixing all day, every day at the Jazz Stage. Many of the most venerable and noteworthy jazz acts are performing, but sadly, it seems as though the majority of the attendees ignore these artists in favor of the larger-than-life pop icons. After my last set I sneak over to the soundboard to surprise him with an iced coffee. I don't want to distract him by hanging around for too long, and I'm starving anyway, so I prepare myself to make a beeline for the food stands. Depending on how exorbitantly long the lines are, I'm either going for the crawfish sacks or the boudin balls first. My stomach snarls in agreement.

There's a new lineup on next. The Anatolian Fusion Project. Drums, electric bass, Nøde organ, guitar . . .

. . . and Aydan on the bağlama. Beaming at the crowd, she is dressed in vibrant textiles with their ancient geometric motifs and brilliant contrasting colors of traditional Turkish finery, yet the clothing is clearly tailored to accentuate her slender body. Her glossy black mane flows freely down her back, yet she doesn't appear to so much as break a sweat in the ferocious heat. Her rosebud lips pucker slightly in concentration.

Her playing is beyond flawless. She blends Sufi singing with complex Western chord changes and Byzantine modes. Her blazing riffs fuse microtonal bends and jazzy blue notes, hands a blur in a dervish of their own. Her cheerful, demure attitude belies her stellar chops and only endears her even more to the rapidly gathering crowd. Her band is clearly digging it, smiling and swaying with the music. I recognize most of these guys from Snug Harbor, and I know that they are loving the challenge.

And of course Rowan is mixing her to sound like an international superstar. His concentration on her music is unwavering. *Does he know that she is lycan, and are they communicating in ways other than musical?*

I've spent so many years in music trying to be a team player and tame my ego that I don't know how to handle jealousy when it strikes. Especially when it's a white-hot slug in the gut like this.

I recognize a well-known music writer standing nearby, murmuring to his buddy. He's out of normal earshot, but helpless to my wolf senses, I hear his commentary anyway. "Do you see that fingerstyle she's using? That's called 'sherpe,' and it's a really expressive technique. I wonder if she'd be interested in doing a cover story . . .?"

His companion is equally enthusiastic. "She was on *Past Your*

Bedtime with Titus and Ronicus recently . . ." Oh, gods! I don't want to listen to this conversation, but I can't help it. Now is not the time for me to find out that it was she who got the spot I'd auditioned for, the exposure that would have been my big break.

I steal a glance back at Rowan and instantly regret it. He is clearly enthralled with the music. And it's a sound that never in a million years could I have thought up.

With that, my hunger is gone, the growling monster in my tummy locked behind bars in a futile effort to cage my envy. But now the free beer in the trailer behind the stage looks really good to me.

◆ ◆ ◆

I desperately want to talk to Sylvia, but she's out of phone range. I should be able to confide in my other packmates, but I am terrified of rocking the boat.

I meet Teddy by the Lagniappe stage, where we're supposed to catch the shuttle to the parking lot. I drunkenly slur to Teddy . . . . "There's this girl from Wolf and it turns out she's a wereturkey . . . ."

"Oh, yeah, I'd heard about Aydan Çiçek through the world music grapevine. Did you know that her name means 'of the moon'? Fitting for a lycan. Then Raúl was just saying that you guys met her at the gym. Um. I *really* think you ought to eat something, or at least drink some water."

I roll the weight of my head in a clumsy *no*. Since I don't have to drive tonight, I want to more than shield myself—I just want to numb these feelings altogether. The harder I try not to dwell on Aydan, the more impossible the task. She could pass for a model, she got the TV show, she has the frontperson diva charm, the musical mind to organize a band, and now my love's respect and admiration—it's all too much for me to handle right now. I reach for another beer. I'll deal with the hangover in the morning.

By the time Raúl meets up with us, I am decidedly weaving. Neither man chides me. I have stopped caring about what signals I am sending out. Teddy waits in the van while Raúl walks me to my door, coaxes me to drink a glass of water and down some aspirin, pulls off my shoes, and rolls me into my bed. Before leaving he gives me a sympathetic look. "Be careful what you piss on, Little One," he softly cautions me. "You might end up marking it as your own."

◆ ◆ ◆

Tonight's gig is The Wild Hunt, which I'm not in the mood for. I hate Bourbon Street, and my head still feels like an exploding spaceship after last night's self-pity party. But the club had provided backline, so all I have to do is find safe parking and stroll through the throngs with only my padded gig bag strapped to my back. Tonight, people don't care that I didn't write or record any of these hit songs. When I play these covers, the crowd comes to life. It's a crying shame that most people are afraid to try new things and explore new original music, but a gig is a gig, and I'm going to milk it for all it's worth.

Going alto unleashes the beast and lends me a commanding beauty for the night. I stare the crowd down, toss my hair, and sling my bass in front of me as if parrying a sword. The façade is a ritual mask that I wear: not innately a part of me, but when I don it, I am one with the role. I am a shaman of bullshit; I am a harbinger of cheap messiahs. *Pace yourself,* my instinct warns me, knowing that

I will be extra-tired tomorrow. I am prepared to go in for the long haul between downbeat and pulling into my driveway many hours from now.

The crowd sways with our parroted repertoire. The tourists want to touch me, they want my attention, or they want a piece of me. It's as if I were the divine creator of this pop cultural echo, and that the guys on the gig and I are the only rock stars in existence. But as soon as they turn their undivided attention away from us, we will be reduced to particles where we were once waves.

But there's a major downside to this simulated glory, especially for a werewolf. Into the fourth hour of the gig the smells of pent-up frustration, vomit, smoke, and ill intent assault my nostrils a hundred times harder than the stench that already makes humans sick. A piercing two-finger whistle emitted by a tourist that wouldn't be out of place in a giant arena slashes at my eardrums in this small club. Musicians rely on their ears, and most of them I know hate this unnecessary sound when done at close range, but for me it's infinitely more excruciating. I wince in pain, much to the delight of the whistler, who does it again. Glaring at him, I bark at him off of the mic, "Dude, that really hurts!" I obviously should have tried ignoring him, because he only repeats the offense longer and louder, grabbing his crotch.

Oh yeah. This is why I hate Bourbon Street.

About three songs later, he wanders up to the edge of the stage with a fresh drink in hand. "Sorry, 'bout that," he smiles. "Me and my buddies are just having some fun. Come on, lighten up! You're in New Or-*leeeeeens*, baby! Have a drink on us!" I carefully take the plastic cup from his hand and unapologetically assess his eyes, his posture, and the way his buddies are all clustered together watching us. I tune into my heightened senses and give the drink a light whiff. *Date rape drug!*

I want to destroy this man. I want to make him suffer in ways that no human can fathom. I want to slowly disembowel him with one claw, a vertical dissection cut that starts with his most secret places. I want him to beg for absolution for crimes he has probably committed over the years to both musicians and females. A burning sensation crawls over every nerve. Breathing through the fury that threatens to consume me, I barely manage to tame the human within. Nothing would please me more than tearing this guy's body into bloody shreds, but I still have forty-five minutes left to play. I whisper my discovery to the drummer before calmly announcing over the microphone, "We need security over here, please." I don't know if security consists of more than our bartenders and bouncer, but this gesture is effective. The drunkard and his posse bolt for the door, leaving me with a glass of potential criminal evidence in my hand. The other band members stare him down, quietly discussing his description amongst themselves. Word of mouth warning is as quick as social networking among the music tribe.

The prickles on the back of my neck cling like burrs for the duration of the gig. *Was he a misogynist out to violate a woman, or one of the unknown enemies out to abduct a shifter?* I'm not sure which would have been worse. The overtones of his piercing whistles still ring in my ears.

Before tearing down for the night, I explain to the bar staff that I happened to have a drug testing strip handy, and no one questions me, especially when I leave the untouched beverage in their custody for anyone to analyze. Date rape drug test strips are so easily found online, I don't doubt that several other people working here have some handy for verification. In his hasty escape, the would-be perpetrator had left his credit card behind the bar, so he is guaranteed to suffer some sort of repercussions if he wants it back. I always make a point of tipping the bartenders on any gig, even if drinks are free or I don't drink anything. But tonight I make certain that I give them a little more than normal. The automatic gratuity added for cards left behind won't begin to cover someone having to deal with this miscreant in the morning—or later tonight, if he's really stupid.

Ready to just get the hell out of the Quarter, I amble down to my parking place on Rampart where I can see a clump of frat boys by my little Honda a block away. My nerves catch fire before this even fully registers. *No!* My *territory!* Somehow I make it over there in a heartbeat and catch an idiot in the act of trying to snap one of my windshield wipers off. This time I had no concern for stage etiquette and let fly a growl that surprises even me. "Party's over, asshole! Let someone trash your vehicle while *you're* trying to get off of work!" I have my unfolding police baton "Thumper" handy, but I'm still trying to decide whether I want to hurt these people— and I want to hurt them very badly indeed—or just make a lasting impression.

The guy holding my windshield wiper is sprawled across the hood of my car, purple baseball cap set tightly backward, oversized beads akimbo. Still determined to get his trophy, he slurs, "Dude, c'mon . . . we're just havin' a good time!"

That settles it. I shouldn't do this, but just for the barest moment, I go into tenor phase. My stage clothes rip as I suddenly grow two feet in height, grabbing the vandal by the shoulder and lifting him as if he were a doll. Swinging him around to face me, I stick a snout full of teeth in his face, letting some saliva drip for added effect. The terror on his face makes this outrage almost worth it, and I savor the stench of his fear before dropping him to the pavement like a bag of trash. The revelers screech and take off down the street like deer after the first warning shot. And in the next instant I am in full human form, loading my bass into my car. No one bears witness to any of this but a lost-looking mourning dove sitting on a nearby wrought iron fence.

Let those obstreperous wastes of human flesh tell the police. Between my shredded clothing, the impossible thing that they have just witnessed, their blood alcohol level, and the fact that they were trying to vandalize my car, who are the authorities going to believe? *Unless some of the authorities are among those out to enslave us shifters.*

I make it home in record time. My friendly porch light has never looked so good. My bed, however, no longer seems like a safe place to sleep. Only a civilized human would rest easily on a soft platform, so readily exposed. Comfy pajamas and soothing tea are the last things I need to feel secure right now.

Yanking the covers off of my bed, I throw them in a pile on the floor in a corner, my new location giving me the advantage of feeling vibrations through the floor. Going into bass form, I prepare my bedding by turning three times. Survival sleep mode kicks in: restful for the body, one tiny section of the mind always on alert. Complacency is dangerous for a wild animal to feel.

◆ ◆ ◆

A dark hunger, a visceral urge ruled by a cycle is what urges me awake. I alternate between walking on two legs and four, snarling all the way to the refrigerator. I care nothing for the repercussions as I feed. *Ahhhh, chocolate* . . .

I try not to delve into self-pity too often, but I can't ignore the fact that being a werewolf with PMS sucks big time. I go through some yoga asanas to try to relieve the pain, but nothing seems to work. My soprano-form human shell feels like it's going to burst. I wonder if I would still be cramping if I changed forms.

Tenor phase comes more easily to me this time. My fingers are tipped with claws, but I still retain the opposable thumb. The pain begins to fade, and I breathe with my whole body in relief. My mind is still more ego-driven human than instinct-based animal, and curiosity gets the better of me. Walking bipedally to my instrument cases, I choose my Music Man, loving the increased capacity of smelling wood and polish and sweat and metal strings. I have to adjust my strap to be able to hold it in this larger form, and it takes me a while to be able to stand upright holding it, as I'm already top-heavy with broader shoulders and heels off the ground. My short tail helps me to balance.

I finally check myself out in the full-length mirror. *Hot damn!* I truly am a monster. My elongated face—neither human nor canine—can't conceal dagger-sharp teeth, even when I try to close my lips around them. My eyes are an unnerving yellow; no wonder we come across as evil. My ears are pointed, and a downy dusting of whitish fur springs along my arms, legs, and down my spine. I am fearsome. I am hideous. *I am awesome.*

I tune my bass down to the recommended slightly lower pitch and immediately feel the difference. Hooked up to my amp, I feel the notes all the way up my spine and flowing out of my throat. The vibrations oscillate in such a way that everything feels inherently *right.* The tones caress and massage me, a giant purring cocoon of sound. I try playing in tenor form, which is cumbersome at first with my longer, thicker fingers. My claws are a hindrance, so I try changing the angle of my picking hand. Mercifully, I still have callouses on my digits. I can't quite sing the way I am accustomed to, with lips that can't quite touch each other to form certain consonants, but I believe that I can eventually manage with enough practice.

The new tuning unlocks something powerful within and my creative juices start flowing. My claws serve as picks, even thought I don't normally use picks for bass. My fingers become a bit more nimble, improvising a quick mantra over the steady drone of my growl. If only my pack and I could play out like this. Who needs a cosplay gimmick when you're in an all-werewolf band? The musicianship alone would put us on the map. We could be famous if only the majority didn't fear us. I raise my growl to a crooning note.

There's a knock at my door. My upstairs neighbor Bob calls, "Buzz! Hey, are you okay?"

Shit, I forgot to ward! "Rust a rinute!" I call, sounding like some demonic Scooby-Doo. I retract my body into soprano form as quickly as parahumanly possible, pull on my sweats and t-shirt, and answer the door as casually as I can. "I'm fine. Just practicing. Why?"

He looks at me askance for a fraction of a second. "Just thought I heard something . . . weird." I assure him that I'm trying to learn some avant-garde new music that all the young people are playing these days, and then we ease into small talk about local politics. And he leaves it at that, and I close the door. *Whew!*

That's enough practice for one day. Calm and pain-free at last, I step into the shower and prepare for another lesson from Rowan.

◆ ◆ ◆

Rowan somehow knows that I have gone beyond alto phase in public even before I say a word to him. He cuts me some slack, but warns me about doing such a thing. Not that the frat boys would have been plausible witnesses, but had our mysterious adversaries been watching, they could have followed me and traced me back to the entire pack. "I can't really blame you," he muses. "The Quarter is getting out of hand, perhaps as bad as it was before Hurricane Katrina. This is why I don't even make that twenty-minute commute if I don't have to." I forget that he's the only pack member who doesn't live in Orleans Parish, choosing instead to hide somewhere in the suburbs of Metairie. He is a little removed from the rest of us in more ways than one.

I'm back at the studio, learning a few more techniques from Rowan before he has a session. It's probably unhealthy, but in times like this I can pretend that we are an item. After all, how many girls does he know who can get genuinely excited about new microphone preamps or can appreciate a three-way analog splitter?

We take a moment to discuss energies of not only people, but the tools of our trade. He talks about vintage boards and mics. "Why do you think people covet them? Why do you suppose they wouldn't just prefer some new state-of-the-art piece of equipment instead?"

I shrug. "The history? The energy?"

He beams, and I try not to melt. "Precisely. It's already been proven that sound imprints itself on the walls, even if there's no way to play it back. But microphones have consciousness. Mics don't just transmit sound. They 'hear.' They receive and retain highly concentrated energy, more intensely than any historical buildings that project ghosts. People prize vintage equipment, sometimes without even knowing why. Microphones especially retain memories, breath, emotions, and the unfiltered things between takes that never even get recorded. They hear all, and only convey the hard cold truth . . . or the raw, undiluted magic. Consoles, too, are like computers that become self aware. The circuitry comes to life, a literal ghost in the machine."

It makes perfect sense to me as I suddenly remember a session I once played at one particular studio where everyone was cooing over a vintage Kohl mic. It was a strange piece, resembling the underside of a horse's hoof, but it was revered for its history with Abbey Road—and thusly named "The Abbey Road Mic" with a kind of hushed reverence. And then I recall historical consoles that engineers covet. There is state of the art equipment being made every day, but everyone wants the ones from C-Saint, from Le Studio . . . the studios that made history.

Already drawn to him as it is, I struggle fiercely to control my urge to wrap my arms around him.

He saves me by showing me the drum room, which is another mystery. Not only is there an acoustic advantage, there is also an implication that part of pentagons and pentagrams traditionally are used for protection based on the same principle as the mysticism of acoustics. Even a wolf paw print can be naturally outlined in a five-sided shape. I can't get enough of this lore, and am just on the cusp of understanding the connection between these tidbits. I am highly tuned to the room, to Rowan, and to the energies surrounding the building. Which is perhaps why inexplicably I feel a lump of dread just before I hear a knock on the door. As Rowan answers, I can sense her, and suddenly will my every emotion under control.

It's Aydan.

When Pandora unleashed the plagues onto the world, I doubt that hope still remained in the box thereafter, because hope is by far the cruelest thing a person can experience sometimes.

I can smell desire on her. And on him I smell nothing. He is shielded to the nines. He could be feeling anything—and why wouldn't he want such a beauty?

Rowan is the one to break the tension. "Aydan is here to record her Anatolian Fusion Project. I suppose it makes sense that a lycan should be the one to produce another lycan."

My shield goes up just in time. I nod a polite goodbye to them both, but walking to my car as fast as possible, I can feel the despair catching up with me. It does not clench my chest—rather it tickles at my thoughts, daring me to scratch. And scratching will rip open a thousand wounds of failures past and present. I try to rise above it. I try to tell myself that I am accomplished in my own right. But the second I focus my thoughts elsewhere, it mocks me. *Only ten percent of all hunts are successful . . .* It's a fact about wolves, but their animal nature enables them to handle failure without crippling regrets. This is more than can be said about humans—or werewolves too, it seems.

So home I drive with my proverbial tail between my legs. I don't permit myself to fall apart until I reach the sanctuary of my little apartment, but once inside I fall to my knees the second my door closes. My chest feels as if it will crack wide open with grief, so I curl up into a little ball, but the pain doesn't stop coming. The old, creeping feeling of being utterly alone seeps into my whole being like ice water. I ward myself as best I can, crawl into bed, and cry quietly, howling very softly into my pillow, *"Rowwwwwan . . ."* Either no one hears me or no one answers.

Everyone preaches about safe sex, but no one ever gives a thought to safe love. This is deplorable, for love is the most dangerous of all natural causes.

◆ ◆ ◆

Journal entry, May 10th: So much I could tell the greedy-eyed spectators, old flings, and my unattainable love. But if I had to choose one thing, it would be this. Do not attempt to revive me with your waters of condescension. Instead, bury yourself next to me in the soil and ash, twisted branches ever reaching upward.

I continue my training and rehearsing with my pack mates, and somehow manage to conceal the deep sadness that follows me everywhere. Sometimes I am able to shake it for an hour or two, but it always eventually continues to pull me down like a lead albatross around my neck, making it hard to even stand up straight. Food no longer tastes good to me. I don't even feel like listening to music.

I try to physically work off the malaise at the New Orleans Athletic Center, but each sighting of Aydan further taunts me. Plus one of the trainers, Javier Del Toro, has gone missing. He was a big bull of a man with a heart of gold, and his unexplained absence hits me hard.

I finally switch my exercise routine to the Downtown Fitness Center, which is smaller and far less glamorous, but it is way cheaper and suits my basic needs. Even still, I can't seem to pull myself up by my bootstraps. Inside my head, my secret sad voices pipe up: *Can I make a living just sleeping all day?* It hurts to breathe, and it hurts to even *exist*. But as always, the show must go on.

The heat and humidity are merciless by now, which means fewer tourists and fewer tips. New Orleans becomes a little more of a ghost town during the peak of summer. This is the time of year when most of the rest of the world is cooler and many bands go on tour or play elsewhere, and I can't help wondering where I would be right now if Slackjaw were still alive. Showering twice daily is an exercise in futility, as every commute to gigs results in a sodden sweatbath, no matter how close I manage to park near each venue.

I am grimly determined to get through this gig at La Balcone. Squaring my shoulders, I take a deep breath and try to get my Kundalini working—or some sort of mojo, anyway—before rolling my rig into the club. I nod hello to Naj and the others, and try to make small talk with Sand while I set up next to her, but she is as distant and aloof as always. She suddenly dashes off the stage, kicking over my water in her haste.

"Man, what is her *problem*?" I ask Naj.

She shrugs. "She's a coldhearted bitch, but she plays a mean set of drums, and she looks good on stage."

I think of the horrible overuse of her cymbals and silently beg to differ, but keep my mouth shut. I don't understand this strange loyalty. It occurs to me that if Naj has her heart set on having a female drummer in the band, I know a couple of very talented ones right here in New Orleans. As I open my mouth to suggest a better player, from the corner of my eye I can see Lydia watching us carefully just for a fraction of a second before seemingly vanishing. "She creeps me out." By this point I have no idea to whom I'm really referring.

Unfortunately, turning my eyes elsewhere proves no more fruitful. I unwittingly lock gazes with a sallow-faced man in drab clothing sitting near me. He raises his Bloody Mary glass at me in a toast from afar. It doesn't take any sort of fine-tuned skills to sense the desperation and self-loathing oozing out of his every pore. I casually move to the opposite end of the bar.

In a split second, he's pulled up the stool next to me. "How ya doin' Birch? Looking forward to hearing ya play. I haven't seen ya since you was with Slackjaw. You look pretty good . . . you were skinny the last time I saw you, but now, you look . . . healthy."

I instantly hate this man and his appraising eyes. I tense up, and begin to feel a little dizzy. *Oh, shit!* He's some sort of shifter, and he is definitely not one of the good guys.

I desperately scroll through my mental notes. *Shield of light* . . . I surround myself with an imaginary wall of compassion, a compassion that guards me, gives him a polite gratification of my acknowledgement, then gently pushes him backward. If I push too hard, he's only going to feed into this. I am the willow tree that bends, but does not break . . .

He begins to drone on and on about his son's failed musical career, despite all the God-given talent. Then he starts in on his assessment of my inevitable fading youth and dwindling career potential, and how he somehow holds the keys to salvation. *Just like Cal.* The burning begins to flare up in my belly. I unfocus my eyes and remember to breathe. In this altered state of consciousness, I gather my thoughts, remember where the office to the bar is, and replenish my energy.

I return, cutting him off midsentence. "Can you astrally project? Then maybe you should get over yourself!" I make a beeline for the restroom and stay there until I calm down, and am pleased to discover that my wits are still about me and my energy level is still high. *I did it!* I fluff my hair, shake out my limbs, and swagger up to the relative safety of the stage.

Overconfidence now carries me in the wake of this triumphant adrenaline rush. Between numbers, Naj is in the middle of introducing the next song with a little story about her connection to it, when a rude tourist interrupts by bellowing out, *"Play it!!!"*

I step up to the mic, ready to defend my makeshift tribe. "Easy, big boy—there are some things that last longer than two minutes!"

Dealing with an unsavory audience member can be tricky. The point is to not only set some boundaries, but also get the rest of the room to sympathize with you in the process, and humor is a good way to diffuse the situation. Over the years my heckler lines have usually been appreciated, not only by the audience, but by other folks on the gig as well. But Naj's brief glower of disapproval sets me straight. Does she think I'm trying to steal her thunder? Likewise, I'm not certain why I seem to be in trouble when later in the night she moves over to the piano and starts a song in the wrong key . . . so I transpose and match it. The horns eventually figure it out and adapt, but something feels hostile now. What was I supposed to do? Play in the assigned key and sound like a train wreck? I am eager for this night to be over. There's a reason that the phrase "that's show biz" is synonymous with "shit happens."

Naj is not in good form tonight. She keeps tugging at the collar of her long-sleeved shirt, sweating profusely in the summer heat. It doesn't take a genius to figure out her mood swings or why she's concealing her arms. I have seen coke and heroin destroy many a great musician, and hope to the powers-that-be that we can soon have the old Naj back; the one who is generous with her smiles, her support for her fellow musicians, and her charisma. She eventually staggers off of the stage and makes a beeline for the ladies' room. Tim grabs the mic and takes over for the rest of the gig, effortlessly belting out staples like *Every Dog Got His Day, I'm Gonna Be a Wheel Someday,* and *Knock on Wood.* The crowd picks up again, gratefully feeding on Tim's natural drive. Even Sand seems to lock in more efficiently.

Lydia is also another saving grace. Around the rest of the world musicians make trombone jokes, especially about them being unemployable. These jokes don't apply in New Orleans, where everyone needs a good trombone player. They are the rock stars of the brass world, and now Lydia has suddenly morphed from a team player into a star soloist. She holds her instrument lightly with a slippery grace. The slide darts back and forth like a forked tongue, deadly and precise like a fencing foil. Sexy and authoritative, she commands the crowd to watch her. Her cornrow braids cascade down her shoulders in serpentine rivers. And her eyes are constantly searching and assessing everything: each individual in the audience, the bartenders, and the rest of the band. She sways with the music, but her gaze could turn the casual observer to stone.

I try to text Rowan after the gig, but no response. Then it hits me that he can't text because he has a session with Aydan. I know that when he's working he never texts and seldom remains on the phone long when anyone calls the landline. After all, he never does anything half-assed, and his focus and intensity are unmatched. He stalks the perfect sound, the ultimate sonic predator. And that's a good thing, right?

I wonder if they laugh easily as they work together, or how efficient her playing is. I pray that she isn't one of those one-take wonders who can nail every part so effortlessly. Trying not to think about it only makes it worse. *Have they developed their own private jokes by now?* I despise this feeling. I have never before been jealous of his female clients—after all, we all have records to make. But then again, none of them have been so beautiful, talented, or obviously after him. I can no longer endure this thought, nor can I bear the guilt and jealously eating me alive, and I need a painkiller.

So I find Yohan down the street at Molly's and accept his invitation to for a drink in a poor attempt to distract myself from the nagging misery in the back of my mind. The cloud of smoke from his cigarette makes it hard to see his features in detail, and I don't know if he's warding, or if I even care. His eyes are like two cornflowers, impossibly blue and guileless looking, but he keeps his sight trained on me like a stalking jaguar. He drones and on and on about his ex-girlfriend and how he will always love her. He says that I am attractive, even though he prefers Asians and redheads. *Don't overthink*, says my inner autopilot. It doesn't even matter what we discuss. His charm is a little too obsequious and his cologne is a bit too heavy, but all I care about is a distraction. I am what my cousin Bonnie back in Scotland calls "skin-hungry."

One thing leads to another, and before long I allow him into my bed. There is the matter of succumbing to the pleasures of the flesh to assuage basic human needs. It's almost like the hunt: something must die, even if it's only an illusion.

There are no harsh words or punishing blows to remind me of Cal. His skin is pale and freckled like mine, and he does not criticize my physique. He attends my body's every need like a skilled auto mechanic: thorough, adept, and impersonal. He flips switches, pushes buttons, and the engine comes purring to life. Skin on skin at last, which I had so desperately craved, a temporary rush. I am finally physically satiated, albeit still empty inside.

Naj has her painkillers and I have mine. Neither of these vices solves a thing.

Once the sound of his breathing slows to that of a sleeping man, I allow the tears to trickle freely down my face. They flow like an open wound, but they barely make a sound when they hit the pillow.

◆ ◆ ◆

It's been awhile since I've played on Frenchmen Street. Sometimes I know I've done my job properly if nobody notices the bass at all. Tonight is very different. I am always encouraged to cut loose with solos and basically be as obtrusive as I want to be.

I enjoy playing with Delta Funk. Salty is on drums, so I know we'll make a solid, friendly foundation. John Lisi the bandleader always shoots me a "rock and roll horns" gesture and a grin when he especially likes a solo I've taken or a groove I've locked into. The blues selection is gritty: Little Freddie King, Hound Dog Taylor, and B.B. King. John likes to throw in some rock as well: ZZ Top, Led Zeppelin, and early Rush. But I like his original songs best of all—they are just plain fun to play. Quirky and driving, there are always refreshing changes, modulations, and unison riffs. No room for musical road hypnosis on those.

I'm catching up with John, whom I haven't seen since The Round Pegs gig, when Gabriel decides to make his presence known, flush-faced and sporting a Slackjaw Harrison t-shirt. Before I can object, he steps right up onto the stage and starts to get in my face. "Hey, man!" John cuts in with his signature polish, "I need you to step off the stage, Daddy-O!" saving me the task of telling Gabriel something less charming. Unabashed, he jumps down but remains right at the edge of the stage, nearly knocking over my mic stand.

"So, Birch! I've been messing around with the guitar some, and I really wanna get together and jam with you sometime!"

I play over two hundred gigs a year and I still can't believe how many people think that I have nothing better to do than to go to their houses—or heaven forbid, have them come to mine—and amuse them. "Gabriel, I would like to help you, but I don't have time to jam with anyone. I always have charts to learn, songs to arrange, and gigs to play."

"It's okay, Miss MacKinlay. I can be patient." His words cover my nerves like a soft blanket of tarantulas, and his unblinking grin brings to mind something hungry and undead. He parks himself at the bar directly across from me and gazes at me like I'm a TV screen.

John grins. "Looks like you've got yourself a boyfriend there!" he teases. I am relieved that John doesn't call me by my nickname aloud. The last thing I need is for this creep to get any more details about my life.

I shake my head. "The cruelest thing I could ever do is to seduce someone who still believes in miracles," I muse more to myself than to John. Pretending to examine a tuning machine on his guitar, I lean into him and whisper, "That guy is really starting to scare me. Just keep your eyes open." We exchange fist bumps of understanding, then it's time for downbeat.

Over the course of the gig the stage becomes a giant dissecting pan. Gabriel hangs onto my every note, occasionally rocking his head and mumbling something to himself. His eyes never leave my face, not even when one of the other guys takes a solo. I try warding myself, which helps a little, but my solos feel duller and the tips don't flow as freely. I can't even let myself go alto because I don't want to appear more attractive. It's turning my blood to lava that one obsessed person is ruining the whole gig. Not just for me but also for the rest of the band, and even for the audience to some degree, because my playing is distracted. I want to charge off the stage and break him in two.

At one point Gabriel leaves his post to stand smack-dab in the doorway. He tries to beckon more people into the bar, which only succeeds in creeping them out and scaring them away. Now I am even angrier, for we make our money on this gig according to the bar ring. Finally I see Holly the bartender tell him something. Her eyes widen as he leaves the bar.

I heave a sigh of relief and try to enjoy the last thirty minutes of the gig, free to be myself at last. But I am now officially exhausted. Holly makes a quick beeline for me and informs me that Gabriel told her that he was my boyfriend. He's now officially banned from the joint, but I am still uneasy. John tries to break the tension as he hands me my money—"Here's a lil' somethin' for your gas tank!" The other guys can see genuine worry in my face as we tear down our equipment, and Salty offers to walk me to my car.

As we make our way toward Royal Street where I am parked, I give Salty a condensed version of the story under my breath. And then as we round the corner, my heart stops for an instant.

Written in the dust on the side of my car is "I LUV U BIRCH." I rip a banana leaf from a resident's nearby plant and wipe the offending words off of my beloved Honda. It also appears that my WWOZ sticker has been ripped from my bumper as a souvenir. I feel a fierce need to reclaim my territory, but I don't think peeing on my car is going to be the answer. Before I load my rig into my car Salty investigates every nearby intersection, and I whip Thumper open and make a point of displaying my police baton. If Gabriel is hiding somewhere watching me, then he'll at least be observing me carrying a weapon. How in the hell did he know which car was mine in the first place, and for how long has he really been shadowing me? These questions trouble me the most.

How easy it is to forget that even predators become prey when there's a madman about.

◆ ◆ ◆

Journal entry, May 18th: Honesty is entirely overrated. One might as well tell it like this: "He said, 'I'm going to shoot you,' right before he pulled the trigger. At least he was honest."

Complete loyalty with a few well-guarded secrets is the way of the wolf.

I have a few hours to kill in the Quarter before my afternoon brewhouse gig, so I stash my bass in the equipment closet there and decide to pay Teddy a visit. I could call or text him on the pack phone to give him specific details, but I decided to try out my warded howl to give him a heads-up instead. Once I get over feeling like a certifiable idiot for howling out loud while walking down Decatur street, I admit to myself that it pretty much rocks to be able to do this while completely unnoticed by passers-by.

A block away from his pad, something odd in the energies hits me, a tiny ripple of an off-kilter wave. This is probably why I have the foresight to look up before knocking, and my brain doesn't quite process what I'm seeing. A person seldom expects to see a Siberian husky standing on the roof, especially one that smells like a trusted friend.

"Teddy, what the *hell?*" I blurt out, aware that warding is still not going to completely hide me, and talking to a dog on the roof might certainly attract attention. Taking the name of my favorite bassist in vain, I continue, "How in Ged's name did you get up there? What have you done to yourself? Rowan is going to kill you for going bass in public!"

He sneezes and contradicts me with a defiant "Nooooo!" before disappearing behind the rooftop. A minute later Teddy the human comes to the front door barefoot and shirtless, and grinning triumphantly at my palpable astonishment.

"It's a technique I've been experimenting with. I got the idea from Raúl's story about casting an illusion of an altered bass form. I've been referring to this doggie trick as contrabass phase, and Rowan has given me his blessing to try it out . . . more or less." While Teddy would never outright defy our Alpha, he is sometimes quite good at bending the rules. This makes me intensely uneasy, and I don't even try to hide this emotion. I sit at the kitchen table, unsure what to say.

He hands me a bottle of water, knowing that I seldom drink alcohol before a gig. Pulling up a chair alongside mine, he stretches to loosen his newly transformed body. "No, seriously. This is something that could help us in the long run. It takes some serious visualization and focus on the subtleties of one's appearance, such as blue eyes, more defined markings, and whiter fur around the face. Combined with physical exercises in wolf form—like curling of the tail backward, and we could convincingly go out in public posing as docile house pets. Anyone who is out to thwart shifters will be on guard if another human is around, definitely so in the presence of an animal that is traditionally associated with wild places. But no one filters conversation around a harmless old pooch, and with so many dog-friendly bars and restaurants in the Quarter, we may be able to do some spying."

I am still rattled from all of the weirdness I have already seen and the suspicions I have harbored. I'm not crazy about any of us risking our hides. On the other hand, I'm even less crazy about the notion of some unknown boogey man or preternatural mafia trying to hunt us down. I agree to play the role of the accomplice if need be, making a mental note to ask Rowan about this.

I end up venting about this new stalker Gabriel. This worries him, for any stalker is a menace, and with the added concerns of someone who might be trying to harm us, this could potentially be very bad news. He offers to accompany me to any gigs that don't conflict with his own schedule in husky guise, not just to offer added protection, but also to sniff out this man's energies in a way that I cannot as long as I need human hands to play. The knot in my stomach unclenches a bit at the notion, and I tell him that I will consider it.

He tells me about how he visualizes contrabass form, imagining the lowest note in the threshold of hearing, coaxing the tail to curve up and over, and invoking the essence of *dog* when wolves and man converged. He informs me, "Everything that you see around you began with a thought. Visualizing is the most important element of creation, and then sound follows. Why do you think so many music teachers advise you to sing along with your improvised solos? It gives your music more intention, direction, and focus. It intensifies your energy. You are simultaneously visualizing and creating, and your magic is stronger that way."

He urges me to try it. By now I don't have a problem undressing in front of a pack-mate, although I secretly wonder if things would be any different should Rowan decide to choose me as more than just a colleague. The thought sends my heart racing, and I can't hold anything else in my mind. I go fully bass, my wolf form suddenly feeling out of place in another person's territory. I try to summon in my mind the lowest frequency I have ever heard– *contrabassoon! Lowest keys on a Bösendorfer piano!* I try to curl my tail and shorten my teeth, but I can't manage to go beyond a lupine body. It seems that I am useless in the wake of my fantasy about Rowan.

Finally I sigh in frustration. "I don't get it. How is this supposed to be *beyond* the quintessential essence of *wolf*? I didn't sign up for all of this training to come across as a harmless doggie!"

Teddy is serious for once. "Don't be a speciesist. Dog shifters have been around since their domesticity to help restore order. I'm sure you've heard of François 'Papa Doc' Duvalier, yes?"

"Dictator of Haiti, and a pretty sick fuck, from what I've read," I reply, slowly donning my clothes. "He died before I was born, but every now and then, something comes up in the papers about him, or about his son. What does this have to do with shape-shifting dogs?"

"Yeah, he was a pretty sinister fellow. He was also a voodooist. Not to knock the voodoo around here in New Orleans, but this guy was a *paranoid* voodooist. At one point he was out of commission from a heart attack and had a man named Clémont Barbot hold down the fort for him. He later began to believe that Barbot had transformed himself into a black dog and was planning to supplant his position. So the nutjob ordered all black dogs in Haiti to be killed. Shifters today still wonder if Barbot was a shifter too. But no one will ever know the answer, because Barbot was eventually killed under Papa Doc's orders. It's a shame; Barbot might have prevented countless executions and tortures. We can only hope that whatever is threatening the shifters now doesn't involve a megalomaniac dictator."

On that note Teddy restores some levity to our vibe with a juicy belch. We swap a few sick jokes and hang out until it's time for me to wander back to the brewhouse and set up. Plus Teddy has some especially juicy gossip for me about The Maestro. Apparently the Dude was stupid enough to attend a recent costume party dressed as a Nazi soldier. He had tried to drive home intoxicated, crashed his car into a telephone pole in a "bad neighborhood," and was thrown into Orleans Parish Prison central lockup near Broad Street—still dressed as a Nazi, of course. The fact that he chose to call Teddy to bail him out is a sad testimonial to how badly he must have alienated himself from the rest of society.

Teddy is grinning so wickedly, I know there's even more to the story. "I ended up getting all of his identity information, which revealed that not only is he much older than he claims to be . . ." He pauses for dramatic effect. "But also his real first name is *Yngschwie!*" He pronounces it "ING-shway."

I don't believe what I'm hearing. "No!" I shove his shoulder hard. "You're making this up! That's just Pig Latin for 'schwing'!"

He shakes his head, clapping in wicked merriment. "Nope! I could never make this shit up. See, this is what happens when you name your kids something that can't be found on the little license plates for their bikes. It makes a person grown up bitter and douchey!"

"It's funny," I muse aloud. "It seems that a great many musicians might also be shifters, but I get the feeling that Yngschwie Holstein isn't one of them."

Teddy gives me a penetrating look. "Gee, ya *think?* If he has any animal trait at all, it's that of a one-trick pony." He snorts derisively. "And one-trick ponies, musical or otherwise, are seldom shifters. Chances are that if a person can't reinvent himself, he probably can't convert his physical body structure either."

Before I leave, he gives me the parting gift of alternate lyrics to Duke Ellington's "Don't Get Around Much Anymore," a staple on casual jazz gigs:

Missed the toilet last night (dunnnn dun, da-dun)
Shit all over the floor (dunnnn dun, da-dun)
Cleaned it up with my toothbrush
Don't brush my teeth much anymore!

On today's gig I am of The Unseen. This is an easy happy hour gig. Most of these folks who are in regular rotation are University of New Orleans music majors, with the exception of Ronnie Twigg, the piano player. The only constant member is the bass player, but he's been missing for a week and the band needs a sub. No one has any idea why he's suddenly vanished, and I certainly can't chime in with my own chilling theory.

I don't play jazz all the time, but I've brought along my doorstop-sized Real Book, the Bible of jazz fakebooks. We are more or less musical wallpaper at the brewhouse this afternoon. The diners do not notice us, but we are nonetheless what make their patronage special. A stronger energy, a real, raw energy that canned music does not convey. We imprint our vibes into them. Some will cherish the experience and we will be indelibly entwined in their subconscious memories. Some will drink too much and eventually become aggressive. We only help to bring out their true natures. What they decide to do beyond that is up to them.

Only one person seems determined to try some one-upmanship with us: a beady-eyed man with slicked back hair and too many teeth in his mouth when he smiles. His expensive suit and clean-cut looks do nothing to cover up for the loose cannon he seems to be underneath his swanky veneer. He never throws so much as a dime into our tip jar, but he makes certain that we see him drop in his business card. Every time we are about to go into a song, he steps up to the stage and tries to cut us off with some saga of his self-importance. The horns drown out his efforts to rope us into some sort of deal with his business in Indonesia. I can't for the life of me figure out why, but it's easier to just ignore him. "I can get you guys a gig in front of someone *very important*," he croons, which reminds me of Cal. A shudder seizes my spine, but I keep playing and don't respond. Finally he glowers at us. "What's wrong with you people? Don't you know who I am?"

I snicker, "Sir, if you don't even remember your own name, I'm afraid I can't help you there!" The guitarist cracks up, saluting me with high fives and fist bumps. Twigg folds himself over his keyboard like a praying mantis at a typewriter, and the drummer gives me a well-timed rimshot. The heckler's obvious failure to unseat us radiates off of his body in palpable angry waves. Just as my suspicions are raised that he might have been trying to flush out some information about us, he dissipates into the background like a wisp of smoke. I later tuck the card away into my gig bag in case he has anything to do with this war on shifters, making a mental note of the tiny angel silhouette and the name of the business: *Chimera Enterprises.*

I reflect intensely on this power struggle afterward as I pack away my bass and stow the restaurant's amp into its equipment closet. I realize that the wolves of the music scene—or simply musicians who fight back—are important for maintaining a natural balance. Perhaps it means that fewer drinkers are in the respective venue as a result, but we bring down only the sick-minded and weak of spirit: those who feel the need to harass an entertainer. Thinning the herd makes for a stronger, more appreciative audience, in which only the most intelligent listeners survive.

I want to find something to do with a pal, but everyone I know is on a gig ... or recording. Realization snuffs out my smug amusement. That sickening feeling in my gut at the thought of that goddess Aydan possibly making love with Rowan right this very moment is more than I can bear, and I can't face my pack-mates in this state. I suddenly and urgently need a painkiller before I go insane.

So once again I track down Yohan, who is in the middle of showing off a picture of some woman to his friends. It doesn't take him long to figure out what I want. He drives me to his pad on Esplanade, in a house not too far from where *Cat People* was filmed.

He takes me more brutally this time, pushing my face down into the bed with surprising force, teeth clamping down on my shoulder, clawlike fingers digging into my hips. *The human must remain in control,* lectures my instinct. *No matter what, do not bite him back.* This is not the time to let things get complicated, and nothing could get more complicated with a lover than inadvertently turning him into a werewolf. I welcome the pain, determined to let it take my mind off of Rowan, Aydan, and my career.

The exhaustion of the long day—trying to go contrabass at Teddy's, playing a gig, and dealing with a shady businessman—forces me into an uneasy slumber in spite of Yohan's jackhammer snoring. In fits and starts, I dream a jumble of gigs, assorted people from over the years all amalgamated into one confusing show. And in every corner I see Sand's scornful glare and my pack is always lost somewhere in the crowd. Then something wipes my confusion clean and starts fresh, and I am suddenly in an ancient temple with Rowan. We are making love on a silk palette. The overwhelming feeling of *rightness*, of goodness and completion moves me to tears and my heart thumps me awake.

My eyes dart wildly around the room. The smell of old nicotine on Yohan floods back into my waking consciousness, and the week-old dishes in the sink reek of rotten food and avoidance. His snoring becomes even more dissonant. I take in the pinup girls smirking down on me from his walls, clearly offended by my mediocrity. The assorted pictures of him posing with various male comrades are fading, but one photo remains pristine: a beautiful red haired woman in a spotless, elegant picture frame. Clearly the one he wants to be with; his ex, I gather from stories he's told me. Or maybe they never really broke up. Realization slaps me hard. I have never been anything in my adult dating life but someone's consolation prize, backup plan, painkiller, comic relief, or a plaything to be eventually discarded. And here again I have allowed it, even sought it out.

With a subconscious swish, one more picture slips to the floor in an afterthought. This is clearly some cosmic invitation to pick it back up and examine it, so of course I take my cue to slip out of bed and pick it up . . . and turn to a solid icicle. It's Yohan sitting at a bar somewhere next to Calvin Quinn. There's no evidence that they are engaged in conversation, but the mere proximity marks Yohan as a traitor in my mind.

How recent is this picture? every neuron screams in my head.

Yohan stirs, drowsily calling, "Is everything okay, baby?"

Long-suppressed anger hits me in a lunatic flood. "No," I snarl. "I am clearly wasting my time. What am I, your bronze medal? Do you take me for some *stupid little bitch?* Goodbye, and have a nice life!" My clothes are on in a flash, my gig bag is strapped to my back, and I slam the door on my way out, hearing his sleepy bewilderment, "Baby . . . baby, what did I do?"

Rage replaces base terror as I storm off into the sweltering gloom. It's somewhere between midnight and pre-dawn, and there isn't a soul on the street. This is an extremely dangerous time to be wandering the Quarter. But between the crushing self-loathing, my roiling anger at Yohan and Cal, and my trusty police baton in hand, I simply do not care. If there are any predators about picking up on my scent, they are probably also picking up on my insanity and steer clear of me. Twenty blocks later I reach my car with a clearer head and the realization of how stupid I was to walk at this hour, and how crazy I must have appeared to Yohan. I drive calmly home and fall asleep with a vengeance.

◆ ◆ ◆

"So what would be the repercussions of being a little husky?" I ask Rowan. We're back at the studio, and I wonder for the umpteenth time why I am never permitted to meet him at his house. I had given him the suspicious Chimera Enterprises card, which he studied with a long frown before tucking it with a strange precision into his wallet. Now am curious to hear his feelings on Teddy's contrabass phase.

He either doesn't follow me or is trying to be funny. "Your voice will sound strained, especially if it's not natural for you to sing that way."

"No, I mean that trick that Teddy does that makes his wolf form appear like a big, cuddly husky dog. Could we effectively go out in broad daylight and get the scoop on whoever is after us?" I sit down on the control room couch and make a concerted effort not to wince from my fresh bruises.

Rowan twists his mouth to the side. "I've been thinking about it. It would make us go unnoticed by humans who can't detect a shifter's ward. But something in my gut tells me to hold back on this until we get more information on who our nemesis is." His gaze hardens as he locks eyes with me in a power play. "You're struggling with something. We need to work on shielding some more. But first, maybe you'd like to tell me what's bothering you?" It's a command, not a question.

I am trying not to let my unbearable tension show. My meltdown with Yohan has rendered me vulnerable, and I am praying that his scent no longer clings to me. It doesn't help that Rowan looks exceptionally good today. He appears to have gotten a haircut that accentuates his widow's peak, and he's wearing his blue Mesa Boogie grease monkey shirt that I love so much on him.

The abrupt clammering of the studio phone rings hacks my thoughts in two. I suspect that even without lycan senses I would be able to hear the conversation just as clearly, the caller is speaking so loudly. He demands, "How much it is to make a song?" With his usual patience, Rowan explains that it is a certain rate per hour, so the price is entirely dependent on how long the artist takes to record.

"Well, I wanna come in right now!" Rowan tells the man that he is booked up until next Thursday, which might even be true.

"Well then, *fuck* yo studio!" The guy hangs up.

Before I can even see Rowan's face, I burst out laughing. His low growl only feeds my hysteria. I don't even care whether or not he is pissed off right now; I simply can't control myself. My love for him and the feelings I can't express collide in the classic mishmash of nerves, where one has no choice but to either laugh or cry. The expression on his face of exasperated concern only makes me laugh harder, and the harder I try to calm down, the worse it gets. Helpless tears are now streaming down my face.

"I think you need to go home and get some rest," he finally tells me, and my giggles slam to a halt. My blood instantly freezes in place. Panic reaches into my ribcage and gives my heart a little squeeze. *He's rejecting me.* I grab my keys and head for the door without even saying goodbye. The sky is darkening overhead, portending a gargantuan summer storm.

I drive home in shock, whispering, "Fuck yo studio," to myself. As soon as I get inside I ward, go tenor, and slash at my shower curtain. The rod falls down with the first swipe of my claw. I let the beast out then and proceed to tear the whole thing to ribbons. The curtain is Cal, it's Gabriel, it's Aydan, and it's the incessant douchebags that make my job miserable. It's my own weakness; it's my own stupidity. The vinyl yields easily to my sharp claws as I snarl, tear, and channel my hysteria and self-loathing into the object. The scent of vinyl, bathroom cleaner, mildew, and rage fills my nostrils. If this is insanity, it's not nearly as colorful as everyone makes it out to be. The tatters become confetti as I shred the ribbons with my fangs. At last nothing remains and I roll in the pieces, the curtain rod a discarded bare bone. I finally exhale and return to soprano form, rising to two legs, covered in scraps and shocked at the damage as my last bit of human nature clicks into place. *Did I really do this?* I am left with a clear head, a huge mess to clean up, and the grave need for a new shower curtain.

Stein Mart is just a mile down the road from my apartment, so I march to my destination, trying to grind gravel and cement into sand beneath my feet. I almost choose a nice curtain that I won't be tempted to shred again—a blend of polyester and vinyl with a Zen-like bamboo print. Then I think better of it and get the cheapest one in the store, just in case I need to let the beast out again someday.

On my walk home the rain begins to kick in: little teasing drops playing cat and mouse with the city, an opening number for what is to come. I get inside before the worst of it hits, remembering that it is now hurricane season. *Bring it on, bitch!* I challenge the powers-that-be. A floor-rattling thunderclap answers my thoughts, and I unplug my computer. Stripping out of my wet clothes and tossing my new purchase into the sink for the time being, I dry myself off, light a few candles, slip into full wolf form, and snarl myself into an uneasy, fitful sleep.

◆ ◆ ◆

On the following gig at La Balcone, I try to keep my game face on. I have no idea who Naj is going to be at any given time: the sweet chanteuse or the unpredictable train wreck. This steady gig has officially become drudgery, and I am always exhausted and drained after each show. I've started to no longer care about my appearance on stage, reverting back to my jeans and t-shirts. My posture has gotten terrible and I keep catching myself slouching, as though trying to protect my heart. I can't even focus my intention into my playing anymore, instead just going through the motions like the zombies I so revile. I was better off on Bourbon Street, which is saying a lot. John Milton and Dante Alighieri may have made terrifying portrayals of what hell might be like, but neither of them ever had to play on Bourbon Street during Mardi Gras. And this gig is getting to be even worse than that.

Naj knows that there's something wrong. Shielded and warded, I still can't keep the trouble out of my eyes. I am still able to maintain my usual verbal deflections toward hecklers. Even though I use passive aggression and humor to try to keep the rest of the audience at ease, some of these attention-seekers are cross with me for not being able to play their game and sulk out of La Balcone. I wish I could get away with using some of the more outrageous comebacks that Teddy uses (such as *Why don't you just shit on your fist and then punch yourself in the face?*). But I know that even in these changing times of equal rights, most people are not prepared to see a woman get so ballsy, so I sacrifice my true sentiments in the name of the audience's comfort level.

Lydia is barely within my line of peripheral vision as usual, but Sand is especially venomous today. She hisses at me to stay in the pocket, even though I am trying valiantly to lock into her fluctuating tempo as best as I can, even watching her foot so that I can try to anticipate her bass drum pedal. I try to get behind the beat with her on *Yes, We Can Can*. Then a straight walking bass shuffle is up next. I lean behind, listening for the cymbal snap, but even that is a bit unpredictable. I am a bass player, not a diplomat. Even so, she is so ostensibly upset I try to break the tension throughout the gig with forced smiles.

Lumbering toward the edge of the stage, a thick-necked man in a business suit rips a dollar bill out of his wallet and dangles it cloyingly over the tip jar. He never spills a drop of the whiskey clutched in his other hand—not cheap whisky either, I can smell—as he tries to tease us as if feeding seals at the zoo. It doesn't take a werewolf to see that he is showing off for his friends, all of whom are watching him. This is clearly a power trip, and I actually don't think he even cares if there is any live music at all or not. In spite of the wide smile plastered across his red face, he smells angry and frustrated. "Can you play any Jimmy Buffett?" he slurs, still holding the dollar as if it were a dog biscuit, expecting us to sit up and beg. The longer it takes the band to confer on this, the more he pantomimes offering and then withdrawing the paltry bill over and over.

I can no longer contain myself. "Sure. Just have the bartender bring over a big enough hoop for us to jump through!"

Like a petulant two-year-old outraged at not getting his way, he snatches away his precious dollar and stomps off into the audience, muttering something under his breath that sounds like "bunch of amateurs."

I grin at the band, but Sand is furious. "Good going, doggie. Now the clients are furious, and you've made us look bad!"

"Sand, do we even *play* any Buffett?" I growl at her under my breath. "This is an R n' B/ funk/New Orleans blues lineup. Are we jukeboxes? That guy was an asshole!"

Before Sand can spit back a response, Naj smoothly calls out the next song. I am simultaneously relieved at the subject changer and unnerved to see Gabriel walk in, wave at Naj, and choose his favorite spot next to the stage as close to me as possible. His eyes never leave me and he claps with the enthusiasm of one who has never heard live music before. Stalkers are the worst kind of vampire ever. He makes a big display of throwing a twenty-dollar bill in the tip jar and Naj blows him a kiss. Luckily he leaves before we finish, sparing me his usual request for us to get together and jam.

It's been a strange day overall. After the gig, I tell the group, "Next week, I'll bring cookies!"

Sand smirks. "How about if you use that time to *practice your bass* instead?!"

Wow. Didn't see that one coming.

I look to Naj for support, but she shrugs it off. "Ignore Sidewinder and chat with me for a bit. What's wrong? Do you need to talk?"

Sidewinder? Is that Sand's surname, a nickname, or something even heavier?

Her eyes are sweet and sympathetic. I haven't confided in another woman in a while, since Sylvia is still out of phone range. For all of her troubling addictions, Naj might understand. She certainly has no qualms about displaying feelings. She is a compelling performer and a lovely woman—when she's sober—but would she know what it's like to fear being upstaged by someone else? Especially when a musician of surreal beauty and virtuosity is working intimately, every day, with one's unattainable true love?

She hands me a drink. "Just let it all out. There's a reason that we all have to unload our venom every now and again."

Relief that she is back to her old self tonight rolls over me in waves. I know the signs of drug use, and wonder if there is anything I can do to help her. Perhaps a little self-disclosure on my part will invite her to do the same.

And so I find an unlikely comradeship in this serpentine woman. I tell her that I am desperately in love with someone that I can never have. Like a floodgate opening, the confessions come pouring out: that there is another woman who clearly wants him, and that I loathe myself for my jealousy. That physical beauty has never been an attribute of mine, and that my bass playing is all I've got. The shots keep appearing on the table in front of us, and I keep sipping without thinking. Still, I am careful to name no names. Since I play roughly two hundred gigs a year with all sorts of bands, these subjects could be anyone. I'm not even letting on that these other people could even be musicians.

"Sweetheart . . . why are you so tough on yourself? You tear yourself down as if expecting someone to pick you back up." *Or before anyone else can beat me to it—like I did to my innocence,* I think to myself.

"It's nice to be raised up, but the effect isn't permanent unless you can do it for yourself," she continues, sniffing avidly. She raises her glass in salute and I take another nervous sip. The room lurches a bit—I have to drink more slowly. "I'm probably thinking too much about an old boyfriend." I elucidate. "He used to remind me that I'm not exactly glamour girl material, let's just put it that way. But I think he's in Vancouver now."

"Vancouver? Are you sure? How long ago did you hear this? If he's that far away, then *what are you afraid of?*"

I wonder if she even knows about this mysterious threat to shifter existence. If drugs are dulling her senses, she could be in even greater danger than those of us trying to remain vigilant. "I'm afraid of a lot of things, Naj! Aren't you?" This question is loaded; I want to see if she brings up the topic, but stress and frustration get the better of me, and I begin to feel choked up.

I turn my face away and she takes my hand. "You have to build yourself up, Buzz. Those hurtful events aren't happening anymore. It's hard to just let go, but you can imagine it in your rear-view mirror. Try visualizing a gossamer bridge from the old to the new. You can cross it if you really want to heal." I manage a smile, weak but genuine, and her sweet face blossoms into warmth. "You're such a great musician. You are a true asset to this band. And you have a following because you're not only talented, but you're attractive. If I could have a girl crush, it would be on you."

Attractive? Me? This is getting strange, even in my intoxicated state.

A slight ripple in the lycan energy—a tiny warning breeze before a storm—sends a tremor down my spine. I glance at my pack phone, but there are no missed calls. Naj raises her brows but says nothing. My lips feel numb, so there's no way I can drive in this condition. It's tempting to text Raúl or Teddy asking them to give me a lift home, but I don't want to raise their concerns. So I message them that all is well, but that I will need a lift to my car in the morning.

By the time I stagger out of La Balcone, I am both lonely and disgusted with myself for allowing myself to get this wasted. Naj ends up driving me to my apartment, seeing me safely inside.

After guzzling a pint of water I lift my eye to the peephole and jump at the sight of Naj still standing in my driveway, examining my house. A ward flares from my energy field, and her brow furrows. She turns, glides back to her car, and her vehicle makes a slow retreat into the night.

CHAPTER

6

BACKWARD MASKING

Journal entry, June 14ᵗʰ: I have become too wrapped up in productivity to notice how beautiful the moon is. I have become too strangled by sorrow to swallow the nectar of the gods. I have become too laden with earthly things to see heaven at the bottom of my coffee cup. If I'm not careful, I'll become one with humanity at last.

As Max said, "Let the wild rumpus start . . ."

Teddy is trying to quit swearing. He believes that purifying his words will help to improve his energies. I don't know if this is possible. All I know is that it's the funniest thing I have borne witness to in ages, and in the haven of his apartment I am more than happy to have something to take my mind off of my misery. As he catches his toe against the bookcase, he hops up and down, trying to make his expletives as nonsensical as Yosemite Sam:

"Gragg fragga nagga nargle krikey narpets!!"

I am just about to ask him what "narpets" are, when he scowls at my amusement and hands me a couple of gilded tickets to some event I have never heard of: The Crescent City Shifters' Ball. "Rowan wants us to be there. I have to do a lot of social networking for Howlapalooza, and this will be one hell of an education for you as well."

I know this is going to open a discussion, but first Teddy hobbles into the kitchen for his favorite remedy: a beer. The stereo kicks on with the live Shakti track "Joy," and we sit in awe of the musicianship of John McLaughlin and company. After about ten minutes of listening spellbound, we both feel like hurting ourselves and never touching our instruments again.

I'm not certain that the idea of a public event appeals to me, so I study the tickets for a long time before asking, "Shifters' Ball? How many different kinds of shifters *are* there?"

Teddy shrugs. "I don't think anyone will ever truly know. It really depends on what is defined by shifting. Some believe that it must be fully corporeal. Others, such as shamans, believe that it isn't something innate, but rather something a person 'puts on,' just as the wearing of wolf skins or bearskins in traditions ranging from First Nations to Asatrú. Whether a person transmogrifies literally or on some astral plane, it is widely accepted that both kinds of change are genuine."

"But a ball? Isn't that a really risky event? Especially with all these attacks on our kind?"

He tilts his head, weighing my question. "No more risky than any gathering for people who were persecuted over the ages," he finally assures me. "Look here's the main reason we need to go: I need to show my face to some bigwigs, and there are some people you really need to meet. We have to form alliances at any cost. Plus, it is officially a masquerade ball. Anything anyone sees may or may not be real. Werewolves are the most celebrated among shifters. Part of the reason that we are so successful is our ability to harness the power of sound. We have made our presence known to the outside world and have still managed to survive. Granted, it was due to the foolishness of some of our kind, and most of us would have preferred to remain a mystery. But what's done is done, and we have ended up with the reputation of being the most fearless. In short, we are the rock stars of the shifters' world. We have not only survived, but also flaunted it. We are the only ones who can transmit our powers through bite. And some shifters are envious of us because the ultimate success is survival, not just in our lineage, but also in our legacy: the books, movies, gaming, anime, and so on. They say there's no such thing as bad publicity as long as they spell your name right in print, you know. Any records that you cut are slices of that immortality.

"What makes lycans such excellent survivors is that we are a blend of two gregarious, tribal-based species. It's harder to find a balance between natures in blended beings if a person is of solitary nature but his animal counterpart is social, or vice versa. Even lycans can sometimes be tortured souls if both parts are not honored, as you can read in Herman Hesse's allegorical *Steppenwolf*, specifically *The Treatise on the Steppenwolf*: the two natures are at war with each other. Remaining unsocialized is bad for the spirit, and mingling with other shifters helps us to remain sane in a world that is even more protean than ourselves. Besides, any outsider who tries to report a spectacle like this would only have his sanity questioned. Fiction and horror movies are the best things that have ever happened to us."

More hiding in plain sight. A little light bulb goes on. "If hints of our various and sundry kind are 'exposed' from time to time, people get accustomed to the idea, and it gets passed off as a costume party . . ."

He flashes his teeth. "Bingo. So it's going to be held at the extra space behind Arnaud's in the Quarter next week. How about if I pick you up earlier that day and you can change here, then crash on my couch afterward? That way you won't have to worry about parking, or even crossing Bourbon. And yes, my couch has been all but sterilized since the Maestro slept on it!"

I chortle in remembrance, but something else is bothering me. "Isn't whoever out to get us going to try to get into this thing? What if these tickets fall into the wrong hands?"

Again the shrug. "I don't think these tickets are for anything but show. Just anyone can't get in there, ticket or not. The security is very surreptitious but thorough, and there are covert operations to keep an eye on everything. SIN agents are supposed to be attending this thing, and even some of the NOPD are rumored to be working for SIN—the shifter cops, anyway. This also might be a way to bait our enemy. But guess what? There will be free food, free music, and free beer!"

Sylvia doesn't return from Guatemala for another three days, so there's no way I can ask what she thinks about this. "Wouldn't you rather ask some glamour girl to escort you?" I half-tease Teddy, stalling for more time. I've never sensed any sexual tension from him, but as long as I've known him, I've never seen him with a girlfriend. As the words escape my mouth, I realize that now I'm slightly curious as to why.

"Alas, my heart's desire is unattainable," he half-teases back. "Marilyn Monroe only consorted with the rich and famous."

"Eeee-*yewww*, she's *dead*, you sicko!" I pretend to cringe, cuffing him on the shoulder. If he doesn't want to tell the truth, then it's really none of my business.

"You say that like it's a bad thing. So . . ." My pack-mate looks me in the eye, flashing his signature infectious grin. "Do you want to check this out? I think it's important for your training."

Part of me wants to just curl up and shut the rest of the world out, but the wild part of me cannot resist. "All right, I'll go."

Thumping me affectionately on the back, he makes a quick dash to his fridge. He hands me a can of NOLA Blonde, cracks one open for himself, and we listen to some old recordings of The Who while sipping, gossiping, and analyzing John Enwistle's bass playing. Before I leave we each try to say *"Boris the spider"* through a single belch. Teddy manages effortlessly but I am laughing too hard to produce more than a gurgle, snarfing the bubbles instead.

Sometimes I truly enjoy being one of the guys.

◆ ◆ ◆

Where is my pack? What am I doing out here on the steppes all alone? I don't even have a body, so I have no way of knowing if I am in human form or lupine form. If I am being this analytical, perhaps I am human. But some wild undercurrent is telling me to run, and I don't even choose a direction, for it doesn't even matter. There's just an energy current that I join. No awareness of ground beneath me; all I sense is speed of the most exhilarating sort.

If only my pack could be experiencing this with me. Nonetheless an ineffable sense of profound *oneness* overtakes me. There is no separation: not from my pack and not from any other souls I know. Not even from the stag I spy grazing twenty paces away.

It doesn't seem unusual in my mind's eye to watch a fourteen-point bull elk glittering like jewels, and smelling like fine wine and deep craving. This creature is made of money, power, food, sex, and music. And it's been expecting me. It lifts its head placidly, gazing into my eyes with a preternatural intelligence before bolting across the steppes so swiftly I barely have time to register its direction.

There is no way that I can *not* give chase. There is no fear of failure, no desperation. There is only motion and desire. It's such a glorious expansion that I wish would never end. I have no legs, but I am the rhythm of padded footfalls. I have no breath, but I am the melody of the wind over the earth and the howl. I have no ears, but there is a bell-like ringing, the chorus of angels and animals —or perhaps they are one and the same—calling to be fed. Shape-shifting angel-beasts, echoing every genius riff ever played and long forgotten, lost chord patterns and lyrics, and torn shreds of songs that every musician hears in dreams thinks that he or she will have no trouble remembering upon waking. My world shrinks to a pinpoint focus on the stag. I am he and he is me, but I am gradually gaining. *I must catch this thing. All of those riches could be mine.*

Just as I spring for that shimmering throat, my fangs slash empty air. My body jolts hard in my bed upon waking as if I have fallen from my leap into consciousness from a physical height.

Some say that dreams don't lie. Some say that they are your brain sorting out all of the garbage it doesn't need and filing away all the important information into storage. Some say that they are divine messages, or at the very least the subconscious trying to tell you something important. I would like to think that whatever this is, it's due to last night's spring rolls before bedtime. But the mysticism and symbolism gnaw at the back of my mind all day as I try in vain to figure out what my dream means.

◆ ◆ ◆

I thought I was familiar with the banquet room of Arnaud's until entering just now. Like *Where the Wild Things Are*, the ballroom has completely transformed into a forest. I recognize a little bit of familiar architecture now and then: brick walls and elegantly arched doorways. But the ivy creeping up walls and grape vines wound around beams lead me to believe that this is some alternate dimension untouched by the business of the mundane. The trees and painted sky give the illusion of limitless space in this building. Somehow even the stars are twinkling. The security guards wearing cheap rubber horse masks at the front door had obviously intended for the revelers to let our guard down and be dazzled upon entering this enhanced reality.

I don't know which conceals my identity more: the elaborate jaguar mask that Teddy has helped me choose or the sexy low-cut gown I had to wear once for a wedding. With my face concealed and my hair flowing freely, I feel almost beautiful. I hadn't realized until tonight that I don't even own a proper handbag, since it's been years since I've been on a real date. At the last minute I finally had emptied a microphone bag, hoping that if no one sees HEIL SOUND on it, the accessory might pass for a clutch purse.

Teddy, good-natured as always about his appearance, sports a half mask of a long-beaked water bird that accentuates his prominent chin and wears a New Orleans Pelicans basketball jersey over his tuxedo to heighten the comedic effect. Some people will be attending half-changed in their natural forms, and some like us will keep the rest of the event guessing. This is a bluffing game in which the stakes are high, but no one can resist playing.

I had no idea that this event would be so surreal. I recognize a good many people here: local figureheads, audience regulars, casual acquaintances, and a great number of fellow musicians. I wonder who among us are shifters and who are humans just being blindly led through this labyrinth of disguise. Many people are wearing masks, some of which are either well-crafted and extremely expensive or perhaps not even masks at all. I see expensive suits and ball gowns complimented by fur, feathers, horns, hooves, scales, wings, and trappings that I'm fairly certain don't exist in nature, at least not the natural world in which I grew up. With so many innovations being made these days in costumes—not to mention the money that some people are willing to shell out for them—it is impossible to tell what is real and what is fake. Many revelers sport ornate jewelry that I could never afford but can certainly admire. I can deduce that the ones wearing silver are not lycans.

I hear a song emitting from the main ballroom: *"A permit for perniciousness, and wild hearts one and all, a license for licentiousness, it's called the Shifter's Ball!"*

There is a central atrium with potted foliage of all kinds, giving the main room a jungle-ish feel. Smack in the middle of the room is a fifteen-foot papier mâché image of Ruthie the Duck Lady frozen in partial transformation, arms extending into wings. Space is cleared for dancing, and the band in the corner is masked. Predators dance with prey, and prey coyly string the predators along. Dominants of the same species engage in terpsichorean one-upmanship. Single males show their bright colors in hopes of luring a mate.

We wander the rooms, each with a different theme. There is a room that contains a fish tank the size of a small movie screen, and some of the guests have already decided to take a dip with the dolphins and seals. One has an assortment of climbing trees, in which guests are lounging. We enter the one that features magical creatures, its main attraction being a giant ice sculpture of a unicorn head. Two little people attend the glacial hunting trophy, pouring vodka into a hole at the tip of its massive horn, ingenious interior plumbing causing the creature to weep chilled vodka tears. The diminutive man hands me a shot glass, smiling with a mouth full of needle sharp teeth bright against his mahogany skin. As I am led from room to room, I catch snatches of conversation. "We all know a neigh is just a bray with vibrato. Those horses don't have anything on mules . . ."

"She can have all the beer she wants, but keep her away from the margaritas! The salt will make her melt!"

"No, there's another reason he only likes missionary position. If he gets flipped on his back, he goes right to sleep! I swear I'm going to make a pair of boots out of him someday . . ."

One guy is already face down at the bar, eyes rolled back in his head and tongue lolling out, but his buddy, a sharp-faced man with tiny eyes and a long nose winks at me. "He ain't passed out! He just don't wanna talk to this gal that's been buggin' him!" The ersatz drunkard rises to give his companion a rough shove, saying, "Shut yer pie-hole, J.D.! You know if her skank sister woulda been here, you'd-a been playin' possum along with the rest of 'em!"

A distinctly wild odor catches my nostrils, obvious enough for even human senses. Whatever it is, it both raises the hair on the back on my neck and piques my curiosity. It's coming from a corner of the room where a number of young men are clustered, blocking my view, although a woman standing next to me sneers, "There they go again. What is it with young men's fascination with cougars?" She isn't kidding. With a small break in the throng I can plainly see a bona-fide cougar lounging on a velvet settee, grooming itself impassively. The jeweled collar and leash that tether it to its resting place don't appear that they would be terribly effective should the creature decide to spring from its perch and snack on a few revelers. I can't help but admire its beauty, and before I can make a remark to Teddy, it looks directly at me and gives me a conspiratorial wink with a jade-colored eye.

A well-known local politician is lounging by the bandstand, flanked by two ostrich-legged cocktail waitresses. The tail feathers sticking out of their skirts appear to move of their own accord as the women snake their bodies around the big man, as if unsure whether to kiss up to him or snap his face off. He accepts a drink from each, tips them both generously, and languidly tastes the air around them with a two-foot long tongue.

My eyes flit next to the tallest woman I have ever seen in my life, tawny-skinned with short black hair, sporting a giraffe mask. No one seems to be disguised tonight as his or her real animal counterpart, so I have a hunch that she's really something even larger. With my ears trained on her I overhear some people ask her if she's going to sing tonight, and she nods her head. With slow, fluid movements she migrates over to the fish tank, mounts the steps on the side, and dives in face-first, her arms making slow flying motions. I can't hear what she says underwater, but people have their ears pressed against the tank, mesmerized. I grab Teddy's wrist and drag him with me to the tank as well and as we press our ears against the smooth glass, a sound resonates through our bones. The sound of bowed basses and crystal bowls are brought to mind. *Humpback whale,* I realize. Their songs have been studied for years, but this is an amazing rare treat to hear it put into lyrics. How quickly I forget that lycans aren't the only shifters with a talent for music. When the song is over, everyone breaks into wild applause. Now that music is singing in my blood, I have to go check out the house band.

It's so strange for me to be attending an event and not be playing. The masked band is a young, good-looking gypsy ensemble, and I don't recognize their scent. My guess is that hiring a group from somewhere else entirely keeps tension from arising among New Orleans groups, especially if some members aren't shifters. The violin, trumpet, saxophone, bass, and drums make for a much bigger sound than five people would normally produce. They are swept up in a frenzy playing a turbocharged *horo,* ensnaring the listeners in their infectious spell. The guitarist spies me studying his fingers and throws me a nod. He turns to face Teddy and me, steps up to the mic, and improvises a quick doggerel: *"The wolf pack chases songs and tones, let no sound go astray! For just as you are what you eat, you're also what you play!"* Well, I'll be darned.

I don't sense any of the other pack mates here. I can't help but wonder what Rowan is up to, and I am even more disconcerted that Aydan isn't here either. My eyes flit to the dance floor and I watch an old man in a wheelchair suddenly glide to his feet, arms outstretched like wings. He appears to grow in height, shifting into some equivalent of alto form. He takes the arm of a woman in a bear mask and they begin to dance flawlessly, captivating more than a few spectators. I find myself wishing that Rowan could see this. In a desperate attempt to focus my mind on something other than my angst, I decide to give the dancing a try. Teddy promises to keep a protective eye on me in case anything goes amiss.

The trouble is that most musicians I know don't dance, and I am certainly no exception. Even though we are required to have a concept of rhythm and motion, we seldom get a chance to cut a rug, since we're always playing for the people who *do* dance. *Or else we are simply the nerds that no one asks to prom* says an old voice in my mind, rising up to burn my gullet. Something tells me, however, that tonight is all about feel and instinct. If I turn off my human ego, pay no attention to choreography and performance, and follow my instincts, I might actually learn something. I remember to lift my rib cage in an elegant posture and stalk to the edge of the dance floor.

A tall man in a gazelle mask sidles over to me as the band strikes up a waltz. Now it gets tricky. He is warded but has let some of his scent permeate his disguise. He moves with impressive authority and I follow his lead, aware of my jaguar disguise and try to appear seductive. *You know you want to fill my belly,* I try to project to this man who would be prey. *Come a little closer,* I silently command, and there is no boundary between our thoughts as he tightens his grip on my arm. I don't know what kind of animal form he takes, but I am now certain that it isn't an herbivore. In fact, he might be something that could possibly give a wolf a run for its money. He is dangerous, but aloof. I get in the back of my mind the image of him lounging in a tree. *Leopard,* I surmise, and I can feel his body tremble in genuine laughter. No wonder he chose me to dance with him: he couldn't resist the joke of my feline mask. He bows, I curtsey.

I catch a snatch of lyrics from the band: *"Celebrate a secret that has never been exposed! The tension mounts between the diametrically opposed!"*

I'm beginning to understand the role of this ceremonial dance. Even in this transient dual nature that we all possess, it is important to pretend to be something that we are not. A predator symbolically experiencing what it is to be prey or vice versa makes for a deeper understanding throughout the shifters' world.

Another man, this time masked as a monkey, takes my arm as the band switches to a bebop tune. I don't know how to swing dance, but he's not leading the standard steps anyway. He initiates a sort of a bobbing and weaving motion, so I mirror him. I can see his eyes through the holes in his mask, and I am trying to not freak out that his pupils are rapidly dilating and contracting. I can't figure out what he craves. I continue bobbing up and down, inhaling the tangy scent of his sweat and aggression. I'm pretty sure that my abs are going to be killing me in the morning. I sense a jungle that would easily be habitat to his simian disguise, but a flash of rainbow feathers out of the cuffs of his sleeves gives him away. If he really is a shape-shifting macaw, then it means that we are actually doing a dance to establish dominance. I relax. Even if my dancing isn't up to snuff, in my animal form I can take him. I let down my warding slightly, and he drops his eyes deferentially. We bow and curtsey like the previous dance and I wander a little dazed back to my pack-mate. I think I've had my fill of dancing. Teddy pats me on the shoulder in sympathy and support.

Something blessedly cuts through my disorientation in the form of a tall, stunningly photogenic man sashaying our way. "Teddy, darling!" exclaims the newcomer, pushing back his otter mask and flipping his long blonde tresses out of his eyes. He hugs Teddy with a flourish of wrists and a girlish foot-pop. His inherent hilarity is infectious, and I can't suppress a snort as the ornamental foxtail attached to the seat of his leather pants sways like a pendulum.

"Dean, you're looking fabulous as always," Teddy chuckles. "Birch MacKinlay, meet Dean deChanteloup; lycan, model, massage therapist, and occasional bartender."

"Hey, what else am I supposed to do with a master's degree in geology?" our new comrade deflects. Turning to me, he remarks, "Girl-child-boo, your mask is *fabulous!*"

Teddy claps the ferociously beautiful werewolf around the shoulders. "Dean is a lone wolf, but a very important part of lycan society. He is a diplomat among the regional packs, and keeps the alphas informed of news. Such a hard life, isn't it, Dean? Your sensitive nose meant that you had to hang out with that food and wine pack of restaurateurs for three days. You will of course, call us if they are doing a gala that needs a live band?"

"I think I already mentioned your pack. Then someone opened a Jerboam of Bordeaux, and I don't remember much after that!"

In a blur of jokes and anecdotes, I rapidly feel comfortable and grounded again. Dean has a laugh like Tom Hulce playing Mozart in *Amadeus*. His energy is friendly, and I sense deep intelligence beneath the flamboyant veneer. Maybe if there are more shifters around like this guy, it won't be such a frightening new world.

I want him to stay with us awhile. "Guys? Who wants drinks?" Abita for Teddy, Jameson on the rocks for Dean.

As I wend my way through the crowd to the bar, the scent and energy patterns of two men seated there catch my attention. One short and plump and the other tall and strong, they seem like a comically cliché duo. Their cockatoo masks are pushed to the backs of their heads, looking like someone has wrung their necks. *Why haven't they warded?* The vibe I get is that they simply couldn't be bothered, so I eavesdrop.

". . .why they think we would even want to drink this shit," says the little man. "You can't even *find* Foster's back home!"

His larger companion shakes his head, swinging his long ponytail off his shoulder. "What do you expect the bar to be stocked with? James Boag and Tassie cider? Be happy they've got Shiraz!"

"Stick it in your date, mate. I don't give a toss about Shiraz! I can drink that at home. It's just the principle. It's like, why would I come to a restaurant in New Or-*leeens* to eat Vegemite?"

Australian, it hits me. *Good gravy, I had no idea this was an international event!*

"Don't get aggro there, Wally. Joey is here representing the whole mob, and you don't want news of an argy-bargy to get back to Old Man Ripclaw." The tall man is clearly enjoying winding up his blunt-nosed friend, and his spicy amusement entices me.

"You're a fine one to talk. You've been acting like a bogan the whole time! Asking that lady this arvo if she'd fancy a root—I'm surprised that she didn't just job you one in the kisser!"

"I just wanted to see how she'd react, mate! You know they like our accents here . . ."

They pick up on my having overheard, and turn to face me. The wave of energy thickens as my own joins in. The longhaired one smiles kindly. His eyes are mild, but their keen blueness holds a reflection of something primal—of clear water and ancient forests. Something is distinct about his scent, like a fox shifter, but wilder and more inviting. "How're ya going, mate?" he inquires politely.

I grin. "I had no clue that this was a global shindig."

"Ah, a babe in the woods!" chimes in his roly-poly cohort, whose wild mess of hair manages to cover his ears but not quite the shiny top of his bald head. "And very pretty, too. Too bad old Malcolm is already making the rounds. He's a bit tired of being such a baby-munching minority in a country full of roos . . ."

"I'm sorry, luv. Wally here needs to stop being so biased towards the marsupials," explains the lean man. "Not even Aussie humans know the full extent of our variety."

Wally blinks his small eyes. "Did you see that local Sheila Miss LaFleur at the bar, playing possum? Or is that 'opossum'? Quite fetching. Marsupials in America . . . who knew? Ah, I do love Lou-weeezee-ana. Great food, as long as I chew some leaves in between meals!" He grips his beer more tightly, and I suddenly notice the oddity. His hand is strangely formed into a configuration of three fingers and two thumbs. *A werekoala?*

But his blue-eyed friend intrigues me even more. "So he's Wally and you are . . .?"

"Darren. Wally's from Queensland and I'm from Tasmania."

"Beautiful there," I volunteer, glad to have some common ground. "I played in Tassie years ago. Launceston and Hobart."

"Hobart, eh? They say all roads lead to Hobart, one-way street hell that it is. 'Played,' did you? So you're a muso, then?" He stretches languidly and the bottom of his shirt hikes up, revealing a strange horizontally striped pattern of birthmarks across his lower back.

I haven't heard the word *muso* in years, and in spite of my overwhelm I smile at the Aussie term for musician. "I am indeed. I used to play bass with Slackjaw Harrison for a few years until he died. I wish I'd had more time to see some parks and such when I was in Tassie, like maybe the Royal Botanical Gardens. I love learning about the flora and fauna of the countries I visit, and now that I know I am, you know . . ." It feels odd to talk about this with a complete stranger. ". . . a shifter, I am trying to get some answers about nature. What is the general consensus down under? Are we natural? Are we more human or animal? What do you think happens if we go extinct?"

Darren flashes an open-mouthed smile, then drops his jaw wider and wider until his abnormally gaping maw looks like something out of a horror film. My suspicions are confirmed. He's a thylacine, known to the rest of the world as a "Tasmanian tiger," or "Tasmanian wolf," long declared extinct. No more wolf than tiger, he moves with a fascinating hybrid grace of the canine and feline. He clicks his mouth shut and takes a swig of his beer, pleased at my reaction.

"We never went extinct, mate. We had to survive the only way we knew how . . . by shifting into humans. Our time to run free will come someday, but even now with attempts to find us, preserve us, and even clone us, it's still too risky. My sister Lucy was one of the last ones to see a human while in her true thylacine form. She too, finally decided to shift. Of course, the most dangerous thing to a human is another human. Even still, we can't resist the laugh. In fact, many so-called 'extinct' species actually walk among us, hiding in plain sight. If you unfocus your mind, you might see a few tonight. And you might see even more after a few drinks!"

Drinks! I have totally forgotten my original mission of procuring libations for my pack mate and his friend. I give Darren my card, say goodbye to Wally, and buy a round of drinks for my pals. Weaving my way back through the crowd, I can see Naj in the far corner, murmuring surreptitiously with Sand and a thin man in a kingfisher mask. As I walk past them, their heads snap up on my approach and the women's smiles for me abruptly turn on like a switch. I have never seen Sand smile before, and the hair on the back of my neck begins to rise. The masked man creeps me out as well, and something about his shape is disconcertingly familiar as I feel his eyes slither over me. I nod and keep walking, trying to appear casual as I shield and remember to breathe slowly through my nose.

In some distant corner, Lydia is sulking alone and sipping a Coke . . . *who twisted her arm to come to this?* I wonder. *If she's not careful, that wet blanket might actually have fun,* is the next thing that crosses my mind, although I'm not entirely convinced that this surreal event could be described as "fun." Further past, my producer buddy Kim is standing in the doorway of a raptor-themed room, chatting up a couple of young chanteuses. We exchange waves, but I am more eager than ever to find my pack mate.

My senses are completely overstimulated now. I can no longer wrap my brain around what I'm seeing, let alone the mixed energies and pheromones now flowing uninhibited from every corner. People are lounging in impossibly high windows, draped around historical rafters, dancing and stomping and fluttering in spirals around the voodoo drummers. Chants mingle with cawing, roaring, howling, braying, and other utterances I can't even place.

Someone jostles me hard then, nearly spilling my drinks. I turn to glare at this perpetrator and a man in a stag costume peers back at me, the mask completely covering his head and shoulders. Something about him creeps me out. I try to get a whiff of identity and my nose is assaulted with the acrid-musky scent of deer urine, easily found in hunting and fishing stores. This man has certainly taken it upon himself to go all-out in his disguise. I also discover that I can't avoid it, because he seems to be following me now. I try weaving my way through clusters of people, but everywhere I turn, those skeletal clawlike antlers are never far away. I try not to panic, ward, and croon The Wild Harmonic under my breath to Teddy.

Teddy has obviously picked up on my signal as he and Dean meander back to me. Teddy sends a warning growl to the masked cervid, who vanishes into the crowd. Dean is animatedly telling Teddy about some prog guitarist he thinks Teddy should join forces with, an Icelandic fellow named Alec Leifsson. I deliver the drinks to him and Dean, we toast, and I drink from my bottle in an attempt to ground myself.

"Oh, hon-*neee*, it's a lot to take in the first time, isn't it?" Dean says in sympathy. "They've been having this thing in New Orleans for a few years, but it's been held in other places over time. Do you see that old couple over there?" He gestures to a remote corner of the dance floor, where an elderly man and woman are weaving together. They are not quite slow dancing, but not really standing either, just sort of moving cheek to cheek, occasionally picking up a foot in a light stamp. "Those two have been coming to these events since anyone can remember. He's from Connemara in Ireland and she's from Camargue in the southern part of France. They hardly speak each other's language, and neither wants to relocate. But it's something you can count on seeing every year. They are just a couple of wild ponies getting to share with each other for a brief moment in their long life spans." My eyes well up behind the eyeholes of my mask. It's incredibly sweet and impossibly sad.

Teddy feels my confusion and claps an arm around me in support. As I slump against his shoulder, I notice that he smells good, familiar. Dear, sweet Teddy Lee. So funny and intelligent, so fearless and musical. Why couldn't I be smitten with him instead of the maddeningly elusive Rowan?

The answer promptly resonates in my skull as palpably as a blow to the head. I cannot splinter from my animal heart. My very nature has me fixated on my Alpha.

My shields back up, Teddy has no clue that for a split second I've even remotely considered more than a friendship with him. "Ready to go?" he asks in a fraternal gesture. I nod and he steers me out into the streets of the French Quarter, now bland and mundane in the wake of the Shifters Ball. The streets are deserted save three people: Teddy, me, and a local character and illustrious drunk known to all as "Moth" because of his incessant staggering from lamppost to lamppost. He is several blocks away, but we quickly and quietly pass him.

I don't know if I have really learned anything tonight. The event only corroborates my suspicion that nothing is ever truly what it seems to be. I glance back over my shoulder to watch Moth lurch around the corner and out of sight. If he's not careful, he will be consumed in the very flame he that craves like so many musicians I have known.

CHAPTER
7

PHASE INTERFERENCE

Journal entry, July 29ᵗʰ: So I edge toward this vast sea that is my double life, impassively walking the plank, animal to one side, vicious killer to the other. It's amazing how fearless one becomes when one has nothing to lose.

Sylvia and I have a lot of catching up to do.

She had a wonderful time in Guatemala, of course. She tells me of the amazing people she met, the splendor of the mountains, the music, and the food.

The mission, she tells me, was full of hard-working people, namely some friendly Methodists who impressed her with their four-part harmonies and their ability to produce mass quantities of food from scratch. Together they had installed water filters to ensure that several villages would have access to clean drinking water, and had helped cook and distribute meals to malnourished children in two feeding centers.

She also tells me of a very special little girl named Lupe who carries all of the traits of one who will most likely be a born lycan, as Sylvia and I were. The family was thrilled to have this Sister Jean-Baptiste establish a bond with the child's parents and offer guidance in preparation for Lupe's impending transition. It appears that my friend won over the entire village so well that they have nothing to fear from this phenomenon and will give Lupe the love and support that she will need when she finally comes of age.

I, on the other hand, am less than inspired. My gob is unstoppable as everything comes shamelessly pouring out of my heart: the mysterious adversaries, the Shifter's Ball, Naj, Yohan, Rowan's infuriating elusiveness, Gabriel, the demanding jerks on my gigs, and Aydan—all of which are wearing me so thin.

My head plops onto her desk at last. "I know I'm not supposed to feel such jealousy," I moan. "Maybe I should invite Aydan out for a drink or something?"

"She doesn't drink; she's a Muslim," Sylvia replies in a soft neutral tone.

In one phrase, my best friend has just spoken volumes. I don't every try to shield this feeling of betrayal. "You've *talked* with her?"

Sylvia sighs. "Yes, I have. She is far away from her pack back in Turkey, and she is struggling with spiritual issues. I have to be available to all who seek counsel, Buzz. She has reminded me of some of the writings of Rumi, actually—namely what he calls 'The Howling Necessity.' And like Rumi, she was crying out in grief. You may find her beautiful, but trust me, you don't want to be in her shoes. She is deeply troubled."

I have no sympathy whatsoever for anyone that stunning. I know in my heart of hearts that my innermost self is being immature and unreasonable. I just want *one thing* to go untouched by this woman. I doubt I could feel sorry for anyone so stunning who is working so intensely with Rowan each day. I feel a tiny prelude to my anger, an itch before the burn, which I immediately quell.

Sylvia's jade eyes are grim. "You cannot influence anyone's decisions or preferences without repercussions—even Rowan's—no matter how much you want him to love you back. But what you can do is control what you do about it, and catch yourself in the act of letting down your guard. The most important words of First Corinthians are 'Love is patient, love is kind.' That's really all you need to remember right now. If it is meant to be, I'll tell you about the rest in good time. What we need to address more than anything is this rage you're feeling."

And so I tell her about the man with the date rape drug. She goes stock still for a minute, closes her eyes, and clenches her jaw. A wash of emotion pours off of her in a tidal wave, which she doesn't bother to shield. My friend may have chosen to walk a path of wisdom and peace, but she is still a person capable of all feelings, including the undiluted rage welling up in her energy.

It suddenly hits me why she stopped playing gigs and went into hiding. I feel like a bucket of ice water has just been dumped over my head. My lungs don't want to work.

Sylvia cannot curse, but she puts so much venom into the word "Philistine," she could make Teddy cringe.

"I'm going to the rectory to give Father O'Flaherty a full report on Guatemala. When you get home try to let off some steam any way you can, so long as it harms no one. We all have to be clear-headed with these mysterious attacks on shifters. In the meantime, I strongly urge you to confide in Teddy and Raúl. Diluting secrets among the pack will dispel some of the tension. They want everyone to be happy, you know." She's right, of course. I grit my teeth with fresh resolve. I love Rowan, and I will not stand in the way of his happiness.

"Oh, and one more thing? Don't be afraid to fight back when push comes to shove. Here's what I personally believe about the old 'turning the other cheek' adage. Jesus didn't actually say to just stand around and let someone clobber you harder. Most people are right-handed, so if someone hits your right cheek, it's going to be a backhanded slap, a degrading gesture. Turning and offering your left is an invitation to an honest fight. It's a dare. I'm just *saying*." We hug fiercely, and I head for my car.

Rolling down Airline Highway back towards Orleans Parish, I ruminate on everything Sylvia has told me. But something is nagging in the back of my mind. I'm not even to Destrehan yet when I get a distinct sinking sensation in my gut. Glancing at the pack phone on the seat next to me, the little device rings the second I touch it. It's Sylvia. My gut ties itself in knots even before I answer.

Even my saintly friend cannot keep the troubled tone out of her voice. "Father O'Flaherty just had a heart attack. He's in River Parishes hospital, although that's little comfort to me. He apparently has had some sort of terrible scare, but won't tell the doctors what it was."

I turn the car around so fast, my tires screech with a sound I thought was only heard in movies.

◆ ◆ ◆

Father O'Flaherty is in stable condition, but looks alarming with oxygen tubes in his nose. "Sister! You and your friend Birch need to do something for me!" Sylvia soothes him and eventually manages to coax his story out.

It appears that the priest had thought he was having some sort of visitation from the Holy Spirit when something had slipped into his room. This being—he cannot describe it—attacked him without warning, demanding information of some sort.

"I have something hidden in my closet that you have to hide. Please, Birch, take it with you. It won't seem unusual if it's discovered on secular grounds." We promise on all that is holy that we will take care of it for him, whatever it is—the frantic old man is paranoid about mentioning it aloud.

Back again at the church, the post-sunset gloom does nothing to reassure us. There doesn't appear to have been much of a struggle in the rectory save a broken window, books knocked off of the shelves, and some scattered pillow feathers. Perusing through Father O'Flaherty's room we find a large red box in his closet, as per his instructions. Sylvia is reluctant to violate his privacy, but I have no such qualms by now. If I'm going to be hiding something secret in my house, I'd better know damn well what it is, especially with all of this mayhem going down.

As we slowly lift off the lid, my mind is reeling. What could this man be hiding that he thinks is so shameful? Forbidden scrolls? Porn?

Comic books. We both fall on our butts in disbelief.

I don't believe this. There is a war being waged on shifters, a priest is attacked in his room, and he's worried that someone will find out about his *comics*. What sort of dogma did they teach this man back in Connemara?

Sylvia breaks the silence with a flutter of laughter that is somewhere in between amusement and hysteria. I am unable to resist joining in, until we are both laughing and crying with grief, stress, and ridiculousness. We sound more like a pair of hyenas than wolf people, but we release the adrenaline though the sound. "It's the Illuminati! *The Spider Man Code!*" Sylvia wheezes, and by now I am so convulsed, I think I might be sick to my stomach.

A rustle from somewhere in the room has us immediately back on our feet, and we are deadly quiet once more. Sylvia never gets scared, and the scent of her fear has me panicked more that whatever has invaded us. My best friend's saintly veneer is ripped away as a guttural snarl tears from her throat. This is sacred territory, and we will fight to defend it. We stand back to back, slipping into tenor phase, fangs and claws ready to do their worst. We smell no people, but we quickly dismantle the room, startling only a dove that must have flown in through the damage. It sails out of the broken window, its wings whistling like a tiny smoke alarm. In one dramatic exhale, we slide back into soprano and fall back to the floor in relief. Whatever attacked Father O'Flaherty is nowhere to be found.

"You're a holy terror, do you know that?" I ask my best friend. She smiles weakly, promising to brief Rowan and the others on the incident. We hold each other for a very long time before I leave, breathing courage into one another, a feedback loop of best friends' trust.

"Text me when you get home safely, okay?" she murmurs.

The second I lock myself into my apartment I reassure her of my safety and that the comics are hidden. She texts me back to inform me that Father O'Flaherty is in stable condition and will be back to work in a week.

So often as little kids, Sylvia and I had tried to get frightened for kicks. I wonder if we somehow sealed out fates that way.

◆ ◆ ◆

"Comic books? Is that man out of his mind? Is that some sort of eighth deadly sin?" Raúl is so incredulous he nearly drops his appetizer.

I make a cursory glance around the swanky interior of La Coquette even though we are warded. "I don't get it either. Oh, by the way . . . happy birthday, my friend."

He raises his glass. "Cheers, Little One. It works out well that we can grab a bite before playing this gig together at the Banks Street bar tonight. Nothing against the fare of the Banks Street, but I think your idea is much more festive."

I feel a warm glow inside, relaxed for the first time since the attack on Father O'Flaherty. Dining out is good therapy right now. Like most musicians, I have to keep a close eye on my budget for food, but I have tired of my own cooking, which is usually a souped-up version of mac and cheese with some canned tuna when I'm in a rush. As famous as it is for its unique cuisine, New Orleans has had to up the ante in its restaurants to keep from being a culinary one-trick pony. Instead of the usual gumbo, jambalaya, red beans and rice, or po-boys, Raúl and I are starting with appetizers at La Coquette: sweetbreads in a blueberry glaze and rare tuna with marinated cantaloupe. For our main course we will make our way to La Boca, an Argentinian steak house— I am dying for rare American Kobe tenderloin. I will even splurge and have a glass of Malbec, since they carry a few kinds that can't be found anywhere else in the city.

Several hours later and with bulging bellies, we begin setting up our gear. This is going to be an interesting gig for sure for the reggae band. Although we are getting paid a guarantee, this is for a showcase benefitting the Louisiana Modified Dolls: the local chapter of a national organization that enlists tattooed and pierced gals to do charity work for the community. There will be a "naughty balloon pop" –one of the local burlesque dancers will have balloons taped all over her body, with each balloon containing a tiny scrap of paper. The paper will either be good for a donated prize—ranging from bags of homemade cookies to discounts on tattoos—or a spanking from Mistress Genevieve, who is lounging at the bar. Other acts are The Tomb of Nick Cage, described as a "New Orleans horror and Illuminati punk band," and a suspension act, whatever that is.

Having tuned his drums, Raúl is warming up with his usual routine of high hat cadences. I know them all by the rapidly spoken words that are supposed to mimic them:

Pea soup, pea soup, pea soup, pea soup! Look at the cat, look at the cat, look at the cat, look at the cat! Boots and pants and boots and pants and boots and pants and boots and pants! Stick and a fuck and a stick and a fuck and a stick and a fuck and a stick and a fuck! Bucket of fish, bucket of fish!

One of our horn players is sick, but I haven't really wondered about who might be subbing until a familiar brazen slide cuts through the sonic disarray. Raúl's head suddenly jerks up as if he's snapped out of a reverie. The prolonged look between him and Lydia King is fraught with tension. I introduce the two of them with as much polish as I can muster. Lydia is aloof as usual, but I remind myself that this isn't a precarious gig with Naj Copperhead and that all will be well.

Soundcheck over, we decide to mingle a bit with our fellow musicians. Gabriel is already here, and the hairs on the back of my neck stand at attention. Raúl's hand lands on my elbow. "Is this the guy stalking you? Do you want me to serve him up for dessert?"

I grit my teeth. "I'm sure he'd love that if there's a chance that I'd be eating part of him," is my grim reply. "But he hasn't actually been seen near my house or my car. He's just . . . weird. Not enough proof to have him thrown out. And since I am onstage all the time, I can't exactly tell him to stop looking at me, can I?"

"Well, don't worry, Little One. I can at least make him very uncomfortable." And with that Raúl never leaves my side, his attention only wavering to sneak glances at Lydia. She is by herself as usual, eyes roving the room, occasionally glancing solemnly at us. *Perhaps I can fix her up with Gabriel,* my malicious little inner monologue pipes up. *Creepy attracts creepy.*

The Tomb of Nick Cage makes for a smashing good kickoff to the night. Lead singer Kym Trailz, with her green leopard-patterned Mohawk, commands the attention of all, including me. Perhaps it's my comparatively mild appearance that surprises people when they find out that I actually like heavier bands. Secure in Raúl's presence, I can relax enough to appreciate the absurdity of the myriad balloons and cookies as a backdrop to the heavily distorted guitars. The suspension act—called The Suspendables, of course—is preparing for their show outside.

A huge crowd has gathered around the old oak tree outside the bar. I smell booze, cigarettes, and above all, antiseptic and adrenaline. And now I learn what a suspension act is.

With the boom box blaring the sounds of Kyuss and Mastodon, the three willing participants of the act take turns getting their flesh pierced and then hoisted into the air by the freshly imbedded hooks. I can't look away. The scent of blood is not only affecting Raúl and me, it's also whipping the crowd into a frenzy. Some of these people could be shifters as well, but any human being can be easily affected by the vibe.

A young man takes two rings through each forearm, crosses his arms over his head, and a rope is threaded through the bloody jewelry. Someone loops the rope over the sturdiest branch of the old oak tree, hoists him up, and gives him a push like a grisly tire swing. He kicks his feet off the ground, oscillating like a pendulum. His face is tight with pain and adrenaline, veins standing out on his neck. If his arms were to become fatigued enough for him to let them fall, it's obvious that the rings would rip out of his arms completely.

"Dude!" someone gasps, "this is the most *metal* thing I have ever seen!" I have to agree.

A young woman in a corset and trailing skirt is up next, her face completely covered by a white expressionless mask. This time my jaw drops as I watch the piercers slide several long meathooks under the muscles in her back and hoist her aloft. Someone grabs the trailing rope and swings her around and around in a wide arc until her trajectory makes her appear to fly. The rope is let go and she sails in a circle above us, her face a graven image, her arms outstretched like some masochistic angel.

The scent of so much blood, pain, and adrenaline is driving me wild—literally. Without exchanging so much as a word, Raúl and I look at each other and decide that it's almost time for us to go inside and wait onstage. It appears that the other group members are like-minded, for everyone else is perched by the bandstand, having had enough of the suspension act. Little by little the overstimulated spectators trickle back into the bar, followed by the performers with fresh bandages doing little to conceal disconcerting amounts of seeping blood.

We are obviously intended to bring some relief and closure to the night: strong enough to keep the momentum going, but *irie* enough to dissipate all of that manic energy. And to my surprise, Nigel steps down for a song and lets Lydia sing a lovely rendition of "Duppy Conqueror." I find it rather poignant in the wake of whatever demons we shifters must soon fight. The vibe within the band is nice tonight, only marred during the last twenty minutes when Gabriel approaches the stage, snatches my set list, and gleefully flees with his prize like a coarse American tourist stealing a beer mug in Germany. I don't care to chase him to get it back, but the hubris of his act sets off the burning within. I can look off of Nigel's set list, but that particular one had all my personal notes on it—when to watch for cues, when to not rush, which songs have hard endings, and so forth. My stalker is now officially tampering with my livelihood. I take a deep breath, suppress a growl, and finish the show with as many memorized notes as possible.

One more hurdle to go. I am glad that Raúl and I are carpooling in his van, but I am not wild about Gabriel being able to identify any vehicle associated with me. I can't imagine that anyone would be so stupid as to cross Raúl, but I hear the familiar annoying scurry of footsteps approaching as I hoist the cymbal bag into the back. "Birch! Hey, Birch! Didja figure out when would be a good time for us to get together and jam?"

Raúl takes a protective stance beside me, growling softly as I stand my ground. The reflection of the streetlights on my stalker's glasses makes it hard for me to make eye contact with him, but I put every ounce of menace into my voice. "Look, Gabriel. I am an extremely busy person with too many irons in the fire as it is. We are not going to jam—ever. And your incessant attention is beginning to get really unnerving . . . okay?"

He freezes in his tracks. Even in the shadows cast by the streetlights, he appears flushed. "You don't appreciate all the support I've given you!" he retorts. At Raúl's cue, we haul the last of the gear into the back of his van. *Just ignore him* is the silent advice. Even still, I can't repress a shiver when he begins to scream at our retreat, "You're a real *buzz kill,* do you know that?"

I glance in the rearview mirror. Gabriel appears to have stepped back into the shadows somewhere, but Lydia is standing outside the bar, watching us slowly disappear.

◆ ◆ ◆

I am on the steppes –was I here before? I don't have the sensation of walking, but I am suddenly facing my shining stag. We resume our stare-down, and its eyes are sorrowful. Something is different. It is made of fame, adoration by others, and lofty status. Balance is good, but now it's time to ride this wave of obsession. I give chase once more. These fangs are very handy. This is like being able to run with a knife and a fork without worrying about falling.

I am gaining with easy speed and am soon upon the creature, which goes down without a fight. *A successful hunt!* This time my teeth snag its shining hide, which slides easily off of the creature's body in one piece, like an old blanket or a cheap costume. The exposed skeleton turns to regard me with empty eyes. Something squirms within its ribcage . . .

I bolt upright in bed with a gasp before my mind can register what else was underneath those bones. I have a chilling feeling that I should just stay in bed today. But the show must go on.

◆ ◆ ◆

Driving up Esplanade toward La Balcone, I feel an uneasy lump in my gut. By this time, I have learned to trust this instinct, but I still feel that I have to show up for my gig no matter what. In the past I have played through extreme illness, personal crisis, major fatigue, and tendonitis, so why should I back down just because now I have the heebie-jeebies?

When I arrive at the venue, I immediately sense that something is wrong. For one thing, there's already a bass rig set up. My first impulse is that it belongs to whoever played the shift before me, so I open my gig bag and strap on my Rickenbacker. Then as the rest of the previous band clears out, it dawns on me that someone else is on this gig tonight, and no one bothered to call me. There's no sign of the rest of the band. This pisses me off, but before I can ask anyone what's going on, Naj walks briskly over to me. A dark vibe washes over me, almost palpably slugging me in the gut.

"Oh, Buzz! Check out the engraving on the jewelry! Does this look like Scots Gaelic to you?" she bursts out before I can ask any questions. She's holding a brooch in her hand. It appears to have some sort of ancient inscription on it, but at a glance there's no telling if it's anything genuine or just a bunch of nonsense. As I lean in for a closer look, she suddenly pretends to fall against me, jabbing the pin of it an inch deep into my forearm.

"Oh, my God . . . I am *so* sorry!"

My knees buckle. White-hot pain shoots from the tip of my

pinky to my armpit and blossoms through my body like a chain of fireworks. I am suddenly overcome with a weakness and fatigue. Too late I realize that the brooch was made of silver. How could I be so *stupid?* Even my instincts were trying to warn me. I grip the wall for support and glare at Naj. Sand has quietly crept up behind her in support.

Her smile is all dimples and sunshine, but her eyes are ice. "Birch MacKinlay, did you really think we needed you on this gig? We need a George Porter Jr. or a Donald "Duck" Dunn or a James Jamerson to bring this group to the next level. Not you. All you do is shapeshift your genres. You're a jack-of-all-trades and a master of none. It's a major handicap for us, and we all have to *dumb down our playing* to accommodate your drama queen ass!"

I don't understand. In over twenty years, no one has ever had a problem with my playing before. *No one.*

"And okay, I'll admit that you can handle rolling with the punches, say when I start in the wrong key or forget an intro or something. But that's *still no excuse.* You can't un-white your playing, get into the groove, or get greasy."

Even though this bitch drummer can't keep a steady tempo? It's my last clear thought before the silver begins to infiltrate my private thoughts. Coils of ancient fears begin to tighten around my chest.

"You have to be a major pocket player and really have a highly developed understanding of playing in the pocket, playing a groove, and having a facility in the genre." *Who does this bitch think she is?* I rage, and then the self-doubt seeps into my nervous system. *I'm a bad musician . . . I deserve to suffer . . . people only hire me because they feel sorry for me . . .*

"You are nothing but a whiny little victim and a band liability," she cheerfully continues, while Sand nods from the background. "Even your pack doesn't need you, especially now that you've put it in jeopardy. There are two bass players in your little family. You know there's going to finally be a musical balance when you disappear and they get that Turkish beauty to replace you. You are so pathetic and needy that you actually spilled your guts to me—someone you barely know. You've given us enough info to help us, and for that I would at least like to thank you."

Smiling sweetly, Naj cups my face and kisses me on the mouth, sinking her teeth hard into my lower lip. I taste the burst of blood over my tongue, even as it goes numb from the poison. Suddenly the lights dim, as if on cue. My eyes quickly adjust, but the rest of the room is oblivious to my shock and disbelief, while the neurotoxins quickly permeate my bloodstream from the bite.

And without fanfare, standing right in front of me is none other than Calvin Quinn. My eyes see, but my brain doesn't want to believe it. *Betrayed with a kiss* . . .

His face is as deadly and charming as I remember it, and likewise his smile has no warmth. *What the hell is he doing here?* He opens his mouth to expose a set of fangs and languidly extends a forked tongue at me, like a deadly child teasing a rival. And his body elongates, grows and my disbelieving eyes can't quite comprehend the man with a python's body from the torso down.

Naj cozies up to him, he slides his arms around her waist, and he slips a wad of bills into her hand. He pauses to give her a lusty kiss on her throat, murmuring for her to keep the silver brooch as her tip. *Thirty silver pieces* is all I have time to think before he lunges forward, grabs my shoulders, hoists me upright, and slams me up against the wall. Splinters of pain bore into my eyes.

My skull sounds like a hollow crack against the bricks and stars fill my vision.

My beloved black and white Rickenbacker bass falls to the ground with a horrible clattering twang, an instrument's yelp of pain. An instant later I too slide to the floor in complete paralysis. The three fall onto my gear, which flies everywhere. They disembowel my gig bag and ropy coils of cables spill out. My tuning pedal gets hurled against a brick wall. I cannot turn my head to see my bass, but I hear the sound of wood cracking and the discordant jangle of strings going limp. Sand kicks my rig hard directly in the speaker cone and the head falls off of the cabinet in a mechanical decapitation.

My head still rings from the impact, and my vision blurs – perhaps I have had a concussion or maybe I am in tears. Pain, anger, humiliation, and despair don't even begin to describe the wreck of emotion that seizes me. Cal returns for me, his hand closing around my throat, his other hand searching my possessions. Helpless, I can only stare in horror as he rummages through my gutted gig bag and then my jacket, where he finds my secret pack cell phone. All of our numbers, all of our texts, correspondence, plans . . . *oh, dear gods!*

The thud of padded metal makes him jerk and let go of my windpipe, as in an instant Lydia King arrives on the scene, drops her trombone gig bag, and with inhuman speed leaps on his back grabbing him in a chokehold. His eyes bulge as she constricts more and more tightly. With a hiss, she wrests the phone away from him, one arm still around his trachea, and dials a number—I can only hope it's the emergency number on the screen. She shoots me a look of extreme apology and whispers, "Not all snakes are poisonous."

There is a pain that passes understanding. A quick fade swallows me whole, and then the world goes black.

CHAPTER
8

GROUND LIFT

Drifting in and out of awareness. I have no senses, only a knowledge of my own existence. Sometimes I feel more than hear a blend of frequencies cocooning me, and I know it is the rest of the pack singing to me. Driving the toxins out of my blood. I hear the occasional canine whine of concern, but mostly human voices.

Fever dreams consume me. I have no idea how much of this is reality and how much of it is in my mind. At times it feels more vivid than anything I have ever experienced before. Images flicker until I finally let go and allow myself to be swept away.

I don't know how I ended up in this tunnel. *Is a near-death experience, or I am actually dying?* But from what I have heard, the near-deceased are swept away, not trying to squeeze themselves through a low crawlspace in pitch darkness. Neither would the passage walls have a rough surface with dirt crumbling under my hands, if I actually have hands. Just as I am trying to figure out whether or not I have a physical body, the tunnel widens into a natural antechamber. I am filled with a sensation of space as I look beyond into a natural apse.

There are wolves in a firelight cave, shaggy and familial smelling, consulting one another in a tightly knit group. This feels like what any den should have, even bones on the ground, presumably from previous meals. But there are paintings on every surface created by sentient beings, petroglyphs depicting animals of all sorts: stags, bulls, birds, and horses. There are also depictions of men in the process of shifting into stags. A central fire is crackling, a human made resource that the animals don't fear. The firelight makes the painted animals appear to move and the people to morph. This is no world of forms. It's something more profoundly abstract.

This preternatural apse is the place where dreams come to die and prepare for rebirth. It's where ideas are formed, where all forgotten music goes, and ideals go to their final resting place. It is a point of primal origin, a womb of solid stone. It's small and it's infinite, as the domed ceiling casts an image of space without time overhead. I try to comprehend as much as I can with my mortal mind, which is about as effective as trying to capture the ocean in a butterfly net.

I blink my non-existent eyes and the wolves are now humans clad in robes of fur, standing in a circle with arms raised; male or female I can't tell. *Male or female doesn't matter in spirit . . .* I don't even question the voice that has just inserted itself into my head. The wolf people don't appear to notice me, but I am being given answers nonetheless, swept on the hypnotic currents of shamanic drumbeats. *Lub . . . dub . . .* I shift my perception to figure out how I can be experiencing the smell of sage burning, the heat of flames and the texture of the stone if I am only a spirit. I want Rowan by my side more than anything else in the world. I want him to explain this to me. I want him with my whole being, even as I don't have a physical body here. I wonder if the closeness of the pack can transcend the boundaries between physical and spiritual as I try reaching out to Rowan in my mind.

He is a holy man, the voices reply to my emotional vibrations. *No one can ever truly have him.*

Despair tears through me like a winter howl, blasting a hole straight through my core of consciousness.

One I don't hear the word, even in my mind, so much as feel its frequency.

Your connection to him will always be there, but with a price. The price is the pain of never truly having him, but you will receive the gift of always being connected to him.

I still cannot see faces, but the singing begins, and the tempo increases. Both primitive and intricate, the music becomes so beautiful, I feel like my heart is about to break . . . and yet the longing deepens to an aching beyond fathoming. *So odd that we are gifted with the wonderful ability to pass out from physical pain, yet emotional agony is relentless,* I muse. *Dissociation is as close as it gets, even in the spirit world.*

And then nothing exists but the eternal echo.

One

◆ ◆ ◆

The pungent smell of alcohol and worry is everywhere. Even before I open my eyes I know that this is not my bed and it's too quiet to be my apartment. First it is sound that I perceive: the hush-hush of padded sneakers going by in the hallway, carts rolling, and call button beeps that sink into my brain before I can fathom anything else. I've got tubes coming out of my arms, and the steel railings of this hospital bed feel like a cage. I am agitated in my confusion and let out a primal growl. Sylvia is at my side in an instant, soothing me, urging me to settle down. I close my eyes and feel a cool cloth across my forehead.

My whole mouth tastes like seawater, caustic and salty, and I wonder how long I've been on the saline drip if it's permeated my saliva. My sluggish face feels like a meaty mask. I reach up to touch it gingerly and discover a rough surface: stitches in my lower lip where Naj bit me. There is still a ringing in my head like an eternal splash cymbal. I'm fairly certain that there are stitches across the back of my head as well where Cal slammed me against the wall. The room is still a little too bright. Sylvia notices, and closes the curtains.

"Safe?" is the only thing I can blurt out. My voice is raspy from disuse.

Sylvia looks deeply into my eyes. "Everyone is fine," she reassures me.

"Nagas . . . they are supposed to be benevolent," I croak.

Sylvia's mouth is grim. "In my line of work, it has come to my attention that even angels can go bad—big time. It appears that there is something about you that was worth serious money to the wrong people. Money for which Naj Copperhead was so desperate, she betrayed her fellow shifter. It appears that she was especially

fond of speedballs—the combination of heroin and cocaine—
responsible for so many celebrity deaths. By injecting, she could get
her high without damaging her voice, although her performance
suffered from far worse than mere vocal shortcomings, as you know.
I suppose she thought that being a naga would make her invincible,
since nagas seem to be immune to blood borne illnesses."

So much I still don't understand. "Lydia King . . ." I try again.

". . . is a SIN agent. Turns out your serpentine ex Calvin Quinn
was involved in all kinds of illicit things, mostly sex trafficking
and the distribution of illegal drugs. Not only that, according to
SIN intelligence, he is linked to our enemy, possibly in allegiance.
He was chased by the cops not long after you were rushed to the
hospital."

I am not surprised to hear this about Cal, although mortified
that I never caught on to how truly nefarious he was. Or that Lydia
was actually on my side the entire time. Only in New Orleans: a
secret good guy in the guise of a bone player, and a naga to boot.
"She turned on her own," I remark.

Sylvia shakes her head gently. "Lydia did what she had to do in
the name of a higher purpose, which was restoring justice—and
saving you. Nagas are no better or worse that any of us. There just
happen to be nasty folks in all of the races out there. There are bad
humans, bad lycans, bad nagas . . . even angels themselves have been
known to fall. Lydia went beyond loyalty to her kind and did what
needed to be done to end a very toxic cycle. Wouldn't you have
stepped up to the plate if you'd known that you could stop a lycan
from such evil? Especially if it meant one fewer lycan out there
giving the rest of us a bad name?"

One fewer . . . A horrible thought startles me. "Cal will be even more deadly when he gets out of custody, even if he goes to prison for a long time . . ."

Sylvia reaches for my hand and holds it tight. "He disappeared, love. While Cal was being detained for questioning, he went ballistic and attacked the cops. He was shot in self-defense, but then took off running and disappeared somewhere around the Moonwalk, presumed to have fled into the Mississippi River. In any case, he's a wanted man now, and won't be showing his face around New Orleans anymore. But he's rumored to be dead."

The world reels. Shock sends me into a tailspin of disorientation. Sylvia grabs my hand and croons a note intended to steady me. I take a deep breath and the bed stops lurching, but the burning starts in my belly.

Now I will never exact my vengeance on Cal. I wanted to kill him. It was my right to be the one to rid the world of his cruelty, to make him feel even a fraction of what he had inflicted on me as well as his many victims. Instead he may have survived a gunshot, thriving in exile somewhere. I am seething on the inside, uncontrollably growling.

Sylvia hums a soothing lullaby to me, but something is wrong. The melody sounds flat and one-dimensional. Then I realize that I cannot find the pitch. My sense of pitch is completely gone. I panic as if discovering that I've had a limb amputated. The roaring in my head resumes, and I can stay conscious no longer. The last thing I recall is the feeling of Sylvia's hand still tightly holding mine.

◆ ◆ ◆

The stitches finally come out of my lower lip. There is an angry white slash across the swollen red skin. I wonder if it will still be visible when I fugue. I am still too weak to sit up by myself. Pain is an indicator that I'm still alive. Sometimes being a survivor really sucks.

Pack members pay me visits. A few flowers surround my bed: tasteful blossoms like orchids, some sweet freshly-cut magnolias that save my sense of smell from the constant antiseptic madness, and a coral cactus, which looks like a tiny Roger Dean painting— no doubt this was Sylvia's gift. I am secretly grateful that no one has brought me Mylar balloons, as I'm not up to seeing anything silver or even remotely lunar-looking. Someone was even thoughtful enough to place my Rush bobblehead dolls on my nightstand, which comforts me more than I can express. Once I had slipped out of consciousness, only to awaken and discover Teddy's precious copy of *The Adventures of Lord Iffy Boatrace* tucked into my arms like a teddy bear. They come and go. Only Sylvia never leaves my side.

I am blessedly awake during one of Rowan's visits. When his face swims into view, I believe myself to still be dreaming until he speaks. I attempt to sit up then, which only slaps me with vertigo.

"Stay in bed," he orders and I accede. Countless times I'd wished that he would come to my bedside, just not with me being a convalescent train wreck. *It's not so much that you should be careful what you wish for,* I muse, *as much as you have to include every specific detail.*

I attempt to spew out all of my concerns, which to my ears sounds like psychobabble, and is perhaps even less coherent to the man I love. "Shifters in danger . . . someone knows about the pack . . . deadly people out there in the music community . . . innocent lives at stake . . . I'm a bad bass player . . ."

He laughs then—*laughs!* How dare he? I realize that my

last concern is paltry compared to the bigger issues, but it's still devastating to me. "There is nothing wrong with your bass playing!" he chuckles. I don't have the energy to be angry at his amusement.

Assuring me that the pack will be safe now, he touches my forehead and the room begins to darken. The last thing I manage to mumble before I slip back into unconsciousness is, "Fuck yo studio . . ."

As I gradually get stronger, I get impatient, then downright subversive. I don't know what day it is, but I can hear Raúl's footsteps approaching down the hall. I pick up on the energies of him flirting, presumably with a young nursing assistant—a female one, anyway—and I pick up his scent even among the harsh sterile hospital odor. I am ready to cause trouble, and as he walks into my room, I feign fever dreams. "Uncle Remus, come back, come back . . . Uncle Remus, come back . . .!"

He laughs so hard that he drops the bouquet of flowers he had been carrying. Sylvia tried to shush him, even as a couple of staff glance into my room and glare warningly.

He isn't alone, either. Someone else has joined him for visitation, and now I know the object of his affection: Lydia King, a completely different Lydia King. She is nothing like the distant person I had known on the gigs. She seems a little shy, but for the first time, I see a genuine smile reach the corners of her eyes. I don't know whether I am more surprised to see her or the fact that she and Raúl are hand in hand.

My first knee-jerk reaction is prejudice. After all, it was a Naga who rendered me this way. And then I remember the prejudice that caused the animal collector to kill his own daughter and break my pack-brother's heart. I look at the peace on his features, a look I've never seen before. Then I turn my gaze to this woman who saved my life and I see the admiration for him in her eyes.

The Creole beauty sheds her aloof persona like an old skin, baring her true self to me for the first time. The real person turns out to be very warm and affectionate, revealing her emotions like an olive branch. Her voice is like lemon and honey as she gently informs me, "We now know that the Shifters are divided. Some have chosen to try to sell the rest of us out in exchange for their own protection, with an added bonus of heroin or cocaine. I am making reports and gathering information on these incidents. We are trying to figure out whom Calvin Quinn was connected to, as he is the shifter liaison between our traitors and the enemy, refusing to align himself with either. Naja Copperhead on the other hand was just a desperate addict, a crisis queen not capable of machinating more than musical dramas and getting her fixes. The shifter community might eventually forgive her, but the music scene will always regard her with suspicion. As for Sand, well . . . she was just a complete bitch."

"I jeopardized all shifters . . ." I venture.

Lydia holds up a graceful hand. "Please do not blame yourself. There have been numerous attacks far and wide. We believe there may have been other shifters spying in their animal forms, especially if they are inconspicuous like insects, bats, or birds. High on the suspect list are migratory shifters, or ones that are common all over the North American continent and may have a network."

Raúl beams proudly at his new companion. "The King family has done a lot over the years for social justice. The harvest moon will be upon us before we know it. Rowan has been keeping me informed of his plans for the rally. Now that one of our own has been harmed, we have more incentive than ever to give one hell of a musical showcase to send out our warnings, not just to other lycan packs, but to as many Shifters as possible. Also to let the traitors know that this will not be tolerated."

The King family. Like regal king cobras, or the king snakes that kill and eat their venomous relatives? I have a dream that someday this won't even matter. There is clearly a lot of emotional detox ahead for me. Tears slither down my face as I stretch out my arms and hug them both close to me. I can't stop crying, whether from shame or relief I have no clue.

A day later I am discharged. Sitting upright for the first time in my wheelchair, I am now strong enough to worry about how I am going to pay for the medical bills. A nurse seeks me out, as Sylvia is about to roll me to her car. He informs me that an anonymous benefactor has paid for all of my expenses, down to the last rubber glove. The only identifying information that can be disclosed to me is that this mystery person wanted to be known as simply "your guardian angel."

Gabriel. It doesn't take a genius to figure this out. He probably was wondering why I haven't been on any gigs lately and could have easily found out which hospital held me.

I'll deal with him later. For now, I just want to go home.

◆ ◆ ◆

A cool hand on my brow, a soothing incantation, and the lights come on. I am lying in someone's bed. A worried face hovers above my own. Familiar objects around the room begin to register in my mind, but it takes a while to realize that I am in my own tiny apartment and that the face belongs to Sylvia. It slowly seeps into my awareness that I have had another night terror. I take a deep breath and take in my surroundings. My clothes are hanging neatly on the rack across the bedroom, my Rush posters are exactly where I hung them all, and the doors to the bathroom and the kitchen are both cracked open to let some light through. Sylvia briefs me that various members of the pack have taken turns tidying my little place for me and there is enough food in my fridge to feed a pride of lions. I wonder if they just feel sorry for me.

"Sylvia," I whimper, "is the pack going to get rid of me?"

"Shush now, don't you be worrying about that," she says firmly, sounding a bit like Father O'Flaherty for a second.

"My playing!" I sob. "I had no idea that my playing was so deplorable! All these years . . . why didn't anyone ever tell me? *Why didn't you tell me?!?*" I grip the sides of the bed to keep from lashing out.

My best friend cradles me to her without fear. "Breathe with me, dear heart. No one is getting rid of you. That's the poison talking. They not only poisoned your blood and your body, they also poisoned your soul. Your self-esteem is sick. Even as you are too weak, you have to fight it anyway. What other choice do you have?"

"I could choose to not drag down the pack," I moan.

My best friend is stern for once. "If you love the pack as much as you claim to, then you will heal. Remember how Jesus said, 'Love you neighbor as yourself.' Well, if you don't love yourself, then you can't very well love your neighbor, can you? I often wonder if that's what He meant. You are bonded to this pack whether you feel worthy or not. We leave no soldier behind. Now are you going to help us and heal?"

I don't think she's even being rhetorical. I take a deep breath and look into her speckled green eyes. "I will try," I promise. For now, that seems to be enough for us both.

CHAPTER
9

DOMINANT PREPARATION

*J*ournal entry, *August 29*[th]: *Force yourself into exile, and be free of this tyranny that you call your deepest wish.*

This is what I tell myself daily. It's far easier to break a drug addiction than it is to break a thought addiction.

Home alone and self sufficient at last. I normally thrive in my solitude, but something in me has changed. Curled up in bed, neither sleep nor wakefulness claims me. I don't know how long I remain in this state, but something needs to change. A push up with my forearms, and the rest of me follows in a disjointed follow-the-leader.

I drag myself to the bathroom, brace my hands on the sink, and examine my face in the mirror. My own appearance shocks me, but I shouldn't have expected anything different. Dark circles ring my eyes, my hair is greasy, and I am now certain that the white slash across my lower lip will mar my face for the rest of my life.

I wonder if it will be visible in wolf form, and am reminded that I should attempt to shift. So I begin my Kundalini yoga and meditations in preparation.

I recall that Kundalini is sometimes called "Waking the Cobra" and recoil as if yanked from my state by a harsh elastic band. And then I experience subtler but infinitely more devastating recoil—for I realize with horror that I have developed a bitter prejudice.

Here in New Orleans, especially in the music scene, all races have to not only coexist, but also truly get along. I occasionally hear people denigrate the Deep South for presumed racism, but from my personal experience, we are all just bands in one fucked-up spectrum called the human race, and we have gigs to play.

Now I harbor the very thing that once infuriated me about others' attitudes. *Snake people. They can't be trusted.* One bite has poisoned my entire view. Can I overcome this? I reach for my phone.

Within half an hour, Raúl and Lydia are in my apartment, encircling me in their arms as hysterical sobs rack my body. Unable to look either of them in the eye, I can barely stammer my inner turmoil, overcome with shame and self-loathing. Fear or loathing of snakes has never in my life been an issue for me. Now being overcome with a generalization against an entire group of snake people is shaking me to the core.

My darkest question finally comes tearing from my throat, "Am I prejudiced?"

Raúl's face is grim. "The fact that you are in such distress over this mind-sickness should be your answer, Little One," he replies at last. "No, you are not prejudiced, but you must address this fear immediately."

Lydia's voice is warm and brimming with sympathy. "People develop fears of all kinds based on experiences, be these fears of ethnic groups, authorities who abuse their power, situations, and so on. Your task is to try to search your soul to a time before you had any such notions."

They sing me through the Kundalini. I know that Raúl managed to overcome his fears in spite of terrible abuses that he suffered the last time he fell in love, so perhaps there is hope for me as well. Lydia is still practically a stranger to me, but I trust Raúl's choice in her. I close my eyes and try to open my heart chakra, but it is still clamped shut in fear. This distresses me, for the heart is the gateway to consciousness: between animal and human. And fear is the base of all prejudice, like the discordant bass note that can drag down the entire song. Even still, they continue to sing healing.

Wolves and snakes. Two creatures vilified by the human race, yet so essential to the balance of life on this planet. I reach out to them, I *trust* them.

When I open my eyes I discover that they have both changed. Raúl is his exotic African lupine beauty and Lydia . . . is too lovely for words. Her coils are dazzling, black with shimmering gold flecks that form a pattern resembling hieroglyphics. Her large velvety eyes are rich with love, humility, and strength. Her exquisite human torso is smoothly muscled and well-defined, a warrior's body. The glow that seems to radiate from her tawny-bronze skin draws us in. She wraps her arms around Raúl's furry neck and cradles me in her smooth coils, letting her compassion flow over us both.

They comfort me and let me cry, let me laugh, and let me cry some more until all of my fear of the mortal coil has dissipated. We three form a nucleus of animal and human, wounded and healing. And letting go of all pretenses I sink into my wolf form, quieting the mental chatter that has plagued me for weeks and allowing myself to just *be*.

I would die for my brother Raúl. And I would likewise sacrifice myself for the mate he has chosen. I am proud to have her as part of my extended family. Even in the wake of my injury, someone I love has healed because of it. I hold a tiny morsel of hope that I too may be restored.

◆ ◆ ◆

By now most of the pain in my body is mostly from depression, but it's no easier to manage than physical damage. I have to regain some self-esteem, even if it only starts with a shower. I have a near aversion to the process, but the water and sweet smelling soaps dilute my thoughts. Perhaps my greatest source of relief is cutting my fingernails. Even on days I don't have gigs, I can't stand to have the tiniest bit of length getting in the way of my fingers, and by now I nearly have claws befitting a comic book werewolf. Some women find long nails a mark of glamour, but they probably don't understand that good chops are glamorous as well.

Physical beauty was never my attribute, and music is the only thing I've ever had going for me. So getting back to it has to be done, even if it's by taking baby steps. If I can only make myself open one of my bass cases, I'll have accomplished something today.

Which bass? I can't even think. I don't want to go on. I just want to sleep forever. The pack took my Rickenbacker to be repaired, but I can't bring myself to look at it, not just yet.

I open my gig bag instead. My cable unrolls perfectly like a lasso. I know that style. Only Rowan could have done it. I am caught unprepared by a wave of love for him that nearly knocks me to my knees in spite of myself.

Courage fills me, and I assess my silent stringed minions again. My Music Man Stingray 5-string, perfect for reggae gigs. My 1961 Fender Precision, a must for studio sessions.

Do I dare . . . ?

I take out my fretless Fodera six-string. I had inherited it from my late friend, Cajun bassist Jack "Tracas" Guilbeau. He was one of the kindest people I'd even known and one of many musicians of his generation to die of hepatitis-C. Trying to channel his love and support, a blanket of good energy seems to cocoon me. I could potentially play a range sweeping four octaves. And the lack of frets . . . I can bend the notes . . . *a greater range of notes. Maybe even Turkish microtones.*

I pick it up with reverence, the weight a sure sign of how badly my muscles have atrophied. My fingers graze the strings to play . . . and instantly burn as if my beloved instrument is plugged into an electric fence. *What the hell?!?*

My strings. I may have survived the silver brooch breaking my skin, but the metal alloy of my strings is like poison to me now. Did Naj plan this demise for me as well?

Panic sets in. What am I going to do if I can't play? I've never had any other form of income: never clerked in a store, served up a drink, waited a table, nothing. And what if I'm useless to the pack?

I have to overcome this. Every day, I grit my teeth in agony as I reacquaint myself with my old friend and coax the sounds out of my Fodera. Every day the strings burn me and I struggle with my lost sense of pitch, having to bumble around the blank fretboard and guess at the accuracy like a commoner. And every night I fall into bed in hopeless weeping.

Teddy comes over with assorted instruments to troubleshoot. I try to see if the reaction is due to electronics, electrical currents, or string substance. We try his upright bass, and acoustic bass guitar, and even a bass ukulele with no pickup and nylon strings. All produce the same excruciating effect. This is some sort of dark magic that makes no logical sense.

One morning Raúl brings me a CD of chakra mantras. Each chakra corresponds to a musical note of our Western scale, and I slowly being to retrain my ear as I do my Kundalini.

My healing comes in baby steps. Some days I make a little progress: able to touch my strings and play through the pain, able to shift, and able to sing. And some days I am so full of despair I crawl into bed, too depressed to move. If I am going to hold the pack back, I would prefer that they move on without me.

◆ ◆ ◆

Journal entry, September 1ˢᵗ: Biding my time, biding my time. It's amazing how the mind can go into sleep mode when there is nothing else to do. Unfocus the consciousness and see what magical images await you on the other side. Most of them are obscure, but it is a relief to let go regardless. Fall in, sink down to the bottom of the pool and rest indefinitely. It's pure meaninglessness, but it's my meaninglessness.

My phone buzzes. It's Sylvia.

"Get the hell out of bed!" she says firmly. "We're going shopping."

"How did you know I was in bed?" I mumble. "I could have been deeply engrossed in practicing for the big showcase. Rowan told me that as one who survived the betrayal, I am to step out and convey my story through a bass solo before the rest of the pack starts. I could have been channeling my muse!"

She snorts. "Not with that heavy energy you're radiating. We can all feel it from miles away. Now get in the shower before a normal human being can smell you. First, I'm taking you for a nice breakfast, and you're going to eat something. Then we're going to Victoria's Secret."

"Where?" I'm not sure I'm hearing her correctly.

"Victoria's Secret," she repeats firmly. "You absolutely cannot play the most important gig of your life in a plain bra."

"Don't you think it's going to be kind of weird for a nun to be traipsing around Victoria's Secret?"

She cackles. "You know how Jesus ate with sinners and all that? Well, imagine the places He'd have gone if He had been a *woman!* I'll be there in forty-five minutes. Pick some good prog rock for us to listen to on the way. The weather is beautiful today, and we're going to take the scenic route."

◆ ◆ ◆

Sunlight through the oak trees dapples the River Road as we take what appears to be the longest route possible. I roll down the passenger window to feel the air on my face, grinning to myself at how utterly canine this proclivity is. It's good to feel some sunshine at long last. Motion is another thing I've been missing.

I've assembled an impressive playlist for her car. She may be a nun now, but she's a progressive rocker forever and she lightly taps out every complex rhythm on the steering wheel. King Crimson, Genesis, Van Der Graaf Generator, Rush, Yes, Gentle Giant, and

Kansas shuffle their way through her stereo. "Time Waits for No One" by Ambrosia pops up as I finally crawl out of my mental shell at last and let some sunlight kiss my skin.

My black-hooded companion and I are regarded with mild curiosity at the Dante's Kitchen brunch as we stuff our faces with bacon praline cinnamon sticky buns, shrimp and grits, and bread pudding French toast. Passers-by display an increased interest as we wander the Lakeside Mall. But when we enter Victoria's Secret together, bystanders begin to gawk shamelessly. Sylvia feigns oblivion to their curiosity, although I notice that she's humming *Pie Iesu Domine* to herself a tad too loudly to be strictly for her own benefit. She never once cracks a smile, but her eyes are positively twinkling with mischief.

Sylvia herds me into a fitting room and runs the task of throwing an assortment of bras in the most outrageous patterns she can find at me over the dressing room door. Occasionally she joins me in the tiny pink-lined booth to lend an objective eye. For the first time since my hospitalization, I can feel myself start to laugh. I finally get into the spirit as one of the young sales ladies tentatively approaches her asking, "Um, can I help you . . . Sister?" It doesn't go unnoticed by me that at this very moment Sylvia is holding a lacy G-string and still maintaining a placid smile.

"Yes you can, my child. Do these come in leopard print?"

◆ ◆ ◆

I am surprised to see the stag still grazing in my dream. I circle it cautiously. It flicks its ears at me impassively. I sniff thoroughly, but catch no scent this time, only a distinct feeling or energy. The creature tilts its head almost inquisitively before trotting away, gradually picking up speed into a graceful lope.

Shall we dance?

As I resume the chase, I am the flow of a song through time. I have no body because *I am music.* My quarry is likewise made of music. The distance between us is always some sort of interval, the tension and release between dissonance and harmony. And I can never really catch that stag, because if I do the song is over.

It is not in the felling, but in the chase, I remember from my moon run with my pack. Of course. There was a time when the creation of song was like this. There were no material possessions and no ego.

Loop it, put it on endless repeats, and I will forever be an event, not an artifact. Ever eternal, ever transient, I leave no tracks.

◆ ◆ ◆

When I open my eyes I am slightly surprised to discover that it is early morning, and that I have actually slept the entire night for the first time since my snakebite. I smile to myself. Because I am my own incessant company, it's usually difficult for me to see if I've made any progress. I give myself a mental pat on the back for this tiny thing, and a phrase comes back to me: *You have to build yourself up.* I chuckle to myself at the irony. Enemies and other unlikely messengers sometimes deliver the most useful truth. *Okay Naj,* I think to myself. *Here comes my best revenge: I'm actually going to take your advice.* I go through my stretches and decide that I could use some sunlight.

I emerge barefoot while the day is still relatively cool and just stare quietly. The back end of the Audubon Zoo is only a few paces away from my front door. Stepping from pavement to lawn, I try to feel the energy of the earth, but I'm only aware of the fact that I could use some coffee. The only activity from its resident fauna that I can ever see without the price of admission is the occasional passing giraffe, huge reticulated neck bobbing like moving scenery behind the trees. I listen to the sounds of sleepy creatures demanding their morning fare. Monkeys and seals, and some sort of bird that I can't identify. Their myriad energies are mixed, but the message I'm receiving is universal.

Run.

Minutes later, I've donned my running shoes and find myself trotting to the edge of the adjacent Audubon Park. The joggers present all seem to be in their own little worlds, a warding of their own. I do a few slow stretches, trying to wake my kundalini energy, and hit the track gently at first. No earbuds for me—the only music I need is birdsong and the mantra of my footfalls and heartbeat.

Run it off. Run it all off.

I feel the burn, I skirt the edge between agony and adrenaline. Doubt begins to melt away; I sweat poison out of my pores.

Run it out of your system. Run it out of town.

The sun begins to rise, baking the mist away, glaring through the canopy of heavy oak branches. Familiar humidity starts seeping into my pores.

I will *do this. What other choice do I have?*

The beast within me knows instinctively that we will fight, not flee. The human within me gathers courage. We are in agreement.

One

A sharp ripple of energy smacks me, and I change course in an instant, bolting toward one of the live oaks out of raw instinct. Someone was careless—having neither warded nor shielded—and is about to be killed.

On a thick root of the massive tree is a purple martin with a struggling walking stick insect in its beak. I growl and the bird briefly flickers to the image of a beautiful brunette before pulling its form back to avian. With a speed I didn't know I possessed, tenor form flows over me. I pounce on the little bird in a savage attempt to swallow it whole, but it slips from my clawed hands and disappears into the air.

The stick insect now stands before me in human form like an El Greco painting, a sad-eyed ectomorph that I recognize as Ronnie Twigg, the piano player from the brewhouse gig. I try to avert my gaze from his concave chest and sharp hipbones and address the problem with exaggerated eye contact, bowing backward to glare up at him. "What the hell were you doing?" I snap. "Don't you know that we're in danger, and here you are in flagrante delicto! What were you doing in public with another shifter in your animal forms?"

His long, angular jaw clenches in an attempt to grin. "The timing could not be worse. I hope you'll see the humorous side to all this. I didn't know this chick was working for the enemy. We were on a date, and things . . . happened . . ."

I sigh, falling back into soprano. "Come on," I growl. "Get back into your insect form, and I'll take you to my place and give you some sweatpants before you get arrested. Then get the fuck out of here."

He turns his back on me and I flinch. I really could have gone without seeing his backside. *It would have been a disappointing day in nautical archeology,* I muse, *to discover a sunken chest but no booty whatsoever.* When I glance back, he is nowhere to be found until I look down. He is almost completely camouflaged against a dry stick. Designed to blend in with his surroundings, his antics could have gotten him killed.

I take him on my shoulder with the care of transporting a newborn infant and head to my apartment in a smooth rolling gait, as if a hard step might dislodge him. If we ever have to play a gig together again, I certainly won't tell anyone he's a shifter. The hard part will be forgetting what he looks like naked.

◆ ◆ ◆

Back at my apartment I flip through some of Father O'Flaherty's comics. He has a very strange selection, ranging from Woody Woodpecker to the Mutants. Some appear to be quite valuable, and some are possibly rubbish. I still can't figure out what on earth is wrong with any of this unlikely contraband.

It's one lone booklet that catches my eye, called *The Stygian Mode*. Devoid of a recognizable publishing company and drawn fairly crudely, it depicts people changing into sea creatures, mammals, birds, and unrecognizable hybrids typically seen in medieval art. There is a scene in which a man is being attacked by a dove that suddenly has my alarm system going off. *Father O'Flaherty thought it was the Holy Spirit. Shifters attacking their own . . .* Something clicks into place. That damned dove in the rectory *was* the thing that attacked Father O'Flaherty. It may have also been the same dove that watched me go tenor on the drunken tourists trying to vandalize my car near Bourbon Street. According to everything Sylvia has taught me, doves are no holier than wolves or snakes. It's the archetypal labels forged by humans that are deceptive, certainly to me.

I call Lydia with the new revelation. She thanks me profusely and I tell her that she is welcome to the book for further analysis. We have to win this war.

◆ ◆ ◆

Journal entry, September 20th: The hole in my heart grows smaller. This means that either my heart is becoming smaller too, or I am filling it up with music.

We have pack rehearsal, the last one before Howlapalooza, and I am utterly sick with nerves. The poison is either still in my system, or it's been replaced by genuine self-doubt.

Am I the weak link of the pack?

But I show up in my jogging suit, bass in hand, and am moved to tears at the warm reception with which I am greeted. I am scooped up in a sea of human hugs and human tears along with yips and whines. *Oh, my pack!* Every member is important. Even with wolves, the loss of one member can throw the whole pack out of balance. Whether in musical groups or true wolf packs, there must be some sort of hierarchy. And yes, there is sometimes tension, and sometimes there are power plays and struggles for dominance. But everyone has a role.

I am shy about meeting Rowan's eyes, but his embrace is so full of genuine warmth, I steel myself against inwardly gushing. I will always be in love with Rowan. I don't know whether or not he's seeing Aydan, but he is still part of my pack and we have an irrefutable bond, regardless of his personal choices.

Moving toward my usual spot in the room, I am not sure what to say now. But this is no longer about me. Now that there is no man down, an issue bigger than me has to be urgently addressed. Sylvia cuts right to the chase about the Stygian Mode. Encrypted in the graphic novel I'd discovered, she and Lydia had put their heads together and found records of a musical structure bearing this name, also called "the Death Mode."

"In spite of the name, it's certainly not a mode, and it's not a scale. It's more or less a rough framework of ascending and descending pitches in a subtle but confounding order," Sylvia tells us. Her voice is calm, but she isn't shielding around us, and the scent of her creeping terror has us all on edge. "I'm going to give you guys a tiny demonstration, just enough to show you what it can do. Somehow the frequencies of each note create an energetic collapse when played in this sequence . . ."

She shuffles reluctantly to her keyboard, shudders, licks her lips, and hacks out a pattern of notes. We all recoil in unison. It's more than a discordant, unpredictable, and unstable melody. It's as if something has just sucked all the light out of the room. For a moment, my brain is seized by an unprompted thought that the world would be a better place if only I would just die—*right now!* Rowan gives a low grunt and the music drops dead in its tracks. The room brightens again, and all five of us search each other's faces, damp and tight with fear.

"That was the most unnerving . . . *excrement* I've ever heard!" moans Teddy. "Never mind the violins in the soundtrack to *Psycho.* That was beyond creepy." He breaks the tension, but his lips are still pale even as he rushes the keyboard, nudges Sylvia aside and bangs out "Chopsticks."

Our token funny Omega, so essential to our survival, brings us back to earth with the latest news about the Maestro. In this new chapter of "Teddy to the rescue," our comic relief had to drive Yngschwie Holstein home from the hospital. Details are vague, but it appears that the flaxen-haired guitar fop got intoxicated at a dive bar and picked up a beautiful large-breasted woman—who later turned out to be a beautiful large-breasted man. Teddy was not privy to the hospital records, but the ensuing incident involved a can of olive oil cooking spray and a string of Christmas light bulbs. We all have a much-needed laugh, and are ready to play now.

We sing together to strengthen our bond. We express healing, we prepare to send our message, and we sing *Waheguru*. The howl over, we pick up our instruments. This time, we are deadly serious. We go over the music to be played at the showcase. I play in fits and starts, ignoring the pain as long as I can until it grows too much to bear. The pack keeps holding down the groove whenever I intermittently drop out and shake my hands to cool them. I stop worrying about being a hindrance and start focusing on the magic of our vibe.

Once we have all of the kinks ironed out of our song, a jam develops in a funky little 5/4 groove. Raúl gives it a jazzy snap, Teddy opting to put down his bass and blaze a solo on his mandolin. And then something miraculous happens, something crucial to wolf society and to musicians everywhere. We dissolve into ridiculousness.

Teddy starts it, of course. Why didn't it occur to me sooner? *Play is vital to the pack.*

This is basically the musical equivalent of a food fight. Teddy starts a riff in a weird Balkan meter, and each time Raúl and I figure it out and join him, he switches again. Sylvia decides to throw a wrench in the clockwork and smashes some dissonant chords on top of it all, and Rowan is somehow soaring above the whole mess with his guitar, actually making it sound good . . . until he throws in a cheesy lick from a cartoon theme.

Teddy is laughing and holding his mandolin in an outrageous parody of every hair metal guitar hero we've ever seen. He loses his balance but manages to fall on his ass, saving his precious mandolin.

And he swears like the good-natured, foul-mouthed Teddy I have always known and loved. *Oh, gods, he's swearing again! He's back! Maybe there's hope for me yet!*

Before we adjourn, Rowan gives us the logistics and the skinny on our showcase. Every single person to be involved is a shifter, from the bouncers to the bartenders. I don't know how Rowan has managed to pull these strings, but I am not surprised. Nor am I surprised that this will indeed be taking place at The Howlin' Wolf. We will sing healing into the hearts of our fellow shifters and warn the parahuman populace worldwide that there is an agenda threatening us all. And we will howl to announce our territory.

On my way home, I reflect on an old memory, my college mascot. We were not called the Wolves, not a bunch of individuals. We were called the Wolfpack, a single unit, a complex organism. I never attended a single basketball game while attending Loyola New Orleans, but something clicks into place nonetheless after all these years.

◆ ◆ ◆

I absolutely have to get some sleep. I wish I'd paid better attention to Raúl's advice about resting. I was beginning to make some pretty poor choices right up to getting bitten. I meditate and try to wind down, but my entire body feels fidgety. Then I realize that I am too restless and that this feeling is more than just apprehension. There's something outside, hanging out in the tiny backyard that I share with the other tenants. I begin to silently bristle, listening for anything unusual besides the night sounds. The only noises in the foreground are cars going by, frog music, and the soft coo of a dove. *Son of a bitch!* Why didn't it occur to me sooner?

Trying to remain calm, I open my back door a crack and leave it ajar. I slip back into my bedroom and strip down. If anyone spies, it will be a final show. I desperately call on the techniques Teddy was trying to explain to me and flow into my full wolf form . . . and focus even harder. *The point where wolf befriends man,* I think as my tail curls over my back, feeling the contrabass phase fit my body. A quick glance in the mirror reveals me resemble nothing more than a big cuddly Siberian husky. Fully warded, no one will see anything but a big dog harassing a scared little bird—if we're seen at all.

I step out into the sticky night air, already too warm for my thick coat. "It's over, motherfucker," I intone, doing a darned good job of producing human speech through a canine facial structure. "Everyone knows that doves are daytime birds."

There is no response. Even the frogs go quiet, as if holding their breath. I speak again, "Give it up, Gabriel! You have a lot of explaining to do, you sick fuck!" *Even angels themselves have been known to fall.*

My hunch is correct: he is too obsessed with me to be scared off, lured instead by my calling his name. In a whistle of wings he descends before me. I'm sure that he would try to manifest a halo as well if he could. His large, dark eyes are liquid and guileless as he spreads his limbs outward in a saintly gesture, fine-boned feathered arms awaiting crucifixion. I don't give him a chance to explain, pouncing on him and pinning both wings to the ground with my forepaws.

He pecks madly at my feet. "Birch MacKinlay, I'm the only one you need! Don't you understand that I've been trying to keep you safe?"

"Safe?" I roar. If he ever wanted to get close to me, he's about to get more than he ever bargained for. I expose my fangs just inches

from his head. He struggles and tries to shift back into human, but I pit my stronger energies against his own.

"She told me you were special, the boss did!" he begins chittering. "I was madly in love with you even before she sent me down to get information on you! Our boss is the world's most powerful shifter, she wants to trap or kill all the other shifters, wants all the power to herself. I kept you safe. I only shared your information with Copperhead and Quinn. Never the boss, never the boss."

"Well, isn't that kind of you," I sneer. "So it's been another shifter killing and abducting us all along. Aren't you a hero?"

He panics. "You don't understand, Birch MacKinlay, Birch, Birch, Birch, Birch MacKinlay! *I* am the only one who can keep you safe!"

"Safe from *what?*" I demand. I press down harder with my forepaws, feeling the delicate wing bones snap. Gabriel screeches but persists.

"Safe from *them!* Those other lycans! You could be with me, and we could be absolved together by the boss, we could be protected, we could be happy together forever while war is waged on the rest of the shifters!"

"And just *why,*" I continue, wondering why I don't bite the head off of this idiot right now, "do I need protection from my own pack?"

"*Bad people!*" he cackles. "*Bad people, bad people, bad people, bad people!* You deserve better! Maybe you would have liked me better as a macho stag, the way I was at the Shifter's Ball. You were so amusing, Birch MacKinlay, letting prey chase predator! Hind's feet in high places, Birch MacKinlay!"

All of my adult life I have been trying to tame my rage. First

I stifled the beast within, then I studied meticulously with my pack mates, who had honed their own skills for years. Do I really want to blow it by killing this guy? If I snuff him while he's in dove form, I can just bury him in the back yard and no one will miss him. But I will be stuck with the knowledge that I've killed another person. Even someone twisted enough to betray his own, who thinks that his obsession with me is love. I growl as deeply as my voice will go.

Gabriel suddenly goes still. "I was afraid that you wouldn't see it my way, Miss MacKinlay," he peeps. "Now there's no choice but for us to see the Kingdom of Heaven right away. We will be together for all of eternity!"

"Oh right, you're going to try for a suicide-homicide now." I am amazed at how much sarcasm can be conveyed from a dog's mouth. And then I see the silver band he has attached to his leg. There's a tiny glass vial on one end and a tiny dart on the other. *Oh, no you don't! No more poison ever!*

I snarl as loudly as I can, but he is too insane to show fear. "I could have killed you right away!" he cries. "I would have kept you cold and stiff and beautiful in my car, to hold you and tuck you in every night, to finally show you some kindness! Not what that idiot Yohan was doing to you!"

He spied on that too? I am almost too incredulous to be sickened.

"But you rejected me!" he accuses. "We were destined to play music together, but you had eyes only for that group of barbarians you call your *pack!* And one of them was always hanging out with that priest, yes that priest, I had to try to kill him, for the Church constructs *lies* about our God! And then you were in love with that *spic,* not to mention always playing gigs with that *ni—*"

His head pops off in my mouth so easily, I can't believe it's really over just like that.

◆ ◆ ◆

"I shouldn't have killed him," I moan between retches. "I didn't want to kill another person, and I could have gotten more information out of him." One last dry heave wrings out my gut, squeezing tears from my eyes. Because I am a werewolf, the taste of blood in my mouth should be expected from time to time, but having killed another person is more than I can handle right now. One's own near death experience is one thing, but I am no soldier trained to keep his own team safe in combat. Even with the coolness of the porcelain sink and tile floor, I can't ground myself. My bathroom begins to feel too small to contain enough oxygen. A final flush, a rinse of my mouth, and I manage to stagger out.

Lydia catches my shoulders before I lose my balance. "You did the right thing, Buzz. Letting him live would have been too risky, even long enough to wait for us to arrive."

"He is connected to our nemesis," I tell her. "It's an individual female with minions rather than an organization. He simply called her 'the boss.' I don't think he meant Springsteen. He said that she was the world's most powerful shifter. We're facing a parahuman dictatorship and totalitarian regime."

She checks my eyes for something. "Buzz, I think you need to relax now. You're shaking and your t-shirt is on backward. You're still panicked, and Raúl and Rowan are waiting outside for you. I will take custody of the body. The poison dart will also be analyzed. We have also added the Chimera Enterprises business card to our files. The only fingerprints we found on it were yours, indicating that the man who handed it to you was able to shift his skin somewhat. It's definitely an inside job."

"One more thing?" I tell her. "I can't believe I hadn't thought of this before. Gabriel paid all of my hospital bills. Whoever he's working for has deep pockets. The records can probably be traced back to the head honcho." She nods. "I'm on it."

Dazed, I descend my front steps where my two packmates await me. They enfold me into a healing group hug, sharing their good energy with me, counteracting the ambiguity of shock. The fight-or-flight adrenaline leaving my body is suddenly replaced with raw emotion and I burst into tears. They set me down onto the cool grass of the sparse front lawn, literally grounding me. I am shaking and sobbing so hard, I don't know if I'll ever get up. I suppose we are warded, for no neighboring tenants come to investigate. The frog songs begin to calm me at last, and Raúl begins to hum a soothing mantra. My body unfolds at last and I sprawl out onto the ground, letting every limb touch the earth, letting the earth absorb all of the excess bad energy. *Corpse pose,* I think to myself. *How appropriate.*

"Listen to me, Little One," says Raúl at last. "You have brought us some very good leads on the enemy. I don't know everything that was involved, but it was obviously at a terrible cost to you. We are here for you whenever you are ready to talk about it." I nod knowing that some tales will have to remain untold, at least for the time being, such as Gabriel spying on my trysts. It would be helpful to mention that he was a racist, but I can never repeat what he said to me verbatim. Raúl has already been through too much.

Lydia appears at the door, and my pack-mates hoist me up and carry me inside. I am wearing nothing but a t-shirt and a pair of sweatpants, but I still feel like an idiot as they place me into my bed and tuck me in. Raúl and Lydia offer me a soothing goodnight, but Rowan lingers for a minute.

He sits at my bedside and pats my hand. "Hey. You did good, kiddo." In spite of my shock, a happy glow begins to kindle in my belly, not a burning, but a friendly candle flame. I think it reaches my eyes.

He kisses the top of my head. "Get some rest. I'll lock up." For now, it is enough.

I dream no dreams.

◆ ◆ ◆

It's impossible not to keep peeking out of the club tonight at that huge pumpkin-colored moon. I try to stay put in the green room, but I am brimming to the max with anxiety and a need to pace.

I had briefly seen Rowan backstage, conferring with a local committee of Alpha shifters and SIN agents. He looked as if he hadn't slept at all, but his eyes were fever-bright as he approached me for a quick kiss on the cheek. I had a hunch that the mastermind had been discovered at last, and he affirmed my query with a brief nod, his mouth at a grim angle. Patting me on the shoulder, he made his way out into the club toward the sound console, instructing a couple of young technicians. This gathering is going to be broadcast on some encrypted frequency only known to shifter leaders and SIN agents worldwide. Anyone else will only perceive it as an entertaining concert. Who knew? I push the gravity of the situation out of my mind. I have a job to do.

My Fodera bass is tuned—although I keep checking it every fifteen minutes—and I have a fresh battery in my pickups. Lucky leopard thong and matching bra are soft beneath my clothing. I've worn my most glamorous stage clothes. My ferocious eye makeup rivals that of Diamanda Galás, but I haven't bothered to try covering my scar with lipstick. Instead I flaunt it tonight as a warning to others. I'm hydrated, warmed up, and pumped up like a horse in a starting gate. I also feel slightly sick to my stomach. I so seldom get stage fright or feel nervous before a show that when it does happen I almost don't know how to cope with it. I tell myself that since I could perform the English horn solo in *The Pines of the Appian Way* at age sixteen, I should have no problem pulling this bass solo off tonight. I try to ignore the little voice in my head that tells me that people's lives didn't depend on my ability to play *The Pines of the Appian Way* back then, and look around for something else to focus on.

Teddy and Raúl are goofing around off to the side of the stage. Teddy has been teaching Raúl a favorite childhood rhyme of his called "Piss-Pot Pete," and they are gleefully reciting it like a couple of schoolboys. I don't doubt that this is deliberately intended for me to overhear and to ease the tension that is threatening to crack me in two. Then Sylvia joins in and I fall into hysterics.

And without warning, the canned music fades, the lights dim, and Aydan takes the stage. A few members of Anatolian Fusion Project have already begun playing the freely improvised *acis* prelude, allowing Aydan to make a sweeping entrance and pick up her bağlama. She introduces her number as an original piece of music set to the poetry of Ahmet Yesevi, a poem about longing for peace. The other players launch into a vamp that walks a fine line between East and West—unapologetic jazz with Byzantine echoes—while she goes into an unmetered improvisation that Teddy tells me is called *taksim*. She barks a quick cue to her band, and the song changes, picking up in speed and intensity. Aydan whips the audience into a frenzy with her blazing fast riffs over a dance tune—*Kolbasti* from the Black Sea, I remember from Teddy's CDs. Her voice sometimes floats above the heavy groove in the spine-tingling Sufi chant, although I'm not versed enough in the music to know what type of Sufi song. But it's like a call to prayer, a lover's kiss of raw silk, and a dark, hypnotic siren. They come to a hard stop, a lightning strike of triumph. The thunderous applause makes me feel caught in a sudden heavy downpour.

And now I'm up: a one woman, one six-string fretless bass spectacle. The stage is huge, and I am tiny. The last time I embarked upon an ambitious endeavor like this I failed, but I have to try again. I freeze the echo of rejection and tuck it away in the back of my mind to deal with later. I can smell apprehension, but the room is dark and the spotlight makes it even more impossible to tell who is out there or how they are reacting. But this is not for them anyway. I cannot base this performance on audience reaction—only the here and now.

I am in alto phase. If it makes Rowan or any other males notice my enhanced appearance, so much the better, but now I need to be in this mode to have my sharpest hearing possible. Even my calloused fingertips need extra sensitivity, even thought I know it's going to hurt like hell.

I take a deep breath and hum a mantra to myself. The vocal mic won't pick it up, but the hum grounds me and gives me courage. And the others can feel it. One by one each member of the pack— *my* pack—joins me. I feel them strengthening my note, a perfect unison, unlike the ever-changing toning that we usually do.

The primal urge to yank my hand away from a hot stove seizes me with the first note, and still I play. There is no going back now. No second chances, no overdubs, and no excuses. I reach for microtones without even gut frets to guide me. The notes ease into one another like a human voice . . . or a subtle howl. My fingers are like figure skaters: they leap and land on a playing field with no markers. Every nerve screams an acid burn, scalding water, fire ants, blistering and boiling, and I exhale hard through my nose and keep on. My jaw is clenched hard enough to shatter my molars. I have to push this pain to the farthest corner of my mind. *Fuck, fuck, fuck, fuck, it hurts* . . . I try breathing it out, mentally separating myself from my body. It doesn't work. A tear wells up in my eye and I think I might be growling. *Concentrate!*

My heart cracks just then, sending lighting bolts of shocks through my ribcage. It breaks wide open, and the music comes pouring out. My thumbs hit the drones of my lower strings as I work my way up the neck and rake through a hypnotic mantra with subtle melodic variations across my higher strings. Each variation is a wordless chapter of my confessions. I play for the hatred instilled in me by Naj and Sand, the vengeance by Cal, the regret for hurt I have caused others, and the rage over endless bullies I have fought from the playground to the venues. I play for my friends and pack-mates in danger. I play for love, and this life of mine that I would gladly lay down for them all. I play through every sorrow and relive every tear I have shed for shattered ideals, failed endeavors, and unrequited love for Rowan. I harness every fear of being discovered as a fraud, and of dying alone. I send my vibrational warning to my fellow shape-shifters, my voiceless testimonial of what may become of us all if we do not wake up and fight.

I shape notes into arrows, ready to take down our adversaries. I shape them into blocks of defense, and I shape them into hard diamonds, cutting and rare. I shape notes into round circles, open but unbroken.

I think I may have tears streaming down my face, but I am long past any dignity. The show must go on. Every note sears my skin, every emotion skins me alive, and I strive to make it sacred. For this moment I rip my heart out and channel it through my rig. It's raw and ugly; it's delicate and pristine. It's my story, and it is real. What musician hasn't felt this? To keep striving for the ultimate beauty, even as every note tears a person in two?

The pain and I dance like old lovers. I am one with the agony; I am the fire, and I am not the fire. *I am the spark that ignites it all* ... And then only the flame remains while the pain recedes. I can almost see its energy radiating off of me, away from me, like ripples in water. Like sound waves. I keep playing. I am the element of fire. *I am the vortex through which fire enters this universe* ...

It's amazing what sounds a person can coax out of an instrument when suddenly no longer racked by excruciating pain. My head clears, my heart soars, and the music becomes the finest thing I have ever created.

I am truly in my own element. Flame is a symbol of what it is to be a lycanthrope. It represents the delicate balance between beast and man. It is the chaotic razor's edge between creation and destruction. Animals cannot invoke it, and humans cannot wield it responsibly. We are intended to be the peacekeepers, taming the human within. We bring the fire and its light and warmth to all.

And one by one, my pack joins me onstage. Rowan on guitar, channeling a signal through his emotional control. He is water. Teddy on bass, laying down a low, steady groove under my improvisation, a pattern of communication and intellect. He is air.

Raúl on drums, creating a strong rhythmic foundation, a physical pulse to be felt in the body. He is earth. Sylvia steps up to the keys, the snarling Hammond B-3 sound an unmistakable sacrament. She is spirit. Even though we all face the audience, we are situated in a circle, forming a wolf-paw pentagon of protection. We form a strong groove, vamping over Rowan's improvisation.

I am in complete control, and yet I let go. Something inside me opens. If I could put cognition into limiting words, this would be labeled as my heart chakra. It is alchemy. Fears melt, impurities burn, all things radiate from the heart. To be broken is to be whole, and now I understand.

Why did no one tell me that I am the heart of the pack? I feel no ego and no pressure . . . just an all-loving center that pumps the blood of life to the unit that is collectively known as a pack.

I feel some sort of energetic gate opening, but I cannot break my concentration to take in the details. All I know is that there is some vast interconnectedness within the room and far beyond. There is not only a strong interconnected pull within the group, but also outward to a network. We are all a part of something much bigger. Our pack is one of many constellations, and I channel the energy. We are a giant satellite, broadcasting our message to be passed along to packs all over the world. Word of howl, and we leave no tracks.

Rowan steps up to the vocal microphone to deliver his warning. His voice is not that of a lead singer, but it carries authority and power, and when he sings, people listen.

Madwoman, self-coronated
On her brow a crown of schemes
Forces tribute without merit
From her throne of stolen dreams

Cult of traitors seeks her mercy
Begging at her feet for scraps
She will slay them all and sundry
Where her kingdom overlaps

We herald the end of this top-secret era
Beware of the woman they call the Chimera!

The story continues to unfold in lyrics about what the SIN has finally discovered: a woman of multiple aliases known as the Chimera, and a shifter herself. A rarity that could shift into not one animal form but several, she began to fancy herself some new messiah. She began a cult some years ago, brainwashing her first followers by denying them food, sleep, and autonomy until they began to develop what is known as Stockholm Syndrome, the dysfunctional need for a victim to protect his captor. Now she usurps the animal form of every shifter she overtakes, growing more powerful, more deadly, and more insane. *She can tell creation to unmake itself...* The unfolding truth I hear makes me quiver, and I grit my teeth, determined to add my strength to this broadcast.

We cannot turn corporeally onstage of course, if only because none of us can play our instruments without long fingers and opposable thumbs. But we converge in bass form on the astral plane, a network of energies, a collective consciousness. Now our message is amplified beyond the range of hearing.

Down below my hands are working expertly. But my extended self is running with the rest of the pack. We touch souls and stand as one. Five people, five digits together, combined to make one strong fist held high in defiance. I gaze out into the audience. *As above, so below.* They cluster bodily around the stage, their animal forms dancing high above with us on the astral plane.

Gradually others trickle onto the stage to join in: Lydia with her trombone, Aydan with her bağlama, and even Tim on his clarinet. Then the floodgates open and more musicians swarm us, adding their voices. I know most of these people, and love a great many of them, even though I didn't realize they were shifters. I am incredulous, for among them I see members of The Round Pegs, Descendientes, The Tomb of Nick Cage, Delta Funk, and a dozen other staple bands of New Orleans. Even Father O'Flaherty is lending his sweet tenor voice, making his way onto the stage like a great waltzing bear. My heart is tight with emotion: gratitude for my allies, overwhelm at the staggering number of shape-shifters who dominate the music scene, and angry resolve toward these unknown adversaries. They strengthen the message, and in one unified crescendo we launch our signal.

Our collective message is sent, spreading outward in concentric waves. A moment later I feel an echo of response in my gut and running strongly up and down my spine. I can sense that everyone else feels it too: the other musicians, the audience, the staff and the technicians. We are read loudly and clearly.

I don't know how long the song lasts—twenty minutes or an hour mean nothing to me. I only know that it reaches a blissful peak and we all end together on Rowan's cue, letting the sound and the message resonate for a second before the wild cheers set in.

My pack is elated. They are all clustered around me, hugging me. Sylvia presses her cheek to mine, crooning, "You did it, Buzz! It was your strong survivor spirit, stronger than the rest of us combined. You were the flame that ignited the warning fires, that launched our signal when you played through the poison, and you converted our message into waves. Like Saint Francis, you transformed and freed yourself."

We did it. We did it together. I am drunk on raw emotion: relief, pain, love, and a dozen other vibrations that I can't even identify right now.

I feel even more responses coming back at us from all over creation. The message is viral now. My whole body resonates like a violin.

One

CHAPTER

10

"Well, you are doubtlessly the darling of the pack!" exclaims Sylvia blithely. She brings me another cup of coffee from the barista. We are sitting at a table in CC's Coffee on Magazine Street, not far from my apartment. "See, I *told* you the bra would help!" she teases.

I sip my coffee and grin foolishly. While I don't doubt that an inflated sense of pride is a sin, it's probably innocuous enough to be happy with one's accomplishment, especially when it involves possible salvation of all blended beings. My spoon slips and dings against my saucer in a perfect C sharp. *My pitch is back! Thank the gods!*

"One more thing," my black-clad confidante says tentatively. "I've been curious about something. Now that you have survived two types of toxins that are harmful to lycans, I've been curious to see if something I once read is true. Hold out your hand."

I extend my palm trustingly, but wince as I see her withdraw a small velvet pouch from her pocket. She gingerly grabs the silver rosary with a small cloth, keeping it away from her own skin and pours the object into my open hand before I have a chance to object. And nothing happens. Whatever fusion took place in my system as the toxins were mixed then expelled, I am now immune to silver. This is fantastic. It's one more way I can go undetected as a lycan if I am wearing some sort of bling that is obviously silver. I play idly with the rosary in wonder.

"So what happens now?" I ask.

"So it appears that *someone* is going home to Turkey for a spell; in fact her taxi should be pulling up at the airport soon. She says her visa has expired, but she plans to come back. And she has news . . . for you."

"News?" My heart suddenly pounds, and I cannot touch another drop of coffee. "Sylvia, what is it?"

She sighs. "You know I have to hold confidentiality sacrosanct. Let's just say that I have a *feeling* that there is something she would like to tell you . . . ."

I bolt for the coffee shop door, nearly leaving my car keys behind me on the table in my mad dash.

◆ ◆ ◆

My car screeches to a halt in front of the curbside kiosk where Aydan is waiting in line to check in. She smiles sadly. I can tell she's been expecting me.

She is as gracious as always. "Birch! I am glad that you came to tell me goodbye. I have had such a great experience playing here and learning so much. The people are amazing, and the *food . . .!*" She forces a smile. I don't know what she's working up toward, but I feel as though I am about to have a heart attack.

"And Rowan was such an amazing engineer and producer. I can't wait to play this Sufi-funk fusion CD for my friends at the conservatory back home. Rowan really made it come to life in a way that only a lycan can."

She drops her bags and lets her hands fall to her sides. "Look, I didn't just come over here for the music. Last year my brother was abducted, and my family believes that it was connected to the attacks on shifters everywhere. My brother Kemal is a fine percussionist, and played with Rowan years ago. So I thought that Rowan could help us, since he is one of the top musical Alpha lycans . . . Rowan and Sylvia were sworn to secrecy about this, but I think things would have been easier if I had told you as well."

I wish she would just get to the bloody point. Her eyes drop to the ground as she says slowly, "You do know, don't you, that werewolves mate for life?"

I still don't understand, but I nod miserably. I don't want to think about this. I can't endure thinking of him with someone else, especially with this exquisite creature that I can never hope to be. I can barely contain myself. "What's your point?" I spit in a fit of impatience.

The whine of a jet overhead sends us both cringing, hands over our sensitive ears. When the noise subsides, she turns to face me again, ignoring the impatient grumbles of the people in line behind her.

She gently lifts my chin with her hand, forcing me to look

her in the eye. "Don't you think that a werewolf would have to be extremely careful choosing a companion? Especially one descended from a long line of Alphas?"

I still don't get it. My vision is blurred with tears again.

She sighs. "He's had to hold out for so long to make certain that the timing is right and that his judgment is accurate. Birch, he loves YOU."

I stare dumbly at her. The words don't register.

She drops her eyes. "I never stood a chance with him. Just as we are trained to pick up frequencies, I knew from day one that you two had a special resonance."

I refuse to let myself be flooded with hope. Or I try, anyway. Maybe I just desperately want this to be true.

"It's not your looks, or even your musicianship, although you should be happy with both. It's your untamed spirit. I envy this about you." This surrealistically beautiful woman, this genius musician, envies *me?*

"But Buzz—may I call you Buzz? You are already a very pretty woman. Strip away another layer or two of the poison you've been infected with over the years. It's still warping your self-esteem, and it's going to hold you back on your musical journey unless you learn to love yourself. Be well. Perhaps we will play together somewhere down the road." A car horn blares, urging me to either unload something or move on. I glance in the reflection of the window and for once decide that I can live with what I see.

Without another word, Aydan rolls her baggage to the skycap. I slip back into my car and head back into the city, astonished.

I still hate her a little.

◆ ◆ ◆

I don't know how I know that he's parked outside my house. I also don't know how I manage to get there from the airport so fast without getting a speeding ticket.

He's waiting for me by his truck, eyes hidden by shades, expression unreadable. I am led by blind faith, but as my legs automatically carry me toward him, we simultaneously reach for each other. And the next thing I know, our arms are around each other, mouths are pressed together, passionately but tenderly . . . more like some sort of long-forgotten homecoming.

I can no longer maintain my cool. Tears blur my vision, and my hands refuse to quit shaking. All I can do is whisper, "Wow . . ." I feel as though all of the oxygen was momentarily sucked out of the atmosphere.

Something is different, new. Then I realize that Rowan is neither shielded nor warded in any way. He has completely let his guard down around me. For the first time I smell affection and desire on him. I am utterly dizzy with incredulity as he pushes back his shades. His expression is still unreadable, but his eyes are kind. And when he speaks, I hear a completely different tone of voice—feather-light and intimate.

"Do you want to go inside?"

And somehow we are now inside my apartment. There is him, and there is me, and there is us. The rest of the world simply does not exist. I have never experienced such completion, not even with the pack.

His lovemaking is nothing lupine . . . it's all so blessedly human. The human within that needs no taming. No shielding. No heightened scents or sounds, no fur or posturing . . . just bare skin and hands and lips, experiencing everything anew. Foreheads pressed together, faces touching, slowly exploring each other's bodies. I am so hungry to experience everything at once, but he gently but firmly leads the dance, compelling me to take it slowly and savor it. Some sort of inexplicable telepathy—he knows my yearnings before I can even guide him, and know his. I taste no pheromones, no spices . . . just a man who is sometimes as vulnerable as I am. Wonder blossoms across his face, and I know in this perfect moment that this is a new height for him as well. Two hearts pounding, gradually slowing and falling into synch with each other. It's the most powerful transformation I have ever experienced. And then the cycle begins again.

I had no idea that it could be like this. Awareness explodes in my brain.

Many hours later, my every nerve is still resonating like vibrating strings. I prop myself up on one elbow and watch him sleeping. I take in the sleek strength of his broad, powerful shoulders, his long black eyelashes fluttering faintly in his dream. His face is youthful in his repose but his breathing is heavy, like that of a world-weary man. His perfect lips, curved into a hint of a smile. His hands, so expert on the fretboard or on my body, now tucked against his chest like a day-old pup. He's so breathtaking . . . and he has chosen *me*. I am still beyond amazed.

Perhaps he had waited for me this whole time—not to put me to a test as a suitable partner for him, but to allow me to come into my own. This conclusion feels right in my gut. *I had to take a path that no one else could do for me.* It was so that I may permit myself to be tested by my new world, and overcome every demon even through heartache. By waiting for me, he gave me the chance to build up the strength, skills, and courage to be a true warrior. For the first time in my life, I *belong* somewhere. And I still have all my bass chops.

Was my fever dream real? Is he really a holy man? He has certainly performed a miracle just now. Maybe some part of him will never truly be mine, but I can accept that. For now, it is enough.

Gravity suddenly drags me down like an external force—or perhaps it really *is* an external force—what do I care, as long as it's benevolent? I can swear I see Rowan stir in his sleep just enough to make some room for me to snuggle against his warm body. And as I do, my two selves blend into one. I breathe in the scent of my mate, a scent meant for only me. Even in repose, his heartbeat is immensely strong. I nuzzle the back of his neck, drape my arm across his chest, and sigh deeply. As unconsciousness begins to settle over me like a soft blanket, all I hear is the distant echo of two howls, slowly blending into a perfect note . . .

One

INTERMISSION

Story nothing without connection
Funny nothing without foolishness
Honor nothing without respect
Idea nothing without dream

—Note found in Birch's tip jar

ACT III

VARIATIONS ON A THEME

"Cage an eagle and it will bite at the wires,
be they of iron or gold."

—HENRIK IBSEN, *THE VIKINGS OF HELGELAND*

CHAPTER
11

AMBIENCE SYNTHESIS

It's been two weeks since we've had a pack meeting. I can't really say that I have noticed. I've been too immersed in the joy of once again playing bass without searing pain. Plus Rowan has had me . . . distracted.

Back in the Fontainebleau room, I still have to pinch myself from time to time. I feel as if I am living in a dream, a perpetual state of disbelief. But the twinkling in the eyes of my pack assures me that this is no head trip as Rowan gives me a quick kiss on my temple before we take our places. Bliss scurries down my neck as Raúl appears knowledgeable, Sylvia conspiratorial, and Teddy slightly wistful.

Rowan is all business now, but flashes his white teeth at Raúl. "I believe that someone has an announcement to make," he says, the velvet pads of his voice carrying his tone perfectly. I am snapped out of my reverie state like a toggle switch.

Raúl cannot stop beaming. "I asked Lydia to make me the happiest man in the world. And she said that it would take a while for her to get Zildjian to come out with a customized line of cymbals for me . . ." He doesn't really finish his joke, but he does a rimshot with his eyes. The air around us has gone completely still. "Seriously, she continued to play dumb until I got down on *both knees* and asked her point blank to marry me."

Sylvia lets out a squeal. Teddy gives him a convivial thump on the back, although his smile doesn't quite reach his eyes. I throw my arms around Raúl, but I sense Teddy's pain, trickling off of him in a slow leak. He still hasn't let on more about his own heart's desire, but this double whammy of recent happy developments is definitely taunting him.

Raúl's eyes are shining with tears. "Because of her connection with the shifter intelligence network, she has contacted my family! They are so relieved to know that I am alive . . . and now they will be able to come to the ceremony . . . I get to see them all again . . ." His voice breaks like a tiny pane of glass and we flood in through the cracks to envelop him in a collective hug, the occasional wordless whine of emotion surfacing from one throat or another.

Slipping from him one by one at last, we turn back to Rowan, who has commanded us with his silence. We still haven't heard the details of the insane mastermind behind the shifter attacks, and are anxious to figure out what to do next.

"I guess it goes without saying that you guys were awesome at the showcase," he begins. We all fist bump each other, and Teddy gives us polite golf claps. "Now that everyone has rested, it's time to give you guys an update," he continues. "Once I was able to put two and two together on this cult and the madwoman behind it, shifter leaders from all over the world began working around the clock to pinpoint her location. There hasn't been any success with that, but we have still collected some information on her.

"There are a few reasons why she is called The Chimera. I'm sure that you guys know the original Greek legend of Bellerophon battling the fire-breathing creature with lion, goat, and snake heads."

We've all heard the myth, but need reminding, so Teddy gives us all a rundown. "The Chimera," he tells us, "was a lionine beast with a lion's head, a goat's head growing out of its back, and a tail that ended in a snake's head. All three heads could breathe fire; I'd seriously love to know the biological mechanisms behind that! It was the offspring of Typhon and Echidna, which were monsters, although their names sound like afflictions of embarrassing places. Anyway! Bellerophon was ordered by King Iobates to fight the monster from the back of Pegasus, for some seriously fucked-up reasons that I'll tell you guys another time. Some say that he himself had the idea to use lead weapons, some say that a goddess told him in a dream. He had the height advantage of fighting from the back of Pegasus, but it was the lead that did the Chimera in. He had a lead-tipped spear that he managed to lodge in its throat, but other sources say that he threw a ball of lead down its mouth. In any case, the lead melted into the creature's stomach, killing it. Personally, I'd rather be tarred and feathered, but The Legend of Teddy Lee remains to be told some other time."

Rowan dips his head in approval of our pack folklorist before bringing us back to the current situation. "In modern genetics, *chimera* is a pretty broad term, sometimes used to categorize humans with two different blood types or two sets of DNA.

"*The Stygian Mode* discovered in Father O'Flaherty's possession turned out to be a heavily encrypted codex for all shifters following the Chimera. O'Flaherty himself was trying to solve the mystery as discreetly as possible, so concerned was he over being discovered by the wrong people."

"He told me that he had tried to pass himself off as a comic book enthusiast," supplies Sylvia. "Some of his fellow berserkers, the bear people, had donated some rather valuable items to make for a convincing alibi. If he had been caught with *The Stygian Mode* in his possession, he knew could feign ignorance about the book's true purpose, not to mention report anyone trying to retrieve it."

Rowan nods. "Lydia and her intelligence team were able to decipher the code and verify the identity of our nemesis, confirming my suspicions. The woman responsible for all this chaos is a polyshifter, a shifter who can assume two or more forms. Her real name is Idona Brume. Some theorize that she was the offspring of some biopunk; however, she was born long before any such studies in genetics were ever made. In reality she is the offspring of a lycan and a kelpie.

"She is reported to be able to shift into over two hundred forms, or combinations thereof, making her a 'splitter,' a polyshifter who can take features from several beasts at once, like griffins or manticores. This is how she almost always transmogrifies, although she prefers to keep her own face, narcissist that she is. The team handling the scientific part of the case believes that it has something to do with the manipulation of viruses, which can replicate DNA.

"Financial reports reveal that she has tremendous fiscal backing, which is officially named Chimera Enterprises. We have already seen evidence of this in how Gabriel paid for Buzz's hospital expenses from the Chimera's coffers. Brume may not have even noticed, so deep are her pockets. Her allegedly inviolable stronghold is estimated to have cost around nine figures."

Sylvia murmurs, "Just think of how many impoverished communities that kind of money could feed . . . provide clean water, housing, education, medicine . . ." She trails off, but her eyes are ferocious.

Raúl's eyes are troubled. "She accrues it criminally, of course," he says. "Lydia told me that one shifter in business with her managed to escape her snares, but didn't live long enough to tell the whole story. This man had been a canny stockbroker. Brume had offered him power, luxury, and protection from her forthcoming war in exchange for a loan of an exorbitant amount of money. But when the time came for him to collect, she was reported to have assumed a dragon form and replied, 'Let's just think of this as a tribute gift, shall we?' and promptly bit off his head. I doubt that Brume realized that in his cockroach form he was able to survive decapitated for an entire week. So she did not bother to squash him as he shifted and scuttled away. He somehow managed to report to some shifter leaders—mostly insect forms—with signals, written cues, and pheromones before finally dying. But even he was unable to pinpoint her location."

Rowan shakes his head in sorrow. "It appears that she will stop at nothing to unite all shifters on her side, eliminating the ones who do not comply, as well as annihilating innocent humans."

Teddy wrings his hands. "Damn, she is guano-crazy!" We pause until he elucidates, "Bat shit."

"That she is," admits Rowan. "She is a commanding, intense woman. Back when I knew her, she desperately wanted to be the center of attention at all times. She has gone even more power-mad since I last saw her. Back then she was addicted to exercise, and sources say that this has only gotten worse—linked to her obsession with her own beauty and the subjugation of others."

"How did you know her?" asks Teddy.

He does not drop his gaze, but as his mate I can smell his extreme discomfort in spite of his shielding. "We used to have a bit of a thing going."

It feels as if I have just taken a cannonball to the chest. Everyone seems to make a point of not looking at me.

"It was back in the 1930s," he discloses. "'Talkies' were beginning to replace silent films, and I was bouncing around from gig to gig, shifting from a pianist to a guitarist. The depression was fully upon us, but we never really felt the effects in Manhattan. I met this woman at one of my shows, and she was the first polyshifter that I had ever known, her blended heritage allowing her to switch from lupine to equine bodies when she chose. She was a runway model and a social butterfly. But the huge fly in the ointment was her ego and her jealousy. As they used to say, 'if she can't be the body, she won't go to the funeral.'

"She especially had an agenda against one of her peers and fellow models, a Scottish lycan named Dottie. Dottie was a fascination to many for her beauty and charming accent, but was loved by all who came to know her for her kindness and generosity of spirit. The words that people often used to describe her were 'elegant,' 'poised,' and 'graceful.' At any party, she could be completely holding court, but it was largely because she expressed so much genuine interest in everyone else. She did not think of herself as remarkable at all, and had a vested interest in helping others.

"Eventually Idona and I parted ways, as I couldn't take any more of her attitude and volatile mood swings. I still saw her from afar on the scene, as I had gigs to play that crossed into her own world. She immediately hooked up with a naga for several weeks. The official story was that he fled New York after they broke up, but no one ever knew where he went next. He was rumored to be dead. And Idona began to take on some of his traits that might further her career, her gait becoming more slippery as she glided down the runway. She began to possess three main animal traits instead of two, and craved more.

"One night after attending a New York Philharmonic performance, Dottie and her husband were seen conversing and laughing with the legendary conductor Arturo Toscanini. Idona had just about had it. Dottie's husband was soon murdered—found with a pair of fang marks to the ankle. At the funeral, I went alto to more effectively eavesdrop and I heard Idona's whispered bragging about this 'warning.' How she could have just killed her rival, but that she wanted to make her suffer first, before executing her plans to take Dottie out. I had smelled that Dottie was with child by then, and the thought of Idona killing not only another innocent person, but also her target's most precious hope was more than I could endure.

"As people began to leave the graveyard, I pretended to offer Idona a lift to her flat. As soon as she got into the passenger seat, I warded and went full on tenor. Rage didn't even begin to describe what nearly consumed me, nearly drove me to kill her—if only I had! She was so full of herself, she couldn't even smell my lycan rage, choosing to believe that I couldn't resist her and that I wanted her back as I bound her hands. I drove her to my apartment and managed to detain her in my bathroom, threatening to blow her cover if she tried to escape. For several hours, she laughed at what she thought was a game. In time she became bored, realized that I was not going to take her, and hissed at me that I was hardly a man for refusing her. And like water, she flowed into snake form, slipped out of her bonds and under the door, slithered out of an air duct, and I never saw her again.

"Several days went by before some hawk shifters spotted her. They reassured me that by the time Idona was on the warpath, Dottie had already vanished. And I decided that if I wanted to stay alive, I would do well to evacuate as well and go back to my native El Paso. Dottie was said to have escaped unharmed and lived on elsewhere. I don't think I even knew her last name."

My blood feels like putty in my veins. I swallow hard. "I know what her story is. Her surname was MacKinlay." I feel the collective jolt from the pack, and I take a deep breath. "She was my grandma, and came down to Louisiana to raise my father. She always said that it was because New York was no place for a widow to raise a child, which never made any sense to me. I guess she didn't want to trouble us with the knowledge that she had been in danger, especially if it were to raise awkward questions."

This is the first time I have ever seen Rowan appear incredulous.

My head spins, but I meet my lover's eyes. "If you hadn't detained Brume . . . I might never have been born." I can't bring myself to say her first name, as if speaking it aloud will somehow invoke her—or his old feelings for her.

Teddy breaks the tension, pointing back and forth from our pack leader to me. "Rowan is a cradle robber, Rowan is a cradle robber," he chants. The whole pack explodes into laughter, and I am so grateful to Teddy right now, I could almost give him my prized Fodera bass.

I pounce so hard on the opportunity for a subject change I can practically hear its neck break. "So, Raúl. Where are you guys gonna get hitched? There's a great spot not far from my house . . . a bona-fide labyrinth. Don't worry, it's only ankle-high, so you can't get lost." Raúl agrees to swing by with Lydia and check it out.

Teddy and I exchange sympathetic glances. How is it that we all can sense each other's emotional states, yet still feel the need to disclose so little? Perhaps privacy is the last remaining luxury of lycan life.

As we all hug goodbye, Rowan's pack phone rings, startling us all into an instinctual state of hyperawareness. He says very little when he picks up, but his mouth goes grim. Even with the encrypted frequencies and foreign words, we pick up vocal tones of extreme distress.

When he hangs up, the silence in the room is almost a vacuum. "Aydan's been taken," he tells us in a flat tone. "She never even made it to her plane out of New Orleans."

A surge of guilt rises in my gut like bile. *I could have stopped her,* is my automatic irrational thought. Rowan swings his head to meet my gaze. "No one could have possibly known," he assures me, reading my energies, smelling my emotions.

Turning to face us all, he says, "This I promise to you all: no harm will come to anyone at the nuptial ceremony. I will personally see to that. We have much to be joyful about." No one questions him.

◆ ◆ ◆

The wedding is like no other I have ever attended or played for. It's small and informal, but there is no way anyone could ever try to recreate such a ceremony. The first cool weather of the year has everyone in high spirits, and the overall joy is infectious.

A cluster of small children runs through the little clearing at the edge of the stables not far from Audubon park. Their bright eyes and ebony skin make it easy to imagine Raúl as a little one, and these nieces and nephews of his warm my heart as they romp like puppies in this strange new terrain.

I'm not certain what theological aspect is being observed. Father O'Flaherty is to perform the ceremony, but I know that Raúl's religious views are centered around the ancestral worship of his Tsonga people. And I'm not even certain what Lydia observes. Like Raúl, she is older than she looks, and I seem to recall her speaking about her roots in Voudoun.

The altar contains two figures: an image of the nearly-forgotten Asherah, wife of Yaweh, holding a pair of snakes. The other is of Hecate with two dogs, or possibly wolves. The little arch is interwoven with wisteria vines, the clusters of flowers like floral bunches of grapes dropping purple blossoms in a lazy shower.

Sylvia had tried to explain it all to me. "We are having a traditional shifter ceremony, and religion is simply out of the picture. What is the Divine but one eternal shifter, anyway? It shifts form according to where we are born and how we are raised. The Divine does not care about Its image. We are as little children fighting each other for the attention of our parents, each trying to win the most favor by capturing the most accurate depiction. Only we kill one another, much to the sorrow of our loving Source."

Speaking of which, Teddy and Sylvia are now off to the side of the altar, pretending to argue about theology, which dissolves into the two of them trying to kick each other in the butt. It's some sort of discussion on the Flying Spaghetti Monster versus the Church of Subgenius. I have only caught the tail end of it, but I double over watching the two of them in action. Teddy puffs out his chest and states, "To quote Connie Dobbs, 'I kick habits while the nuns are still in them!'" His subsequent attempted roundhouse is way off mark and he loses his balance. I am relieved to know that there is at least one other werewolf around who is as clumsy as I am.

I recognize a few guests, including the flamboyant Dean deChanteloup from the Shifter's Ball, hired to organize the caterers and florists, choosing only lycans with the most discerning noses. He's chatting with P.H. Fred, who is enthusiastically proclaiming that while it must be glamorous to be a lycan, folks like us will never understand the simple pleasures of peeling a banana with one's own feet or flinging poo. Dean is cackling his infectious laugh, and I insert my way into this animated discussion until the music starts.

Sylvia has her Triton and a small amp set up, and Father O'Flaherty is standing patiently at the altar. My black-clad best friend begins to play a lovely Scarlatti selection. Lydia's father, a majestic black man to whom she had introduced us earlier, leads the bride towards the arch, and as we stand to see her, the collective sound of breath catching in everyone's throats flutters like breezes through branches in the little congregation.

Lydia is the most stunning creature I have ever seen. Her cornrow braids are interlaced with one another like Celtic knotwork, shaped to her head in a sleek, intricate cap. Her adaptation of a traditional Haitian gown is at once classy and otherworldly, as if the fey had spun a flowing silver karabela dress, tailoring it to accentuate her curves. Raúl is grinning so brightly, it almost hurts to watch him.

Father O'Flaherty raises his musical voice that needs no amplification.

"So as you transform yourselves, you now transform one another. Beast and human, man and woman, wolf and serpent. Musician to musician and friend to friend. I wish for you both:

"Instinct to listen to each other.

Strength to support each other.

Speed to defend each other.

Reasoning to temper each other.

Joy to lift each other.

And love to encircle each other.

Do you, Raúl, take this naga . . ."

I can't focus for a minute. Less than a year ago, I didn't even know that there were other lycans here besides Rowan, and now this whole other world is widening faster than I can keep up. Rowan senses my overwhelm and squeezes my hand, grounding me.

They walk the path of the labyrinth together, symbolizing their journey ahead. I sense powerful warding around the ceremony, but neither bride nor groom is asked to transform. A wedding, it seems, is an entirely human thing, and the transformation is within. I blink rapidly, realizing that we are getting to the good part.

". . . by the powers bestowed upon me—oh, for the love of Saint Brigid! Would you all stop crying?" A watery giggle ripples throughout the little congregation and Teddy blows his nose with a massive honk.

"I now pronounce you . . . the most disgustingly sweet man and wife I have ever seen! Go on then, you may kiss the bride before I develop diabetes!"

Dean shouts, *"Mazeltov!* Oh, shit, wrong wedding!"

The recessional is Aaron Copeland's "Hoedown," á la Emerson, Lake, and Palmer, of course. Sylvia looks like a novelty greeting card: a nun gleefully rocking out, oblivious to religious mores.

At the reception, the music of Gharwane piped is through someone's jam box, and I hear people greeting each other in Haitian vernacular: *"Onè"* (honor) and *"Respè"* (respect). I take Sylvia aside. "I found this stuck in my gig bag the other night." I hand her a folded piece of paper. "Someone wrote this little piece on the back of a flyer. I figured that you of all people would be able to make heads or tails out of it. It's compelling, even if it doesn't rhyme."

Sylvia nearly trances out, mouthing the words silently. A wondrous smile begins to flow. "Ah, but it does rhyme," she breathes. "Just not on paper or spoken aloud. This appears to have been written by a deaf person. Their concept of rhyme is not in the way that words are written—for how can you explain a word like 'through' rhyming with 'new' by sight? Their rhymes and meters are according to the visual similarities and flow of signs, and where they are in relation to the face or body. The meanings still carry vibrations, even though there is no sound. For all thought is vibration.

"Many deaf people enjoy music as much as any of us do. They just perceive it in a different way. There are even some very accomplished deaf musicians. Not all deaf people are into music, suffice to say, but there is an entire subculture of deaf poetry, punctuated by things like eyebrow movements and facial expressions. I'm been to some deaf poetry slams, and it is unfathomably beautiful, even if it goes over my head. I still can appreciate it like a kind of dance that I can never hope to perform."

I still have so much to learn. I tuck the poem into my jacket pocket for luck. An odd tingle down my spine leads me to believe that it will come in handy someday.

◆ ◆ ◆

My hair finally dry, I give it a few more strokes with the brush before tucking it into a ponytail. Rowan slides up behind me and kisses the back of my neck. We'd had a blissful morning giggling like a couple of loons watching a few episodes of *The Mighty Boosh*, before the laughter heated up into a carnal urge that had to be attended immediately. A private glow fills me at the new delight of discovering Rowan's outrageous strength firsthand. I don't recall being so happy, ever—even if a cold lump occasionally grows in the pit of my stomach thinking about the Chimera. But for now, all shadows have fled my mind.

"Where is the gig again?" he asks, his arms around my waist.

The drug of happy disbelief has overcome my mind so strongly that I have to think really hard about the answer. "Private party just north of Jackson," I recall at last. "Some people from a Mississippi blues society are honoring Slackjaw's birthday. They've hired some of their local musicians, but are apparently over the moon at getting his old bass player to join them. I seem to be the only member of his former band who was available. I guess the other guys already had gigs."

He frowns. "Do you know these folks?"

"My contact was somebody named Angeles. Look, I've played all over the world, and driven a good deal over it as well. I'm going to be fine. Jackson is always cool. The annual Jubilee Jam is huge, and turnout was always good at Hal and Mal's whenever I played there, so I expect this to be a good crowd."

He appears troubled, but can't seem to put a finger on it. And I secretly feel similar apprehension, but I can't pinpoint it either.

"This gig is an easy commute for me," I continue to reassure him. "I've made the drive to Jackson so many times, I could almost do it with my eyes closed. Once I get over the Mississippi state line, I no longer have to stay in the right lane." We step out of my apartment together and I lock up with my usual little obsessive compulsive doorknob check.

As I slide my bass into my hatchback, I savor the sight of his car parked next to mine, and the ensuing butterflies in my stomach rise in a cloud. He kisses me one final time, and I lean in with unabashed greed—I can't get enough of those lips of his. "Be careful," he murmurs.

"Fuck yo studio," I reply in the same caressing tone. It is as close as we ever come to saying *I love you* and *I love you too.*

Off I go to a chilly late autumn sky, blasting the sounds of Crack the Sky from my stereo.

◆ ◆ ◆

By the time I get to the Mississippi Welcome Center just over the state line, the lump in my stomach has returned. I had always imagined that winning the love of my life would result in the fabled "happily ever after" so common in fairy tales—which is why they are classified as fiction, of course. I hate the fact that I am still so insecure.

I'd tried to distract myself on the way, finding a little mom and pop antique store just off of the I-55. Nothing had interested me except for a tiny headless toy soldier made of lead, obviously forged before anyone cared about getting sued over lead poisoning. I thought it would be a perfect addition to my collection of discontinued deadly toys—including my lawn darts and Ice Bird Sno-Cone grater—and so I'd bought it for five dollars and tucked it into my jacket pocket.

But later with the endless stretches of pine trees lining the roads, I was having a hard time keeping my thoughts away from this former model who was my lover's ex. *And addicted to exercise at that*, I reflect. I had been keeping myself in shape throughout my training, of course, but I will never be athletic. I have a poet's body: meant to be venerated only after I am gone.

And now this looker had enough power to influence a sizable portion of the shifter population. My key to true love and belonging somewhere at last, tainted by this bitch. I shake myself. If I don't get a grip and focus, I won't be in good form for the gig tonight.

I roll into the parking lot and shut off my engine. In the privacy of my car, I permit myself a good, cathartic growl, lip lifted. Not even swearing makes me feel better. Then I remember my mother's way of letting off steam by pretending to angrily call people by the names of counties and rivers of her native Mississippi, so I give it a try. "You Tishomingo Yalobusha Homochitto Buttahatchee!" I yell at the top of my lungs. "Issaquena Yockanookany Sucarnoochee!" It does, in fact, bring a smile to my face. I recall Sylvia and me gleefully trying this in grade school with parishes and rivers of Louisiana— we had gotten our mouths washed out with soap, especially over "Tangipahoa" and "Tchfuncte." I let fly an undignified sigh before unbuckling and stepping out into the sunshine with an outwardly normal affect.

The Welcome Center might have some free coffee in the main building, amid their maps and pamphlets advertising points of interest: museums, symphonies, historical houses, and zoos. But the ladies room is my main priority, so I make my way down the unnecessarily labyrinthine walkway to the back of the site. Even after I reemerge I am still agitated, and need to let off a little steam. The grove of trees beyond makes for a good spot to discreetly jog off my frustrations, so I trot towards it, as far away from the parking lot as I can go.

I don't hear any bees or hornets, so the sharp sting between my shoulder blades catches me completely by surprise. I reach back to swat the offending insect and dislodge a small dart instead. The sudden drowsiness that fells me to the ground is somehow less surprising. *This is getting really old,* is all I have time to think before I black out.

◆ ◆ ◆

Pain in my joints—shoulders, elbows, hips, and knees—is what hits me as my eyes open. Having one's wrists and ankles tied in the same position for what may have been hours will do that. I try to go bass to slip out of my bonds, but I can't somehow, and the panic sets in. The large animal crate that confines me is just large enough for me to stretch out my back, although I wouldn't have been able to stand up in it even with my limbs free. I feel the erratic vibrations of a moving vehicle carrying me somewhere. I clear my throat and the acoustics tell me that I'm in a van. Through a grid in the side of the crate, I can see weak sunlight trying to permeate the tinted windows.

And I'm not alone. There's another woman in the crate with me. There is something familiar about her willow-thin body and her too-red hair, now dulling at the roots. Even as she rolls over to face me, I can't quite believe that I am once again stuck with Naj Copperhead. By the look on her face, it's obvious that the astonishment is mutual.

"Buzz? Oh, Buzz, I am *so* glad to see you!" she gushes, trying to smile. Tear streaks have cut furrows through the dirt on her face. She struggles to regain her charm. "I hope I didn't insult you with my critique of your bass playing. Nothing personal, huh? I was just trying to help you. You're like a sister to me, and we shifters have to stick together. Where do you think they are taking us?"

"Just shut up, Naj," I growl.

Her eyes flick down to the scar on my lip, and she does indeed hold her tongue. I don't even want to waste my energy with angry words. The only thing breaking our strained silence is the sound of tires on the road. I feel her eyes upon me, so I roll over to turn my back on her, drifting in and out of tranquilized stupor.

The light gradually fades as we are swept on a current of utter helplessness into the night. As the crate gets colder, I begin to wonder slightly about her silence. I am unable to tap into my wolf senses much, but my human eyes can still see that her skin is graying, and her stillness abnormal.

"Naj?" I call softly. She doesn't move. "Hey, Naj!"

"Buzz . . ." she hisses with almost no air. "I'm . . . cold-blooded . . ."

Oh, fuck. I hate this bitch beyond fathoming, but I can't in good conscience just let her die. I wiggle my way across the crate and press my body against hers. Her skin is morgue-frigid, and I don't try to hide my shuddering.

I try again to shift, but nothing happens. *Why can't I become the wolf?* I wonder. I could keep us both warm more effectively if I could go bass and let my fur do the insulating. Even still, my body heat is sufficient, and we eventually both fall into a hard, drugged sleep.

◆ ◆ ◆

There's no telling where we are or how long we have been imprisoned when the crate begins rocking and we are flung from side to side like pebbles inside a maraca. Cold sunlight blinds us as the latch opens and the crate tilts sharply down. Naj takes a hard jolt and pisses herself as she lands, but I manage to hold my aching bladder as we are dumped onto a dirt road like garbage. A gruff voice barks down at me, "Too bad your little friend thought she was going to get her halo without proper training. And you! Looks like you won't be playing any Slackjaw tonight. Not that you ever were going to. You're in the hands of the angels now."

Angeles. Angels. *Damn it!* Incidents flash back to me: the drunken man who said I needed a guardian angel after the Pegs gig, and the gutter punks with their Angel Ministries cardboard box, Cal's talk of halos and wings, and Gabriel, who fancied himself an angel with his name and his deluded beliefs that he was working for a greater good. But this man is certainly no angel. I try to glare at him, but my neck is so stiff that I can't even turn my head.

Our captor hunkers down to my level and reveals himself to be a cold, beady-eyed man. He looks familiar, but I can't put two and two together until he smiles and flashes his abundance of teeth. A new level of fear seizes me as he sneers, "You should have shown me some respect back at the Crescent City Brewhouse. You didn't know who I was then, but you will certainly know me now. You will call me Azrael, since I am one of the Chimera's many angels." I am shocked to see how frightening this man is without the expensive suit barely concealing his true nature. The memory rushes back to me: *Don't you know who I am?* And I had mocked him at my brewhouse gig that day.

His rough, stubby fingers fasten a thick silver collar around my neck. "This is for your own good," he says sternly. "Only angels can keep you safe from sin. How can you feel secure knowing that the shifter intelligence is abbreviated S-I-N? But we are merciful to the sinners who convert." I think of Sylvia and her dedication to helping others and remind myself, *Angels and sinners are only names.*

Refusing to answer, I feign weakness and pain, although I am now immune to silver. I can't help wondering in the back of my mind how many hungry families that much precious metal could feed. Angeles unties my limbs, and a new pain stabs me as my joints finally move in the wake of prolonged immobility.

"You, doggie!" he shouts at me. "You can go mark those trees over there, since the boss doesn't want you stinking up her nice complex." A long rope leash is clipped to my collar, and I shamble off to the nearby grove.

All thoughts of danger momentarily desert me in the primal act of relieving myself. Still I think up a quick, desperate idea. I retrieve my pack phone from my pocket and hunch down, trying to dig without claws. What I lack in wolf skills I make up for in adrenaline fear, and I bury my phone six inches in the dirt. It still has a third of a charge, and I hope it's enough for my pack to track me.

I carry this out just in the nick of time, as my captor returns and gives me a cursory pat-down—even though he assures me that no weapon could ever harm the boss. Satisfied at finding no large guns or knives, he grabs my leash and hitches it to the one holding Naj, who is collared at the ankle. He pulls a couple of armbands out of his jacket and tags us each on the left upper arm. Then comes a violent yank on our leashes again as if we are rebellious mules instead of drugged, hungry hostages. I try to close my ears to the harsh words he mutters like a mantra as he takes us to the edge of a densely wooded area.

We are dragged down a trail that is barely visible for all the trees obscuring the sunlight, but Naj and I are able to pick our way through it with our latent instincts. I am struck by the profound absence of birdsong and insect noise, as if everything is either dead or holding its breath. Amid the scents of pine and numerous plants that I don't even recognize is the overwhelming stench of greed, fear, and anger. A tiny ramshackle cabin protruding from a large hill meets us at the end of the trail. It leans to one side, a wounded warrior of rural architecture. Only the hill, subtle and ominous as a burial mound, seems to keep it from collapsing.

I hear the click of a gun and feel cold metal against my temple. "See now, you will either pass the Chimera's test or your brains are gonna decorate this wall. We can't just drag any hostage in here. You have to get through the boss' warding—like the way you lycans do it, but infinitely superior and impenetrable. See, this is a hidden world we have to step into, and you have to access these little dimensions sideways. If you can do it, maybe you will be worthy to be her guest."

He pushes me against the wall. "Now unfocus your mind a little and make yourself flat. When you feel the next world forming around you, shape yourself to it, like a puzzle piece. You'll feel yourself sort of snap into place. Wait just a little while, and you'll know when it's time to step out."

I comply, feeling the surreal push and pull of nonphysical energies squeezing me into position. *Forced through a thick energy.* Three deep breaths later, I can move my fingers. I pull away from the wall and tear out of the shed . . . into a bright atrium.

CHAPTER
12

The blond guard waiting for us introduces himself as Metatron as he collects us from Azrael. I am still trying to take in the nature of the atrium. There is light shining from windows across the top, but I can't tell the direction of the sun. I glance at my watch and my blood runs cold as I watch the hands pivoting back and forth erratically, like two compass needles in a roomful of magnets. Azrael's meaty hand darts out and grabs my wrist. With a flick of his knife he severs the leather strap on my timepiece. The second it falls to the floor, he crushes it under the heel of his boot. "You won't be needing this ever again," he sneers. "There is no time in this underworld. You can rot here for a hundred mortal years before your neighbors will begin to notice that your newspapers are piling up."

This is a lie, that much is obvious. There's enough of a palpable magnetic field that might trick a person into suspending disbelief, but this is no magic place. It is, however warded beyond fathoming. The energy trick itself has a strong scent of uniform overwhelm, like hundreds of creatures with only one scent. *This is the scent of Brume, the Chimera. Many bodies, one mind.*

Metatron looks at my armband, and says, "English? Very well, then." I am American, of course, not English, but I say nothing. I don't have time to wonder about this place as I am dragged through a side door and down a spiral ramp.

The cold humidity that envelops me is like the blood of something long dead. *Not a good place to store instruments* is my instinctive thought.

The corridor is little more than a tunnel with cells dug into the sides. There is the occasional ventilation grate cut into the ceiling, the overhead light creating shadows of the bars, like hollow rib cages. Weak electrical lights cast a greenish pallor over everything, illuminating the forms of things that may or may not be people.

All shifters, none of whom can change. I sense only this, nothing more. Even to my human nose, the acrid stench of piss, shit, blood, barf, and sweat sends tremors though me. *Bodies, cramped like living meat in a slaughtering chute, dying from the inside out.*

I thought I'd known fear before, but that was from quick, fleeting attacks or things that in hindsight were menial. Now I am truly terrified to the core of my being. I look back for Naj, but I am the only one being led to the cells. I can only guess that she was too weak to survive the transition into this underworld.

As I pass endless cells on either side of me, I hear a car wreck of voices in more languages than I can identify. The tunnel keeps going on indefinitely, as if expanded with need. I am finally brought to the last cell on the left and shoved in with more force than necessary. The iron gate that swings shut is almost a cliché.

There is another man in my cell. His deep-set, sad eyes are hollow and haunted. A mop of dark curls falls over his oversized ears. His long nose twitches as he sized me up, and he strokes his scraggly beard self consciously. He greets me softly in French and I suddenly get it. They labeled me "English" by language, not nationality. There must not be enough holding cells for each prisoner, so language groups are split up to prevent communication. We are in some labyrinth of Babel. But they must not have known that I am from southwest Louisiana, and had first begun learning French in nursery school. My command of the language is rusty, but I am relieved that I can communicate.

His name is Jean-Michel Lapin, he tells me. He is a biochemist, and being forced to research the many sets of DNA that the Chimera possesses, which now number in the hundreds. Like me, he is unable to shift into his animal shape, and knows that he could probably dig us out if he could retain his rabbit form.

The door shrieks open again, and Azrael's face leers into mine. "MacKinlay! You are to make an appearance! Don't disappoint her—the Chimera is very curious to see how an ordinary lycan could survive a Naga bite. She may have . . . *use* for you!"

Lapin doesn't meet my eyes as Azrael attaches a chain to my collar and leads me back out. The muffled voices of the other prisoners frighten me more than the prospect of what awaits me.

◆ ◆ ◆

On the way over Azrael tells me that I am in the Chimera's center of operation. After all the efforts by the shifter leaders to find the precise location of this hellish nest, the dramatic irony does not escape me. Light suddenly sears my eyes as I step out of the gloom into the foyer, and I clutch at my face in agony. Azrael does not wait for me to adjust to my new surroundings. Another rough shove to my back, and I am pushed into the royal hall.

The throne room is sparsely furnished but impressive. Columns spring up like fountains of white marble, or perhaps alabaster . . . I wouldn't know. I am but a poor musician. The hall is lined with gothic arched windows, sturdy and commanding, but smoked glass reveals nothing to me of the outside world. An enormous single rafter crosses the upper half of the room, neatly dividing heaven and earth. An overhead oculus beams light down onto the empty dais, wide enough to hold three people. I don't doubt that this is a deliberate form of intimidation, a way to cast a royal or divine illusion of my nemesis. I refuse to be awed, whatever it is I am about to face.

Her henchmen are in attendance, and they command me to address them by their official titles. They are all named for angels: Raphael, Metatron, Azrael, and Uriel. No Gabriel, of course.

I try crooning the wild harmonic. All of the angels except the one called Metatron turn to glance at me.

Waiting for the Chimera to make her grand entrance, I am already plotting her demise. I don't even lie to myself about the hatred I feel. She is killing the happiness I have finally found with my pack, and now she has gone after me personally. Trying to aggrandize herself wasn't enough, nor could she merely remain a megalomaniac. She is a dictator, she is an abomination . . .

The curtains part from a side door and she enters. She is a *goddess*.

The woman called the Chimera stands in palomino centaur form, her golden blonde hair cut short like the crest of some prehistoric bird. Butterfly wings the size of my car spring from her back, each wing marked like the tip of a peacock feather. A single narwhal tusk springs from her forehead.

Her face is perfectly symmetrical, an exquisite work of art. Her brushstroke lips curve into an amused smile as she meets my gaze. Her eyes are a thousand colors at once, each more beautiful than the last. Each of her angels kneels before her and she bestows her blessings: bags of white powder, chunks of resin, and syringes. They scuttle off to receive their divine messages, leaving the two of us alone.

She extends a graceful hand to stroke my head, and I feel the urge to grovel at her feet. *Did Rowan grovel at her feet?* a tiny voice within me asks.

For once my jealously saves my life, and I instantly jerk back a split second before she can grab my hair. I growl. This time she is genuinely delighted. Peals of musical laughter echo and bounce around the throne room like light from a prism.

"Such bad manners, you little bitch!" Her voice is like honeyed opium. "My angel Ezekiel, better known to you as Calvin Quinn, was right: you are nothing but a stupid little bitch! You can only change into one form, and you show no respect for your gods. Even if you could change into different animals, you would lack the intelligence and power to take on multiple attributes!" I bite back the overwhelming urge to beg her forgiveness. *No! She is wielding some sort of mind control!* I hum to ground myself, and the feeling vanishes.

She changes forms like water pouring from one fantastically shaped vase into another. *A splitter. Dividing into multiple signals.*

She now appears as the Sphinx, lion body lean and athletic, gargantuan wings stretching up from her back until they touch at the tips. Her claws flex in and out, and she lashes her tail to whip the air inches from my face. Laughing as I jump back, she lowers her voice to a purr.

"Answer me this, little cur:

The bitter fruit of lame defeat

Produced a wine that tasted sweet

Terror is as terror does

Meek and ugly as it was."

"Your mom!" I snarl without a second thought.

Her face does not change expressions, but her eyes become laser-piercing. Her wings extend like satellite dishes, trying to tune into my frequency. "That is correct. My mother was a she-wolf like you. She was hideous and weak. Yet she produced *me!* But she lacked the finesse to raise me to the immediate glory I so richly deserved.

"Things that were once legendary are now a reality because of *me!* I am the incarnation of all the humanoid therianthropes: centaurs, mermaids, fauns, minotaurs, bat-winged angels, and serpent-tailed imps. They were depicted in art because people witnessed shifters in mid-change. But they were nothing more than stories.

"And now, I am here to bring all shifters to full glory. We will hide our true natures no longer. All humans will die, and all shifters will worship me." She sits up on her haunches for effect, wings cleaving the air in bass notes like slow helicopter blades. Dropping back to all fours, she reaches a massive paw toward me and pins the leg of my jeans to the floor with a single claw.

"I could kill you now as originally planned, but it seems that it would be more beneficial to keep you alive for a while. You are resistant to so much. I could use a strain of that. Perhaps you would like to pay tribute to me? Passing along your DNA will be a way for you to immortalize yourself in my mission. But hold . . . you smell familiar." She pauses, nostrils flaring.

"Well, well, well . . . aren't you a *special* little bitch? I should have known, given your musical connection. I know that smell of Rowan's passion, little worm—oh, yes I was *well* acquainted with it once. His standards seem to have fallen awfully low!" In spite of myself, I can't help agreeing with her. "He's such a fighter. I should have killed him in his sleep!"

I imagine my mate slumbering next to this beautiful creature, this demon-beast, and growl in spite of myself. A lightning jolt of mad energy, and she is a mermaid with deadly lionfish spines down her supple back. A webbed hand grabs me by the throat, and a talon sharper than a broken seashell nicks my skin. My will to live suddenly overrides all else and I remain as still as possible until the angels take me away, back into the underworld that is my new home.

I am guessing that no one hears me growl, "Oktibbeha Tallahatchee," under my breath, because no one cuffs me.

◆ ◆ ◆

By the time they drag me back to my cell, I am foaming at the mouth. Lapin says nothing, just hums while I curl up into the farthest corner and snarl. The snarls become soft howls, howls diminish into weak sobs.

"How long is she going to do that?" I hear a new voice query.

There is now a third man in our cell, compact and powerful. Lapin glances around for any signs of approaching guards before saying, "Birch, I present to you our secret ally, Petit Puce. He is the smart one of the two of us, for he hid in my fur well enough to escape the anti-transformation dart. I hope you don't mind sharing your cell with a flea."

Petit Puce looks like a cartoon strong man: exaggerated muscles, shaven head, even an outrageous mustache that would probably be a handlebar if we weren't prisoners of war. I inhale until my lungs creak, trying to ground myself. I force a tight smile and extend my hand. "Enchanted. Some of the best bass players are fleas."

A crescendo of heavy footfalls, and by the time a guard walks past us, Petit Puce has vanished entirely. Only Lapin remains, sitting on his hands in an effort not to scratch his beard.

I understand. Petit Puce is so healthy because Lapin lets him feed in his animal form. He would be a formidable defender if we weren't so grossly outnumbered by the henchmen, or angels, as they are called. But as a spy and go-between, he is perfect, and I am lucky to have this flea in our cell.

◆ ◆ ◆

And so begins my chthonic life. I had thought that mere incarceration would be the worst of it. But the lack of sunlight nearly drives me insane, causing me to almost look forward to being taunted by the Chimera in her bright throne room.

The guards, or "angels," are all shifters. They frequently slip into their forms of cicadas, birds, and other night singers. They whisper messages while we get whatever sleep we can: our lives are meaningless. We must become useful to the cause or die. The only henchman that does not shift is Azrael. He remains in human form the entire time, and I am too groggy to wonder why.

The hunger pangs surpass anything I have ever felt before. I am desperate to fill my belly with anything at all, even if it's inedible. I search my pockets and come up with nothing but my little lead soldier, the folded poem penned by someone who cannot hear, and a dirty Kleenex. After another day, I begin to eat the Kleenex in hopes that the fibers will at least settle my stomach.

At least there are toilets in the cell, albeit little more than outhouses dug into the floor. No privacy, of course. Lapin and I are courteous enough to look away from each other, but we cannot spare each other the indignities of sounds, especially during frequent bouts of sickness.

The most maddening thing is the airhorns. They blast every hour or so. Not only can I get little sleep, but the constant startle has my nerves permanently on edge.

"Why doesn't it hurt the henchman's ears?" I ask Lapin one night—or perhaps it is day—as the blast sends us both quivering from our blankets.

"Petit Puce says that he is deaf. The Chimera has named him Metatron. He can speak and read lips, but takes no auditory cues. He is the only person who can carry out the tasks of his mistress without going mad, including hearing the screams of the tortured and executed."

There are other auditory tortures. The guards form a discordant choir, singing a strange harmonies on odd sighing voices, like the lowest possible scream. *The Stygian Mode,* I realize. It's clearly a structure designed to break people's wills, not unlike the higher-pitched music intended to agitate World War II prisoners. I mumble my favorite Rush lyrics to myself under my breath each time those broken voices swell, hoping to counteract the weight of those notes that insist that I give up the fight.

One day, food is delivered to our cells. We are hog-tied first, forcing us to eat facedown on the ground. Our fare is little more than cornmeal mush, but we are suddenly grateful. Several fights over the rations break out in other cells, as many cellmates do not speak each other's language and begin to forget their empathy toward each other.

After several weeks, I begin to fantasize about food. It would be so divine to have cornmeal mush with chicken. Or perhaps cornmeal mush with chocolate. All I can ever imagine are variations on my staple diet. On the occasions that Lapin is sleeping and I am not, I fight the voice in my head that reminds me that his shifted form is a prey animal. I am always brought back to my senses, either with a song or a needle-stick itch on my skin, as fleeting as it is sobering. Our tiny stowaway reminds me that the smallest of creatures feed upon us all.

There is without a doubt some sort of drug in our food. After each feeding, I feel complacent, and my wolf counterpart is very far away. Something to facilitate mind control, and an anti-shifting drug, the same one used in the tranquilizer dart, is what Lapin theorizes. So I cling to the memories of my wild self and my loved ones, refusing to give in.

I sometimes compose letters in my head to Rowan. Impossibly, his scent floods my senses, as though he were close enough to embrace. The hallucinations are alternately comforting and cruel. I send out thought vibrations to him, but wonder if we are even in the same world. I often take out my little toy soldier—now slightly misshapen from my body heat—and imagine him marching as to war, scratching little diagrams in the dirt floor. I sing little songs to him: *You have no head, you should be dead, perhaps you are a cockroach instead.* I use him to scratch pictures of wolves on the walls, thinking of the cave artists from my vision so long ago. They may not have been trying to immortalize themselves or further their careers. Perhaps they were just trying to stay alive.

The guards are in constant rotation in both human and animal forms, always keeping us awake in various ways. They never call me by my name, first or last. They address me as Chimera's Bitch until each time I hear it, I know that they are talking to me. If I try to speak to them, they only parrot my words back in my face. At some point I finally fight back and tell the male guard known as Ramiel, "I have no penis!" just to see if he will actually say it back. He freezes and we study each other's faces. As he pulls a slow grin, I can see that his teeth are pus-yellow, set in swollen red gums. His eyes are rotten cores where intelligence should be. He lets out a childlike giggle, then punches my face, knocking me to the ground. The pain almost blinds me, rattling me from jaw to shoulder blades. He spits on me before walking away to taunt other prisoners.

As the stars clear from my eyes, I push my tongue around in my mouth to feel for broken teeth, but they all seem to be intact. Since I still care about my teeth, that must mean I still have my pride. This gives me the tiniest hope, the span of a dragonfly's landing, and then it's gone even more quickly.

◆ ◆ ◆

Metatron visits our cell the next day. Lapin is dragged out to do some sort of work, and I don't see him for hours. He returns smelling fed. I am about to tell him how lucky he is for being granted permission to leave his cell, to walk awhile, but my first words die in my throat. Lapin has a look as if he would be better off dead.

The deaf henchman and I lock gazes, and a spark of his true nature surfaces for the first time. His blue eyes are searching, confused, and afraid. He doesn't want to be here any more than I do. *What happened to this man, that he fell into such desperation?* There is the faint crackle of paper bending in my pocket, which I know he doesn't hear.

My hand instinctively closes around the paper, and something makes me hand him the poem. I observe how cautiously he unfolds it. His hands tremble as he reads, sending me furtive glances the whole time.

I only know some basic signs. I draw my index finger across my palm. *What . . .* My index and middle fingers of both hands extend, then stack across each other. *Name.*

His eyes flood with tears. *T-r-o-y* he finger-spells slowly.

B-i-r-c-h I respond, and he suddenly turns on his heel.

He walks back to the compound, and there are no airhorns that night.

◆ ◆ ◆

Lying face down in the dirt, I don't have the energy to get up. My stomach is beyond growling. I never knew it was possible to feel this hungry. It's like a dull knife constantly pressing in my gut.

"You know, if you're hungry, that means you're losing weight."

I know that voice. I raise my head to find Cal crouched in front of me.

This can't be right . . . he's dead, I think. But not even Sylvia could confirm it. *Oh, gods, he's back to work for the Chimera.*

"You should know better. You have to look good for the cameras."

I cannot change, but lift my lip in a snarl anyhow. Words seem to have eluded me anyway, and this is the only way I can make myself understood.

Cal rises to stand above me in my filthy cell, smiling his familiar winning grin that charmed even the most hard-nosed cynics. With his glossy hair and expensive bomber jacket, he could not look more out of place. He takes my elbow and hoists me up. "You know I was right. You couldn't have sold any records if you couldn't fit into those stage clothes. You never looked as good as those girls in the peeler joint, but you were okay as a sideman. But only that."

I have never been what the tabloids would call pretty, but I am worn out from being reminded of this every day. Why is he talking about my career as if nothing cataclysmic has gone down? *Where am I?*

"You were getting too big for your britches, literally," he chides me. "Food is pain, don't you remember? *Food is pain!*"

He turns and lifts the lid of a covered dish. A sumptuous meal appears before me: half of a spit-roasted chicken, red beans and rice, and cornbread. I defy Cal's admonishments and snatch a mouthful of chicken, which is inhumanely hot and sears me to the skull. Pain and starvation engage in battle within. Eyes streaming, I let my jaw flop open to release the steam and the skin on the roof of my mouth peels away in one piece.

Cal laughs. "You will never learn, will you? No. Because you're nothing but a stupid little bitch."

Digging into his pocket, he produces a small cassette recorder and pushes a button. There's a phone ringing somewhere in the tiny machine. The click of an answering machine takes over, and the fiberoptic crackle of my parents singing happy birthday to me resonates in the cell. *My parents!* My throat tightens and I crawl toward the sound, a near infantile instinct.

Cal's body stretches and uncoils, and an enormous serpent now flexes before me. I have never seen him in full snake form before: a thickly muscled rope extending thirty feet, graceless head blunt and unsightly. The meaty serpentine tail whips out, grabbing me so hard around my waist that my diaphragm forces my breath out in a vocal grunt. My parents continue their cheery message, oblivious to my creaking ribs.

Dragging me back to face him, the snake says, "So touching. Like you deserved some sort of special treatment, a reward for *aging.* Your parents took such pity on you. That's only because they have no clue as to what you really are. Someday I am going to call them up and set them straight. I'm the only one who knows what's best for you, and they know it too. Who are they going to believe? A failed sideman, or a successful businessman?"

His tail pushes the button again, and I hear the sound of a mic check in the darkness. Cal sets me down hard onto my feet. "You have a show to put on for the Chimera in a few weeks. And you'd better not fuck up in front of her. Last time I saw you perform you made seven mistakes. *Seven.* There's no excuse for a pro to be doing that . . ."

"I was hungry," I mumble my protest. "I couldn't concentrate. I was lightheaded . . ."

The tail lashes me across the face. "Missing a meal won't kill you, trust me! And you shouldn't have even looked at the monitor man once your levels were set. If you don't want to be treated like a whore, you'd better stop acting like one."

Somewhere, wolves are singing. The firelit cave forms around me once again. *They cannot take away the wolf within! Fight, my child, fight!*

I am too weak to attack him, but I use my body weight and gravity to fall at him, aiming for his neck on my way down. He hisses, slithers out of my cell, and another man suddenly stands in his place. I snarl at the new intruder.

"*Mon Dieu!* Birch, it's me! Lapin! That snake man played on your hallucinations!"

I am horrified. "Lapin, oh gods, I am so sorry!" I sink to my knees and he crouches next to me, stroking my shoulders and reassuring me that I haven't hurt him. The horror of reality sets in again, the reality that Cal is still alive and that I am dying.

I would cry, but I have no tears to spare. A howl tears from my throat, and Lapin lets go of me at the sound of fast approaching feet. We cannot be seen in alliance with each other, we have to appear hostile or at least uncomfortable in each other's presences.

A flashlight cleaves the air, slashing across my face. Keys jangle, and Ramiel is yanking me to my feet so hard, I worry that my arm is going to pop out of its socket. He spits in my face and says, "Feeling sorry for yourself? We can't have any crying here."

A hard cuff across my face, my ear ringing from the blow. He drops me to the ground, kicks me in the ribs, and says, "Consider yourself lucky. Next time you might end up on the pile. The Chimera has no use for a whiny little victim."

His words mirror Naj's so long ago. I bite back a groan until his footsteps have faded. Lapin and I feel for broken ribs, but everything seems intact.

After that, I train myself how to cry without getting caught. I blink at the ceiling, and if I am hydrated enough for tears, they slide backward and down my throat. I control my breathing through my nose, slow and steady. I let my vocal cords go limp. Only my belly goes crazy in silent jerks and spasms, voiceless screaming for a humanity that will never return.

◆ ◆ ◆

I have completely lost my sense of time. Lack of light prevents me from tracking the passage of days, and now, due to the severe living conditions, my menses have stopped. Stripped of my lupine traits, I can't even sense the moon anymore.

It appears that every prisoner serves a purpose to the Chimera's agenda. At some point or another, everyone is led out, presumably brought before her, and returned to his or her cell smelling of food, sedatives, and despair—obvious even to my human senses.

I can pick up a few familiar scents of prisoners here. Wally the werekoala and Darren the thylacine-turned-human from the Shifter's Ball are in separate cells, but their energy patterns flicker into my awareness as I am led past. And somewhere in a cell removed from the rest of us is Aydan.

On some sort of regular rotation, I am taken to the Chimera's medical research laboratory. Even if I still had my lupine senses, the astringent tang of alcohol would be enough to confuse my nose. The only female angel I have seen thus far rules this domain. Slight of build, she is completely anonymous in a nurse's uniform, surgical mask, cap, and goggles, only wearing a nametag that reads ARIEL for identification. Each time, she draws my blood, jabbing the needle so hard into my arm, it gives me flashbacks to La Balcone. Sometimes Ariel rips my hairs from my scalp, and sometimes she chops off a strand close to my head. When my hands find their way to my head, my locks feel jagged and irregular, further degrading my appearance.

I still don't understand what the point of this is. Lapin thinks that she is trying to get a poison resistant strain of DNA. But mainly, this seems to only accomplish weakening my body and spirit.

Even more maddening is that I am marched past Chimera's exercise room en route to the lab. The wall to her fitness haven is made of glass, and I am helpless to get a glimpse of her as she runs the track that encircles the perimeter, spars Jiu-Jitsu with a captive trainer, or shoots arrows at a wolf-shaped target. In the center of the room are also weights, gymnastic bars, and machines. A simulated palisade for climbing spans the entire far wall. There is a massive fish tank for swimming rather than a pool, and it's clear that she expects to be admired as she furthers the glory of her body.

On one trip, she is swimming in her giant tank in the form of an icthyocentaur—a centaur with a dolphin's tail, when Azrael climbs up the side and dives in to join her, transforming as soon as he is submerged. And now I know why can does not change forms with the other angels. His shifter animal is a shark. They glide in conspiratorial patterns of infinity around each other, sharing secrets.

After one particularly excruciating lab procedure with Ariel, I am led back to my room and gladdened to see Petit Puce standing before us once the guards retreat. He reports that the Chimera's prisoners include scientists, financial experts, political strategists, and even psychics, for her ambitions include mind control over others. There are personal trainers for her incessant exercise and endorphin fixes. Drug lords and spin-doctors are brought into the fray as well to provide rewards and hyperbole among the increasing network.

The musicians are held to serve multiple purposes. We have some sort of energetic power that she wants, and Puce says that she is going to force us to play Stygian Mode structures to weaken the other captives. She also intends to put together a massive musical spectacle in celebration of her eventual victory and coronation.

All are shifters, and all are doomed. Prisoners are all given sunlight, food, and promises of protection so that we will come to crave visits with this mad dictator. The shifters who end up serving no purpose are eventually dispatched. The rest of us just try to survive.

I hate my own scent. Filthy and thick with fear, I wish I could scrub myself into oblivion.

One man finally caves—or does he resist where the rest of us have caved? In any case, he is found dead in his cell, his mind having overcome matter in his hunger strike. The angels make a public display for us of throwing his body in an undignified heap onto a wheelbarrow, before bearing him off to his afterlife on the trash heap. *No*, I try to remind myself. *The hermit crab is free at last, only his shell remains.*

My smartass spirit—the very thing that once got me kicked out of class and in trouble on gigs—is the only thing keeping my mind whole. I lack the ability to conform, even when my life depends on it.

Lapin and I keep ourselves sane by clinging to ordinary things. We swap anecdotes of home in an effort to remember our true selves. We also pass the time with jokes, which is a good mental exercise for me. I analyze them to see how many of them could work translated into English. My cellmate's laughter brings to mind a falling star: dazzlingly bright, but so fleeting that there is never enough time to make a wish.

He tells me one that I'd already heard years ago, just not in

French. "There was a man who wanted to visit Beethoven's grave," he begins. "When he gets there, he hears some very strange music emitting from it. So he fetches the caretaker, who tells him that it is Beethoven's Fifth playing backward. The man asks why it is playing backward, and the caretaker tells him that Beethoven is *decomposing!*" It's grim joke, but I smile anyway, more at Lapin's enthusiasm.

I wonder what Beethoven played in reverse would really sound like, and a wild idea slinks into my mind. "Lapin, have you ever heard of DNA Music? I saw something in a documentary when I was a kid about DNA codes used as melodies."

He chuckles. "What biochemist has not heard of it? It's also called Protein Music or Genetic Music. I believe it was pioneered by Joel Sternheimer. There are several ways to convert protein sequences—such as genes—into musical notes. There are computer conversions that enable you to feed in the DNA sequences and come up with music." He frowns. "Without a computer there is still a way to do it. The codons can be converted into hertz frequencies. It can be done with a paper chart, although it's tedious. But my little friend here can be working on it while I am slaving over the Chimera's helixes."

"Petit Puce, can you find a way to retrieve some of the DNA records? Maybe hide on Lapin to get in the office and wait. Go back into human form after hours, slide the papers under the door, go back into flea and get yourself out of there . . . "

"I get the idea. What do you propose to do?"

"If I can find a way to musically link my energies with those codes, I can sing them backwards and unbind them."

◆ ◆ ◆

Mental journal entry, date unknown: Hope springs eternal even when reality gives me the finger. I just wish the two would slug it out while I get some rest, and get back to me with a verdict.

It is impossible to tell the passage of time, but what feels like a span of two days later marks my first attempt at wave genetics. My cellmates talk me through a brief overview, as if I can possibly understand biochemistry in a short tutorial. Still, I hang onto every word. They tell me about the four nucleobases: adenine, guanine, cytosine, and thymine. To me it is arcane and unfathomable. Looking at the diagrams drawn in the dirt, I try to think of them as scales with pentagonal and hexagonal variations. *More like Indian ragas*, I think, but unlike Indian ragas, I don't have two years to learn each one. After scratching the surface of the subject, they assure me that my main task is to just learn the music backward and put my intention into the unbinding. Which is all I have the energy for, anyway.

Figuring out the hertz frequencies is the hardest even with a chart hidden on a piece of paper. I assiduously carry out the task to the highest accuracy possible, and I don't dare sing the notes forward. Keeping my voice nearly inaudible, I croon the wild harmonic and try to think of a chord structure on my mind that will make the note sequence make sense to me.

I may not be able to shift bodies. But I can emit vibrations. Everything is vibration: instinct, emotion, and intention. I defend myself against the Chimera's anger that is jamming my circuits.

I recall in the back of my mind a word: *Waheguru*. It was taught to me by someone . . . Raúl, I think his name was. I hum it softly, and feel energy creep up my spine, water seeking absorbency. I cannot grow a tail, but the energy extends out from my root chakra, as if my tail still existed. Something is overcoming the drug, or perhaps I am hallucinating from lack of sleep.

I don't know if I have accomplished much, and I am drained from the effort. Collapsing onto my pile of blankets, I manage to get a few winks of hard sleep before the first airhorn blast.

◆ ◆ ◆

I am brought back before the Chimera four cornmeal feedings later. Her laugher echoes through the entire chamber like a disco ball.

I look around but see no one. She could be anywhere . . . unless she is omniscient.

"Up here, you stupid bitch!" I raise my head to see a giant harpy with a lyrebird's tail perched in the ornate beams. I immediately hate myself for responding to the word.

Her face is magnificent, her human arms rippling with muscle. Each day, the aspects of strong creatures come together to build the perfect beast. And yet something else nags at the back of my mind. *What is beauty?* A different countenance snaps into my memory: a smiling dark-skinned Creole woman with cornrow braids in a white wedding gown, a woman with a beautiful and noble heart. I think she might take on the form of a snake. *Who is she?* My thoughts are muzzy, but I wish she were by my side.

A shriek from the Chimera brings me back to the present. "So . . . *MacKinlay!* It appears that you have a forebear I might have known, hmmm?"

"I don't know," is my automatic response.

She flutters down from above to meet my eyes, hers blazing the color of glowing iron in a forge. *"Liar!"* she screeches. "You had a grandmother who decided not to pass along my legacy. *I* was the one who discovered her talent. I suppose she didn't tell you that, did she?"

I shake my head, assuming that this is a lie. The woman formerly known as Idona Brume would have never lifted a finger of her hand for anyone else, unless there was something in it for her. Still, the cherished memories of my grandma begin to blur.

"She would have been *nothing* without me. You owe your very existence to me, you know. Even as Dottie MacKinlay got all this praise—oh, let me tell you, she just ate it all up, she really believed they liked her—it was I who had the real genius. Like you, your grand-bitch could only change to one animal counterpart. Mediocrity seems to be a genetic trait! She could never have aspired to assume the forms of beasts that were once only the stuff of legends and nightmares."

Shifting headfirst and then gradually down her sleek body, she goes into what appears to be a manticore form: a human face, lion's body, and scorpion's tail. It is as effortless for her as a metaphysical costume change, a velvet glove slipping across a core of raw energy. Just as the long tail feathers begin to morph into the expected stinging appendage, something goes wrong.

The end piece struggles like a sad little withered sprig reaching feebly for emergence. It finally collapses into a flaccid tendril and retracts into her spine.

I try to still my thoughts. *The DNA music . . . it's working.*

The Chimera hisses. "I am not finished with you, bitch. You are no paragon yourself." Sitting on her haunches, she abandons ceremony and becomes a giant insect. She snaps open prehistoric-sized wings, and becomes something crossed between Mothra and a siren.

The lights dim, and projected onto each wing is some sort of motion picture. I don't know where this video footage comes from. It can't have possibly been filmed, as I have only seen these events before in my mind. They could only have been experienced trough my own perspective, yet here they are for all the world to see.

It's like a video montage of my every mistake and failure. And the soundtrack playing from somewhere is unmistakably The Stygian Mode. Any remaining shred of self-worth drains from me as the images bore into my skull and the music cajoles me with thoughts of death, for I am beyond worthless.

I jeopardized the pack with my carelessness. I allowed Yohan to use me. I failed my audition for the prime time show.

Hecklers who hated me over the years suddenly line up in my projected memory like a firing squad. *You suck, you should be shot, spread your legs, show your tits, you whore* . . . The memory of their every hurtful word suddenly plays back like a long forgotten answering machine tape resurrected by obsolete technology. I would deflect their attacks with humor and theatrics, then cry all the way home.

Drowning in a sea of failed relationships, I am the butt of every joke. My old lovers leer as they walk off with my hard-earned money. *I am never good enough.*

Time continues to move backward. Running through the woods, slashing wildly in my rage . . . *I hurt living things.* I get smaller and weaker with youth as I bomb my first recital. I can't do math. I can't pay attention in school, and begin failing to the point that I am tested for brain damage. The other kids in school hate me. *You're a loser, a nobody,* they tell me. *You don't deserve to even be alive.* I feel the punches to my head, my feet being kicked out from under me, the slaps across the face ringing in my ears. In this case boys have no qualms about hitting a girl, since I am not considered to be female. Only a dog, as I am told over and over again.

Now I am even smaller. There are things that I was supposed to love, and I let them break. I don't want to be a precious ballerina—I want to be a wild animal, and I disappoint the grownups. I accidentally tear a paper lamb, and there will be no Christmas cookies for me now. I've wet my diaper. I am being born, and I am hurting my mother . . . I am making her bleed.

I am a mistake.

There is nothing but an electrical buzz in my ears. *Buzz* . . . it's a funny word, but it carries some meaning. It resonates with something that connects, a friendly vibe. *Friends. My friends call me Buzz.*

I fight the mental assault, pulling myself back to the present by humming a soft "om." It occurs to me how an *ohm* is a unit of resistance, and now I resist the mind games. My cognitive mind is back, and I remember to scream out loud in hopes of fooling the Chimera. Any shapeshifting opossum, hognose snake, or ptarmigan would be proud of my theatrics.

The visual montage stops and the lights go back on. And then the Chimera is crouched on the floor next to me, presenting me with food. It reminds me of the comfort food I had while visiting family in Scotland: roast lamb, potatoes, and steamed cubed carrots and turnips—with just the right amount of pepper. This time my desperation is real, and I eat ravenously on the floor, disregarding the silverware provided me.

She croons. "I asked the angels to give you concession. They only do so because I tell them to. You can't trust anyone, certainly not your cell mates. Only I can keep you safe. Do you understand?"

This is a cult, I remind myself, *or trying to be. Just go along with it.* I nod, keeping my eyes on the now-empty plate on the floor. Even playing along, it's hard not to really believe it all.

"You are dismissed. Remember that I am ever merciful to you, my little bitch."

As I am led back to my cell in a daze, doubtlessly smelling of food and fear, I completely understand Lapin's plight now.

CHAPTER

13

SPLICING BLOCK

I have whittled down to the Chimera's two basic DNA codes. I'm as ready as I'll ever be to battle this demon, and hope that the other prisoners will lend their energies, even if they don't know what I'm about to do.

No one speaks anyone's language. There's no common lexicography, anyway. But I know one thing: Everyone can respond to music.

I am almost self-conscious that all the songs I hope everyone knows are in English, which seems to have overrun the pop culture world like locusts. But there are worse things than coming across as an insular American at this moment.

I'm not going for a fresh repertoire here. I'm going with the tried and true. I won't start loudly—everyone is sleep deprived. But if I start with an inaudible hum, I can invite people to my frequency.

I start with "Amazing Grace." I am so sick of that song, I could cry, but hearing the corridor begin to stir and come to life as others join in miraculously give it new meaning.

"Let It Be" is what finally reins everyone's attention in. When traveling with Slackjaw, there were many Japanese musicians who spoke little or no English, but everyone knew Beatles songs. And it appears that everyone, shifters from all four corners of the earth, can connect now on this classic song.

My message is clear: I want them to sing with me. And they do, tremulously and timorously at first. Something begins to flow around the prison and connect us all. We are like effects linked together on one electrical current. I feel more than hear them join me, sympathetic strings vibrating, concentric circles rippling in water, a chain reaction growing.

I feel something, as if my wolf senses are returning, if only faintly. Somehow there are other shifters running free just outside, oblivious to the Chimera's stronghold and the horrors within. If our signal strengthens, we can send a wave of instinct, of gut feeling.

Help us.

This time I sing the new melody; a simple form of the Chimera's kelpie code in reverse. Then I switch to her lycan code and alternate back and forth in a call and response antiphon. I feel an unbinding as my voice gets stronger. As others join in, I can feel the fortress begin to rumble.

Some animal energies begin to surface. A woman down the hall calls out in an indiscernible tongue, then resumes the song. I can feel her swan energy in her raised voice, even as she is dying.

I reach out to the Chimera's angels, even the one who punched me so long ago, and unbind their addictions. Most of them had drugs as their vices, but a few clung to sex and food. One was simply mislead and afraid to break away . . . *Troy*.

I splice the spell binding us all as easily as wielding a razor blade. I go even deeper and reach for the subtle microtones of the music. Mental chains begin to slip away.

The gate swings open. Troy reaches his hand to me but does not meet my eyes. "You, Birch! The Chimera wants to see you at once!" I don't think he realizes he's called me by name.

He does not see Petit Puce suddenly standing behind him in human form. I desperately want to believe that he pretends not to notice my tiny ally stealing the keys from his back pocket. As we hurry down the tunnel, he does not hear the clank of metal on metal as Petit Puce unlocks the first cell.

◆ ◆ ◆

The queen is not amused. She takes the form of a red-eyed hawk, save her human face. Perched in the rafters, she spreads her wings, and feathers begin to drop off.

"What is this treachery you are sowing, little worm? It has to be you, with your musical witchcraft! Metatron, kill her!"

Troy glances at her with no comprehension in his eyes. She grabs him by the face and turns his head, forcing him to look at her, hissing, "I know you didn't *hear* me, so read my lips. I have endowed you with a blade. Now prove to me that you know how to use it."

He takes a step toward me, extends his knife arm, and opens his hand in defiance. I don't doubt that even he can hear the clatter of his blade onto the floor. "No," he simply states.

"As you wish." She glides off her perch, stoops and strikes. Nabbing the knife, she slits his throat as calmly as if peeling an apple. I have seen enough death already, but the bright red geyser spewing from the arterial wound is too much for me to bear. He falls to the floor like a feather unable to remain aloft by itself. His eyes stare sightlessly at the oculus, hopefully reading some divine poetry of mercy from above.

She ignores the blood that has just sprayed her from face to talons. "Fine then. Like teeth in a shark's mouth, I always have another one ready to take its place. Ariel!"

The new second in command angel called Ariel turns out to be the lab technician who drew my blood and tore out my hair. Still wearing her white coat, she peels off her mask and goggles, slithering to the leader's side with liquid grace. I am so taken aback by the presence of my tormentor that it takes me a moment to realize that Ariel is Naj Copperhead. As she locks gazes with me, her blue eyes are smug, as if she's beaten me in a card game.

"Ariel, kill this piece of shit." The Chimera tries to extend human arms from her hawk form, but something goes wrong. The stumps of flesh shrink back into her core, like time-lapsed footage of a new plant in reverse.

I hum one of the DNA melodies, unbinding the Chimera's form. This time, her arms extend, but her wings fall off. She can no longer be a six-limbed creature without being an insect.

Another wave of vibrations plays my body like a string. My wolf self begins to reintegrate. I feel the energies of prisoners escaping below, of newcomers rushing to join us.

"Boss, all you have to do is eat her!" cajoles Naj. The insane polyshifter suddenly swells to become a dragon. She tries to sprout wings, but her fire vanishes. She roars in outrage, then finally sacrifices the extra limbs for the flames. They are weak, but still hot enough to really hurt, and my nose is scorched with the stench of burning hair—most likely my own.

I search my jacket for any sort of weapon and feel something in my pocket: the tiny lead soldier. So simple. *Bellerophon!*

I fight fire with fire. I *am* fire, and I am in my element.

Her maw widens, ready to consume me whole, and in that hungry mouth I see a ceaseless craving for domination and the pain of others. A flashback shakes me: the little dead mockingbird that was Alma, who had never hurt a soul. The cries of the prisoners, the false promises to the lackeys she called angels, the sightless eyes of Troy, the terror of each and every shifter just trying to survive . . . and Rowan. *My* Rowan. I'm starving, bleeding, dirty, stinking, and one angry werewolf. A voice snarls, "Why don't you take on *this* shape, you monstrous bitch?" It only registers after I hear it that the words are my own.

With all the fury of my being I fling the lead toy down her throat, sending my little soldier on a kamikaze mission. There is sizzling sound like meat on a grill amplified a hundred times, and a volcanic sulfur stench. Weakened by the unbinding, the lead poisoning hits her almost instantaneously.

The Chimera wraps her short, scaly limbs around her belly. She writhes and screeches, and the various forms of her captive DNA flicker to the surface as they are freed. I watch the specters of horses, raptors, peacocks, felines, spiders, and dozens of other creatures rise from her shrinking body and disappear into the air. At last she simply dissipates . . . *into a mist.* Nothing remains but a small hissing puddle of molten lead.

My soldier died an honorable death. In the midst of this turmoil, I feel a pang of animism for the poor little guy.

Naj beams at me. "See, Buzz? I got her to open her gob. I was on your side the whole time!"

"I'm serious, *Ariel*. Shut. The fuck. Up."

And she does, because just then all hell breaks loose.

CHAPTER
14

SIGNAL FLOW

Now that the queen is dead, the spell is broken, and the shifters regain their abilities. Stripped of its warding, the compound has collapsed like a kicked anthill, a colony of people, beasts, and different stages in between—all running amok. Newly freed captives regain their abilities to shift, and press forward in a wall of talons, hooves, and claws. Guards, prisoners, and rescuers fight hand to hand and in clusters. In their animal forms, I can't tell who is on whose side, although the more emaciated and beaten creatures seem to be the ones in need of rescue. It's like the Shifter's Ball in reverse. Weak and disoriented, I abandon the idea of joining in and look for any exit I can find. The main entrance to the throne room is blocked. *Think, think, think, why can't I think?*

My fangs come out even before I have hackles to raise. I switch to a lupine body so fast my clothes tear from me as I make my escape, too terrified to feel the familiar relief of my old wolf form back. My new limbs tremble from the exertion and malnourishment . . . I stagger in a dizzy headrush.

And Azrael comes charging at me through the fray, dead-eyed and determined. Something is wrapped around his wrist and trailing behind him. It's some sort of cast net—I recognize it from my childhood days of fishing in the bayous. This man who first caught me is either going to try to kill or reclaim me, and I don't intend to let him do either.

Fast approaching footsteps drive me in the opposite direction as I weave my way through the twisting, bloody clumps of combatants. The vibrations on the marble floor get stronger, and Azrael's salty scent pushes me into overdrive. I find a low side door that has been blown ajar. There's no telling if it's a garbage chute or a secret passage, but I manage to wriggle through it, bruising my unpadded ribs in my panic. Fresh air lies beyond, and that's all that matters. There is the shock of intense cold, and the first sunlight I have seen in forever stabs at my eyes. Rolling and tumbling, I thrash and skid until I find footing in snow. I inhale a scent map into my mind and stumble away from the destruction. Since my abduction in Mississippi, I have no idea how far I was transported, but the dry winter weather tells me that we are not in the Deep South. The leaning shed through which I first entered squats in the distance, so I stagger toward it, hoping to retrace my steps to civilization.

Bursting from another direction, Azrael cuts me off at the path and throws the net. It drops in a perfect circle around me, tightens around my body as easily as a snake, and snatches me off my feet. I thrash my legs to find an opening between the weights, which have become attached to each other. *Dammit, he's got magnetized weights. He uses this for more than just fishing,* my thoughts scream. My eyes roll back hard enough to see my captor twist some sort of clamp, and the grid-like fibers constrict me harder, as if trying to wring me out like a wet mop. I gasp though my nose in desperation, filling my lungs as much as my ribs will let them expand. Even a well-fed lion is no match for a net, and my teeth are useless while I am bound so tightly that I can't even open my jaws.

The assertive thud of heavy boots on the frozen ground gets louder as he approaches, and in an instant his face is next to mine, separated only by the nylon grid that binds my muzzle. His beady eyes are triumphant. "This little contraption makes it easy for me to snack on dolphins whenever I want to swim in the deep and enjoy the best of both forms," he gloats. "But you . . . you will be much more useful that a temporary snack!" And then only his boots are in view again. With a vicious tug, my woven pod and I begin to move across the icy ground, through the shed's door, and then back into the compound as we slide along the marble. The sudden wall of battle sounds hurts my ears: shrieks, roars, and terrified human screams. The air is thick with scent of blood, fear, sweat, and offal—acrid and metallic. Back into the war zone, back toward the passage that leads to the prisons. "It's every man for himself," he snarls down at me. "All the other angels are taking what they can from this place, but I know where some of the Chimera's assets lie, and believe me, it's a better location than this stinking shit-hole!"

He drops his voice to silky condescension. "You're working for me now. You have two choices. You can cooperate and enjoy a fulfilling life recruiting new shifters from a swanky Indonesian resort. Or else you can struggle, and I will have your pack killed.

I strongly suggest that you choose the former, for I can assure you that I did my research while I was in New Orleans! If you do work with me, you will be famous, you know. My new army of shifters will submit to the woman who took down the Chimera."

A screech from the rafters right above us makes Azrael pause in his tracks. A vaguely familiar voice shouts in a massive crescendo, "Drop beeeeeeaaaaaarrrr . . .!" The impact of a large koala suddenly upon me knocks the breath out of my lungs, but I recognize Wally's scent and within moments the net begins to loosen as the werekoala severs the fibers with his sharp claws. I gasp lungfuls of air, my jaws free and my ribs no longer constricted, and gather up some fresh strength.

Wriggling through the widening hole, I can turn my head just in time to see Wally suddenly launch himself onto Azrael's face. One furry fist slams itself into the man's mouth, then the claws begin shredding at the thick jaw. Azrael staggers backward, but his furry cannonball has only a limited time before the shark man delivers a vicious blow with his right arm. Wally is hurled from his perch with such force he sails a good twenty feet before hitting a wall.

Azrael slowly turns to face me again, bloody and hyper-focused, and pulls a slow rictus. One front tooth is missing from Wally's punch, and to my horror, another neatly slides into place. His human mouth is unfit for biting, but he draws a pistol. Unable to change into his shark form on dry land, he is nonetheless a dangerous foe, especially to a half-starved werewolf. Silver or otherwise, I am invincible to no bullet if it hits me in the wrong place.

My legs won't support me. Exhaustion brings about delirium, for it feels as if my whole pack is near me again. Their energies resonate in my bones, the sounds of their arrival thrum at the base of my skull. I raise my head, and the apparition of Rowan in wolf form looks so real, I can even smell him. Only I have never seen him so angry or ferocious.

He knocks me down and pins me to the floor, and a split second the gun goes off, the bullet whining right above my head. Then it hits me that this is no hallucination. *My mate! My pack!*

And Rowan is circling Azrael now, while Teddy and Sylvia appear at my side. Whimpering, they nose me to my feet. I glace backward to look for Raúl, who is fighting three minions at once.

Another wolf staggers into view, and her scent floods my memory. *Aydan.* Her eyes are sunken, her hip bones jut out at a painful looking angle, ribs protruding through her patchy black coat. A ragged shell of her former glory, there is still a terrible beauty in her resilience. She has eyes only for Azrael right now, and the gentle musician reveals herself to be the powerful lycan that she really is. Her rage smells acrid, her energy is smoldering. Nose bunched backward to reveal wicked fangs, she emits a guttural snarl of deadly intentions. And then she speaks as clearly as a human.

"You killed my brother, you might kill me now, but you will never get away without a fight!" Her jet-black hackles run down her back like spines. Wally begins a broken crawl back toward the so-called angel of death, dragging one hind leg. Eyes glowing red, his slitted pupils are trained on the back of Azrael's neck.

Before Rowan can dive in to assist, something slithers into view. I have no choice but to tune out the frenzied sounds of combat coming from the cluster that is Wally, Aydan, and Azrael and heed this new threat approaching us. Cal appears walking upright, but his slippery movements alert me that he is about to change.

Like water blasting from a hose, he goes serpentine so quickly that neither my mate nor I have time to react. He winds himself around Rowan's legs, tripping him and yanking him off of his feet. Rowan pins his ears, thrashes his legs, and flips himself back onto his feet. Dancing around the twisting coils, he punches his head out and strikes with his fangs more quickly than I knew was possible for a wolf to move. His teeth get a secure death grip on Cal's tail, and my tormentor's skin merely slides away, leaving fresh skin that is lacerated but nonetheless free.

Cal cranes his neck this way and that, finally pinning me with his gaze. His smile never reaches his eyes as he addresses me, "You see, you're about to find out what happens when you don't do as you're told, you stupid little bitch. Biting back has its consequences!"

And as four limbs sprout from Calvin's sides, a new horror grips me. I recall Teddy telling me that werewolves are the only shape-shifters that can transmit their abilities through a bite, and how I'd fought back and bitten Cal so long ago. Now as the new wolf stands over the weakened Rowan, I drag myself over to defend my mate in spite of my exhausted state. Self-preservation is not an option, not even when Rowan gives me a warning growl to stay back. Even still, I am too weak to keep up with the action unfolding before me.

Cal launches himself at Rowan so hard, I feel the impact. I don't understand why Rowan isn't fighting back. "I don't even need to be in my primary form to take you down. I will be known as the wolf that defeated one of the most powerful musical Alphas."

Rowan continues to simply sidestep Cal's attacks. The naga-werewolf polyshifter becomes increasingly frustrated, and frustration begins to show in his attacks. His strikes begin to miss, for he is clearly not accustomed to his secondary wolf body.

But Cal is showing off. In lycan form he lacks the natural wolf instincts, and is still no match for Rowan. Cal raises his head as if to flare a hood like a cobra, and Rowan chooses that perfect moment to fight back. Lupine to the core, the Alpha strikes Cal's jugular faster than any snake. The spray of blood drenches us both, and something primal sings in my veins.

The lesser wolf gives a high, hissing yelp, twisting his body in a desperate attempt to shift again. But it's too late, and his legs convulse before the death rattle hisses out of his lungs like a guttering steam engine. And the man who tormented me for so many years slumps to the ground in a lump of dead meat and fur. His eyes are frozen wide open in a serpentine stare of shock. I want to tear Cal's body to shreds, but I can't afford to be distracted.

If I couldn't be the one to kill him, I'm glad it was Rowan. And I sense that Rowan was glad to be the one to kill him too. My mate sidles up to be, gives me a quick nuzzle, then bolts into the melee to defend other innocents. I try to follow, take a few shaky steps, and fall to my haunches. All I can do is watch and hope that I can lend whatever remains of my energy.

Surveying the room with a cursory glance, recognition of a dozen or so prisoners fighting for their lives gives me another surge of determination. Sweet, friendly Teddy has his jaws locked around the throat of the madman Ramiel, who draws in final gasps that still sound like maniacal laughter in his spotted hyena form. A snarling Sylvia is protecting Lapin and Petit Puce, who are have remained in their less vulnerable human forms, but are still no match for the large gray lizard circling them. I wonder if she gravitated toward them because they probably smell like me. My best friend darts and snaps, always eluding the reptile's whip-like attacks. She gets a few decent bites into the creature's back before it lashes its tail at her again.

I lose track of the score as Naj appears before me in human form, hissing in my face. Her blue eyes are fever-bright, but her mouth is stretched into a rictus, fangs exposed. Like a switch being flipped, she suddenly brightens as another person joins us: Lydia King. Naj begins, "Lydia! Thank the gods you're here! With Cal gone, I was afraid I'd be the only naga . . ."

Lydia's eyes are ruthless as she replies, "I've wanted to do this since our very first gig together, bitch!" She whips out a pistol, and shoots Naj in the temple, the report deafening me for one awful moment. The assault on my sensitive ears sends me reeling so hard that I almost miss the horror of having to witness the spray of blood and brains. It doesn't even register in my mind until Naj falls to the floor like a cold coil of meat, her eyes bugged in two directions, even in death unsure whose side to be on.

The hall is clearing. All that remain are the dead. The scent of so much blood makes me gag, even for a predator, for it is tainted with fear, desperation, and cruelty. Azrael lies in the center of the room, disemboweled. Cal's serpent body still lies on the floor like a length of giant intestine. Scores more of unidentified slain litter the room. There is no telling where the survivors have gone. Perhaps they have been recaptured, although I would like to think that they somehow escaped. Among the dead, there are no signs of Aydan, Lapin, or Petit Puce, only the residual scent of their adrenaline.

Furry bodies press all around me with familiar yips and whines, and my pack encircles me in the closest thing possible to a group hug. A low moan tears from my throat. I had lost hope that I'd ever see them again. Reunited at long last, I wonder how I could ever carry on without my closest companions.

And then I hear is a familiar voice sobbing, "Wally . . . Wally, stay with me, mate!" Darren has taken on his human form, his lower back still striped, but the outline of his body blurry in his grief. His long hair falls over his face as cradles the motionless koala to his chest. Wally stirs to mumble, ". . . dog's breakfast, mate . . ." before slumping at an odd angle. We all feel his energy pass.

Darren cannot seem to hold his human veneer any longer and retracts back into his true form, a formidable six foot long carnivore that cannot be compared to anything I have ever known, like a creature that never quite finished evolving to fit the modern era. Something wild and unfathomable lies behind his dark, expressionless eyes. His distinct scent is thick with animal grief. He emits a few barking coughs, then drops his jaw and lets forth a wheezing cry, undulating in his devastation. His stripes give him the appearance of still being behind bars.

I try to move in to comfort Darren, even as Raúl urges me with a growl to stay back. But he doesn't know that I too must honor the brave shape-shifting koala saved my life, and possibly took his mortal injury in freeing me. As I limp over to sit beside the suffering thylacine, his rounded ears swivel, then press against his skull. At first he hisses at me, but then picking up on my scent, he slumps in acceptance and we rest our muzzles together. His snout is smooth and boney . . . definitely not canine, but somehow familiar. We share several long breaths, wordless exchanges of comfort, as only two people who have suffered the same hell can.

Bipedal footsteps behind me signal that my time is up. Everyone has gone back to soprano form except Rowan, who remains hyper-vigilant and dangerous. "Come on, Little One," says Raúl at last in the softest voice I have ever heard him use. "You did well to bury your cell phone, for it was the only way that the SIN agents were able to locate this place. We were looking straight at the compound for days and unable to see it until you killed the Chimera and broke her warding. But time is running out. We don't have a choice, we have to get out of here now. You there . . ." he addresses Darren, but with a hiss the thylacine refuses any help and resumes his grieving.

The rest of the pack is strong enough to move on, but I am too weak to walk. Raúl hoists me over his shoulder like a sack of potatoes, and we make out way toward the waiting van and freedom. I take one last look at the bereaved Darren, sitting on his haunches all alone among the dead, and I suddenly can't stop howling. Raúl pets me soothingly, but his pace remains firm. Darren's cries ring in my ears long after we make our way through the main portal and into a blast of cold air.

The starry night sky is surreal. I have no idea how long the battle must have gone on, or even how long since it's been since I last saw stars. The rhythm of Raúl's feet crunching in the snow and the rocking of his body begin to calm me down and I go deadweight in his arms.

Carried backward away from the compound, a glimpse of the building's true form in the distance—with the Chimera no longer alive to ward it—creeps into view. It's not the palatial exterior I'd have expected. It's an abandoned-looking gray cement block building obfuscated by vegetation. Ivy and kudzu form a shaggy network around the exterior, giving the fortress the appearance of a harmless butte.

Along the trail we find a partially frozen stream. With only minutes to spare we wash the worst of the blood off of ourselves. Everyone goes bass in order to better avoid hypothermia. Then it's back to three people and two wolves, and then Raúl's van rises like a specter by the old dirt road. Heavy doors slide open, and from all sides loving arms wrap me in thick blankets.

I shiver uncontrollably. They place me in the back of the van, with Rowan curled protectively around me. Raúl's van smells so familiar, so much like New Orleans and pack and musical equipment, I almost can't stand it. Raw emotion shoots through me—relief, terror, grief, solace, and confusion.

But there's no time for anyone to comfort me. The urgency to get the hell away from here is still far too pressing.

In a wash of tingling someone wards the van, for a vehicle containing three naked humans and two wolves would most likely pique the interest of any state trooper.

Once the van begins moving, I begin to panic, triggered by the memories of my abduction. Rowan wraps his body around me more tightly, shudders, and in one breath slides into his soprano human shape. At long last I surrender to my own form as a woman, allowing him to spoon against me like the perfect puzzle piece. He wraps his arms around me, strokes my hair, and murmurs comforting words. His scent flooding my senses is the best drug ever. He kisses the top of my head—the way he first did after I killed Gabriel, I realize— and familiarity rushes back. *My mate.* And then I think no thoughts.

◆ ◆ ◆

There is no telling how much time has passed before Raúl pulls the van over. "We are a safe enough distance from that hell hole," he reassures us. "I think it's time to join the land of the living." Duffel bags full of clothes come out. The pack must have left in such a rush that there was no time to swing by my house and get my own clothes, but they had hastily found some cheap truck stop coverings for me: a t-shirt with a bald eagle and an oversized pair of Tweety Bird pajamas. I just hope that they can help me to ward whenever we finally have to be seen—a filthy, half-crazed, half-starved woman in mismatched clothing would definitely get the attention of authorities.

Teddy and Sylvia open an ice chest and try to coax me to drink some water and eat some sliced turkey. The moon is high in the sky, a gibbous disc from which I draw a little strength. And then we are back on the road, putting more miles between us and the compound with every passing minute.

I'm in some sort of mental haze that might be half-wakefulness, or perhaps the world is really that blurry. Their soft voices communicating with each other surround me—worried tones, relieved cadences, unresolved chord progressions of speculation.

Artificial light streaming through the window hurts my eyes. Something feels like a hard bubble around me, but flexible like a curtain—more warding magic. No one looks my way as they help me make my way across the parking lot to the truck stop, with its promises of food, supplies . . . and a *shower!*

◆ ◆ ◆

The first thing I do is cut my nails. My callouses are gone, and it is so strange to have tender skin, I might as well be missing teeth or claws. But I am still a musician, and need to feel prepared for anything. So many things I will never again take for granted: a toothbrush, enough room to stretch my limbs, and *water*, so much water! I can get it from the tap any time I am thirsty, I can even bathe my whole body in it.

Sylvia and Lydia stand guard by the truck stop shower. They hum soothing frequencies to me—*take your time* is the message I feel. They ward themselves and shield me with patience, while I sob and cry and laugh, and bark my frustrations that the water can't wash away the filth and rot I feel to the very core of my being.

"You guys all came for me," I sob to Sylvia. "Once again, I was the weak link of the pack . . ."

"Look at how far you're come, Buzz," she whispers. "In just under a year, you went from not knowing that there were other lycans out there—aside from Rowan—let alone other kinds of shifters, to taking down Public Shifter Enemy Number One. I think you're doing okay."

I still can't wrap my head around all that has passed. Did I truly take down the public shifter enemy number one? Or did I just kill my lover's ex?

She wasn't my lover's ex, I correct myself in my mind, *she was merely my opening act.* My own guffaw startles me. It's been so long since I've laughed that it feels like some external force shaking me like a rag doll. My packmates look at me with alarmed concern, but I hold up my hand to indicate that all is well.

Stumbling back toward the van, I smell a rat even before my eyes find the large rodent by the nearby dumpsters screeching at us, *"Escapeeeeeeees!"* Sylvia snarls a warning, and as if on cue a barred owl stoops out of nowhere and strikes. The bird swivels its head backward at us, throwing us a wink before carrying off its prey.

◆ ◆ ◆

"How did ye get so bloody far away?" my cousin Bonnie demands over Lydia's pack phone. The morning sunlight streams in through the windows, and I am finally able to sit upright in a seat. We still have a couple of hours to go before we cross into Orleans Parish, and her voice forces my anxiety to the back of my mind.

My non-shifter parents have apparently been spared the news, but Bonnie had heard the whole saga while in her wolf form. The "official" story that I have been found after a camping trip gone wrong has been announced to human family, friends, and followers of my music, and I've been notified that the guestbook on my website has been flooded with prayers and well wishes over the past few months. Maybe people don't suck as much as I once thought they did.

I shouldn't have been surprised that Bonnie turned out to not only be a shifter, but also one working for SIN as well. Next to Sylvia, she can keep a secret like no other. Phone communication is still circumspect until we are certain that all of Brume's minions are either dead or in custody. But undercover shifters like Bonnie and Lydia have an extra level of encryption in their lines. So if I cannot talk directly to my family, at least I have my wild kinswoman, and her voice is a magical elixir to my psyche.

She continues her interrogation before I can answer. "Was this some sort of Mary Poppins leaping into a painting? And if it was that easy, then when the fuck are ye gonna come and visit again? I haven't seen ye since we caused all that trouble in Oban!"

I chuckle at the memory. That was over ten years ago, when we were two bored young women splitting the Isle of Skye for the weekend. It was an adventure. First there was a hitchhiking race between us and a pair of girls from Vancouver that we'd met on the ferry. We'd lost because we'd tried to kidnap someone's lamb on the way. Then after a mighty session of traditional fiddle tunes, we'd ended up chaperoning a night-blind accordionist named Aleister, whom we kept having to hoist up every time he fell into a ditch. And somehow we all had ended up in a trailer with six travelers and a Scottish deerhound. The cheap wine had turned my lips blue, and when I fell asleep, everyone had freaked out because they'd thought I'd stopped breathing.

Good times. Nothing can take that away.

"Oh, and by the way, I'm supposed to relay a message to ye," she continues, her accent exaggerated in her buoyancy. "Some Turkish chickie named Aydan says congratulations for being the number one hero, and thank ye for helping her to learn the real words to 'Let it Be.' She says for years she and her sister Reyhan were singing it as *ver ipe.*" Bonnie pronounces it *very pee,* with a trilled *r.* "Which is Turkish for 'give me the rope!'"

I laugh for the first time in months. It's a comfort to know that my former rival survived, and I find myself proud to know this tough and troubled woman.

"Also a man named Jean-Michel Lapin was asking for ye. He says that Crick and Watson would be proud, whatever that means." Neither do I, but I am relieved to know that he is safe, presumably his mighty flea of an assistant as well.

"So, in all seriousness now," she asks a bit more softly, her accent softening. "How in the world did you get almost to the Canadian border?"

It would take a long time to explain how I was abducted in Mississippi, held prisoner in the upper Midwest, with my buried phone sending a signal to the allies, and just tried to survive as best as I could, somehow coming up with a solution that would weaken the Chimera's power. I promise to tell her everything once

I'm settled in before handing the phone to Lydia, who turns out to be a colleague of my cousin's.

The pack would have been proud of my skills. I managed to keep my wits about me for the duration of what turned out to be three months. Now I can only hope that I am not too damaged to be an asset to the pack and play my bass again.

◆ ◆ ◆

When we arrive at my apartment, my little Honda waits in the driveway, crouched like a contented cat glad to see its human at long last. Even my bass and rig are safe, as I discover the second I walk in. My home is alien in its familiarity, as if I don't know where I am, but am being hosted by someone who shares my taste in music and trappings. This is coming home to live in a childhood fairytale, a place that ceased to be, yet never stopped existing.

Rowan undresses me slowly, trying to kiss away every scar within. We don't leave my home for a very long time.

◆ ◆ ◆

The careful *snick, snick* of the scissors in my hair causes an involuntary shudder in me. Dean pauses and places a hand on my shoulder. "It's okay, honey. Remember to breathe, okay? Do you want some ice water? The cold might ground you."

I shake my head. "Thank you, no. Let's just do this. I have to get back to work in a few days, and I can't go onstage looking like a six-year-old just tried to play barber with me."

"Just let me know if you start to get triggered." Dean's house is comforting, full of modern art and soft lighting, with the pungent-sweet odor of sage burned on a regular basis. He resumes his magic on my hair, evening out the parts where it was hacked off in my confinement. Wisps of mustard-colored locks fall from my smock to the ground, and I draw in a huge breath through my nose, gripping the arms of the chair. My fellow lycan begins humming a low, soothing melody. Between the healing energy of his song and the exhaustion that still consumes me, it has a soporific effect, and I allow myself to drift off to his music.

"Buzz, honey?" he whispers. "Why don't you have a look?" How long was I out? Blinking hard, I lightly swat my own cheek to rouse myself. Dean spins my chair around, facing me at an image. It takes me two entire heartbeats for me to realize that what I'm looking at is my own reflection in his mirror.

Dang . . .

He's given me a shaggy, layered bob that looks edgy and fierce. "Wow, Dean," I tell him. "I don't know how you did it, but you've made me look like a rock star."

He unclasps my smock, whisking it off and giving me a gentle peck on the cheek. "Well, you *are* a rock star, girl-child-boo! You do realize, don't you, that you are the most celebrated werewolf of the century? Not only did you beat the Chimera *mano a mano,* but also you're also immune to silver. Packs far and wide call you 'Silver Birch.' You're a heroine among all shifters. How does *that* feel, sweetie?"

I stare for a long time into his kind blue eyes before dropping my head. "It doesn't feel like anything, really," I finally answer. "It just is what it is. No silver lining is worth that kind of cloud."

"I know, baby." He draws me to him in a hug, and the last of my confusion drains from my body. "But somebody had to save us all. I'm proud to know that it was you, and . . ." He releases me, pulls me to my feet, and coaxes me into a smile. ". . . now you look *fabulous!*"

A chuckle leaps out of me like a fish after an insect. "Dean, you are a genius. Is there anything that you *don't* do?"

"Yes. I don't do girls!"

♦ ♦ ♦

It's a time of turning in so many ways, and we are the ones on top for now. Our practice room at the Fountainbleau has never felt so sacred, or so homey.

"Housewarming party soon!" announces Raúl. "We couldn't do it with the heart of the pack missing!"

My four closest companions are still holding me in a group embrace. It's hard to know who needs the most reassurance, them for my safety or me for their presence. *Oh gods, we're all together again!* And now Raúl's news is just what we all need—tidings of life going on.

"Can you do a blessing?" he asks Sylvia. "We need a holy woman, and would prefer pack. Just a general one—holy water and sage—with a quick nod to Asherah."

"Asherah? As in the wife of Yahweh?" queries Sylvia.

"Yes. What do you think?"

My best friend smiles with a faraway look in her eyes. "I always liked to think of Mother Nature as being God's wife."

"But doesn't that go against your . . . line of work?"

Sylvia snorts. "Hey, if I thought that women had no business in sacred stuff, do you think I'd be wearing this ridiculous outfit?"

Teddy chortles. "Don't knock it. The Bible wants women to be modest."

Sylvia gives him a look. "Bite me. The holy book is full of outdated values, most of them misogynistic. I know I'm supposed to teach the Bible, but in my humble opinion, too many authors spoiled the plot."

"What did you say?"

"I said too many authors . . ."

"No, before that."

"Bite me."

Teddy springs at her with playful nipping teeth. I don't think he knew he was going to kiss her any more than the rest of us did. Maybe she was the only one who saw it coming, because she kisses him back with the ferocity of a long wait.

His unattainable love . . . Of course. And then it hits me: *That's why he'd tried to give up swearing!* I could have told him that he didn't need to change, so to speak.

The spontaneous applause floods my very soul with a warmth and goodness. Everyone is happy in the pack.

One

CHAPTER

15

OUTRO

*J*ournal entry, February 14*th*: *I'm not ready for happily ever after just yet. The movie's only just starting to get really good now.*

What remains to be seen?

All music, like the animal kingdom, evolves. From Stravinsky's *Rite of Spring* riot to Bob Dylan going electric, all change in music frightens people. There is also fear that comes with changing times, such as equal rights and alternative fuels. Taking baby steps is the key, not instant results that can throw everything out of balance. We can savor each moment that way, replaying it for family and friends and generations to come. No matter how good the intention, any change that is too much too soon is more than most people can handle.

Now that Sylvia has both the pack and Teddy, she doesn't need the isolation of the convent for protection. Now I pick up Teddy for pack meetings. Sylvia shows up in her habit, changes clothes before the end of the night, and leaves with Teddy. She doesn't disclose much, but she obviously isn't torn. She intends to eventually break away from the church. But for now, baby steps.

Teddy has finally broken his ties with the Maestro, finally refusing to be associated with him at all. Endorsers of the same string company, they were asked to attend the NAMM (National Association of Music Merchants) conference together. The Maestro had said something outrageously insulting to a guy from Line 6, who promptly beat the shit out of him. Teddy was a witness, but refuses to testify in a court case over the damage to the Maestro's hair plugs. My pack mate is now working with the Finnish prog guitarist Alec Liefsson, whom Dean had mentioned at the Shifter's Ball. They have just recruited a legendary lycan drummer named Dave Peartnoy, and are planning some sort of epic record. Because they can all shift into husky form, I suggested that they call their band "Mush," but no one seems to go for that idea.

Raúl and I are doing session work together for the solo project of our reggae singer Nigel. The fact that we get to do it at Rowan's studio makes it even more magical. Working with the whole lineup with horns, keys, and guitars makes for an amazing vibe, as we three hold the most precious secret ever. Each night after the rest of the band leaves, we frolic in wolf form until Lydia comes by to pick up her mate.

I am back home from my happy hour gig, relieved that I don't have to be out tonight. Driving to the Quarter was a hassle, as people are beginning to flock to New Orleans in pre-Mardi Gras festivities. Tourists are basically human deer. Once there are too many of them they will develop a tendency to bolt in front of my car without warning. But it is my duty to defend New Orleans, not thin the herd.

This was my last gig for a while. The city is too much to deal with after my plight. Earlier today I overheard someone say "bitch," and I barely fought off a panic attack. Because of airhorns, I won't be watching any Saints games for a while. I'd also seen Sand from a distance. We exchanged cool stares and nothing more. Word has it that she didn't know that she was in league with Chimera sympathizers, but her recent ignominy among shifter musicians is hurting her career. Even still, the sight of her had made my palms sweaty and my hair stand on end.

Rowan and I have agreed that I should not be subjected to the stress of Mardi Gras and are planning a real getaway together during that time. He's found a place in West Virginia where a wolf can be a wolf, and Father O'Flaherty has a cousin with a pub not too far away from it. I still have night terrors, so Rowan stays over, and it fills my heart with relief to come home and find him waiting in my apartment, his scent purifying my sacred space. The healing will be a long process, with lots of therapy. But every day that I am alive is a triumph.

Baby steps.

In the wake of all that has happened, I had completely forgotten about the Sarya Sheepsour album, which went gold twenty days after its release. It is a very strange feeling to discover that I have not only become a shifter hero, but that I am also on a gold record. All I ever wanted was to be a great bass player in my own right, and between my hearing and longevity, it may actually happen in time. Sarya's manager has offered me a job touring with her this summer in Europe, then Australia this winter—which is summer in the Southern Hemisphere. This means that my musical travels are far from over now. I am glad to see things unfolding for me, but I will never let my skills or instincts dull. Someday I will tell the young wolves, "If you think you kick ass, you're not paying attention."

In the meantime, I will be resuming my schedule of steady gigs around the time of our pack's one-year anniversary. They are the most amazing family ever. Teddy is volunteering to bring several cases of beer to the Fountainebleau, as well as a piñata filled with meatballs. He may be kidding, but I doubt it. I'd much prefer a moon run, but any time that I spend with my pack is precious in and of itself. Even with increased longevity, life is still short.

I watch Rowan string his guitar. The memories of our recent lovemaking are erased from his face in his complete absorption in the task. Changing strings is a sacred ritual for many.

And I laugh. Of course no woman will ever truly have him. He is a musician. Just like no man will every truly have me. We are holy people in our own rights. We are as devoted to each other as any two people can be, but some harmonics are meant to be wild.

And I finally get it—more than career, more than love, the most important thing is that I finally have my own life back. Beyond the adoration of an audience or a lover, beyond belonging to a pack, beyond the confines of a prison cell, *I belong to me.*

I hear the strings call out and find each other as Rowan's guitar inhales itself into tune. A few experimental strums, and he begins to play. I know that chord progression instantly, and my bones resonate with power.

Let it be.

The birdsong coming from the windowsill makes me smile. A pair of eavesdropping mockingbirds is joining in with Rowan's playing, and it's widely known that they are canny at mimicking music composed by people. But when the warbles fall in perfect synch with the melody, I snap my head around to face them. As soon as their jeweled eyes meet mine, they halt in their song and fan out their wings, bowing until their beaks touch the sill. Something in their energies feels sad and humbled. What are they trying to convey? They rise and cock their tiny feathered heads at me before disappearing into the air like a pair of striking gray and white windborne leaves, leaving me to ponder their message in their wake.

PLAYLIST

Author's note: What I have here is more or less a do-it-yourself soundtrack. Some of the music in my head can't quite be replicated by anything I've found, but this is still some recommended listening that I feel moves the plot along. All of these tracks can be found online. If you find yourself drawn to any of them, I encourage you to buy the downloads—or better yet, if some song really speaks to you, why not try to find the entire album in physical form? You will then hear a broader range of frequencies that the songwriters, musicians, recording engineers, producers, and mastering engineers intended you to hear.

1.   Glass Tiger: "Animal Heart," *No Turning Back*

2.   Adonai and I: "Adon Olam (Minor)," *Adonai and I*

3. Garmarna: "Varulven (Werewolf)," *God's Musicians*

4. Illapu: "Se Alumbra La Vida," *Mis Mas Grandes Exitos*

5. Sheila Chandra: "Lament of McCrimmon/Song of the Banshee," *Roots and Wings*

6. Allen Toussaint: "Yes, We Can Can," *Our New Orleans*

7. Huun-Huur-Tu: "Prayer," *The Orphan's Lament*

8. Trä: "Täss'on Namnen," *Hedningarna*

9. Balkanika: Balkan 2000, *The Best of Balkanika*

10. The Stranglers: "Golden Brown," *Feline*

11. The WooHoo Revue: "R'Ambo," *The Moreland's Ball*

12. Petra Haden: "Psycho Main Title," *Petra Goes to the Movies*

13. Sweet Cicada: "Fingerprints," *Switch (EP)*

14. SAVAE (San Antonio Vocal Ensemble): "Hanacpachap Cussisuinin," *La Noche Buena*

15. Adonai and I: "V'nemar," *Adonai and I*

16. Ambrosia: "Time Waits for No One" *Anthology*

17. Portnoy, Sheehan, MacAlpine, and Sherinian: "Apocalypse 1470 BC," *Live in Tokyo (Disc 1)*

18. Blake Hunter: "Famed Creators" *Skylights*

19. Ghorwane: "Salabude," *Kudumba*

20. Crack the Sky: "Surf City," *Crack the Sky*

21. Alanna O'Kelly: "One Breath," *Lament (Real World Compilation)*

22. Kronos Quartet: "Doom: A Sigh," *Black Angels*

23. Carol Woods and Timothy T. Mitchum: "Let it Be," *Across the Universe (Music from the Motion Picture), Deluxe Edition*

24. Crimson Glory: "Red Sharks," *Transcendence*

25. Daniel Lanois: "*The Maker,*" *Acadie*

26. Peter Gabriel: "The Time of the Turning (Reprise)/The Weaver's Reel," *Ovo*

From Birch's Bookshelf . . .

1. *Bug Music: How Insects Gave Us Rhythm and Noise* (David Rothenberg)

2. *Jaco: The Extraordinary and Tragic Life of Jaco Pastorius* (Bill Milkowski)

3. *The Music Lesson* (Victor L. Wooten)

4. *A Confederacy of Dunces* (John Kennedy Toole)

5. *The Real Zappa Book* (Frank Zappa and Peter Ochiogrosso)

ABOUT THE AUTHOR

Beth W. Patterson was a full-time musician for over two decades before diving into the world of writing, a process she describes as "fleeing the circus to join the zoo." Her first book is a compilation of her lyrics and poetry entitled *Mongrels and Misfits*, and she is a contributing writer to fourteen anthologies.

Patterson has performed in seventeen countries across the Americas, Europe, Oceania, and Asia. Her playing appears on over a hundred and thirty albums, soundtracks, videos, commercials, and voice-overs (including seven solo albums of her own). More than a hundred of her compositions and co-writes have been released. She studied ethnomusicology at University College, Cork in Ireland and holds a Bachelor's degree in Music Therapy from Loyola University New Orleans.

Beth has occasionally worn other hats as a body paint model, film extra, minor role actor, recording studio partner, record label owner, producer, and visual artist. She is a lover of exquisitely stupid movies and a shameless fangirl of the band Rush. You can find her at BethPattersonMusic.com